MM | | WAB
16-03-16 | |
13/9/16 | |
7/7/17 | |
21.7.18 | |

Please return this book on or before the date shown above. To
renew go to www.essex.gov.uk/libraries, ring 0845 603 7628 or
go to any Essex library.

Essex County Council

RITA BRADSHAW
writing as Helen Brooks

PENNY JORDAN

CAROL WOOD

Orphans FROM THE *Storm*

MILLS & BOON

This edition published in Great Britain 2015
by Mills & Boon, an imprint of Harlequin (UK) Limited,
Eton House, 18-24 Paradise Road, Richmond, Surrey, TW9 1SR

ORPHANS FROM THE STORM © 2014 Harlequin Books S.A.
(Originally published as *Winter Waifs* in 2007)

The publisher acknowledges the copyright holders of the individual works as follows:

Bride at Bellfield Mill © 2007 Penny Jordan
A Family for Hawthorn Farm © 2007 Helen Brooks
Tilly of Tap House © 2007 Carol Wood

ISBN: 978-0-263-91559-4

056-0515

Harlequin (UK) Limited's policy is to use papers that are natural, renewable and recyclable products and made from wood grown in sustainable forests. The logging and manufacturing processes conform to the legal environmental regulations of the country of origin.

Printed and bound by
CPI Group (UK) Ltd, Croydon, CR0 4YY

Bride at Bellfield Mill

Penny Jordan

Penny Jordan, one of Mills & Boon's most popular authors, unfortunately passed away on 31st December 2011. She leaves an outstanding legacy, having sold over a hundred million books around the world. Penny wrote a total of one hundred and eighty-seven novels for Mills & Boon, including the phenomenally successful *A Perfect Family, To Love, Honour & Betray, The Perfect Sinner* and *Power Play*, which hit the *New York Times* and *Sunday Times* bestseller lists. Loved for her distinctive voice, she was successful in part because she continually broke boundaries and evolved her writing to keep up with readers' changing tastes. *Publishers Weekly* said about Jordan, 'Women everywhere will find pieces of themselves in Jordan's characters.' It is perhaps this gift for sympathetic characterisation that helps to explain her enduring appeal.

Penny Jordan also wrote World War II sagas as Annie Groves, published by HarperCollins.

To my wonderful editor, Bryony Green,
for her encouragement and support.

CHAPTER ONE

'I CAN'T take you no further, lass, seein' as I'm bound for Wicklethwaites Farm and you're wantin' Rawlesden,' the carter informed Marianne in his broad Lancashire accent, as he brought the cart to a halt at a fork in the rutted road. 'You must take this turning 'ere and follow the road all the way down to the town. You'll know it before you gets there on account of the smoke from Bellfield Mill's chimneys, and then you keeps on walking when you gets to the Bellfield Hall.'

'Why do you say that?' Marianne asked the carter uncertainly.

She needed to find work—and quickly, she acknowledged as she looked down into the too-pale face of the baby in her arms. A lone woman with no work and a baby to care for could all too easily find herself in the workhouse—as she knew already to her cost.

The rich might be celebrating the Edwardian era, and a new king on the throne, but nothing had changed for the poor.

'I says it on account of him wot owns it—aye, and

t'mill an' all . There's plenty round here who says that he only come by them by foul means, and that the Master of Bellfield wouldn't think twice about ridding himself of anyone wot was daft enough to stand in his way. There's one little lass already disappeared from these parts with no one knowing where she's gone. Happen that's why he can't get no one working up at the hall for him. No one half decent, that is…'

'He doesn't sound very pleasant,' Marianne agreed as she clambered down from the cart, and then thanked the carter as he handed her the shabby bundle containing her few possessions.

'I still dunno wot would bring a pretty lass like you looking for work in these parts.'

Marianne could tell that the carter was eager to know as much about her as he could—no doubt to add to his stock-in-trade of gossip. He had already regaled her with several tales of the doings of those who lived in the town and the small farms on the moors beyond it, with a great deal of relish. Marianne suspected it was an enclosed, shut-off life here in this dark mill town, buried deep in a small valley between the towering Pennine hills.

Her large brown eyes with their fringing of thick black eyelashes shadowed slightly in her small heart-shaped face. The carter had referred to her as a 'pretty lass,' but she suspected that he was flattering her. She certainly did not feel like one, with her hair damp and no doubt curling wildly all over the place, her clothes old and shabby and her skin pinched and blue-looking from the cold. She was also far too fine-boned for the modern fashion for curvaceous women—the kind of women King Edward favoured.

'It's just as I explained to you when you were kind enough to offer me a lift,' she answered the carter politely. 'My late husband's dying wish was that I should bring his son here, to the place where he himself was born.'

'So you've got family here, then, have you?'

'*I* haven't.' Marianne forced herself to sound confident and relaxed. 'My late husband did have, but alas they, like him, are dead now.'

'Aye, well, it's natural enough that a man should want to think of his child following in his own footsteps. Dead now, you said?'

'Yes. He…he took a fever and died of it,' Marianne told him. It would not do to claim too close an acquaintance on her late husband's part with anything that might enable others to ask her too many questions.

'Well, I hope you manage to find yourself a decent place soon, lass. Although it won't be easy, wot with you having the babby, and you don't want to find yourself taken up by the parish and put in t'workhouse,' he warned her, echoing her own earlier thoughts.

'They don't suffer strangers easily hereabouts. Especially not when they're poor and pretty. T'master, is a hard man, and it's him wot lays down the law on account of him owning t'mill.'

Despite her best intentions Marianne shuddered—but then who would not do so at the thought of ending up in a parish workhouse?

Images, memories she wanted to banish for ever were trying to force themselves upon her. That sound she could hear inside her head was not the noise of women screaming in hunger and pain, but instead merely the howl of the winter wind, she assured herself firmly.

'You've no folk of yer own, then, lass?'

'I was orphaned young,' she answered the carter truthfully, 'and the aunt who brought me up is now dead.'

'Well, think on about what I just said,' the carter told her as he gathered up the reins and clicked his tongue to instruct the raw-boned horse between the shafts to move on. 'Keep away from Bellfield and its master if you want to keep yourself safe.'

There it was again—the unmistakable admonition that the mill and its master were dangers to be avoided. But it was too late to ask the carter any more questions, as the rain-soaked darkness of the November evening was already swallowing him up.

Picking up her bundle, Marianne pulled her cloak as closely around the baby as she could before bracing herself against the howl of the wind and setting off down the steep rutted and muddy track the carter had told her led into the town.

Marianne grimaced as mud from the uneven road came up over the sides of her heavy clogs and the sleet-laden wind whipped cruelly at her too-thin body, soaking through her cheap cloak. The carter had talked of how winter came early to this part of the world, and how it wouldn't be too long before it saw snow. She had only walked a mile or so since the carter had set her down at the fork in the road that led down off the Lancashire moors into the town below, but already she was exhausted, her teeth chattering and her hands blue with cold. What money she'd had to spare on the long journey here had gone on food and a good woollen blanket to wrap around the baby she was cradling so protectively.

The carter, with blackened stumps where his teeth had been, and his habit of spitting out the tobacco he was chewing, might not have been her preferred choice of companion, but his kindness in taking her up with him had brought tears of relief to her eyes. His offer had come after he had heard her begging the station master at Rochdale, who had turned her off the train, to let her continue her journey—a journey for which she had told him she had a ticket, even if now she couldn't find it. She certainly couldn't have walked all those extra miles that had lain between Rochdale and the small mill town that was her destination.

Now, as she struggled to stand upright against the battering wind, the moon emerged from behind a cloud to shine down on the canal in the valley below her. Alongside the canal ran the railway—the same railway on which she should have travelled to Rawlesden. She could see smoke emerging from the tall chimneys of the mills. Mills that made fortunes for their owners whilst becoming a grim prison for those who worked in them. She had never so much as visited a mill town before, never mind been inside a mill. The aunt who had brought her up had owned a small estate in Cheshire, but it was no mere chance that brought her here to this town now.

The baby gave a small weak whimper, causing her heart to turn over with sick fear. He was so hungry and so weak. Her fear for him drove her to walk faster, slipping and sliding on the muddy road as she made herself ignore the misery of her cold, wet body.

She was halfway down the hillside now, and as she turned a sharp bend in the road the large bulk of an imposing mansion rose up out of the darkness in front of her, its presence shocking her even though she had been looking for it. Its façade, revealed by the moonlight, was grim and threatening, as though daring anyone to approach it, and was more that of a fortress than a home. A pair of heavy iron gates set into a stone wall barred the way to it, and the moon shone on dark unlit windows whilst the wind whipped ferociously through the trees lining the carriageway leading to the house. She had known what it was even before she had seen the name Bellfield Hall carved into the stone columns supporting the huge gates.

A thin curl of smoke from one of its chimneys was the only evidence that it was inhabited. No wonder the carter had urged her to avoid such an inhospitable-looking place. Marianne shivered as she looked at it, before turning away to comfort the baby who had started to cry.

It was then that it happened—that somehow she took a careless step in the muddy darkness of the cart track, causing her ankle to turn so awkwardly that she stumbled heavily against the gate, pain spearing her even whilst she hugged the baby tightly to her to protect him.

As she struggled to stand upright she found that just trying to bear her own slender weight on her injured ankle brought her close to fainting with the pain. But she could not fail now. She must not. She had given her promise, after all. She looked down into the town. It was still a good long walk away, whilst the hall… This was not how she had planned for things to be, but what choice did she have? She reached for the heavy gate handle and turned it.

CHAPTER TWO

IT HAD taken her longer to walk up the carriageway to the house than Marianne had expected, and then she'd had to find her way round to the servants' entrance at the rear. The smell from the mill chimneys was stinging her throat and eyes, and the baby's thin wail warned her that he too was affected by the smoke. A stabbing pain shot through her ankle with every step she took.

Relief filled her when she saw the light shining from a window to one side of the door. Here, surely, despite what the carter had told her, she would find some respite from the harsh weather, and a fire to sit before— if only for long enough to feed the baby. She was certain no one could be so hard-hearted as to send her out into a night like this one. Milo had often talked with admiration and pride of the people of this valley and their generosity of spirit. A poor, hard-working people whom he had been proud to call his own. He had shown her the sign language used by the mill workers to communicate with one another above the sound of the looms, and he had told her of the sunny summer days he had spent roaming free on the moors above the valley as a young boy. He had desperately wanted to come back here, but in the end death had come and snatched him away more speedily than either of them had anticipated.

She raised her hand toward the door knocker, but before she could reach it the door was suddenly pulled open, to reveal the interior of a large and very untidy kitchen. A woman emerged—the housekeeper, Marianne assumed. For surely someone so richly dressed, in a bonnet lavishly trimmed with fur and feathers and a cloak lined with what looked like silk, could not possibly be anything else. Certainly not a mere housemaid, or even a cook, and no lady of the house would ever exit via the servants' door.

The woman was carrying a leather portmanteau, and her high colour and angry expression told Marianne immediately that this was no ordinary leave-taking.

The man who had pulled open the door looked equally furious. He was tall and broad-shouldered, with thick dark hair and a proudly arrogant profile, and both his appearance and his demeanour made it plain that he was the master of the house and in no very good humour.

'If you think you can turn me off with nothing but a few pennies and no reference, Master Denshaw, then you'll have to think again—that you will. An honest woman, I am, and I'm not having no one say no different…'

'An honest woman? So tell me then, Mrs Micklehead, how does such an honest woman, paid no more than ten guineas a year, manage to afford to clothe herself in a bonnet and a cloak that even to my untrained male eye would have cost in the region of ten times that amount?'

The woman's face took on an even more crimson hue.

'Given to me, they was, by Mr Awkwright what I worked for before I come here. Said how I could have them, he did, after poor Mrs Awkwright passed away on account of how well I looked after her.'

'So well, in fact, that she died of starvation and neglect, you mean? Well, you might have hoped to starve me into submission—or worse—Mrs Micklehead, with your inability to perform any of the tasks for which you were employed—'

'An 'ousekeeper were what I were taken on as—not a skivvy nor a cook. I come here out of the goodness of me heart.'

'You came here, Mrs Micklehead, for one reason and one reason only, and that was so that you could line your own pockets at my expense.'

'If you was real quality, and not just some poor brat what managed to marry up into a class what was too good for him, you'd know how the real quality and them that works for them goes about things. Call yourself the Master of Bellfield? The whole town knows there was another what should have had that right, even if they're too feared of you to say so.'

'Hold your tongue, woman.'

The order thundered round the chaotic room.

'You're no housekeeper,' he continued grimly into the silence he had commanded. 'You're a lazy good-for-nothing, a thief and a liar, and I'm well rid of you.'

'You may well be, but I'll tell you this—you won't

find no one daft enough to come looking to take me place, that you won't,' she told him vigorously. 'Not when I've had me say—'

'Excuse me...'

At the sound of her faltering interruption they both turned to look at Marianne.

'Oh, I see—got someone to take me place already, have you?' The housekeeper gave Marianne an angrily contemptuous look, and then, without giving either Marianne or her late master time to correct her, she continued challengingly, 'So where's he had you from, then? One of them fancy domestic agencies down in Manchester, I'll be bound, with that posh way you talk. Well, you won't last a full day here, you won't. You'll have come here expecting to be in charge of a proper gentleman's household, with a cook and parlour maids, and even one of them butlers. There ain't nowt like that here. Take my advice, love, and get yourself back where you've come from whilst you still can. This ain't no place for the likes of you, this ain't.'

Turning away from Marianne, she addressed the man watching them both. 'She won't last five minutes, by the looks of her. She don't look like no housekeeper I've ever seen.'

'I know enough to recognise a house with a kitchen that isn't being run properly,' Marianne told her pointedly. On any other occasion it might almost have made her smile to see the look on the other woman's face as she realised that Marianne wasn't going to be manipulated, as she'd hoped, or used as a bullet she could fire at her employer.

'Well, some folks don't know when they're being done a favour, and that's plain to see,' she told Marianne, bridling angrily. 'But don't expect no sympathy when you find out what's what.' With a final angry glower she stormed past Marianne and out into the darkness.

'I don't know what brings you here,' the Master of Bellfield said to Marianne coldly once the housekeeper had gone, 'But we both know that it wasn't an interview for the post of housekeeper via an employment agency in Manchester.'

'I *am* looking for work,' Marianne informed him swiftly.

'Oh, you are, are you? And you thought to find some here? Well, you must be desperate, then. Didn't you hear what Mrs Micklehead had to say about me?'

'She is entitled to her opinion, but I prefer to form my own.'

Marianne could see from the look of astonishment on his face that he hadn't expected her to speak up in such a way.

'Is that wise in a servant?'

'There is nothing, so far as I know, that says a servant cannot have a mind of her own.'

'If you really think that you are a fool. There's no work for you here.'

Marianne stood her ground.

'Forgive me, sir, but it looks to me as though there is a great deal of work to be done.'

There was a small silence whilst they both contemplated the grim state of the kitchen, and then he demanded, 'And you reckon you can do it, do you? Well, you've got more faith in yourself than I have. Because I don't. Not from the looks of you.'

'A fair man would give me the chance to prove myself and not dismiss me out of hand,' Marianne told him bravely.

'A fair man?' He gave a harsh shout of laughter. 'Didn't you hear what Mrs Micklehead had to say? I am not a fair man. I never have been and I never will be. No. *I* am a monster—a cruel tyrant who is loathed and hated by those who are forced to work for me.'

'As I've said, I prefer to make my own judgements, sir.'

'Well, I must say you have a great deal to say for yourself for a person who arrives at my door looking like a half-starved cat. You are not from 'round here.'

'No, sir.'

'So what brings you here, then?'

'I need work. I saw that this is a big house, and I thought that maybe…'

'I'd be mad to take on another housekeeper to pick my pockets and attempt to either starve or poison me. And why should I when I can rack up at a hotel and oversee my mills from there?'

'A man needs his own roof over his head,' Marianne told him daringly, drawing courage from the fact that he had not thrown her out immediately. She was pretty certain that this man would want to stay in his own house, and would not easily tolerate living under the rule of anyone else.

'And a woman needs a clever silken tongue if she is to persuade a man to provide a roof over hers, eh, little cat?'

Marianne looked down at the floor, sensing that his mood had changed and that he was turning against her.

'It is work I am looking for, sir—honest, decent work. That is all,' she told him quietly. She could feel him weighing her up and judging her, and then putting that judgement into the scales to be weighed against his past experience and his cynicism.

'And you reckon you can set this place to order, do you, with this honest, decent work of yours?'

Why was she hesitating? she thought. Wasn't this what she wanted—why she had come here? The kitchen might be untidy and chaotic, but at least it was warm and dry. Where was she to go if she was turned away now? Back to where she had come from? Hardly. Yet still she hesitated, warned by something she could see in the arrogant male face with its winter-sky-grey eyes. His gaze held a hint of latent cruelty, making her feel that if she stepped over the threshold of this house and into his domain she would be stepping into danger. She could turn back. She could walk on into the town and find work there. She could…

A gust of wind rattled the windows and the door slammed shut—closed, Marianne was sure, not by the force of the wind but by a human hand.

'Yes.' Why did she feel as though she had taken a very reckless step into some dark unknown?

She could still feel him looking at her, assessing her, and it was a relief when he finally spoke.

'So, tell me something of the cause of such an urgent need for work that it has brought you out on such a night and to such a place. Got turned off by your mistress, did you?'

Although his voice had a rich northern burr, it was

not as strong as that of the departing housekeeper. She could hear the hostility and the suspicion in it, though.

'No!'

'Then what?'

'Beggars can't be choosers, sir,' she replied quietly, looking not at him but down at the floor. It had taken more than one whipping before she had known that it was not her right to look her betters in the eye.

'Beggars? You class yourself as such, and yet you are aspiring to the post of a housekeeper?'

'I know the duties of a housekeeper, sir, and have carried them out in the past. On this occasion, though, I was not in any expectation of such an elevated post.'

'*Elevated?* So you think that working for me as my housekeeper would be a rare and juicy plum of a post, do you?'

'I had not thought of it in such terms, sir. Indeed, I had not thought of taking that position at all—you are the one who has done that. All I was looking for was the chance of work and a roof over my head.'

'But you have worked as a housekeeper, you say?'

'Yes, sir.' It was, after all, the truth.

'Where was your last post?'

'In Cheshire, sir. The home of an elderly lady.'

'Cheshire! So what brings you to Lancashire?'

The baby, who had fallen asleep, suddenly woke up and started to cry.

'What the devil?' He snatched up a lantern from the table and held it aloft, anger pinching in his nostrils and drawing down the corners of his mouth into a scimitar curve as he stared at them both. 'What kind of deceit is this that you try to pass yourself off as a servant when you have a child?'

'No deceit, sir. I am a respectable widow, forced to earn a living for myself and my child as best I can.'

'No one employs a woman with a child as a servant.'

It was true enough. Live-in domestic staff were supposed to remain single. Housekeepers might be given the courtesy title of 'Mrs,' but they were certainly not supposed to have a husband, and most definitely not a child.

'I was in service before my marriage,' she answered his charge, speaking the truth once again.

'So you're a widow, are you? What happened to your husband?'

'He died, sir.'

'Don't bandy words with me. I don't have the temperament for such women's ways. There's no work here for the likes of you. You might have more luck in one of the bawdy houses of Manchester—or was that how you came by your brat in the first place?'

'I am a respectably married woman.' Marianne told him angrily. 'And this child, my late husband's child, was born in wedlock.'

'I'm surprised you haven't had the gall to farm it out to someone else, or left it outside a chapel door to add to the problems of some already overburdened parish. Without it you might have convinced me to give you some work.' He was walking towards the door, obviously intending to force her to leave.

It was too late now for her to wish that she had not allowed her pride to overrule her caution.

'Please…' She hated having to beg for anything from anyone, but to have to beg from a man like this one was galling indeed. However, she had given her promise. A deathbed promise what was more. 'Please let me stay— at least for tonight. If nothing else I could clean up this kitchen. Please…'

She hated the way he was looking at her, stripping her of her dignity and her pride, reducing her to nothing other than the miserable creature he perceived her to be.

He gave a mirthless bark of derisory laughter.

'Clean this place—in one night? Impossible! What is your name?'

'Marianne—I mean Mrs…Mrs Brown.'

Something too sharp and knowing gleamed in his eyes.

'You don't seem too sure of your surname, Mrs Brown. Could it be that you have forgotten it and that it could just as readily be Smith or Jones? Where were you wed?'

'I was married in Cheshire, in the town of Middlewich, and my name *is* Brown,' Marianne told him fiercely.

'Aye, well, anyone can buy a cheap brass ring and lay claim to a dead husband.'

'I am married. It is the truth.'

'You have your marriage lines?'

Marianne could feel her face starting to burn. 'Not with me…'

He was going to make her leave…

'If I turn you out, you and the brat will no doubt end up on the parish, and the workhouse governors will have something to say about that. Very well, you may stay the night. But first thing in the morning you are to leave—not just this house, but the town as well. Is that understood?'

He had gone without giving her the opportunity to answer him. Which was just as well, given the circumstances that had brought her here.

For tonight at least she and the baby would have the warmth of this kitchen. A kitchen she had promised to clean in return for its shelter, she reminded herself, as she rocked the baby back to sleep and prayed she would be able to find some milk for him somewhere in the chaos.

Her arms ached from carrying both the child and their few possessions, and her ankle was still throbbing. She limped over to an empty chair and placed the silent swaddled bundle down on it. Her heart missed a beat as she studied the small waxen face. She turned towards the fire glowering sullenly in the range. Ash spilled from beneath it, suggesting that it was some time since it had been cleaned out properly, and she would need a good fire burning if she was to heat enough water to get this place properly clean.

Picking up the lantern, she walked slowly round the kitchen. Half a loaf of bread had been left uncovered and drying out on the table, along with some butter, and a jar of jam with the lid left off, causing her mouth to water at the sight of it. But she made herself resist the temptation to fall on it and silence the ache of hunger that tore at her insides. Everywhere she looked she could see filthy crockery, and the floor was sticky with dirt.

A door opened off the kitchen into a large pantry, in which Marianne was relieved to find a large pitcher of milk standing on a marble slab. Before she did anything else she would feed the baby. Another door opened down to the cellars, but Marianne decided not to bother exploring them. A good housekeeper would keep a domain like this well stocked and spotlessly clean, and it would be run meticulously in an ordered routine, to provide for the comfort of its master and mistress and their family. If the kitchen was anything to judge from, this house did not provide comfort for anyone.

In the back scullery Marianne found a sink piled high with dirty pots. The pain in her ankle had turned into a dull ache, so she found a small pan, unused and clean enough to need only rinsing under a tap before she put some milk in it to heat up for the baby. He was so very, very frail. Tears filled her eyes.

Ten minutes later she was seated in the rocking chair she had drawn up to the range, feeding the baby small pieces of bread soaked in the warm milk into which she had melted a teaspoon of honey and beaten a large fresh egg. He was so weak that he didn't even have the energy to suck on the food, and Marianne's hand shook as she gently squeezed so that the egg and milk mixture ran into his mouth.

It was over an hour before she was satisfied with the amount of nourishment he had been able to take, and then she removed the swaddling bands to wash him gently in a bowl of warm water in front of the range. After she had dried him, she used a clean cloth she had found to make a fresh clout for him. He was asleep before she had finished, and Marianne put him down in a wicker basket she had found in the larder, which she had lined with soft clothes she had warmed on the range.

Was it her imagination, or was there actually a hint of warm pink colour in his cheeks, as though finally he might begin to thrive?

Marianne turned her attention to the range, ignoring the aching misery of her ankle as she poked and raked at the old ashes until she had got the fire blazing brightly and the discarded ash swept into a bucket ready to be disposed of. An empty hod containing only a couple of pieces of coke told her what the range burned, but whilst in a properly organised household such a hod—and indeed more than one—would have been ready filled with coke, so that the range could be stoked up for the night, in this household no such preparation had been made.

There was no help for it. Marianne recognised that she was going to have to go out into the yard and find the coke store, otherwise the range would go out.

The wind had picked up during the time she had been inside, and it tore at her cloak, whipping it round her as she held a lantern aloft, the better to see where the coke supply might be. To her relief she found it on her third search of the yard. But again, just like the kitchen, the store was neglected, and without a cover to keep the rain from the coke. The handle of the shovel she had to use to fill the hob was gritty, but she set her jaw and ignored the discomfort.

She had just finished filling the hod when she felt something cold and wet slither against her ankles. She had lived in poverty long enough to know the creatures that haunted its darkness, nor did it surprise her that there should be rats so close to the house. Instead of screaming and running away, she gripped the shovel more firmly and then raised it, ready to despatch the too-bold vermin.

'Miaouww.'

It was a cat, not a rat. Half wild, starving, and probably infested with fleas. Marianne tried to shoo it away, but as though it sensed her instinctive sympathy for it the cat refused to go.

Perhaps she would put out a saucer of milk for it if it was still there in the morning, Marianne decided, as she shooed it away a second time. She started pulling the hod back across the yard, but its weight forced her to rest several times before she finally reached the back door. She leaned against it, then pushed it open and dragged the hod into the kitchen. Her ankle was still swollen and aching, but at least she had not twisted it so severely that she could not walk, she reflected gratefully.

First thing in the morning she intended to find out if the Master of Bellfield employed an outside man to do such things as bring in the kindling and fuel to keep the fires burning. If he didn't, then she was going to insist that he provided her with a wheelbarrow, she decided breathlessly as she opened the range doors and stoked up the fire. Properly banked down it should stay in until the morning.

She stood up and stepped back from the fire to check on the baby, who thankfully was still sleeping peacefully. When she looked back towards the fire she saw to her be-musement that the cat was sitting in front of it, basking in its warmth. It must have slipped in without her noticing when she had brought in the hod. Its fur was a silky soft grey, thick and long, and beautifully marked. Marianne stared at it in astonishment as it looked back at her with an unblinking gaze. She frowned, remembering how long ago, as a child, her aunt had taken her to visit a friend of hers. She had been entranced by the cat that lived there because of its beautiful long coat. It had been a special and very expensive, very aristocratic breed, she remembered her aunt's friend informing them.

But, no matter how aristocratic its coat, the cat couldn't possibly stay inside. Marianne went briskly towards it, scooping it up. Beneath its thick coat she could feel its bones and its thinness. Surely that wasn't silent reproach she could see in those eyes? Marianne hesitated. It wouldn't hurt to give it a saucer of milk and let it stay inside for a while. It would be company for her whilst she set to work cleaning the kitchen.

Telling herself that she was far too soft-hearted, Marianne returned the cat to the hearth and poured it some milk.

Even the way it lapped from the saucer was delicate and dainty, and when it had finished it set to immediately cleaning its face, before curling up into a tight ball and going straight off to sleep.

Lucky cat, Marianne reflected, as she covered the baby's basket with some muslin netting, just in case the cat should be tempted to climb into the basket whilst her back was turned. Marianne had never forgotten hearing her aunt's cook telling the most dreadful story of how in one place she had worked the mistress of the house had gone mad with grief after her pet cat had got into the nursery and lain on top of the baby, smothering it to death.

The pans of water she had set to boil whilst she had

been out filling the hod were now bubbling and spitting with the hot water she needed to start washing the dirty crockery that seemed to have been left where it had been used. Marianne had no idea how anyone could tolerate so much disorder.

It took her the best part of another hour, but at length the crockery was washed and dried and put back on dresser shelves that she'd had to wipe down first to remove the dust and grease.

She was so tired—too tired now to want to eat the bread and jam that had made her mouth water so much earlier. But she could not sleep yet. There was still the table to scrub down and bleach, and the floor to be cleaned, the range to be stoked up again for the morning, and the baby to be fed again—if he could be coaxed into taking a little more bread. Refusing to give in to her own exhaustion, Marianne set to work on the table.

The mixture of strong carbolic soap and bleach stung her eyes as she scrubbed, and turned her hands red and raw, but there was still a sense of accomplishment and pleasure in being able to stand back from the table to survey her finished handiwork.

The glow from the oil lamps was now reflecting off a row of clean shiny pans above the range, and the air in the kitchen smelled fresh instead of stuffy. The baby gave a small thin cry, signalling that he was waking up, and the cat, no doubt disturbed by the sound, uncurled itself and stretched.

Washing her hands carefully, Marianne headed for the pantry—and gave a small shriek as she opened the door to see three or four mice scattering in the lantern light, a tell-tale trail of flour trickling from one of the many bags of foodstuffs stacked on the larder floor.

A streak of grey flashed past her to pounce on a laggard mouse, before despatching it with swift efficiency and then padding towards Marianne to drop the small body at her feet.

'So, you're a good mouser, are you? Well, then, between us we should be able to get this kitchen into a proper state. That's if the Master of Bellfield will allow us to stay,' she warned the cat, which, having accepted its due praise, retrieved its trophy—much to Marianne's relief.

The baby's basket would be safer tonight placed up on the table, she decided a few minutes later, watching in relief as the baby fed sleepily on his milk and egg bread. Marianne thought he was already a little bit heavier and stronger, and she prayed that it might be so. There had been so many times during the dark days since his father's death when she had feared that he too might slip away from her.

Fed and changed, the baby was restored to his cosy bed, now safely elevated away from any wandering mice daring enough to creep past the cat. Marianne ignored her own tiredness to set to work on the kitchen floor, which she could see needed not only rushing but a good scrubbing as well...

Marianne had no idea what time it was when she finally emptied away the last bucket of water and squeezed out the mop. All she did know was that the kitchen floor was now clean enough for even its master to eat his dinner off, and that she herself was exhausted.

The baby was still fast sleep, and so it seemed was the little cat—who for a while had sat up to watch her whilst she worked, as though wanting to oversee what she was doing. She felt so very tired, and so very dirty. Marianne stretched out in front of the fire, her too-thin body greedy for its heat. In the hallway, beyond the green-baize-covered door that separated it from the kitchen, a clock chimed the hour—but Marianne was already fast asleep and unable to hear it.

Not so the Master of Bellfield, to whom the striking of the hour heralded the start of a new working day. Like those who worked for him, the Master of Bellfield rose early, where others might have lain in their beds, enjoying the comfort and luxury paid for by the success of their mills.

There was no immaculately dressed maid to bring up the morning tea and a freshly ironed newspaper, no manservant to wake his master and announce that his bath had been drawn and his clothes laid out. How, after all, could a man reared on the cold charity of the workhouse, following the failure of his father's business, appreciate such refinements?

The Master of Bellfield knew well what people thought of him—and what they said of him behind his back. That gossip would be fuelled afresh now, following the departure of his housekeeper, he acknowledged as he shaved with cold water, ignoring the sting of the razor. His dark hair, untamed and thick, was in need of a barber, and he knew that at the next Mill Owners' Meeting at the fancy hotel in Manchester, where his peers met ostensibly to discuss business, he would be looked down upon by those who liked to pretend to some kind of superiority. Those who had lost their northern accents, smothered their hair in sickly smelling pomades and generally acted more like members of the landed gentry than mill owners.

That kind of foolishness wasn't for him. It had, after all, been the cause of his own father's downfall— too many nights spent playing cards with his new-found fancy friends, and too few days keeping an eye on how his mills were working and their profit and loss accounts.

His sister could screech all she liked to who she liked that their father had been cheated out of what was right-fully his when the bank had foreclosed on him, but the Master of Bellfield knew better.

He also knew how people had mocked and despised him for the steps he had taken to turn round his own fortunes—until they had learned to fear him and talk about their suspicions in hushed whispers. Well, let them say what they wished. Let the other mill owners' stupid wives, with their airs and graces and their falsely genteel accents, ignore him and exclude him from the fancy parties they gave to catch a husband for their virginal daughters. He didn't care.

He pulled on a cold and unironed shirt, and then stepped into a pair of sturdy trousers made from his own cloth. Only then did he pull back the shabby curtain from the windows and stare out into the darkness, illu-minated by pinpoints of light coming from the various mills. He picked up his pocket watch.

One minute to five o'clock. He waited in silent impatience, only moving when, dead on the hour, he saw smoke billowing from the chimneys of his mills.

In the kitchen, two of its three occupants remained fast asleep when the Master of Bellfield entered the room, the third having padded silently over to the settle against the wall and crawled out of sight beneath it.

The first thing the master noticed was the young woman, lying in front of the fire. The second was the unfamiliar clean smell. His eyes narrowed as he strode against the scrubbed stone floor. The woman was lying on her side, one frail wrist sticking out from the thin shawl she had pulled about herself. He frowned as he looked down at her. He had not expected for one minute that she would be able to make good her claim to clean the kitchen. He had no doubt that she must have worked virtually throughout the night in order to do so. Why? Because she hoped to prevail on him to let her stay?

His mouth compressed as he looked at the basket on the table. If that was the case she was soon going to realise her mistake. Soon, but not now. It was half past five. Time for him to leave if he wanted to be at the mill for six, which he most assuredly did. Those who worked at Bellfield knew better than to try to sneak in later when its master was there to watch them clock in.

No foreman could instil the respect in his workforce that a watchful mill master could, nor ensure that the cloth woven in his mills was of such excellent quality that it was highly sought after. Let the other masters and their wives give themselves what airs and graces they pleased. It was Bellfield wool that was the true aristo-crat of the northern valleys.

He made to step past the sleeping woman, but then turned to go back to the hall. He opened one of several pairs of heavy double mahogany doors that lined it and strode into the room beyond to remove from a fading red-velvet-covered sofa a dark-coloured square of cleanly woven wool.

Returning to the kitchen, he dropped the wool over her, and then headed for the back door. Other mill owners might choose to ride, or be driven in a carriage down to their mills. He preferred to walk. His head bare, ignoring the cold wind and the fraying cuffs of his shirt and jacket, he strode out across the yard, whilst behind him in the kitchen Marianne opened her eyes, wondering for a few seconds where she was, whilst the cat emerged from its hiding place to rub itself around her feet and mew demandingly.

Ignoring it Marianne fingered the fine wool cover that was now warming her. Someone had put it there, and there was only one person who could have done that. A faint blush of pink colour washed up over her skin.

An act of kindness from the Master of Bellfield? She shook her head in disbelief.

CHAPTER THREE

UNEXPECTEDLY—at least so far as Marianne was concerned—after the biting sleet-laden wind of the previous day, the morning had brought a sky washed clear of clouds and sharp cold sunlight, making her grimace as it revealed the grimy state of the kitchen windows.

A commanding cry from the cat had her obediently opening the kitchen door for it. The yard looked a bit more hospitable this morning, and there were even a few hens scratching around it. As she studied them, wondering if and where they might be laying, an errand boy riding a bicycle that looked too big for him came cycling into the yard, grinning cheerfully at her as he brought his bike to a halt and slid off it.

'Charlie Postlethwaite of Postlethwaite's Provisions,' he introduced himself, whilst pointing to the lettering on the bicycle. 'That's me dad,' he told her proudly, 'and he told me to get myself up here,' he announced, opening the basket on the back of the bicycle. 'He said how he'd heard about that old besom that called herself an 'ouse-keeper had done a flit, and that like as not she'd have emptied the larder afore she went. He said that he'd heard that the t'master had taken on someone new and all.'

Having removed a small flitch of bacon from his basket, he was eyeing Marianne speculatively.

'Going' to be stayin', are you?'

'That depends on Mr Denshaw,' Marianne told him circumspectly folding her hands in front of her and trying to look like a proper housekeeper.

'Ooh, Mr Denshaw, is it? We call him t'master round here, we do, 'cos that's what he is. Down at t'mill he'll be now, aye, and ready for his breakfast when he gets back. Me dad said to say how he'll be happy to sort out an order for you if you were wishing to send one back with me.'

'Mr Denshaw hasn't had time to acquaint me with the names of the tradespeople he favours as yet,' Marianne responded repressively, but her attempt at formality was rather spoilt when the baby gave a shrill wail and the boy looked past her into the kitchen and gave a low whistle.

'You've never brought a babby with you, have you?' he exclaimed. 'Hates them, t'master does, on account of him losing his own—and his wife and all. Went into labour early, she did, when t'master were away, and died. Oh, and my cousin Jem said to tell you that if you was wantin' someone to do a bit of outdoor work, he'd be willin'.'

Marianne had never known a boy so loquacious, nor so full of information. Just listening to him was making her feel slightly breathless. The cat, having finished its business outside, ran back across the yard, pausing to stand in front of her, very much in the manner of a small guard.

'Here, that's one of Miss Amelia's fancy cat's kittens, ain't it?' the boy exclaimed in some astonishment as he stared at the cat. 'I'd heard how t'master had given orders that they was all to be drowned. Took it real bad, he did, when she left. There was some that said he'd brought her home from that posh school of hers so as he could make her his wife, and that it were on account of that she upped and ran off. Took her cat with her and all, she did, and when it come back, months after she'd gone, t'master had it killed. Some round these parts said that the cat weren't the only thing he'd done away with, and that he'd killed Miss Amelia an all. Aye—and her cousin, that were t'master's stepson.'

Such a garbled and gothic tale was bound to be overexaggerated, Marianne knew. Nevertheless she found that she was shivering, and that her stomach was cramping hollowly as small tendrils of fear uncurled inside it to grip hold of her.

'Thank you, Charlie.' She stemmed the tide of information, determinedly starting to turn away, hoping that the boy would take the hint.

'Aye, you'd better go and get some of that bacon on. He's got a mean temper on him, t'master has, and he won't be too pleased if he comes back to find his breakfast ain't ready for him.'

'You're right. I shall go inside and cook it now,' Marianne told him swiftly, exhaling with relief when this time the boy finally swung his leg up and over his bicycle.

'So,' she told the cat sitting watchfully at her feet a few minutes later, as she nursed the baby now sucking eagerly at his milky bread, 'We have two good reasons why Mr Denshaw won't want to keep me on. The baby, and you.'

She gave a small sigh. If the Master of Bellfield did but know it, she was as reluctant to be here as he was to have her here. But she had given her promise—a deathbed promise that could not be broken.

The baby had finished his milk. Marianne lifted him to her shoulder and rubbed his back to bring up his wind.

Within half an hour of Charlie Postlethwaite leaving, the baby had been fed and changed, and was back in his makeshift crib, now returned to the floor, whilst Marianne was carefully turning the bacon she was frying ready for the master's return. All the while she kept a cautious eye on the cat, who had forsaken the hearth to go and sit beside the basket, where it was watching the sleeping infant.

'Don't you dare get in that basket,' she warned it.

The cat gave her an obliquely haughty look, that immediately changed to a wary twitch of its ears as it stared at the door, as though it had heard something that Marianne could not.

Sure enough, within seconds, just after the cat had retreated to its hiding place beneath the settle, Marianne could hear the sound of men's voices in the yard.

Hurrying to the window, she saw a group of men surrounding and supporting the Master of Bellfield. His arms were about their shoulders and a bloodstained bandage was wrapped around his thigh.

Marianne rushed to the door and opened it.

'What's happened?' she asked the nearest man.

'It's t'master,' one of them told her unnecessarily. 'There were an accident at t'mill with one of t'machines.'

'Told us to get him back here he did,' another man supplied.

As the two men now supporting their employer struggled to get him through the doorway they accidentally banged his injured leg, causing him to let out a small moan through clenched teeth.

His face was pale, waxen with sweat, and his eyes were half closed, as though he was not really fully conscious. Marianne could see the bloodstain on the makeshift bandage spreading as she watched.

'He needs to see a doctor,' she told the men worriedly.

'Aye, the foreman told him that. But he weren't having none of it. Threatened to turn him off if he dared to send for him. Said as how it were just a bit of a scratch, even though them of us who'd seen what happened saw the pin go deep into his leg. Sheered off, it did, looked like someone had cut right through it to me…'

Marianne saw the way the other man kicked the one who was speaking, and muttered something to him too low for her to hear before raising his voice to ask her a question.

'What do you want us to do with him now that we've brought him back? Only he'll dock us wages, for sure, if we don't get back t'mill.'

Marianne tried not to panic. They were treating her as though she really were the housekeeper, when of course she was no such thing.

'Perhaps you should consult your master—' she began, and then realised the uselessness of her suggestion even before one of the men holding him spoke to her bluntly.

'Out for the count t'master is, missus, and in a bad

way an all, I reckon. Mind you, there's plenty living round here that wouldn't mind seein' him go into his coffin, and that's no lie.'

Instinctively Marianne recoiled from his words, even though she could well understand how a hard and cruel employer could drive those dependent on him to wish him dead. It was no wonder that some workforces went on strike against their employers.

'You'd better take him upstairs,' she told the waiting men. 'And one of you needs to run and summon the doctor.'

'You'd best do that, Jim,' the oldest of the men announced, 'seein' as you're the fastest on your legs. We'll take him up then shall we, missus?' he asked Marianne.

Nodding her head, Marianne hurried to open the door into the hall, trying to look as though she were as familiar with the layout of the house as a true housekeeper would have been, although in reality all she knew of it was its kitchen.

She had time to recognise how badly served both the house and its master had been by Mrs Micklehead as she saw the neglect and the dull bloom on the mahogany doors which should have been gleaming with polish. The hallway was square, with imposing doors which she assumed belonged to the main entrance, whilst the stairs curved upwards to a galleried landing, the balustrade wonderfully carved with fruit and flowers whilst the banister rail itself felt smooth beneath her hand.

Two corridors ran off the handsome landing and Marianne hesitated, not knowing which might lead to the master bedroom, but to her relief the Master of

Bellfield had regained consciousness, and was trying to take a step towards the right-hand corridor.

Trying to assume a confidence she did not feel, Marianne hurried ahead of the men, who were now almost dragging the weight of their master. Halfway along the corridor a pair of doors stood slightly open. Taking a chance, Marianne pushed them back further, exhaling shakily as she saw from the unmade-up state of the bed that this must indeed be the master bedroom.

'We can't lay him down in that, lass,' one of the men supporting the master told her, nodding in the direction of the large bed. He added trenchantly, 'That looks like best quality sheeting, that does, and I reckon with the way he's bleedin' it'll be ruined if we lie him on it.'

He was right, of course, but since she had no idea where the linen cupboards were Marianne shook her head and said firmly, 'Then they will just have to be ruined. How long do you think it will be before the doctor gets here?'

'Depends on how long it takes Jim to find him. If I know Dr Hollingshead, he won't take too kindly to being disturbed before he's finished his breakfast.'

The two men had managed to lay their master on the bed now, and Marianne's heart missed a beat as she saw how much the bloodstain on his bandage had spread.

'Come on, lads,' the man who seemed to be the one in charge told the others.

'There's nowt we can do here now. We'd best get back t'mill.'

Marianne hurried after them as she heard them clattering down the stairs.

'The doctor will want to know exactly what happened,' she told them 'Perhaps one of you should stay—'

'There's nowt we can tell him except that a metal pin shot off one of the machines and flew straight into his leg. Pulled it out himself, he did, and all,' he informed Marianne admiringly, leaving Marianne to suppress a shudder of horror at the thought of the pain such an action must have caused.

CHAPTER FOUR

THE men had gone, but the doctor had still not arrived. Marianne, who had seen all manner of injuries during her time at the workhouse, and knew the dangers of un-cleaned wounds, had set water to boil and gone in search of clean linen, having first checked that the baby was still sleeping.

When she eventually found the linen cupboards on the attic floor, she grimaced in distaste to see that much of the linen was mired in cobwebs and mouse drop-pings, whilst the sheets that were clean were unironed and felt damp.

Her aunt would certainly never have tolerated such slovenliness and bad housekeeping. This was what happened when a man was at the mercy of someone like Mrs Micklehead. Against her will Marianne found that she almost felt slightly sorry for the Master of Bellfield— or at least for his house, which must once have been a truly elegant and comfortable home, and was now an empty, shabby place with no comfort of any kind.

She made her way back down the servants' staircase

to the attic floor and along the corridor to the landing. The departing men had left the door to the master bedroom open, and she could hear a low groan coming from it.

Quickly she hurried down the corridor, pausing in the doorway to the room.

The Master of Bellfield was still lying where the men had left him. His eyes were closed, but his right hand lay against his thigh, bright red with the blood that was now soaking through his fingers.

Panic filled Marianne. He was bleeding so much. Too much, she was sure.

Whilst she hesitated, wondering what to do, someone started knocking on the front door.

Picking up her skirts, Marianne ran down the stairs and across the hallway, turning the key in the lock and tugging back the heavy bolts so that she could open the door.

'Doctor's here, missus,' the man who had been knocking informed her, before turning his head to spit out the wad of tobacco he had been chewing.

Marianne could see a small rotund bearded man, in a black frock coat and a tall stovepipe hat, emerging from a carriage, carrying a large Gladstone bag.

'I understand there's been an accident, and that the Master of Bellfield has been injured,' he announced, without removing his hat. A sure sign that he considered a mere housekeeper to be far too much beneath him socially to merit the normal civilities, Marianne recognised, as she dipped him a small curtsey and nodded her head, before taking the bag he was holding out to her.

'Yes, that's right. If you'd like to come this way, Doctor. He's in his room.'

The bag was heavy, and she could see the contempt the doctor gave the dusty hallway. She vowed to herself that on his next visit she would have it gleaming with polish.

'You're new here,' he said curtly as Marianne led the way up the stairs.

'Yes,' she agreed. Taking a deep breath, she added untruthfully, 'Mr Denshaw sent word to an employment agency in Manchester that he was in need of a new housekeeper. I only arrived last night.' She hoped that the sudden scald of guilty colour heating her face would not betray her.

She paused as they reached the landing to tell him, 'The master's bedroom is this way, sir.'

'Yes, I know where it is. You will attend me whilst I examine him, if you please.'

Marianne inclined her head obediently.

The sheet was red with blood now, and the man lying on the bed was unconscious and breathing shallowly.

'How long has he been bleeding like this?' the doctor demanded sharply.

'Since he was brought here, sir,' Marianne told him, as she placed the doctor's bag on a mahogany tallboy.

'I shall need hot water and carbolic soap with which to wash my hands,' he told her disdainfully, as he went to open it. 'And tell my man that I shall need him up here. Quickly, now—there is no time to waste. Unless you wish to se your master bleed to death.'

'Yes, sir.'

Marianne almost flew back down the stairs, thankful that her ankle, whilst swollen, was no longer bothering her. Opening the front door, she passed on the doctor's instructions to his servant.

'Probably wants me to hold him down,' he informed her. 'You wouldn't credit the yellin' and cursin' some of them do. Shouldn't be surprised if he has to have his leg off. That's what happens to a lot of them.'

Marianne shuddered.

By the time she got back upstairs, with a large jug of hot water, some clean basins and the carbolic, the doctor was instructing his servant to remove the scissors from his bag and cut through the fabric of his patient's trousers so that he could inspect the wound.

One look at the servant's grimy hands and nails had Marianne's eyes rounding with shock. What kind of doctor insisted on cleanliness for his own hands but seemed not to care about applying the same safeguard to others? Marianne's aunt had been a friend of Florence Nightingale's family, and she had been meticulous about adopting the rules of cleanliness laid down by Miss Nightingale when doctoring her own household and estate workers. She had also been most insistent that Marianne learn these procedures, telling her many times, 'According to Florence Nightingale it is the infection that so often kills the patient and not the wound, and thus it is our duty to ensure that everything about and around a sick person is kept clean.'

Impulsively Marianne reached for the scissors, remembering those words now. 'Maybe I could do it more easily, sir. My hands being smaller,' she said quickly.

Before the doctor could stop her she placed the scissors in one of the bowls she had brought up with her

and poured some of the hot water over them, before
using them to cut through the blood-soaked fabric.

The air in the room smelled of blood, taking
Marianne back to scenes and memories she didn't want
to have. The poor house, with its victims of that poverty.
A young woman left to give birth on her own, her life
bleeding from her body whilst Marianne's cries for help
for her were ignored.

Her hands, washed with carbolic soap whilst she had
been downstairs, shook, the scissors slippery now with
blood. How shocked her aunt would have been at the
thought of Marianne being exposed to the sight of a
man's naked flesh. But of course she was not the young
innocent and protected girl she had been in her aunt's
household any more.

Soon she had slit the fabric far enough up the Master
of Bellfield's leg to reveal the wound from which his
blood was flowing. Not as fast as it had been; welling
rather than pumping now.

'Come along, girl—can't you see that there's blood
on my shoes? Clean it up, will you?' the doctor was
ordering her.

Marianne stared at him. He wanted her to clean his
shoes? What about his patient's wound? But she could
sense the warning look his servant was giving her, and
removing from her pocket the small piece of rag she had
picked up earlier, intending to use it to clean the top of
the range, she kneeled down and rubbed it over the
doctor's shoes.

'Good. Now, wipe some of that blood off his leg, will
you, so that I can take a closer look?'

Marianne could hardly believe her ears. Surely he wasn't expecting her to wipe the blood from her employer's leg with the rag she had just used to clean his shoes? Indignation sparkled in the normally quiet depths of her dark brown eyes. She turned to the pitcher of water she had brought upstairs and poured some into a clean bowl.

'Of course, sir,' she told him. 'I'll just wash my hands first, shall I?' she suggested quietly, not waiting for his permission but instead rubbing her hands fiercely with the carbolic soap. She poured some water over them, before putting some fresh water in a clean bowl and then dipping a new piece of sheeting into it.

The only wounds she had cleaned before had been small domestic injuries to her aunt's servants, and none of them had involved her touching a strongly muscled naked male thigh. But Marianne forced herself to ignore that and to work quickly to clean the blood away from the wound, as gently as she could. She could see that the pin had punctured the master's flesh to some depth, and a width of a good half an inch, leaving ragged edges of skin and an ominously dark welling of blood. Even though he was still semi-conscious he flinched beneath her touch and tried to roll away.

'Looks like we'll have to tie him down, Jenks,' the doctor told his servant. 'Brought up the ropes with you, have you?'

'I'll go down and get them, sir,' the servant answered him.

Marianne winced once again, moved to unwilling pity for her 'new employer.'

'Perhaps a glass of spirits might dull the pain and quieten him whilst you examine him, sir?' she suggested quietly.

'I dare say it would,' the doctor agreed, much to her relief. 'But I doubt you'll find any spirits in this household.'

'Surely as a doctor you carry a little medicinal brandy?' Marianne ventured to ask.

The doctor was frowning now.

'Brandy's expensive. Folk round here don't believe in wasting their brass on doctor's bills for brandy. Hmm, looks like the bleeding's stopped, and it's a clean enough wound. Knowing Denshaw as I do, I'm surprised that it was his own machinery that did this. Cares more about his factory and everything in it than he does himself. Your master is a foolish man at times. He's certainly not made himself popular amongst the other mill owners—paying his workers top rate, giving them milk to drink and special clothes to wear in the factory. That sort of thing is bound to lead to trouble one way or other. No need for those now, Jenks,' he announced to his servant, who had come into the room panting from carrying the heavily soiled and bloodstained coils of rope he held in his arms.

'Best thing you can do is bandage him up and let nature take its course. Like as not he'll take a fever, so I'll send a nurse up to sit with him. She'll bring a draught with her that will keep him quiet until the fever runs its course.'

'Bandage him up? But surely, Doctor—' Marianne began to protest, thinking that she must have misheard him. Surely the doctor couldn't mean that *she* was to bandage the Master of Bellfield's leg?

'Those are my instructions. And make sure that you pull the bandage tightly enough to stem the bleeding, but not too tightly. I'll bid you good day now. My bill will be five guineas. You can tell your master when he returns to himself. You may feed him on a little weak tea—but nothing more, mind, in case it gives rise to a fever.'

Five guineas! That was a fortune for someone like her. But it was the information the doctor had given her about the Master of Bellfield's astonishing treatment of his workers that occupied Marianne's thoughts as she escorted the doctor back down the stairs, and not the extortionate cost of his visit. Her heart started to beat faster. Did this news mean that the task she had set herself before she arrived at Bellfield could be nearer to completion? If only that might be so. Sometimes the weight of the responsibility she had been given felt so very heavy, and she longed to have another to share it with. But for now she must keep her own counsel, and with it her secret.

As soon as she had closed the heavy front door behind the doctor she headed for the kitchen, where to her relief the cat was curled up in front of the fire whilst the baby was lying gurgling happily in his basket.

He really was the sweetest-looking baby, Marianne acknowledged, smiling tenderly at him. He was going to have his father's cowlick of hair, even though as yet that cowlick was just a small curl. His colour was definitely much better, and he was actually watching her with interest instead of lying in that apathetic stillness that had so worried her. She was tempted to lift him out of the basket and cuddle him, but her first duty had to be to the man lying upstairs, she reminded herself sternly. After all, without him there would be no warm kitchen to shelter them, and no good rich milk to fill the baby's empty stomach.

Bandage him up, the doctor had said. He hadn't even offered to leave her any bandaging either, Marianne reflected, her sense of what was ethically right in a doctor outraged by his lack of proper care for his patient.

She would just have to do the best she could. And she would do her best—just as her aunt would have expected her to do. Now, what was it that boy on the bicycle had said his name was? Postlethwaite—that was it.

Marianne had seen the telephone in the hallway, and now she went to it and picked up the receiver, unable to stop herself from looking over her shoulder up the stairs. Not that it was likely that the Master of Bellfield was likely to come down to chastise her for the liberty she was taking.

A brisk female voice on the other end of the line was asking her what number she required.

'I should like to be put through to Postlethwaite's Provisions,' she answered, her stomach cramping with a mixture of guilt and anxiety as she waited for the exchange operator to do as she had requested. She had no real right to be doing this, and certainly no real authority. She wasn't really the housekeeper of Bellfield House after all.

'How do, lass, how's t'master going on?'

'Mr Postlethwaite?' Marianne asked uncertainly.

'Aye, that's me. My lad said as how he'd heard about t'master's accident. You'll be wanting me to send up some provisions for him, I reckon. I've got a nice tin of turtle soup here that he might fancy, or how about…?'

Tinned turtle soup? For a sick man? Marianne rather fancied that some good, nurturing homemade chicken soup would suit him far better, but of course she didn't want to offend the shopkeeper.

'Yes, thank you, Mr. Postlethwaite,' she answered him politely. 'I shall be needing some provisions, but first and most important I wondered if you could give me the direction of a reliable chemist. One who can supply me with bandages and ointments, and quickly. The doctor is to send up a nurse, but in the meantime I am to bandage the wound.'

'Aye, you'll be wanting Harper's. If you want to tell me what you're wanting, I'll send young Charlie round there now and he can bring it up.'

His kindness brought a lump to Marianne's throat and filled her with relief. Quickly she told him what she thought she would need, before adding, 'Oh, and I was wondering—would you know of anyone local who might have bee hives, Mr Postlethwaite. Only I could do with some honey.'

'Well, I dunno about that,' he answered doubtfully, 'it not being the season to take the combs out of the hives. But I'll ask around for you.'

'It must be pure honey, Mr Postlethwaite, and not any other kind.' Marianne stressed.

Her aunt had sworn by the old-fashioned remedy of applying fresh honey to open wounds in order to heal and cleanse them.

'A word to the wise, if you don't mind me offering

it, Mrs Brown,' Mr Postlethwaite was saying, his voice dropping to a confidential whisper. 'If the doctor sends up Betty Chadwick to do the nursing you'd best make sure that she isn't on the drink.'

'Oh, yes…thank you.'

At least now she would have the wherewithal to follow the doctor's instructions, and the larder would have some food in it, Marianne acknowledged as she carefully replaced the telephone receiver, even if the shopkeeper's warning about the nurse had been worrying.

Mentally she started to list everything she would need to do. As soon as she had bandaged the master's wound she would have to fill the copper and boil-wash a good supply of clothes with which to cleanse his wound when it needed redressing. She would also have to try to find some decent clean sheets, and get them aired—although she wouldn't be able to change his bed until the nurse arrived to lift him.

Armed with a fresh supply of hot water, and a piece of clean wet sheeting she had washed in boiling water and carbolic soap, Marianne made her way back upstairs to the master bedroom.

Her patient was lying motionless, with his face turned towards the window and his eyes closed, and for a second Marianne thought that he might actually have died he was so still. Her heart in her mouth, she stared at his chest, willing it to rise and fall, and realised when it did that she was shaking with relief. Relief? For this man? A man who… But, no, she must not think of that now.

Quietly and carefully Marianne made her way to the

side of the bed opposite the window, closest to his injured leg.

Congealed blood lay thickly on top of the wound,
which would have to be cleaned before she could
bandage it. Marianne raised her hand to place it against
the exposed flesh, to test it for heat that would indicate
whether the wound was already turning putrid, and then
hesitated with her hand hovering above the master's
naked thigh. Eventually she let her hand rest over the
flesh of the wound. A foolish woman, very foolish
indeed, might almost be tempted to explore that
maleness, so very different in construction and intent
from her own slender and delicate limbs.

Marianne stiffened as though stung. There was no
reason for the way she was feeling at the moment, with
her heart beating like a trapped bird and her face starting
to burn. In the workhouse she had become accustomed
to any number of sights and sounds not normally
deemed suitable for the eyes and ears of a delicately
reared female. Naked male limbs were not, after all,
something she had never seen before. But she had not
seen any that were quite as strongly and sensually male
as this one, with its powerful muscles and sprinkling of
thick dark hair. And, shockingly, the flesh was not pale
like her own, but instead had been darkened as though
by the sun.

An image flashed through her head—a hot summer's
evening when, as a girl, she had chanced to walk past a
local millpond where the young men of the village had
stripped off to swim in its cooling waters. Over it her
senses imposed the image of another man—older, adult,

and fully formed in his manhood. *This* man. A fierce shockwave of abhorrence for her own reckless thoughts seized her. What manner of foolishness was this?

Deliberately Marianne cleared her head of such dangerous thoughts and forced herself to concentrate on the feel of the flesh beneath her hand as though she were her aunt. Was there heat coming up from the torn flesh, or was the heat only there in her own guilty thoughts? There was no flushing of the skin, but her aunt had always said that a wound should be properly cleaned before it be allowed to seal.

Marianne wished that the nurse might arrive and take from her the responsibility of judging what should be done. She had seen what could happen if a wound turned putrid when a young gypsy had been brought to her aunt's back door, having been found on neighbouring land caught in a man trap. His leg had swelled terribly with the poison that even her aunt had not been able to stem, and he had died terribly, in agony, his face blackened and swollen.

Gripped by the horror of her memories, Marianne's hand tightened on the Master's thigh.

When he let out a roar and sat up in the bed, Marianne didn't know which of them looked the more shocked as she snatched her hand away from his flesh and he stared in disbelief.

'You! What the devil? What are you about, woman? Is this how you repay my charity? By trying to kill me?'

'Dr Hollingshead said that I was to bandage your leg.'

'Hollingshead? That fraudulent leech. If he has let that filthy man of his anywhere near me then I am as good as dead.'

Instantly Marianne tried to reassure him. 'I took the liberty of suggesting that I should be the one… That is…since he had—wrongly, of course—assumed I was your new housekeeper…'

'What?'

'It was a natural enough mistake.'

'Was it, by God, or did you help him on his way to making it?'

For a man who had lost as much blood as he had, and who must be in considerable pain, the swiftness of his comprehension was daunting, Marianne acknowledged.

'I…I have a little nursing experience through my aunt, and if you will allow me, sir, I will bathe your wound and place a bandage around it until the nurse arrives. She is to bring a draught with her that will assist you to sleep.'

'Assist me to sleep—finish me, off you mean, with an unhealthy dose of laudanum.' He moved on the bed and then blenched, and Marianne guessed that his wound was causing him more pain than he was ready to admit.

'The bed will need to be changed when the nurse arrives, and that will, I'm afraid, cause you some dis-comfort,' she told him tactfully. 'I suggested to the doctor that maybe a medicinal tot of brandy would help. However, he said that it was unlikely that I would find any, so I have taken the liberty of ordering some from Mr Postlethwaite, to be brought up with some other necessary provisions.'

He stared at her. 'The devil you have! Well, Hollingshead was wrong! You'll find a bottle in the library. Bottom cupboard on the left of the fireplace.

Keys are in my coat pocket, and mind you bring them back. Oh, and when young Charlie gets here, tell him he's to go to the mill and tell Archie Gledhill to get himself up here. I want to talk to him.'

'You should be resting. The sickroom is not a place from which to conduct business,' Marianne reproved him, earning herself another biting look of wonder.

'For a charity case who only last night was begging at my door, you're taking one hell of a lot of liberties.' His eyes narrowed. 'And if you're thinking to take advantage of a sick man, then let me tell you—' He winced and fell back against the pillows his face suddenly tense with pain. 'Go and get that brandy.'

'I really don't think—' Marianne began, but he didn't let her continue, struggling to get up out of the bed instead.

Worried that he might cause his wound to bleed again, Marianne told him hurriedly, 'Very well—I will fetch it. But only if you promise me that you will lie still whilst I am gone.'

'Take the keys,' he told her, 'and look sharp.'

Marianne had to try two sets of doors before she found those that opened into the library—a dull, cold room that smelled of damp, with heavy velvet curtains at the window that shut out the light. There was a darker rectangle of wallpaper above the fireplace, as though a portrait had hung there at some time.

She found the brandy where she had been told it would be. The bottle was unopened, suggesting that the Master of Bellfield was normally an abstemious man. Marianne knew that here in the mill valleys the

Methodist religion, with its abhorrence of alcohol and the decadent ways of the rich, held sway.

There were some dusty glasses in the cupboard with the brandy so she snatched one up to take back to the master bedroom with her.

When she reached the landing she hesitated, suddenly unwilling to return to the master bedroom now that the master had come to himself, wishing heartily that the nurse might have arrived, and that she could leave the master in her hands.

She heard a sudden sound from the room—a heavy thud followed by a ripe curse. Forgetting her qualms, she rushed to the room, staring in disbelief at the man now standing beside the bed, swaying as he clung to the bedstead, his face drained of colour and his muscles corded with pain.

'What are you doing?' she protested. 'You should not have left the bed.'

'I hate to offend your womanly sensibilities, but I'm afraid I had to answer a call of nature,' he said, glancing towards a now half-open door Marianne had not seen before, which led, she realised, to a bathroom. 'And now, since I am up, and you, it seems, are intent on usurping the role of my housekeeper, perhaps you would be kind enough to change the bedlinen?'

He was far too weak to be standing up, and indeed looked as though he was about to collapse at any moment. On the other hand the bloodstained sheet did need to be removed.

Marianne glanced around the room, and then ran to drag a chair over to him, urging him to sit on it.

'I'm afraid Mrs Micklehead has neglected the care of the linen cupboard,' she told him. 'I have, however, put some fresh sheets to warm. I shall go down and get them.' She looked at him and added, 'Would you like me to pour you a measure of brandy?'

'Measure?' He gave a harsh bark of laughter. 'Much good that will do. But, aye—go on, then.'

Very carefully Marianne poured a small amount of the liquid into a glass, and then went over to him with it. When he tried to take it from her she shook her head firmly and told him strictly, 'I shall hold it for you, sir. You have lost a great deal of blood and are likely to be weakened by it.'

'Too weakened to hold a glass? Don't think I haven't guessed why you're fussing around me,' he warned her.

Immediately Marianne stiffened. Was it possible that he had discerned her secret?

'You think to make yourself indispensable to me so that I will keep you on,' he continued.

Relief leaked from her heart and into her veins.

'That is not true,' she told him, avoiding looking at him. 'I am simply doing my Christian duty, that is all.'

'Your Christian duty.' His mouth twisted as though he had tasted something bitter. 'Aye, well, I have had my craw stuffed full of that in my time. Cold charity that starves the flesh and the soul.'

Marianne's hand trembled as she held the glass to his lips. His words had touched a raw nerve within her. She too had experienced that same cold charity, and still bore in her heart its scars. It would be so easy now to open that heart to him, but she must not.

So much that she had learned since coming to Bellfield was confusing and conflicting, and then there were her own unexpected and unwanted feelings. Feelings that a woman in her position, newly widowed and with a child had no right to have. She had felt them the first time he had looked at her.

Like an echo she could hear inside her heart she heard her own voice asking, 'But how does one know that it is love?' and another voice, sweet and faint, answering her softly.

Her body trembled. Her life had been filled with so much loss and pain that there had not been room for her to wonder about love.

And she must not think about it now either. Not here, or with this man above all men.

There was, after all, no need for her hands to tremble, she told herself sternly. What she was doing was no more than she had done for others many times over.

But they had not been like this man, an inner voice told her.

Engrossed in her thoughts, she gave a small gasp when suddenly his hand closed over hers, hard flesh, with calluses and strong fingers, tipping the glass so that he could drain its contents in one swallow.

Marianne tried not to let her hand shake beneath his, nor wrench it away before he had released her.

Already she could see a flush of colour seeping up along his jaw from the warmth of the brandy.

'You must promise me that you will not move from here,' she told him. 'If you were to fall on that injury…'

'Such concern for a stranger,' he mocked her. 'I do

not trust you, Mrs Brown, and that is a fact. You are too good to be true.'

Fresh colour stormed Marianne's face. She did not dare risk saying anything. Instead, she headed for the door and the kitchen.

The baby was sleeping peacefully. He would need feeding again soon. She might try him on a little oatmeal this time, now that his poor little stomach was no longer so shrunken.

Taking the sheets from the maiden she had set up in front of the range, she set off back for the master bedroom, thinking as she did so that surely the nurse and Charlie Postlethwaite should both arrive soon.

Marianne's aunt had firmly believed that a mistress should know for herself the exact nature of any domestic task she asked of her servants, and had taught Marianne the same.

Quickly she removed the bloodstained sheet, noting as she did so the untidy fashion in which the bed had been made, and wrinkling her small straight nose in disapproval of such sloppiness.

Since the Master of Bellfield was now slumped in his chair with his eyes closed, it didn't occur to her to look at him to see if he was watching her as she worked quickly and neatly to place a clean warmed sheet on the bed and tuck in the corners 'hospital fashion', the way she had been taught.

'For one so small and young you have a great deal of assurance as to domestic matters, Mrs Brown.'

His words made her jump, but she still managed to reply. 'It is the duty of a housekeeper to ensure that her employer's house is maintained to the highest possible standard, sir.' Then she added, 'If you think you could bear it, it might be better if I were to bathe and bandage your leg whilst you are seated here, in order to spare the sheet and ensure that you can lie comfortably on clean sheets. I do not know if Mrs Micklehead used a laundry service, but I dare say there is an outhouse in the yard with a copper, where I can boil-wash—'

'That won't be necessary.' He cut her off sharply. 'There is enough gossip about me as it is, without folk saying that the Master of Bellfield can't afford to get his linen laundered and must have his housekeeper labour over a copper, when all the world knows that that is the work of a laundress. When Charlie Postlethwaite gets here you can tell him to ask that uncle of his who runs the laundry to send someone up to collect whatever it is that needs washing.'

Marianne's eyes widened. Did that mean that he intended to keep her on as his housekeeper? She didn't dare ask, just in case her question provoked him to a denial of any such intention.

Instead she picked up a clean bowl and poured some water into it, then went to kneel down at his side.

Somehow her task felt much more intimate knowing that he was watching her. It was, of course, only because she was afraid of hurting him that her hands were trembling and she felt so breathless. Nothing more, she assured herself, as she dipped the cloth into the water and started to carefully wipe away the encrusted blood.

He didn't say a word, but she knew he must be in pain because she could feel his thigh muscles tightening under her hand. With the wound being on the inside of his thigh the intimacy of their position was unavoidable.

'Your hand shakes like that of a green girl who has never touched a man before,' he told her roughly. 'And yet you have had a husband.'

Marianne's heart leapt and thudded into her ribs. 'My hand shakes, sir, because I am afraid of starting the wound bleeding again.'

Did she sound as breathless as she felt?

Marianne could feel him looking at her, but she was too afraid to look back at him.

'The child—is it a boy?' The abrupt unexpectedness of his question caught her off guard, achieving what his earlier statement had not. Her hand stilled and she looked up at him, right into the smoke-grey eyes.

'Yes…yes, he is.'

'I had a son. Or I would have done if—' His mouth compressed. 'The child thrives?'

'I…I think so.'

She had cleansed the wound now, and the width and the depth of it shocked her. She tried to imagine pulling out the instrument that had caused it, and could not do so for the thought of the pain that would have had to be endured.

'I have cleansed the wound now, sir. I will cover it until the nurse gets here.'

'Pass me that brandy,' he demanded.

Thinking he intended to pour himself another drink, Marianne did as he had commanded, but instead he dashed the tawny liquid straight onto his flesh.

Marianne winced for him as his free hand clutched at

her arm and hard fingers dug into her flesh. She knew her discomfort was nothing compared to what his must be.

'Your husband—how did he die?'

Marianne stiffened.

'He died of smallpox, sir.'

'You were not with him?'

'Yes, I...I was with him.' She had nursed Milo through his final days and hours, and it was hard for her to speak of the suffering he had undergone.

'But you did not take the disease yourself?'

'I had the chicken pox as a child, and my late aunt was of the belief that those who have that are somehow protected from smallpox. I think it would be best if you were to lie down now, sir.'

'Oh, you do, do you? Very well, then.'

Automatically Marianne went to help him as he struggled to get up from the chair, doing her best to support him. He was obviously weaker than he himself had known, because he fell against her, causing her to hold him tightly.

He smelled of male flesh and male sweat, and his thick dark hair was oddly soft against her face as his head fell onto her shoulder. The last time she had held a man like this he had been dying, and he had been her husband. Marianne closed her eyes, willing the tears burning the backs of her eyes not to fall.

To her relief the master managed to gather enough strength to get himself onto the bed, where she was able to put a loose clean cover over his wound and a fresh sheet over him, followed by some blankets and an eider-down. She noticed that he was shivering slightly, and resolved to make up a fire in the bedroom as well as heat some bricks for the bed.

She had just finished straightening the linen, and was about to leave when, without opening his eyes, the master reached for the keys she had returned to him and spoke. 'Here—you had better take these, since you have taken it upon yourself to announce to the world that you are my housekeeper.'

Marianne stared at him, but he had turned his face away from her. Uncertainly, she picked up the keys. These were her official badge of office—one that everyone coming to the house would recognise and honour.

Relief swelled her chest and caused her heart to beat unsteadily.

To have accomplished so much and gone so far towards keeping her promise in such a short space of time was so much more than she had expected.

From downstairs came the sound of someone knocking impatiently on the back door. The Master of Bellfield was lying still, his eyes closed, but she knew that he was not asleep.

CHAPTER FIVE

'SORRY it's tekken me so long to get here, missus,' Charlie Postlethwaite apologised when Marianne opened the door to him. 'Only it took me dad a while to get hold of old Harry to ask him about that honey you wanted.'

'You got some?' Marianne exclaimed, pleased.

'Aye. He weren't for giving it up at first, but when Dad said that it was for Mr Denshaw...'

Marianne tried not to frown. Here was someone else telling her that the Master of Bellfield was a man well regarded by those around him. And yet there were others all too ready to tell a tale of cruelty and neglect towards those who had most deserved his care.

'Mr Denshaw said to tell you that he wants to see a Mr Gledhill,' she told him.

'Aye, that's t'manager of t'mill. It's all round the town now, what's happened, and there's plenty saying that they'd never have thought of anything like that going wrong at Bellfield, on account of the way the master is always having his machines checked over and that. Them that work in t'other mills are always getting themselves injured, but not the people at Bellfield. My dad's sent up a chicken, like you asked for—he said how you want to make up some soup with it. Got some turtle soup in the shop, we have, that would suit t'master a treat,' he told her, repeating his father's comment.

'I'm sure it would,' Marianne agreed diplomatically, 'but chicken soup is best for invalids. Will you thank your father for me, Charlie? Oh, and Mr Denshaw said that I was to see if you could ask your uncle at the laundry to send someone up.'

Nodding his head, Charlie headed for the door.

Marianne had no sooner seen him cycle out of the yard and fed the baby then there was another knock on the door, this time heralding the arrival of the nurse.

'I'll show you up to Mr Denshaw,' she told her, after she had let her in.

'There's no rush for that. He's waited this long. He can wait a bit longer. A cup of tea wouldn't go amiss, mind.' The nurse sniffed and wiped her hand across her nose. Her hand was grubby, and Marianne couldn't help but notice the strong smell of drink on her breath.

'You've come from Manchester, then, have you?' she commented, settling herself in front of the range.

'Yes, that's right,' Marianne fibbed.

'Bit young, ain't yer, to be taking on a job like this?'

Marianne said nothing, lifting the kettle from the fire instead, to make the tea the nurse had requested.

'A nip of something in it would go down a treat,' the nurse told her. 'Just to warm me old bones.'

'The doctor said that he would send a draught up with

you for Mr Denshaw,' Marianne told her, pretending she hadn't heard.

'Aye, a good dose of laudanum to keep him quiet, so as we can all get a decent night's sleep. I can't abide nursing anyone what don't sleep. Heard about what happened to his wife, I expect, have you?' she asked Marianne.

'I heard that she died in childbirth,' Marianne felt obliged to reply.

'Aye, and some round here said they weren't surprised, that they'd thought she were daft to marry him in the first place. Ten years older than him, she were, and a widow with a son what should have inherited this house and everything that went with it. Only she had her head turned by him coming along and making up to her, so she let him have what the wanted, like a fool. He married her out of vengeance, so they say. And to get his hands on the mill, of course. See, his pa and hers were in business together at one time. Only his pa decides to go and set up on his own, and then things went wrong for him, and he got himself into debt. Blew his brains out, he did, and him upstairs were taken into t'workhouse.'

Marianne's heart clenched with pity and fellow feeling.

'Poor woman, she must have regretted the day she stood up in church alongside Heywood Denshaw. She'd be turning in her grave, she would, if she knew what he did after she'd gone. Drove her son, what was the rightful heir to Bellfield Mill, away. And Amelia, that niece of hers, as well—the master's ward, what the young master were sweet on. Ran off together, they did. And there's some folk that say as they'll never come back, on account of a foul dark deed being done by a certain person, that they're lying in their graves now…'

Marianne's hands shook, and seeing them the nurse said, 'You do well to look fearful, lass. A terrible man the Master of Bellfield is. If I was you I'd get that babby swaddled nice and tight, so that it lies quiet instead of moving about like that.' She changed the subject to look disapprovingly at the baby in the basket. 'A bit of laudanum in its milk at night and you'll not hear a sound from it. That's what I tell all them I nurse, and I've never yet had a mother complain to me that she can't get no sleep, nor a husband complain that he ain't getting his nuptials neither.'

Her words caused Marianne to go over to the baby and place a protective hand over him. She had seen babies in the workhouse tightly swaddled and fed laudanum to keep them quiet, their little bodies so still that it had been hard sometimes to tell whether they lived or died. She would never allow little Miles to be treated like that.

'Some say that his sister should have given him a home, but I can't see that there's any sense in going blaming a Christian woman like Mrs Knowles for not wanting to take on a bad lot like him. Always in trouble, he was. Ran away from the poor house once and had to be brought back. Anyways, Mrs Knowles and her husband was living away then, on account of Mr Knowles' health. Always delicate, he were, and it's no wonder he went and left her a widow. Luckily for her she's got a good son to do his duty by her. Like I said, she's a true Christian woman is Mrs Knowles. Recommends me to all her friends, she does, when they want any nursing done.'

Marianne tried not to show her astonishment. From what little she had seen of the nurse, she was not only a gossip and partial to a drink, she was also dirty—and, Marianne suspected, all too likely to neglect her patients.

'Does Mrs Knowles live locally? I am sure she would wish to be informed of her brother's accident. It may be that she will also wish to oversee his convalescence,' Marianne suggested.

'Well, as to that, after the way he treated her the last time she tried to help 'im, I'd be surprised if she wanted to set foot inside this house again, brother or no brother. Told 'er he put the blame for his wife dying and taking the babby with her on her shoulders, when everyone knew that it were *'is* fault. Even came over herself when she'd heard his missus had gone into labour, and sent for Dr Hollingshead as well. See, her and the missus were close friends, and she told her that she blamed herself for introducing her to 'er brother. No, there's no call to go sending any message to Mount Vernon to tell Mrs Knowles what's happened. 'Cos even if she was to be Christian enough to come and see him, she ain't there. She spends the winters down in Torquay, on account of her Jeffrey's chest. Won't be back until the spring starts, and by that time… Well, owt could happen.'

It was plain to Marianne what the nurse would like to see happen, and it shocked her that someone who was supposed to care for the sick should show such relish at the prospect of death.

Marianne could see the nurse surreptitiously removing a flask from her pocket and tipping some of its contents into her tea, and her concern deepened.

* * *

By the time Marianne was opening the back door to the tall, thin man who introduced himself as, 'Archie Gledhill, t'mill manager,' the nurse was asleep and snoring, and smelling strongly of drink.

'Yes, do come in Mr Gledhill.' Marianne smiled politely at him. 'I am Mr Denshaw's new housekeeper, Mrs Brown.'

'Yes, I 'eard as to how you was 'ere. And lucky for t'master that you are an' all,' he told her, glancing approvingly round the pin-neat kitchen. His approval turned to a frown, though, when he saw the nurse. 'You'll not be letting 'er anywhere near t'master?' he asked Marianne sharply.

'Dr Hollingshead sent her up,' Marianne told him.

'T'master won't want her 'ere. Not after what happened to his missus and babby. If you'll take my advice you'll send her about her business.'

'If you think I should.'

'I do,' he assured her grimly.

Marianne nodded her head. His words had only confirmed her own fears about the nurse's suitability for her work.

'I'll go and inform Mr Denshaw that you're here. If you would like a cup of tea…?'

'That's right kind of you, missus, but I'd best see the master first.'

'If you would like to wait here, I'll go up and tell him now,' Marianne told him.

She had closed the door to the master bedroom when she had last left it, but now it was slightly ajar.

She rapped briefly on it, and when there was no reply she opened it.

A tumble of clothes lay on the floor: the shirt the Master of Bellfield had been wearing, along with some undergarments. The room smelled of carbolic soap, and there were splashes of water leading from the bathroom.

It amazed Marianne that a man in as much pain as Mr Denshaw had felt it necessary to get out of bed, remove his clothes and wash himself. And whilst ordinarily she would have admired a person's desire for cleanliness, on this occasion she was more concerned about the effect his actions might have had on his wound.

Without stopping to think, she bustled over to the bed, scolding him worriedly. 'You should have called for me if you wanted to get out of bed.'

Immediately a naked hair-roughened male arm shot out from beneath the covers and a hard male hand grasped her arm.

'And you would have washed me like a baby? I'm a man, Mrs Brown, and that ring on your finger and the marriage lines you claim go with it don't entitle you to make free with my body as though it were a child's.'

Marianne could feel her face burning with embarrassment.

'Mr Gledhill is here,' she told him in a stilted voice. 'Shall I bring him up?'

'Aye.'

'I have spoken with Charlie Postlethwaite about the laundry. I have not had time to check the linen closet properly as yet, but I shall do my best to ensure that your nightshirts are…'

To her dismay it was a struggle for her not to look at his naked torso as she spoke of the item of clothing he should surely have been wearing.

'Nightshirts?' He laughed and told her mockingly, 'I am a mill master, Mrs Brown, not a gentleman, and I sleep in the garment that nature provided me with—my own skin. That is the best covering within the marital bed, for both a man and a woman.'

Marianne whisked herself out of the room, not trusting herself to make any reply.

For a man who had injured himself as badly as he had, the Master of Bellfield had a far too virile air about him. Her heart was beating far too fast. She had never before seen such muscles in a man's arms, nor such breadth to a man's chest, and as for that arrowing of dark hair… Marianne almost missed her step on the stairs, and her face was still glowing a bright pink when she hurried into the kitchen to find Mr Gledhill rocking the baby's basket and the chair beside the fire empty.

'T'babby woke up and started mithering.'

'I expect he's hungry,' Marianne told him.

'Aye, he is an all, by the looks of it. Got a little 'un of me own—a grand lad, he is,' he told her proudly. 'I've sent t'nurse packing for you, an' all. Aye, and I've put the bolt across t'back door in case she were thinking of coming back and filling her pockets. A bad lot, she is. There's more than one family round here 'as lost someone on account of her. After what happened to the master's missus, me wife said as how she'd rather t'shepherd from t'farm deliver our wean than Dr Hollingshead.'

'I'll take you up to Mr Denshaw now, if you'd like to come this way?'

This time when she knocked on the bedroom door and then opened it Marianne purposefully did not look in the direction of the bed, but instead kept her face averted when she announced the mill manager, and then stepped smartly out of the room.

It was some time before the mill manager returned to the kitchen, and when he did he was frowning, as though his thoughts burdened him.

'T'master has told me to tell you that for so long as he is laid up you can apply to me for whatever you may need in your role as housekeeper. He said that you're to supply me with a list of everything that needs re-placin'—by way of sheeting and that. I'm to have a word with the tradesmen and tell them to send their bills to me until t'master is well enough to deal wi' them himself. There are accounts at most of the shops.'

He reached into his pocket and withdrew some bright shiny coins, which he placed on the table.

'He said to give you this. There's two guineas there in shillings. You're to keep a record of what you spend for t'master to check. If there is anything else I can 'elp you with…'

'There is one thing,' Marianne told him. 'The house is cold and damp, and I should like to have a fire lit in the master's bedroom. There is a coal store, but there does not seem to be anyone to maintain it, nor to provide the household with kindling and the like.'

The mill manager nodded his head. 'T'master said

himself that he wanted me to sort out a lad to take the place of old Bert, who used to do the outside work. Should have been replaced years ago, he should, but t'master said as 'ow he'd worked 'ere all his life, and that it weren't right to turn him out. Not that 'e'd been doing much work this last year.' The mill manager shook his head. 'Too soft-'earted t'master is sometimes.'

Marianne couldn't help but look surprised. Soft-hearted wasn't how *she* would have described the Master of Bellfield.

'I'll send a lad up first thing in the morning. I know the very one. Good hard worker, he'll be, and knows what he's about. Master said that you'll be needing a girl to do the rough work as well.'

Marianne nodded her head.

For a man who less than a handful of hours ago had barely been conscious, her new employer seemed to have made a remarkable recovery.

'And perhaps if Mr Denshaw could have a manservant, especially whilst he is so…so awkwardly placed with his wound?' Marianne suggested delicately.

The mill manager scratched his head. 'Begging your pardon, ma'am, but I don't think he'd care for that. He doesn't like all them fancy ways. Mind, I could send up a couple of lads, if you were to send word, to give you a hand if it were a matter of lifting him or owt like that?'

'Yes…thank you.'

He meant well, Marianne knew, but that wasn't what she'd had in mind at all. With the nurse dismissed, she was now going to have to nurse her employer, and if what she had experienced earlier was anything to go by, the Master of Bellfield was not going to change his ways to accommodate her female sensibilities.

'T'master also said to tell you that you can have the use of the housekeeper's rooms, fifteen guineas wages a year and a scuttle full of coal every day, all found.'

Fifteen guineas! And all found! Marianne nodded her head. Those were generous terms indeed.

CHAPTER SIX

THE day's bright sunshine had faded into evening darkness, and beneath the full moon which Marianne could see from the kitchen window the yard was glazed with white frosting.

True to his word, the mill manager had sent up a sturdy-looking youth who had spent what was left of the afternoon chopping fire kindling and filling enough coal scuttles to fuel every fire in the house.

At four o'clock Marianne had gone out to him to take him some bread and cheese. He seemed a decent lad, shy, and not quick with his words, but hard-working. He had told her his name was Ben. He had further added that his cousin Hannah would be coming up in the morning, to see if she might suit for the rough work in the kitchen.

A cheerful-looking individual had also arrived, announcing that he was from the laundry, and Marianne had somehow made time to bundle up and list as much of the grubby linen as she could.

She had even had time to run up the stairs to the attic

floor, to seek out the rooms the mill manager had referred to as the housekeeper's rooms. It had been easy enough to establish which they were, and Marianne had decided the minute she saw them that neither she nor the baby would be occupying them until she had given them a good scrub through and got some fresh ticking to cover the mattress. For tonight she planned to sleep in the kitchen again, where it was warm and clean.

The house's nurseries were also on the attic floor, and Marianne had been drawn to them. Once they would have rung with the childish laughter of the young boy and girl whom, so local gossip said, had been driven away by the cruelty of the man who had been stepfather to one and guardian to the other.

The rooms were cold and abandoned, with distemper flaking off the sloping walls where they rose to meet the ceiling. Heavy protective bars guarded the windows, and there was a large brass fireguard in front of the fire, the kind on which a children's nanny would have dried their outside clothes, and perhaps as a treat made toast for nursery tea.

One thing that had impressed her about the house was the fact that the nursery floor had a proper bathroom, with a flushing lavatory and a big bath.

Now, though, she was busy in the kitchen, keeping an eye on the baby whilst she worked busily.

Although she had been upstairs several times, on each occasion the Master of Bellfield had been sleeping, so Marianne had not disturbed him. Now the kitchen was full of the rich smell of the chicken soup she had made for the invalid, and the cat, who had proudly presented her with three dead mice already, was sitting purposefully in front of the range.

As she bustled about, Marianne hummed softly under her breath, mentally making lists of all that she had to do. There was the warming pan to be made ready for the master's bed. Thanks to Ben, there was now a fire burning cheerfully in the bedroom, and tomorrow she would send Ben down to the mill to ask Mr Gledhill if he had any idea where she might find the boiler that should provide hot water for the bathrooms. She suspected it would be in the cellars, but she was reluctant to go down and investigate, knowing that it was by the door that led to them that the cat sat, waiting for her prey. The thought of mice running over her feet as she explored the cellars' darkness made her shudder.

That meant that she must heat water on the range, both to clean the master's wound and for him to shave with, should he choose to do so.

It had caused her several moments' disquiet to discover that nowhere in the linen cupboard was there a sign of any kind of male night attire. There must, however, be a draper's shop in the town, and they would be sure to be able to supply some, she decided firmly. Whether or not Mr Denshaw would wear them was, of course, another matter.

She let the cat out and, covering the soup and leaving it to simmer, gathered up everything she needed to wash and bandage her employer's injury.

This time when she knocked on the door and turned the door handle the Master of Bellfield was not only awake, he was also sitting up, leaning back against the pillows and frowning as he stared out of the uncurtained windows.

'Who gave orders for a fire to be lit?' he demanded brusquely.

'I did,' Marianne told him. 'When a person has received a wound of the magnitude of yours, then it is important that they are kept warm. I have brought you some water and some clean towels in case you wish to…to refresh yourself, before I bring up your supper. But first I must check your…your injury.'

'My injury can look after itself.'

Marianne stood her ground. 'I am relieved that you feel recovered enough to think so, sir, but I would rather check.'

'Very well, then, but I warn you that my belly is empty, and I am in no mood to be fussed over like a mewling babe in arms.'

Marianne ignored him, dragging a chair over to the side of the bed instead and then laying a clean cloth on it.

'What is that for?'

'I thought that you could rest your leg on it whilst I cleaned the wound, so as not to dampen the sheets,' Marianne told him calmly.

'You want me to place my leg on the chair, do you?'

'If you would be so kind, sir, yes.'

So far Marianne had managed to keep her gaze fixed on the wallpaper above his head, and thus avoid having to look at his naked chest, but now, as he moved, the sheet slipped down to reveal more of his torso, at the same time as he pushed his naked leg free of the bedding to rest it on the chair.

Marianne's throat went dry. On this side of the bed at least there was nothing covering him except the shadows of the bed, which mercifully covered those parts of him she should not see. But in order to reach the site of his injury she would have to lean over him, and then…

What was the matter with her? She had attended other injured men, and nursed a dying husband to his death, sponging his whole fever-soaked body over and over again through those long hours.

But this man was different. This man touched something within her womanhood that she had no power to control. Marianne looked towards the door. It was too late for flight now. She had given her word and must stay, no matter what the cost to herself.

Taking a deep breath, she removed the cloth from the wound. The bleeding had stopped, but there was an ominous swollen reddening of the flesh around the puncture. Very gently Marianne placed her hand over it, her heart sinking when she felt its heat. The wound was becoming putrid.

'Imagining me dead already, are you?'

The harsh words made her flinch.

'The wound has some heat, sir, but I doubt that you will die of that,' she told him, with more conviction that she felt. 'I shall cleanse it and bandage it, and then if the heat has not gone I believe you should send for Dr Hollingshead.'

'That quack! I'll not have him near me.'

'Perhaps another doctor, then?'

'Aye, perhaps I should get myself one from Manchester—like my new housekeeper,' he taunted her.

Marianne said nothing, getting up instead to fetch what she had brought with her.

She wiped the wound clean first with boiled water, using fresh pads as hot as she thought he could bear to draw the poison as her aunt had taught her, whilst keeping an eye on him to make sure that she was not causing him more pain than he could stand. And then, when she had done that, she reached for the honey.

'What the devil do you mean to do with that?' her patient demanded angrily, attempting to draw his leg out of the way.

'It is honey, sir. My aunt believed that it has great efficacy in the drawing and healing of wounds.'

'Well, I'm having none of it. Douse the injury with brandy and then wrap it up clean, and let's have done with it.'

Marianne could see that he meant what he was saying. Reluctantly she did as he bade. She could not swear to it, but as she secured the clean bandage over the wound she feared that his flesh already possessed more heat.

'I will go downstairs now and bring your supper, sir.'

His brusque nod told her that he was in more pain than he wanted her to see, she acknowledged as she hurried back to the kitchen.

A faint scratch at the back door told Marianne that the cat had returned and wanted to be let in. When she opened the door she saw that whilst she had been attending to her patient the sky had clouded over and it had started to snow, the flakes whirling in such a dizzy frenzy that she couldn't see across the yard.

Shivering, she closed and then locked the door.

She had found blankets and pillows in the linen cupboards that would suffice for now, and had made herself a bed up on the settle. The range was stoked up for the night and banked down, and the kitchen clean and warm.

The baby, more lively now, held up his arms to her and smiled.

'You should be asleep,' she reproved him as she lifted him from the basket. Surely he was fatter and heavier already.

Marianne laughed to see the eagerness with which he took the small spoonfuls of soup she fed him, laughing again when he crowed happily at the sound of her laughter. The nurse might have wanted to see him swaddled, but Marianne could see his pleasure in being able to wriggle and kick out his legs.

'My, but your daddy would be proud of you,' she told him emotionally. There had been so many times during the arduous journey here when she had asked herself if she was doing the right thing, and now that he was here she was no closer to knowing the answer.

According to the nurse and the doctor, the Master of Bellfield was a man who had treated his late wife cruelly, abandoning her in her hour of need and leaving her to die along with his child. He was a man who had driven away his stepson, surely his rightful heir, and had caused the disappearance of the young innocent girl in his care.

But then his mill manager had spoken highly and warmly of him, and so had others. Who was to be believed? The baby yawned and closed his eyes.

Tenderly Marianne carried him to his basket and laid him in it, kissing his forehead as she did so.

It was gone ten o'clock and she was tired. Once she had cleaned the housekeeper's rooms on the attic floor she could enjoy the luxury of its bathroom, but for tonight she would have to make do with a wash here in front of the fire. Even that was a luxury compared with what she had known in the workhouse.

She started to take down her hair, ready to brush it. She had no nightgown to wear and would have to sleep in her chemise. Perhaps Mr Gledhill might know of somewhere where she could buy some serviceable lengths of flannelette. There was a sewing machine in the nursery, and her nimble fingers would soon be able to fashion some much needed new clothes for the baby and for herself.

Fashionable ladies might wear the new 'health' corsets beneath their expensive gowns, to emphasise the sought-after S-shaped curve that the King so admired, but even if she could have afforded such a garment there would have been no point in her wasting good money on it, Marianne reflected, for she had no one who might fasten it up for her.

Tears weren't very far away as her meandering thoughts brought home to her how very alone she now was. All those she had loved had gone, though her beloved aunt thankfully would never know how cruelly her much-loved orphaned niece had been treated by those who should have cared for her. Her aunt's estate, which should have been hers, had been sold over her head to pay off a bank loan Marianne was sure had never really existed, but at seventeen she had been too young and powerless to be able to prove it.

Life in the workhouse had come as a terrible shock to a young girl reared so gently. But it had been there that she had met and lost her very best and dearest friend.

And her husband. Poor Milo. He had fought so hard to live. She had seen how much he wanted to do so from the look in his eyes when he had asked her to place the baby in his arms one time. Tears stung her eyes, but she wiped them away. She was here in Rawlesden now, where Milo had wanted her to be.

A dab of salt on her finger, brushed round her mouth and then rinsed away, would have to serve to clean her teeth for tonight, and she summoned the courage to push her sad thoughts to one side. She must ask Mr Gledhill if he would authorise an advance on her wages, she decided, so that she could buy a few small personal necessities.

She was so tired that her eyes were closing as soon as she lay down on the settle beneath the blankets she had found.

Outside the snow whirled and fell in the biting cold, obliterating the landscape in deep drifts.

Marianne woke abruptly out of the dream she had been having. Her body felt warm but her mind was not at rest. She thought about the man upstairs and the ominous heat she had felt round his wound. Pushing back the blankets, she swung her feet to the floor.

It was not her responsibility to worry about him, but somehow she could not help but do so.

That flushed and discoloured wound and what it might portend was preying on her mind.

He would be sleeping, of course, she told herself as she lit a lantern, her toes curling in protest against the cold of the stone floor. And no doubt he would be angry with her if she woke him. But she knew that she would not rest until she had done as her aunt's training was urging her and checked the wound, in case her fears weren't merely in her imagination.

The lantern light cast moving shadows on the stair wall, elongating her own petite frame, so that it almost seemed to Marianne that as she climbed the stairs others climbed them with her.

In turn, that led her to think of the other women who had climbed these stairs before her, like the master's neglected wife, her heart perhaps even more heavy than her body as she fought against her too-early labour pains.

And what of the wife's niece? Had she too climbed these stairs in dread?

This house had known so much unhappiness and so much death. It needed the laughter of happy young voices to drive away its sadness.

The lantern highlighted darker patches on the landing wallpaper she had not noticed before, where a trio of paintings must have once hung. The chill of the unheated space drove Marianne on until she reached the master's bedroom. She paused before turning the handle and opening the door.

A fire still burned in the grate, but surely it wasn't just its glow that was responsible for the flush burning on the face of the man asleep in the bed. His breathing was rapid and unsteady, his body jerking in small spasms, as though even in his sleep he was in pain. His face was turned towards the window. On the table beside the bed she could see the bottle of brandy and an empty glass.

Marianne shivered. Were her worst fears to be realised? Putting down the lantern, she walked over to the bed. Leaning down, she placed her hand against its occupant's forehead and then snatched it back again as she felt its heat, knowing that she would have to check his wound. She could smell the brandy he had drunk, no doubt to help him sleep and to dull the pain.

If the feverish heat of his face was anything to go by then his injury had indeed turned putrid. As she went to the other side of the bed Marianne prayed that she would not see on his thigh the tell-tale red line her aunt had warned her meant that the poison was spreading.

She prayed also that the brandy he had drunk would keep him asleep, because this time she intended to have her way and make sure that some cleansing honey was applied to his wound.

He winced when she removed the bedcovers, his face contorting in a spasm of pain, but he did not wake. In the light of the lantern Marianne could see what she had hoped she might not. His thigh was swollen, its flesh drawn tight and shiny, but when she looked closer she saw thankfully there was no red line. It smelled of heat and blood, but not of putrescence.

She worked as quickly as she could, using boiled and cooled water to draw the heat from the wound, and then covering the site with honey before rebandaging it.

She had worked so intently and so swiftly that she

was slightly out of breath, her own flesh warm from her exertion.

Thankfully, through all that she had had to do, the Master of Bellfield had never once opened his eyes, although she had heard him groan on several occasions. Now, with her task completed, she replaced the covers and then, like any good nurse, went round the bed to its head, so that she might straighten the pillows and draw the sheet up to cover at least some of that disturbing breadth of male chest.

Busy at her task, she leaned over her patient and then froze in shock as suddenly his eyes opened and his hand curled tightly into her hair as it lay against his chest.

'Why do you come here to torture me like this?' he demanded thickly. 'Why cannot you leave me be?'

Surely he could not really be meaning to speak so to her?

Marianne guessed that he must be lost in some memory from his past, of another woman. Why should that knowledge bring her such a sharp pain?

'Why?' he repeated, plainly expecting her to answer him.

'I…I'm sorry,' Marianne apologised. 'I had no choice. It had to be done.'

'How sweetly you take the words from my mouth, and how fiercely I long to take the breath from yours.'

He could not possibly mean such words for her. He might be looking at her, but surely either the pain or the brandy must have turned his brain and he was confusing her with someone else. His ward, perhaps, his wife's niece, the beautiful young girl who had loved his stepson and who some said the master had lusted after so dreadfully that he had pursued her to her death?

Marianne tried to pull away, but it was too late. He was too strong for her. Somehow he had managed to raise himself on his pillows.

Marianne closed her eyes on a small sob as his hands slid into her hair, constraining her whilst he kissed her as a man should surely kiss no woman but his wife.

Shockwaves of feeling rushed through her body, stiffening it to outrage, and then softening it to something she did not know or want to know—something yielding and wanton and oh, so pleasurable that she wanted to cast herself upon its waters and let it take her where it willed, like a small craft being guided by the hands of another and taken with the current into the secret shadows.

She felt his hand move, sliding down her bare shoulder to the strap of her chemise, urging it downwards, the intensity of his kiss mirroring the intensity of his desire to expose the female flesh of her breasts. She was surrounded, possessed by his heat and his urgency. She could feel it in his kiss and in his touch, and she shuddered to see the strong male hand covering the pale flesh of her breast whilst he kissed her throat and then her shoulder.

Her knees buckled beneath her and she fell against him, bare flesh against bare flesh. What she was permitting was wrong, a sin, and yet…

'You have possessed me—do you know that?' His words were slurred and thick, the cry of a man in torment as he pressed fierce kisses against her skin.

She must stop this. She raised her hand to push him away, and then felt beneath it the thick softness of his hair. Her palm rested against his head, holding him to her as she leaned over him. This was so wrong—and yet hadn't she known deep down inside herself that she was drawn to this darkness and to him? Her chest rose with the passion of her thoughts and her breathing.

'Why do you do this to me?' His angry cry filled the room. He turned from her as though in revulsion, and then cried out again, this time in pain, as he moved his injured leg while reaching for the brandy.

She tried to stop him but it was too late. He had raised the bottle to his lips to take a deep draught from it before collapsing back against the pillows, his eyes closing and his grip on the bottle relaxing, enabling Marianne to remove it from his hold and then straighten her chemise.

It could surely only have been her concern for his wound that had kept her in his hold instead of struggling to break free. It must only be that concern; she could not, dared not, allow it to be anything else, she told herself fiercely. He was asleep now, thanks to the brandy he had drunk, but it was not an easy sleep, she could see. And neither would her own be. Not now and, she suspected, not ever again.

CHAPTER SEVEN

MARIANNE looked from the bed, where the Master of Bellfield lay in an uneasy sleep, his breathing shallow and punctured by wild, unintelligible mutterings, to the view beyond the window.

It had snowed heavily during the night, and now everywhere was blanketed in thick white snow. Piled into huge drifts by the wind, the snow had left the house cut off from the town. The Master of Bellfield, though, was unaware of this.

She had been so afraid of facing him this morning, after the events of the previous night, but when she had eventually found the courage to push open his bedroom door she had very quickly realised that her concern should be for the deterioration in his health, not her own guilt.

She had gone back downstairs, hurrying to pick up the telephone, hoping to summon help, but the line had been dead—she assumed as a result of the heavy snow.

Twice now she had checked the Master of Bellfield's wound, hoping that she might see some improvement, but on both occasions she'd been forced to recognise that there was none. Just the pull of the bedding against his skin had been enough to make him cry out in agony, even through his unconsciousness.

It was plain to see that the wound had become putrid, though thankfully as yet there was no red line. Where the flesh had sealed tightly it pulsed and throbbed and burned against her hand.

Marianne looked towards the fire, knowing what she must do.

The wound needed to be opened and the poison allowed to drain out. It was a task for a doctor, or at the very least a nurse, not someone like her. But there was no one else, and nor could there be whilst this snow lay imprisoning them here. Her employer's condition was worsening, and if she delayed until the snow had gone…

But what if by attempting to lance the wound she made matters worse? The snow could not lie for ever. Might it not be best to simply wait…?

For what? For him to die?

She thought of the baby downstairs, and she thought of her dead husband and the promise she had made him. What she must not think of was last night, with its dark, hot sweetness and her own wanton surrender to it.

A harsh agonised cry from the bed had her banishing her own thoughts to go over.

'Lucinda… I must go to her… The baby…'

He was sitting bolt upright, his eyes wide open as he spoke, but Marianne knew that he was not seeing her. She had seen fever like this before, stealing over a person and then consuming them, until there was nothing left other than the pitiful agony of their breathing and then the harsh rattle of death.

'Shush…shush, sir,' she quietened him gently. 'All will be well.'

The pillows on which he had been lying were soaked with his sweat. She could not delay much longer. The wound must be lanced.

Marianne checked that she had everything that she needed, her stomach coiling tightly and her heart hammering against her ribs as she stared at the small sharp knife lying on the tray in front of her. Alongside it lay clean bowls, and next to them new bandages and more honey. She had scrubbed her hands with the hottest water she could stand and carbolic soap. The bedding lay folded back to reveal her patient's leg. She looked at the bottle of brandy. She had poured some into a glass, ready, knowing the pain she was about to inflict.

Picking up the knife, she held it in the fire's flames, waiting until the tip glowed red before removing it and going over to the bed.

The pulse of the wound was like a wild thing now, the putridness beneath the sealed flesh clearly visible. She took a deep breath and then, as swiftly as she could, slit the seal to the wound.

Pus spurted from the broken seal. Nausea clogged Marianne's throat at the sight and the smell of it, but she ignored it to work quickly and determinedly to remove the poison and make the wound clean.

Only when she was as sure as she could be that the

poison was removed did she pick up the brandy bottle and dash some over the still open wound.

The man in the bed gave a great cry of pain, and this time when he looked at her Marianne knew that the Master of Bellfield knew exactly who she was. To her relief, though, the pain was such that his senses quickly deserted him, leaving her to apply the honey and bandage the cleansed wound.

The air in the bedroom smelled of brandy and heat and her own fear, Marianne recognised as she cleared everything away.

An hour went by, and then another, as her patient slept—surely a little more easily. Marianne had to force herself to leave the bedroom to see to the baby and her other responsibilities, telling herself that sleep was the best healer of all, as her aunt had used to say. Except that sleep also stole life away… But she must not think of that.

Downstairs in the kitchen she fed the baby and told him how much his father had loved him, and why she had brought him here.

The baby slept in her arms. Her gentle words to him lingered in her mind. Had she done the wrong thing in waiting? Should she have confronted the Master of Bellfield with the truth right from the beginning?

'Your father begged me to bring you here because this was his home,' she told the now sleeping baby softly, confiding to him the secret of their presence here and the worry that lay on her conscience.

The Bellfield Hall Milo had remembered and talked to her of so often had been a happy home for him as a boy. He hadn't been able to remember his father, who he had told her had been killed by a runaway carriage in Manchester. He had, though, told her of his anguish when his mother had died in childbirth, and her child with her. He had told her too of the anger and the bitterness he had felt against his stepfather.

'I blamed him for my mother's death. It was the mill he loved, not my mother, and I could not understand then... I didn't know then what love can move a person to do.'

Marianne blinked away her tears as she remembered that conversation.

'I am dying, Marianne,' he had told her. 'We both know that. I want you to take baby Miles to my stepfather, and I want you to give him this letter I have written to him. He is a hard man, but a fair one. He will, I know, recognise his duty to my son—for after all I am his heir, and my son after me.'

Marianne hadn't wanted to argue with a dying man, but she had promised herself that she would say nothing of her real purpose in coming here, nor of baby Miles' true identity, until she had satisfied herself as to the way the baby would be treated. The master had, after all, driven Milo away from his home. He had married a woman he did not love in order to become Master of Bellfield. He was a vigorous man in the prime of his life; what if he should marry again and father children? What, then, would be the fate of the baby she was supposed to entrust to his care?

She had planned everything so carefully, but she had not planned for what had happened the night before, and the way it had made her feel.

Marianne got up, still holding the baby, pacing the kitchen floor as she tried to calm her agitated thoughts.

The day passed slowly, long hours dragged out minute by minute, and the Master of Bellfield slept whilst Marianne tussled with her conscience. Was it wrong of her to want to be absolutely sure before she revealed the truth to him? She had, after all, given Milo her promise that she would see his son to *safety*.

A dead wife, a dead stepson, and a ward disappeared without trace. Was this truly a man fit to have charge of a helpless child?

And what about her own feelings? A widower who had married for gain, and who had by all accounts passionately loved a young girl who did not return his love. Was this truly a man fit to have charge of her vulnerable heart?

Where her heart was concerned it was too late for her to save it, Marianne acknowledged. But for the child she would fight with the strength she hadn't been able to muster on her own account.

It was evening before Marianne could finally assure herself that the wound was clean and the Master of Bellfield's sleep was a healthy, healing one.

Her duty to him was done. Now she must attend to that duty which had brought her here.

For every voice that gainsaid Milo's stepfather there was another voice to praise him. Milo himself had said that his stepfather had shown him great kindness in the early days of his mother's marriage to him.

'It was only after my mother's death, when I told him that I wanted to marry Amelia, that he changed towards me,' he had told her. 'He said we were too young, that I had no money other than the allowance he gave me. I cursed him then for persuading my mother to make him my trustee.'

CHAPTER EIGHT

IT WAS hard to believe that three short days could make such a difference, Marianne acknowledged. The snow had gone from the town, and from Bellfield Hall, even though snow still lay on the hilltops, and the sun was shining. The Master of Bellfield was improving in strength by the hour, his wound was clean and healing well, his fever was gone, and his irritation was growing along with his recovery.

He had made no mention of the subject she had been dreading, and Marianne had grown to believe that he had no memory of that fever-driven intimacy. That knowledge was the greatest relief to her—of course it was. How could it be otherwise? That ache within her heart was a foolishness she should sweep out with the same vigour with which she had been sweeping out the housekeeper's rooms.

That, though, had been this morning. The improvement in the weather, combined with the spread of the news through the town of the Master of Bellfield's recovery had brought a growing number of visitors to his front door to enquire after his health.

The ever-cheerful Charlie had delivered a parcel discreetly and firmly wrapped up and tied with string. Inside, Marianne had discovered a smart new frock, and an apron to go over it, along with a note from the mill manager explaining that it was being supplied to her under the Master of Bellfield's instructions. It had not come a minute too soon in view of the status of her employer's visitors. Mostly they were eminent men from the town, including his fellow mill owners, although there had been no return visit from the doctor—nor, thankfully, from the nurse.

Now, wearing her new uniform, and with tea trays and china cups at the ready in the kitchen, Marianne felt confident enough to face the mayor of the town itself on her employer's behalf if necessary.

She could face the mayor, perhaps, but she was certainly not confident enough to face the increasingly intent and probing gaze of the Master of Bellfield himself.

A knock on the front door heralded the arrival of yet another visitor. This time the visitor announced himself not as a fellow mill owner but as the Reverend Peter Johnson. He was tall and stooped, his face thin and his cheeks sunken, and the zeal shining in his eyes reminded Marianne of how Milo had described the Reverend—how stern and zealous the churchman was, and how Amelia had been in fear of him. Milo had told her that local gossip said that as a young man he had yearned to work as a missionary, and that being disappointed in that hope had soured him and caused him to preach of the hellfire awaiting his flock if they should slip from the path of righteousness.

Milo had also told her, with a small laugh, of how the Reverend had read out a fierce lecture from the pulpit after he had seen Milo and some of the other young men from the town wearing fashionable trousers with turn-ups.

Whether it was because of that memory, Marianne did not know, but the burning-eyed look the Reverend turned on her made her feel that she had been found wanting.

'I'll inform Mr Denshaw of your arrival,' she told him, intending to show him into the library—now polished and free of dust, with a warm fire burning in its hearth.

But before she could do so the Reverend shook his head and told her sharply, 'My business will not wait. Take me to him immediately.'

Marianne did not dare refuse to obey him. Her heart was hammering against her ribs as she led the way up the stairs and then knocked on her employer's bedroom door.

At his 'Come' she pushed it open.

The Master of Bellfield was seated at the small desk he'd had brought into his room by a couple of stout men from the mill, so that he could work whilst his wound healed.

'The Reverend Johnson, sir,' she informed him, before starting to back towards the door.

'Wait,' the Reverend ordered her, then addressed the Master of Bellfield. 'The woman must stay to hear what I have to say, since it concerns her and her presence here in the house of an unmarried man.'

Marianne folded her hands together tightly, unable to bring herself to look directly at either of the two men, although she could sense that her employer was looking at her.

'I could not believe my ears when it first came to my attention that you, sir, a single man and a widower, were allowing a young woman to act as your nurse and to perform such intimacies for you as must cause repugnance and shock to any decent person who came to hear of them. This woman must be sent from your house immediately, whilst you yourself must repent of your sins in allowing her to be here.' The Reverend's voice was thundering now, as though he was speaking from his pulpit.

Marianne looked up at him, and wished that she had not when she saw the burning anger in his gaze.

'It is a sin for a man and a woman such as yourselves to live beneath the same roof when—'

'I am glad that you have called to see me, Reverend Johnson, since I was on the point of requesting my manager to ask you to do so.' The master's voice was calm but cool.

'You wished to see me?'

'Yes. I wished to speak with you so that I might advise you of my intention to marry Mrs Brown, and to ask you to put in hand the arrangements for that marriage as speedily as you can.'

Marianne didn't know which of them was the more shocked. The Reverend Johnson or herself.

Both of them had certainly turned to stare at the Master of Bellfield in equal disbelief. But it was towards her that he limped, taking hold of her hand and squeezing it in warning rather than affection as he asserted meaningfully, 'There you are, my love. I told you that we must not linger over making our plans known in case others misjudge the situation.'

'You are to marry?'

The Reverend's face was flushed, and Marianne wondered if perhaps he was more resentful at being deprived of the prospect of denouncing them both from his pulpit than a true man of God should have been.

'You are the first to know, Reverend, and I know I can rely on you to speedily dismiss any gossip that may be being spread.'

'When...when is this marriage to take place, may I ask?'

The Reverend's voice was stiff with what Marianne suspected was angry disapproval.

'As soon as it can be arranged. Certainly I wish to be wed before Christmas, so that we might celebrate it as man and wife. Now, if you will excuse us, my bride and I have much to discuss and arrange. I dare say you can see yourself out?'

Marianne might have laughed at the expression on the Reverend Johnson's face if she had not been in such a state of shock.

The moment the door had closed behind the affronted minister she turned towards her employer, intending to demand an explanation, but before she could say anything he had swept her into his arms and was kissing her with a ruthless determination that made it impossible to do anything other than allow him to continue to do so.

When he finally released her she was trembling so

much that she was actually leaning against him instead of moving away from him.

'I… You… We… You cannot mean to marry me…' she finally managed to get out.

'I cannot do aught else, Mrs Brown—especially not now, after having treated you so fiendishly. Surely you must agree with that?' he said. 'After all, have I not taken advantage of you in the most vile manner, pressing an intimacy upon you that no man should press on a woman to whom he has not offered the respectability of marriage?'

'You *have* kissed me,' Marianne agreed. 'But—'

'That kiss was merely a mark of our betrothal,' he told her softly. 'The intimacy to which I refer was the one that took place in my arms and in my bed when I—'

Marianne's face burned. She covered her ears and shook her head, telling him frantically, 'Sir, please—I do not wish to talk about that. It is best forgotten.'

Instantly his expression changed, a look of triumph darkening his eyes.

'So it *did* happen, and was not solely something I conjured up from my imagination. Well, Mrs Brown, there is no getting away from it now. We are both condemned to one another, and we have no choice but to commit our flesh and our sins to the sanctity of marriage—as I am sure the Reverend Johnson would be the first to tell us.'

Was he actually daring to laugh? Marianne could see that he was.

Her thoughts were in the most painful kind of turmoil. On the one hand—yes, she must admit it to herself there was nothing she wanted more than to give herself where she had already given her heart and become his wife. On the other, she was bruisingly conscious of how much she had deceived him, kept him from the truth.

'You cannot want to marry me, Mr Denshaw,' was all she could think of to say as she made to move away from him.

'I find it telling that whilst you say that I cannot wish to marry you, you say nothing of *you* not wishing to become my bride, Mrs Brown, and that leads me to infer that in fact you do not have any objection.'

The colour came and went in Marianne's face.

'I…I am your housekeeper, sir. A servant. Naturally…'

'Naturally you would not refuse to become my wife? Is that what you were about to say? Well, it may interest you to know that it is not the humble Mrs Brown, widowed and with a child to nurture, I wish to marry. No, it is the delicious woman who came to my arms and my bed, who gave herself to me with such sweet abandon, that I intend to make my wife—and for reasons that would no doubt cause the sour Reverend Johnson to call down hellfire and brimstone on my head if he were to know of them. But of course he won't. It is only you, Marianne, to whom I shall whisper them, in the privacy of our marriage bed, when I kiss every inch of your quivering silk-fleshed body, when I silence your sweet cries of pleasure with my own greater cry of need to share that pleasure…'

'Sir… Mr Denshaw…'

'Heywood, Marianne. My name is Heywood, and I have ached badly these last days to hear the sound of it on your tongue…'

His words dizzied and enraptured her, and Marianne knew that if he were to take her by the hand now and lead her to his bed and those pleasures he had spoken of she could not and would not deny him.

'You are saying that…that you wish to marry me, sir…*Heywood*…and…and make me your true wife in every way there is?' How her voice trembled and shook with the force of her feelings and her hopes.

'I am saying exactly that, Marianne.'

'But we have only just met. You hardly know me.'

'I know that you saved my life, and I know too that you are a good housewife.'

Marianne looked up at him and saw that his last words were meant to tease her. Suddenly the grey eyes were sparkling with fun and laughter. Her heart turned over inside her chest.

'You are also a good mother.'

Marianne's heart became as heavy as a stone. 'Sir—Heywood…'

'The child—what name does he have?'

'It is Miles…' Marianne answered him quietly.

'Miles…'

She knew that Heywood was looking at her, but she could not lift her own gaze to his. She felt too ashamed and too guilty. How much she wished now that she had been open with him right from the start. How hard it was going to be now to tell him everything.

'He…he is named for his father,' she felt obliged to add.

The silence in the room was such that Marianne could hear the unsteadiness of her own heart.

She *had* to tell him.

'Sir…I mean Heywood…there is something…'

'Here is Archie Gledhill just arrived. Show him up will you, please, my love? Unless I am mistaken he has some important news for me.'

Numbly, Marianne nodded her head. Now was plainly not the time to unburden herself to him.

CHAPTER NINE

Two days from now she would become the Master of Bellfield's bride, and another week on from that it would be Christmas. Marianne's heart gave a lightning leap of mingled delight and dread. So much had happened since the afternoon of the Reverend Johnson's visit that she could scarcely take it all in.

The mill manager had been given his orders, and within a matter of days she had not only been measured for her trousseau, she'd also had a chaperon, in the shape of a sweet-natured elderly second cousin of Heywood's, who had been persuaded to give up the comfort of her pretty house in Harrogate to come and stay at Bellfield Hall until after their marriage.

Marianne had had to move from the housekeeper's room to a prettily decorated room on the first floor, along the opposite corridor to the master bedroom, and she had not been surprised when her chaperon had explained to her that it had once belonged to her husband-to-be's ward.

'Such a pretty girl. Heywood was distraught about

her and the boy leaving. Such a dreadful tragedy, as neither of them were ever found.'

Marianne had nodded her head and said nothing, but now the memory of that conversation pricked at her conscience.

Heywood was everything any young woman in love could hope for in her husband-to-be, and if their chaperon was of an age when she preferred to retire to her room for a sleep after luncheon, leaving the two of them alone together, Marianne was not going to complain.

Those stolen kisses they had shared had been so sweet, and their more intimate stolen caresses sweeter still. She trembled with delicious pleasure just remembering the hard warmth of Heywood's hand against her breast, and the feel of his body firm and male against her own.

Only yesterday, whilst he held her fast in his arms, Heywood had demanded roughly, 'Tell me that you love me, Marianne.'

'You know that I do,' she had whispered.

'Aye, I do know it,' he had agreed, with a smile that had made her heart swell with pleasure. 'I knew it the night I first kissed you. But I still like to hear you say the words.'

'I love you, Heywood Denshaw,' she had told him then, laughing softly, and then not laughing at all when he had kissed her.

Such precious and wonderful memories. At least she would have them to hold if it should be that when he knew the truth—

Her heart thudded painfully. It was no good. She could not go to the altar without telling him—even though that meant that she might lose him.

It was four o'clock, and her chaperon was safely asleep. Heywood was in his library, his injury now having healed sufficiently for him to be able to climb the stairs with ease. Miles was asleep, and in the care of the young nursery maid Heywood had insisted on hiring.

Marianne smoothed her hands nervously over her hair and took a deep breath.

When she opened the library door Heywood was looking at some papers on his desk, and she allowed her gaze to delight itself to the full, absorbing every tiny detail of the preciousness of him until he looked up and saw her.

'There is something I…I want to talk to you about, but if I am disturbing you then you must say—' she began, breaking off when he laughed and got up to come towards her.

'You always disturb me, my precious love, but in the most delightful way. However, if you wish to discuss with me yet again your plan to provide every child in the whole of Rawlesden with a Christmas gift, then…'

'Not every child, Heywood dearest, merely the children of those who work for you,' Marianne protested, distracted from her purpose by his reminder of her plans for the children of his workers.

'A dozen or a thousand—it matters little to me in truth, just so long as you smile at me so sweetly, my love. Can it really be another two full days before I can make you mine…?'

Inside her head a small voice whispered to her that if she were to lose him then perhaps she should ensure that she had something special and wonderful from him first. She had, after all, only promised herself that she would tell him before they were married—not before she gave herself to him. But even as her longing filled her Heywood was gently releasing her, as though somehow he had sensed that he needed to chaperon her desire for him as well as his own.

'Of course you don't disturb me, Marianne. Indeed, I have been thinking this last half an hour that it has been far too long since I last saw you.'

'We had luncheon together,' Marianne reminded him with a small smile.

'A lifetime ago,' he replied with mock solemnity.

When she did not respond his expression became more grave and concerned.

'You look distressed. If someone has upset you…'

'No one has upset me. But…but the truth is that perhaps I deserve to be distressed, because…' She stepped back from him and began to pace the room, her agitation straining her voice and her expression. 'The truth is, Heywood, that I have behaved most deceitfully.'

'You don't love me after all?' he demanded.

'*No*. Never that. I love you with all my heart, and I always will,' Marianne told him passionately.

'How so have you deceived me, then?' he asked calmly.

Marianne bit her lip. 'It is a long story,' she began huskily, 'and…'

'And it is one that began when a caring and loyal young woman agreed to marry a young man in order to carry out his dying wishes,' Heywood supplied for her, whilst Marianne stared at him in disbelief.

'You *know*… But—'

He shook his head, commanding her silence, and

continued. 'When, through the most unfortunate of circumstances, you found yourself in the workhouse you befriended another young woman you met there. Pretty, and plainly used to better, she confided to you that she had run away from home with her sweetheart. They had planned to marry, but nature and their love for one another had overwhelmed them and she had become pregnant. Without money or any means of support they had been taken up by the town worthies and sent to the poorhouse where, as is the custom, they were separated. She to the women's quarters and he to the men's, although he managed to get permission to leave and go in search of work.

'She was afraid, alone, and with child, and she turned to you and made you her confidante and friend. The weeks and then the months passed. The young woman's health suffered badly, despite you doing what you could to get her extra food, even giving her your own when she went into labour. After many days of dreadful travail her child was born—a son—and his birth cost her her life. The child too would have died if you had not taken charge of it—against the rules of the workhouse.

'You were in despair, knowing that the child would be taken from you and put in an orphanage, when a young man came to the workhouse asking for the young woman. It was her sweetheart, who had finally secured a job working on a farm. The work was hard and the hours long, but he had finally managed to get together enough money to come for her. When you had to tell him of her fate he was bereft. All he had to live for now was his child. He asked you to go with him to the farm where he worked, where he had a small cottage, so that the child could be cared for.

'Out of love for your friend you agreed, but then he too became ill, and that was when, knowing that he would not survive, he begged you to marry him—so that the child might be protected. You felt you had no choice other than to agree. As he lay dying he told you about his childhood and his home. He begged you to take his child to that home and hand him over to the person he believed he should be with, and you gave him your promise that you would do just that. But at the same time you had heard such a harrowing tale of this person's cruelty that you vowed you would not reveal the child's identity until you had assured yourself that the child would be safe.'

Marianne couldn't restrain herself any longer. 'You do know. How can you…? When did you…? I—'

'I knew from the first…before that, even. Had you tarried so much as a day longer on your journey my agents would have found you and brought you to me.'

'Your agents? You had sent someone to search for me?' Her fear escaped into her voice.

A look that contained both pain and sadness darkened his eyes. 'I can understand, given what you knew of me then, that you might once have found it hard to accept that I cared so deeply about both my stepson and my ward that I would do everything in my power to find them and bring them home safely, but I had hoped that with what we have recently shared I might have shown you a different side of myself from the one Milo must have described to you.'

'No—please, you must not speak like that or think like that.' Marianne cut him off immediately. 'It is true that when Milo and Amelia ran away together they were both filled with anger and bitterness. Amelia, I think, more than Milo.'

'Aye, beneath that sweet gentleness there was always a strong determination.'

'She feared that you meant to marry Milo to someone else. She was very conscious of the fact that she had no inheritance to bring to their marriage, and I believe it was she who prevailed upon Milo to leave. Milo had only the happiest memories of you until you spoke so harshly to him, forbidding his engagement to Amelia, especially coming as it did so close on the heels of his mother's death.'

'They were so young, and I knew that Lucinda, who had seen what was in the wind, wanted them to wait until they were older and sufficiently sure of their feelings. I blame myself for not explaining this to Milo more fully, but at the time there were problems with the mill. Other mill workers were going on strike, and I was involved in meetings in Manchester with regard to that and to other associated matters. Of course there was also the burden of guilt I carried for not being here, as I should have been, when Lucinda went into labour, so I was less patient with Milo than he deserved. I missed Lucinda's calm hand on the household and on all of us. She was a good woman, and despite all that is said of me and my reasons for marrying her I honoured her for what she was. Even if I could not love her as…as a man loves the woman who has his heart.'

There was a small silence, and Marianne could feel tears stinging her eyes.

'From the moment I knew they were gone I tried to find Milo and Amelia, but too much time had been lost and they had covered their tracks too well, using false names. Milo's choice of Brown being particularly effective. Eventually, though, we did track them down. But by then it was too late. All my agents could tell me was that my stepson had contracted a deathbed marriage to a young woman by the name of Marianne Westall, to whom he had entrusted his child. I instructed my agents to make contact with you, and to beg you to agree to a meeting, but by that stage you had already set out on your journey here. Not knowing where you were going or what you planned, initially I told my agent to follow you, but he lost you in Rochdale—the small matter of a railway ticket?'

Marianne nodded her head.

'He telephoned to tell me of this, and to ask for instructions, for by this stage we had deduced that you were making your way to Bellfield. Everything my agent had reported about you seemed to point to a young woman of great courage and fortitude—a young woman, moreover, possessed of tremendous loyalty and honesty. And with everything I learned I grew to want to know this young woman more and more. Indeed, I felt that in part I already did know her, and her grave sweetness of expression, plus her concern for the weak and the vulnerable. Foolishly, perhaps, I even began to think that she might bring me not only the child that belonged here, through whom I might make atonement to my stepson and my ward, but also the warmth and laughter and the love that this sad house and I both lacked.'

Marianne couldn't speak. There was a huge lump in her throat and she felt overcome by emotion. When she did find her voice all she could say was, 'You knew I would come here, but when I arrived you said *nothing?* I thought you were going to turn me away. I feared—'

'I admit that at first I didn't realise who you were—it was only when I saw the child… But by then we were at odds, and since *you* had said nothing to me—'

'I…I wanted to. But I needed to be sure, for baby Miles' sake.' Her voice broke. 'I am sorry. I should have trusted you—especially once I had begun to love you—but somehow that made it harder.'

'My dearest love, please do not cry. I should have said something, and would have done so had it not been for my accident.'

'And you really love me still? Despite—'

'My sweetest love, there is nothing in this world nor the next that could stop me from loving you.'

'But why did not you say anything about Miles?'

'Why did not you?'

'I was afraid it might change things between us, and that I might lose your love.'

'I felt the same. I feared that whilst you loved me you did not entirely trust me to have Miles' best interests at heart. I knew that Milo and Amelia must have entrusted you with their confidences, and I knew too that there was still gossip in the town about them.'

'They say that you refused to allow them to marry because you wanted Amelia for yourself.' Marianne gave a small sigh. 'But of course I knew that was not likely to be true because of the way in which Amelia had talked to me of you.'

'You cannot know how much I wish that I had been less harsh. If I had—'

Marianne went to him and placed her fingers against his lips, telling him, 'Hush, my love, you must not blame yourself. The truth is that Milo wanted to come back, but Amelia begged him not to. She refused to believe, as he did, that you would relent and allow them to be together—especially once she was with child. Milo told me that he pleaded with her to let him ask you for your help, but she was beyond reason and said that she would destroy herself if he did. I believe she was thinking of the Reverend Johnson, who I know she feared.'

Heywood's face darkened. 'Between them he and that wretched man Hollingshead have a lot to answer for. The one of them puts the fear of God into your sex for their natural inclinations to show their love, and the other sees to it that they are killed by the results of those inclinations. If I had my way they would both be run out of town.'

'Milo entrusted to me a letter he wrote to you. I have it in my room. It explains everything and…and begs for your forgiveness and your love for baby Miles.' She made to go to the door, but Heywood stopped her, reaching for her hand and pulling her into his arms.

'There was no need. I am the one who should ask his forgiveness, and I would that I could. As for his son, I shall treat him and raise him as my own. Milo's mother left his inheritance in trust, and that trust will always be there for Miles. I wish with all my heart that he and

Amelia could know how much I thank them for sending you to me, dear heart, my love, my bride-to-be…'

'I'm honoured to become the Bride of Bellfield,' Marianne whispered softly to him—before abruptly remembering what she had still not told him. She stiffened in his arms, her colour deepening, her expression anxious.

'What is it?' Heywood asked with concern.

'There is still something I have not—that is…I should… The truth is that whilst Milo and I did marry, he did not…I was not actually ever a true wife to him,' she managed to whisper. 'So I am afraid that I do not…I am not…' She fiddled with one of the buttons on his shirt, her gaze downcast. 'I realise that from…from my behaviour on a certain occasion you may think that I am a woman of experience, and thus be disappointed when—'

His shout of laughter stopped her in her tracks.

'My dearest, darling girl, you are adorably absurd. Of course I have known from the outset that, despite your claim to the title of Mrs, and your marriage lines, you are in truth still chaste and untouched. I would have known it anyway, from the way you tremble and sigh at my slightest touch, and the look of sweetly shy uncertainty in your eyes when your body responds to mine. However, even if I had missed those telling signs, there could have been no mistaking your reaction when you realised that I sleep in my skin.'

'I was shocked,' Marianne admitted.

'It is not your shock to which I refer,' Heywood teased, causing her to blush warmly as he drew her back into his arms and proceeded to kiss her very thoroughly.

* * *

It was Christmas Eve, and the new Mistress of Bellfield Hall was busy about the same business as the rest of her sex: preparing her home for the celebration of Christmas.

Hams had been baked, poultry bought and plucked and left to hang, and puddings bought—for it was true that this year at least there was no time left in which to make them. Extra pairs of hands belonging to the newly important and scrubbed clean older daughters of the master's workers, in their pretty tartan frocks and white pinafores, hurried to restrain the excitement of their younger siblings as they were all admitted into the hall, with its wonderfully decorated Christmas tree—so tall that its angel brushed the ceiling, and so wide that there was scarce room for the children to gather round to admire it.

'Just look at them, Heywood,' Marianne whispered as they watched their young guests from the shadows of the galleried landing. 'It was truly generous of you to do this.'

'There is nothing I would not do for you, my precious love. Nothing,' he told her emotionally.

'You wouldn't wear the Father Christmas robe and beard I made,' she reminded him, teasing.

'Ah, yes… That is because I did not want to deprive Archie of the pleasure of playing such a role,' he answered, tongue-in-cheek. 'Have I told you yet today how much I love you, my Marianne?' He was leaning towards her as he spoke.

Suddenly one sharp-eyed little lad amongst the excited throng in the hallway below looked up and yelled out, 'Look—t'master's kissing t'mistress!'

After that there was no gainsaying their young

guests. The Master of Bellfield and his wife were made to come down and be thanked for their generosity, with cheers and, in the case of the littlest ones, big hugs and happy kisses.

Marianne smiled to herself. It was far too soon to know yet, of course. She was after all a bride of a matter of days only. But she felt it was not too out of the question for her to hope that by this time next Christmas the Bride of Bellfield Mill would be a mother, and would have presented her husband with a very special Christmas gift indeed.

In the busy hallway the mill manager was raising a glass of Christmas punch, calling out, 'A Christmas toast. To the Master of Bellfield and his bride. God bless them both.'

'Happy?' Marianne heard Heywood asking her.

'How can I not be when I am with you?' Marianne whispered back lovingly.

* * * * *

A Family for Hawthorn Farm

Rita Bradshaw
writing as Helen Brooks

Helen Brooks lives in Northamptonshire and is married with three children, two grandsons and a granddaughter. As she is a committed Christian, busy housewife, mother and grandma, her spare time is at a premium, but she likes nothing more than to curl up with a good book or take her dog for a walk. Her long cherished aspiration to write became a reality when she penned her first novel at the age of forty and sent it off to Mills & Boon, where it was accepted first time.

As well as writing contemporary novels for Mills & Boon, Helen also writes sagas set at the beginning of the twentieth century for Headline publishers, under her own name Rita Bradshaw. These are usually set in the north-east of England. The fascination and affinity with the north which shows so clearly in her stories first began as a child. A branch of the family from the north-east would visit Northampton and tell stories of their life there, and when Helen began writing sagas she says they flowed from the bottomless well deep inside.

If you enjoy *A Family at Hawthorn Farm*, you might like to read recent titles by the same author, writing as Rita Bradshaw, published by Headline.

CHAPTER ONE

The North-East of England, 1899

'IT'S coming down thicker than ever. Me gran said we'd be in for a packet this year and she was right.'

Connie Summers raised her head from where she was standing peeling a mountain of onions and looked out of the grimy window of the pickling factory. She could see the snowflakes dropping to rest in their white purity on the roof of another factory opposite, and the heavy sky was laden.

She nodded a reply to the girl who had spoken but said nothing, knowing if she opened her mouth the bitterly cold air—which was only a few degrees warmer than that outside—would bring on her cough. All she wanted was to get through the last few minutes of her twelve-hour shift and get home.

'You all right, Connie? You look bad—really bad.'

Again she nodded, forcing a smile before lifting the massive tin bowl full of onions and carrying it over to one of the big vats at the far end of the factory floor, trying to stifle her racking cough as she did so. The last few days she had found that every time she carried the bowls, which always threatened to tear her arms out of their sockets, the strain seemed to aggravate her wheezy chest. How she was going to walk home tonight she didn't know, but she'd have to. She couldn't afford a penny for the tram. But she'd manage. She always did.

When Bill O'Dowd, the foreman, blew his tin whistle ten minutes later Connie took off her apron and hung it on the peg behind the table where she worked, before taking down her hat and coat. She had a job to do up the buttons of the coat, her hands were so red, raw and swollen, but she was used to that. It had been the same for the last three years, since she had left school at thirteen. All the women who worked at the pickling factory suffered in the same way on account of the work they did.

But she wasn't complaining. As Connie began to file out of the factory she gave a mental nod to the thought. Most of the girls she had been at school with had gone straight into service, but that hadn't been an option for her—not with her mam being so poorly and her younger sister and brothers to see to in the morning and at night. She couldn't have been away all week, they wouldn't have managed. She'd been lucky to get this job.

She stood for a moment on the snow-covered flags in the factory yard, catching her breath. The burning in her chest and back was worse tonight, and the pain when she coughed seemed to radiate out to every part of her. But she couldn't be ill. She couldn't have any days off work. They were already behind with the rent, and Tommy had holes in his boots and Flora couldn't do her coat up, it was so small for her. Whatever was she going to do? Oh, Mam, Da, help me. I've tried so hard to keep us all together, like you'd have wanted. Don't let it be for nothing. Show me what to do. Somehow show me.

She swayed slightly, her head feeling as though it was full of cotton wool. She could feel her face was damp with perspiration, in spite of the freezing night, and the thought of the long walk home from the factory in the East End of Sunderland to the room they were renting in a house on the outskirts of the town was daunting. But it was no use standing here in the cold.

Pulling her felt hat more firmly on her head, she walked out of the factory gates, shivering as the raw north-east wind hit her. The sky lay low over the town, and the big fat snowflakes whirled and danced in the wind. The pavements underfoot were treacherous, with a layer of ice beneath the freshly fallen snow. It was quite dark, being seven o'clock on a late November evening, but as she passed the entrance to the old market in High Street East the smell of hot meat pies wafted out on the bitingly cold air, mixed with tripe and onions.

Connie walked on a few paces and then leant against a shop wall. Normally the smell from the old market made her mouth water, but tonight it had brought on a feeling of nausea.

By the time she had reached the tangle of mean terraced streets on the west of the town, close to the grim high walls of the workhouse, Connie was feeling very strange. Added to the sick dizziness in her head and the excruciating pains in her chest and back was a consuming exhaustion. It made her want to lie down in the snow, just where she was, and go to sleep.

But she couldn't do that. She forced herself to keep treading on. Flora was waiting for her, and Tommy and David and Ronnie. They wouldn't have eaten yet. They always persisted in waiting for her, even though she told Flora to feed them all when they got in from school with the stew she prepared each night once her sister and brothers were in bed. What she would feed them on tomorrow, though, she didn't know. She had eked out the scrag-ends and vegetables until there was only enough for a meal tonight, and she didn't get paid for another two days. But she'd worry about that tomorrow. For now it was enough to get home. If she could just rest for a few hours she'd be all right.

As she turned the corner into Howarth Street, where they rented their room, any relief she might have felt was swept away by the feeling that she was going to faint. Clinging on to a lamppost, the main street behind her and Howarth Street obscured by the driving snow, she willed herself to go on as the dark buzzing in her head increased. She thought she heard someone say her name. It sounded like Mrs Briggs from three doors down. But as her hold on the lamppost slackened and the darkness took over she slipped to the ground into…nothingness.

'…too much for her. I mean she's a slip of a girl, there's nothing to her, and to work all day at that factory and then be mam and da to the rest of them—it couldn't go on. I knew something like this would happen one day.'

'What happened to the parents? How long have they been gone?'

She could hear the voices, but from a great distance, as though she were under water, and the lead weights on her limbs prevented her from making any movement.

'Mr Summers—grand man, he was—he died in a fall at the mine over twelve months ago now. Just after their mam was took with the fever. Been ill for years though, had poor Annie. Always sickly. They lived in a house in the next street then, but with only Connie's wage coming in they couldn't continue there. There was talk of the younger ones going into the workhouse, but Connie wouldn't have it. She's fought tooth and nail to keep them all together, but I reckon this is the end of it. Poor lass. Still, you can only do your best in this world.'

'Mrs…Mrs Briggs?' Somehow she found the strength to pull herself out of the enervating exhaustion and open her eyes. 'What's happened? Where are Flora and the lads?'

'It's all right, Connie. Don't fret, lass.' Mrs Briggs bent over her in the next moment. 'You passed out in the street, right at me feet, and I was just wondering what to do when this kind gentleman stopped. He brought you home in his horse and trap. That was nice of him, wasn't it?'

Horse and trap? Connie wanted to sit up. She wanted to ask a whole lot of questions. But she could feel herself slipping into the darkness again when she tried to move.

'Keep still.' The male voice was deep and authoritative. 'The doctor has been called and he will be here shortly.'

The doctor? They couldn't afford a doctor. There

was barely a crust in the house, and nothing for tomorrow's dinner. A doctor was the last thing she wanted. 'No.' This time the room didn't spin so fast when she struggled to sit up. 'I don't want a doctor.' Her vision clearing a little, she saw Mrs Briggs's worried face at the side of her. 'Tell him I'm all right,' she said feebly. 'Please, Mrs Briggs, tell him.'

'But you're not.' Mrs Briggs's voice was unusually soft. 'Now, just you lie back and rest a while. You're in my kitchen and our Elsie has gone to see to your lot. Mr Briggs went for the doctor over fifteen minutes ago. They'll be back shortly.'

For the first time Connie realised she was in her neighbour's house, lying on the kitchen settle, a blanket over her. 'No,' she said again. 'I have to get home, Mrs Briggs.'

'For the moment you're going nowhere.' There was a movement behind her and then the owner of the voice she had heard came into view. He was tall—lying on the wooden bench as she was, he seemed to tower over her—and handsome in a rugged sort of way. His face was tanned, as though he was used to being in the open air, and his hair was black. But it was his eyes that held her weak gaze. They were grey, a deep smoky grey, and his lashes were thick and long, but it was the forcefulness emanating from them that was so disconcerting. Even before she had taken in the quality of his clothes she had gathered this was a man who was used to being obeyed.

Nevertheless, she opened her mouth to argue—only to shut it again as Mr Briggs and the doctor came into the kitchen from the door which led into the hall.

Mrs Briggs stayed with her while the doctor examined her, and Connie was glad of this in view of the shock of his diagnosis.

'Pleurisy. You will need to go home to bed and stay there for the next few weeks. And make sure you take the medicine I give you at regular intervals. Plenty of liquids, good nourishing soup once you feel like it, and don't overtax yourself unless you want to end up in the hospital or worse. And keep warm. Both inside and out.'

Connie stared at him. Every word he had spoken was impossible. She tried to tell him so, but the bout of coughing this caused had her lying weak and helpless at the end of it.

Mrs Briggs showed the doctor out, and Connie heard him talking to Mr Briggs and the stranger in the hall but couldn't hear what they were saying. Not that it mattered. She gazed round Mrs Briggs's homely kitchen, the glowing fire in the black-leaded range and the well-fed cat sitting on the big, brightly coloured clippy mat in front of it telling her what she knew to be true—here was a family where the father and three teenage sons were all in work. This home couldn't be more different from the one room they were renting, with its damp walls, tiny fireplace and bare floorboards. Everything smelt musty, no matter what she did.

It was clean. Her small chin rose a fraction, as though someone had suggested otherwise. She and Flora had made sure of that when they moved in, scrubbing every inch of the place before they had moved the boys' bed and the one they shared into the confined space. But with the table holding their pots and pans and plates and cutlery, the wooden chest containing their meagre few items of clothing and the personal belongings she had kept when she had sold the contents of the house—which had fetched a paltry sum—and her mother's old rocking chair, there wasn't room to swing a cat. She had tried to maintain a semblance of decency by putting the boys' bed in a corner of the room and stringing an old curtain up, so she and Flora had some privacy when they washed and undressed, but the last twelve months had been hard for them all. And the grim shadow of the workhouse had always been there. Threatening them.

Connie pulled herself into a sitting position, holding on to the high back of the settle as the room whirled. She wouldn't let the younger ones go there. She *wouldn't*. And if she gave in to this sickness that was what would happen. Maybe she'd just have the next day off work and send Flora to explain to the foreman. She had always got on all right with Mr O'Dowd—he'd keep her job for a day or two, but no longer. The manager didn't hold with folk being sick. But two days would be enough.

Pushing the blanket to one side, she brought all her considerable will to bear and swung her legs over the side of the bench. Ignoring the rushing in her ears, she stared down at her ugly, heavy-looking boots without seeing them. She had to get to her feet and show them she was all right. She had the doctor's fee now, on top of everything else; she supposed the Briggses had paid him, but she would have to settle up with them.

She managed to totter a few steps before the door opened and Mrs Briggs and the man came in. He caught her as she keeled over, and she heard him swear under his breath as he whisked her up and carried her back to the settle, dumping her unceremoniously on the flock-cushioned seat.

'For crying out loud, girl, stay put. Do you want to pass out again? Just lie still.'

It was a growl. If she hadn't been feeling so ill, Connie's temper, which went with the red in her chestnut hair, would have been roused. As it was, she managed to say fairly strongly, 'I need to get home now. I have to see to my sister and brothers.'

'I rather think it will be a case of your sister and brothers looking after you for the immediate future,' he said flatly.

Connie stared into the dark face. He didn't have a clue. In spite of Mrs Briggs explaining their circumstances, he had no idea how things were. It was hurting her to breathe, and she wanted nothing more than to lay her head down on the flock-stuffed cushions and go to sleep, but still she said, 'I'm going home.'

As she tried to stand up he muttered something that sounded like, 'Damn little fool,' but Connie didn't have time to reflect on that. He had bent and lifted her into his arms again, holding her against his black overcoat as he said to Mrs Briggs, 'I'll take her home. She can't walk back. Perhaps your husband would be good enough to bring the medicine round later?'

'Aye, aye—he'll do that, and I'll pop round in the morning and see how she is. Poor little thing. She's worn out.'

They were talking as though she wasn't here. The thought came, but barely registered. All her senses were taken up with the fact she was in a man's arms for the first time in her life. In spite of her physical state, the fresh clean smell of him, the effortless strength with which he held her, and the fact that his hard square jaw with a dusting of black stubble was inches from her face rendered her dumb. She didn't even make a token protest as he carried her out of the house. Which wasn't like her.

Once in the snowy quiet street, he looked down at her, his eyes glittering in the darkness of his face. 'Which house is yours?' he asked abruptly. 'What number is it?'

He wasn't wearing a cap. All the men and lads hereabouts wore a cap. But as they'd left the house Mrs Briggs had handed him a hat, like the gentry wore, which was clasped in his hand right now. And yet he didn't talk like the gentry.

She watched the starry snowflakes settle on the jetblack hair, her head muzzy, and then caught sight of the horse and trap some yards away. He had tied the reins of the horse to a lamppost. It was just as well it was such a terrible night or else the urchins from miles around would have congregated round it by now. She couldn't remember anyone ever being visited by someone rich enough to own a horse and trap, and it was a fine horse too, not like the rag and bone man's old nag.

Connie suddenly became aware he was waiting for an answer to his question. 'It's three doors down,' she said quickly, beginning to cough as the cold air hit her throat.

It only took him a couple of strides to reach the house, but she was coughing so badly and felt so dizzy she couldn't tell him the door was never locked. With an old couple in one room upstairs, a spinster lady in the other, and a family of six occupying what had been the kitchen when the house was first built, the hall was merely a thoroughfare. She and her sister and brothers had the front room, and everyone shared the privy in the backyard, along with the tap for water.

Flora must have seen them arrive through the front room window, though, because the next moment her sister opened the door, bursting into tears as she did so. Mrs Briggs's Elsie stood in the doorway to the room, gnawing on her thumbnail as they entered the hall, then springing to one side to let them pass.

As her coughing subsided, Connie gasped, 'Thank you. I'll be all right now.' But he didn't put her down as she'd expected. Instead he stood surveying the room from the doorway.

Tommy, David and Ronnie were sitting huddled under their thin blankets in their bed, mouths agape, and the small fire burning in the grate was heating the steel shelf fixed over the hot coals on which the pot of stew stood, but doing very little to warm the room. She saw the man's eyes linger on the stew for a moment, and on the five bowls Flora had put to warm on the hearth. She knew what he was thinking. Not much to feed five people. She agreed with him, but there was little she could do about it. If ever the day came when she could let Flora and the lads eat until they were bursting, she'd know they'd landed in heaven.

The grey gaze moved to the curtain over the boys' bed, which at the moment was pulled back and tied to a hook on the wall with a bit of string, then to the old rocking chair next to the battered table holding their pots and pans. Finally it focused on Flora, who was still sobbing unrestrainedly. And very loudly.

Acutely embarrassed now, Connie murmured again, 'Thank you. You've been very kind, Mr…' It was only then she realized she didn't even know his name. 'But we can manage now.'

He didn't acknowledge that she had spoken, turning with her still in his arms and speaking to Elsie standing in the hall. 'Tell your mother I'm taking Miss Summers and the rest of them home with me tonight, so I shall need the medicine your father's fetching the minute he gets back. I shall call and have a word with your mother tomorrow, when I come to collect the necessary belongings, but I live at Hawthorn Farm—past High Ford and the old quarries. Can you remember that? Hawthorn Farm?'

Elsie stared at him before nodding. She seemed to have lost the power of speech. Connie didn't blame her.

'Go and wait for your father and then bring the medicine straight here,' he said slowly to Elsie, as though she was dim-witted. 'We cannot leave until we have it. Do you understand?'

Elsie nodded again, and then turned and flew out of the house as though she had wings on her feet.

Finally Connie found her tongue. Trying to instil some strength into her voice, she said, 'We can't go anywhere, Mr…'

'Hudson. Luke Hudson.'

'We can't leave here, Mr Hudson.' She wriggled as she spoke, and he walked across and placed her in the rocking chair, looking down at her with unfathomable eyes as she continued, 'I have a job, and the children have to go to school—'

'You won't be able to work for some time. Hasn't that sunk in yet? You're ill, Miss Summers. Very ill. If you don't do exactly as the doctor ordered you may well find you will be leaving your sister and brothers for good. Have I made myself clear? I've no wish to frighten you, but the doctor was explicit.'

Her face was chalk-white, and she was as weak as a kitten, but still she argued. 'You don't understand. If we lose this room we won't be able to get anything else if I can't find another job. I have to go to work.' Her breath caught in a little sob which was more frustration at her own weakness than anything else. 'I have to. There's no other choice.'

'One of the labourers' cottages on my farm is empty as of last week. You and your family can stay there. When you're feeling better you can help my mother in the farmhouse. She's been thinking of getting someone to assist her for some time. There are jobs your sister and brothers can do when they get home from school to earn their keep too. I'm not offering charity, Miss Summers. You'll all work in some capacity.'

The grey gaze was cool—distant, even—and with her head swimming as it was Connie found it difficult to take in what he had said. 'You mean…?' She paused, brushing a strand of hair from her face with a trembling hand. 'You're saying it would be permanent? The cottage, me helping your mother, everything?'

'If you so wish. You would be free to leave at any time, of course, if you find the arrangement does not suit you.'

He was offering them the moon, and he must know it, but he was so cold, so aloof. But he was saying there was a cottage—a *cottage*—and she would be helping his mother. No more pickle factory, where even when she was well she felt sick with exhaustion at the end of the day. 'But why?' she said dazedly. 'Why would you do this for us? You don't even know us.'

His eyes narrowed. 'Like I said, you would earn your keep, all of you, but I like to think I offer a good day's wage for honest work. For the moment you need someone to take care of you, if these children aren't going to be left alone, and my mother is an able nurse. You'll be in good hands.'

It wasn't really an answer, but she felt too ill and too weak with relief to care. She wanted to say thank you. She wanted to express her thanks for the most miraculous, wonderful thing that had ever happened to them. But instead she found herself falling into the darkness again, and the only difference to last time was that now she could hear Luke Hudson swearing softly as he gathered her into his arms once more.

CHAPTER TWO

'How is she?' Luke appeared in the doorway to the scullery, rubbing his hands dry on the big rough towel his mother kept there for that purpose when he came in from the fields.

He watched her close the kitchen door which led directly on to the big stone-flagged yard at the back of the farmhouse. The farmhouse's front door was situated in the huge, oak-beamed sitting room, and this opened on to his mother's front garden, which she kept as neat as a new pin in the summer, when the flowerbeds were a riot of colour. It was his mother's boast that no other farm in the district had a front garden, and in this she was probably right. When his father had been alive he had indulged his mother's love of flowers, and Luke saw no reason to do otherwise.

His mother shrugged her plump shoulders, glancing at him as she said tartly, 'Same as she was this morning, and lunchtime, and mid-afternoon.' She walked across to the massive black-leaded range, opening the oven door and taking out the big tin holding a joint of stuffed roast breast of lamb which was their evening meal. She had taken a pot pie over to the cottage earlier.

Luke eyed his mother's stiff back. She had been furious when he had turned up with Connie and the others that evening three weeks ago. Having said that, she'd bedded the lot of them down in the farmhouse and then sat up the whole night with Connie, who had been delirious. But for his mother's nursing those first few days he doubted the girl would have survived.

'What did the doctor say when he called this afternoon?' Luke walked across to the big scrubbed kitchen table and took his place at the head of it. Since his father had died five years before, his mother had always insisted he sit there, and if they had guests and used the dining room next to his study she again set his place at the head of the long mahogany table.

She was a strange mixture, his mother. It had been she, along with Flora and a couple of his labourers' wives, who had cleaned and aired the empty cottage for Connie and the little ones when the doctor had pronounced she could be moved from one of the spare bedrooms in the farmhouse two weeks ago. The cottage had been left in something of a state by old George, the previous tenant, who had got too old and arthritic to work and gone to live with his married daughter in Newcastle. But when Luke had bought some bits of furniture secondhand to furnish the place she'd raised her eyebrows and muttered under her breath about some people not having the sense they were born with. A couple of days later he'd noticed curtains at the windows of the cottage, which had never been there in old

George's day, and he knew for a fact she'd taken a load of their old sheets and blankets for the little family, along with towels and such.

'The doctor?' Maggie Hudson placed the joint in front of her son for him to carve, and busied herself with the roast potatoes and vegetables. 'He's pleased with her progress, by all accounts. He reckons this time next week she'll be able to get up and sit in front of the fire, but she's got to take it steady. He's of a mind the pleurisy is only part of it. The lass was worn out long before that. At the end of herself, he said she was.'

'I'm not surprised. I told you what their room was like, didn't I? Our stables are warmer, and a darn sight more spacious.'

His mother said nothing to this, but once they were eating she suddenly put down her knife and fork and turned to him. 'I'm going to say it,' she said flatly. 'You won't like it, but I'm going to say it nonetheless. We know nothing about this girl except where she comes from—and that's none too good. Now, she might be all right, but we don't know that, and I believe the proof of the pudding is in the eating. I'm holding my horses with regard to the lot of them, Luke. It might be she sees this place as a welcome refuge, or on the other hand as a soft touch.'

'You mean me. She sees *me* as a soft touch,' he said quietly. He wasn't offended. He believed in plain speaking.

His mother tossed her head. 'Perhaps.' And then, her voice softening, she said, 'She's a pretty little thing, I'll give you that, and being in need like she was it brought out the protective side to a man. But the thing is…' She bit her lip. 'I don't want you hurt again. That's what I'm trying to say.'

He surveyed her for a moment or two before shaking his head slowly. 'She's a child—they all are. Barely out of nappies.'

'They've all been out of nappies a good while,' his mother said tartly. 'And Connie is going on seventeen. She's a little wisp of a thing, admittedly, but she's a woman, Luke.'

'And I'm a twenty-eight-year-old man who buried his wife and child two years ago,' he ground out harshly.

'Oh, lad, I'm sorry. I didn't mean to rake things up.'

'It's all right, Mother.' A muscle worked in his jaw, and he breathed in and out a few times before he said, 'I had eighteen months of marriage, and believe me I don't intend to repeat the experience—as you well know. Once was enough for a lifetime. For several lifetimes,' he finished bitterly. 'I brought them here because I could do little else. It would have been a death sentence for her and the workhouse for the rest of them if I'd walked away that night. I couldn't have slept easy ever after.'

Maggie nodded. After a moment, she said, 'Eat your dinner,' and her voice was placatory. 'You don't like your food cold.'

It was much later that night, after Luke had checked on his favourite horse, which had had a touch of colic during the day, that he left the snug stables and walked outside into the frosty darkness. He didn't make for the farmhouse, but turned and walked away in the opposite direction, up the slight incline that led to the top of a low hill. Here the night sky stretched above him like black

velvet, the stars twinkling like so many glittering diamonds and the full moon sailing resplendent in her inky
sea. It had snowed again on and off all day, and the
countryside was clean and white and sparkling. If he
turned his head and looked towards the farm, his labourers' cottages, four of them in all, had light shining from
the windows. All except one. But of course Connie and
the children would be asleep by now. He'd noticed they
were always the first to be abed.

In his mind's eye he pictured Connie as she had been
yesterday evening, when he had stopped by for a brief
visit once Flora and the lads were back from school. He
always made sure the children were home when he
called, and this in itself gave the lie to what he had
declared to his mother—that he considered Connie a
child. She had still looked very pale and fragile, lying
propped up against the pillows, but there had been a
touch of colour in her cheeks and her deep blue eyes had
had a sparkle in them.

He shook himself, as though dislodging a weight, and
turned to face the countryside again. Anyone looking at
him would consider him a most fortunate man, and he
supposed he was, he thought, drawing the biting air
deep into his lungs. Not only did he own a farm of some
two thousand acres, a large part of it providing rich
good soil for crops and luscious grass for his cattle, but
he had never known want in his life. Not of the material
kind anyway.

A shooting star blazed across the sky for a moment
and then was gone, and his eyes could see it no more.
That was the way love—or what he'd naively assumed

was love—had blazed into his life over six years ago, and its exit had been just as final.

Christabel Ramshaw—the beloved and cossetted only child of neighbouring farmers and the belle of the countryside. And out of all of her many suitors she had chosen him. And so he'd begun courting her, visiting the Ramshaw farm twice a week on Wednesday evenings and Sunday afternoons. They'd have tea in the parlour with her parents, or the two of them would take sedate walks—weather permitting—but always with her mother and aunt, who lived with the family, bringing up the rear. They had never been alone before their wedding day. Not once. He'd barely held her hand.

A barn owl screeched somewhere in the night, shattering the peace and quiet, but within moments all was silent again.

Their wedding night had been a nightmare, and she had made him feel a brute even when he had just tried to hold her. After two months, when the marriage had still been unconsummated, her mother had come to the house on his request and talked to Christabel. After this his wife had allowed a certain degree of intimacy, but once their son was conceived had declared 'that nasty kind of thing' was over for good. He'd finally had to accept that he'd married a woman who was not only frigid, but lazy, spoilt and selfish into the bargain. She hadn't lifted a finger to help his mother in the house, had insisted on travelling about the countryside visiting her friends in the horse and trap every day, and had flatly refused to have anything to do with their son once he was born. If he'd objected, she'd gone hysterical.

It had been shortly after one of her jaunts that she'd complained of feeling unwell. Within three weeks the scarlet fever had claimed her life, and their son had followed a week later. He had been just three months old.

Luke lifted his face to the sky, the anguish as real as when he had carried the tiny white coffin from the church to the cemetery. He'd watched his son being laid to rest in the same grave which held the body of his wife, and he had wanted to snatch him up and shout to the mourners that there would be no comfort for the baby with his mother. That Christabel hadn't wanted him, had refused to feed him, insisting she had no milk, had barely even held him in his short life and had finally been responsible for his death. That his son's wet nurse and grandmother had been more of a mother to the child than Christabel.

But of course he hadn't. Christabel's parents had been half demented with grief as it was, and his mother had been pitiful to see that day. So he had held his tongue, and his bitterness had been all the more profound for it.

He swung his body round, looking down to the dim shadow of the cottage wherein Connie was sleeping. He had sworn that day at his son's graveside that he would never allow himself to become another woman's fool. He was done with love—if such a thing existed. Which he doubted. Never again would a woman hold him in the hollow of her hand and lead him on until he gave her his name. *Never again.* Nothing was worth that.

He began to walk towards the farmhouse, the faint smell of the bonfire two of his labourers had made earlier, when they had been clearing a section of wood-land and cutting logs for fuel for the next few months, giving the cold air a timeless fragrance. He sucked it into his lungs, relishing its bite.

This was real. He pictured the rolling fields and woodland, the low scrub hedges, drystone walls and outcrops of rock and shale shelves that made up his domain to the boundary of the land he owned. The earth, the air you breathed. He was master here. He gave orders and they were obeyed. He was in control. And it would remain that way.

He approached the house with measured steps, his face cold and set, and he did not glance towards the silent cottage deep in the shadows of the night again.

Being made a fool of once was one thing. Every man was allowed to make one mistake. But to repeat the exercise… That bordered on insanity. His life was now set in order once again, and it ticked along fairly well on the whole. The seasons came and went, the farm prospered, and he was answerable to no man. Or woman.

He opened the farmhouse door but paused, glancing across his land, as somewhere in the far distance the owl hooted again.

He was content. His eyes narrowed. As content as he ever would be. And with that he shut the door.

CHAPTER THREE

CONNIE sat quietly, her hands in her lap, gazing into the glowing fire, her mind and senses still touched with the wonder she'd felt ever since arriving in what she privately termed heaven on earth. She still found it hard to believe they were really here.

It was Christmas Eve, and for the first time in a week it wasn't snowing. Flora and the three boys had gone into the wood with their next-door neighbour's wife, Rose, a warm, comely soul, to dig up one of the small fir trees growing there. They were an old couple—older than her parents, at least—but they had taken an interest in the younger ones from day one, and Connie was grateful for it. Rose was going to help Flora and the lads decorate the tree with pine cones they were planning to paint in bright colours. She had told them she'd done this with her own children when they were young, and little Ronnie had made himself sick with excitement the night before. Even Tommy hadn't been able to sleep.

She liked Jacob and Rose. She liked all Mr Hudson's

men and their wives. Everyone had been so kind to them. So welcoming.

Connie's gaze left the fire and moved to the shining black-leaded hob, an oven to the right of it and a nook for pans to its left. She was sitting in a shabby but comfortable armchair which was one of two set either side of the range, divided by an enormous thick clippy mat where her brothers liked to sit of an evening, toasting their toes on the fender.

The kitchen also held a table, with two long benches either side of it, a rickety dresser against the far wall and her mother's rocking chair. And in the tiny scullery leading off it an old tin bath stood on its side, with a large bowl on a stout stool used for all purposes that required water. Two bedrooms, each with a double bed and a chest of drawers, made up the rest of the three-roomed cottage—a cottage Connie could still hardly believe was their home. With no rent man knocking on the door either.

If she and the rest of them worked for Mr Hudson every day for the rest of their lives they would never be able to repay him for all he'd done for them. She had been more ill than she had realised and he'd saved them. He was a kind man, so kind.

Here Connie's thoughts gave a little hiccup, and as though to repudiate something she said out loud, 'He is. He's so kind.'

She stood up, walking over to the kitchen window and peering out into the snow-covered world outside. The hard frost which had fallen the night before was holding, coating everything with a film of silver which sparkled in the weak morning sunshine. She would have loved to go out with the others in the fresh biting air, tramping through the snow and making sport, but she knew she wasn't well enough for that yet. Hopefully it wouldn't be long.

Sighing, she wandered to the kitchen table and sat down, beginning to scrape the potatoes for their evening meal. Until this last week, when she had begun to feel much better, Mr Hudson's mother had brought their dinner in each night, but she was glad this was no longer so. She was longing to be able to help in the farmhouse and dairy, and start to earn her keep. She'd felt such a burden to Mrs Hudson these last weeks. And to him.

Her hands stilling, she stared into space. He had never said anything, of course, but the way he was, so distant and cold, made her feel he had regretted bringing them here almost since day one. Or was it her he didn't like? She frowned to herself. She had watched him on the occasions he had called by, and he wasn't so chilly with Flora and the boys. Tommy and David and Ronnie had been full of the fact yesterday that he had stopped a while to have a snowball fight with them and the other children of his employees, once they had all finished clearing and sweeping the paths and doing some odd jobs for his mother.

A knock at the door brought her head swinging round, and as she called, 'Come in,' and stood to her feet her heart began to pound—even as she told herself it didn't necessarily have to be him.

It was, though. As he filled the aperture her heart beat even faster. Sometimes when he called by he was in his working clothes because, as Rose had put it, 'The master isn't afraid of getting his hands dirty,' and was known as a man who liked to be out of doors. Other times, like now, he dressed as befitted a well-to-do farmer of a large and thriving farm. The thick dark brown tweed coat was three-quarter's length, and cut in such a way that the powerful shoulders looked even broader, and his trousers and shining leather boots were clearly of the best quality. He was holding his hat in his hands and the jet-black hair had a sheen to it.

'Good morning.' He glanced round the room. 'All by yourself on such a beautiful Christmas Eve morning? The others out?'

'Yes, sir.' All the labourers and their wives and the farm children called him master, but somehow she couldn't bring herself to do that—possibly because it had been her father's boast that he had never dipped his cap or bent his knee and called a man master, poor as they were. He had been a proud man, her da, and that had mattered a great deal to him.

He nodded, but didn't come into the room. She had known he wouldn't. He never did if she was alone.

'Rose has kindly taken Flora and the lads to fetch one of the small fir trees,' she said quietly. 'They're going to decorate it later. The lads are half mad with excitement. They've never done anything like it before.'

'Not even when your parents were alive?'

She shook her head. There had been no time or energy for things like that, although she and her mam had tried to make sure the younger ones always had an orange and an apple and a sugar mouse Christmas morning, to make the day special. One Christmas Eve, before Ronnie was born, her father had managed to get a big fat turkey from the old market at gone midnight, when the last of the stallholders was packing up. The stallholder had haggled at first, but when her father had held out the few coppers he'd saved the man had suddenly relented, muttering something about it being Christmas as he'd shoved the turkey into her father's arms. That had been a lovely Christmas. She missed her mam and da.

Whether something of her thoughts showed in her face she didn't know, but to Connie's great surprise he pulled the door shut and came fully into the kitchen, saying, 'You must have found it hard after they went. Weren't you ever tempted to put the children in the care of the guardians and just fend for yourself?'

'The workhouse?' She stared at him. 'Have you ever seen inside that place?' And then, realising her tone wasn't what it should be to her employer, she added, 'Sir.'

'No, I haven't. But they would have been provided with accommodation and food, surely?'

'Along with the stigma of being workhouse brats and more degradations besides. They would probably have been split up and—' She stopped. He would never understand, never, but when she had gone with her mother to visit one of their old neighbours the hideous uniform of the female inmates and the smell of the infirm ward had made her sick all night. The foul-smelling atmosphere, the silent misery, the way families were separated had left her deeply shaken. 'I would never have let them go there after what I saw,' she finished flatly.

'It was worse than that one room and you all slowly starving?' he asked quietly. 'Because that is what was happening.'

She had lowered her eyes, but now she looked straight into the rugged handsome face, her own expressing far more than she was aware of. 'It was hell on earth.'

'I see.' He was quiet for a moment. Then he said, 'I've interrupted you working,' as he gestured to the potatoes she had been scraping. 'Please don't let me hold you up.'

'Oh, I've got all day to get the evening meal ready.' She hesitated, and then said very quickly, 'I've never thanked you properly for all you've done, sir. I know I wouldn't be here now if it wasn't for you. The doctor's made that plain. And bringing us all to this cottage, and the furniture and food and fuel…' She didn't know how to adequately express what it meant.

There followed a silence during which their eyes met and held. Hers were the first to drop away, and she felt a shiver trickle down her spine. She didn't know how to explain the effect he had on her except, as she put it to herself, he was the most masculine man she had ever met. It wasn't just the height of him, or the breadth and strength in his shoulders and arms which she had been conscious of that first night, when he had carried her so effortlessly, it was something else. Something powerful and potent and altogether disturbing. Rose had told her he had been married and his wife and son had died of the fever. After that, Rose had said, he'd become a different man. It must have been wonderful for his wife to be loved so much by a man like Luke Hudson. Even if their time together had been so short.

Her thoughts made her flush, and now her voice was even more rushed when she said, 'I'll be ready to start work after Christmas, sir. And in the spring and summer, when Flora and the lads can work in the fields till late, we'll start to pay you back some of what we owe you.'

'Owe?' His brow wrinkled. 'You owe me nothing, Connie.'

It was the first time she could remember him saying her name, and the intimacy, slight though it was, made her cheeks flush warmer still. 'But we do,' she stammered. 'It's been weeks now, and you've provided food and fuel and—'

'You owe me nothing,' he repeated firmly. 'My mother will appreciate the help in the farmhouse once you're fit enough. She won't admit it, but she tires more easily these days. Rose and Bess assist in the dairy, and Seth's wife looks after the pigs and chickens, but there's still far too much for her to do now she's getting older. Of course she still thinks she has the energy she did when she was twenty,' he added with a smile.

'I'll do anything she wants, sir. And I'm stronger than I look. Well, normally, that is,' she finished awkwardly.

His smile widened at this. 'I doubt it, but you are improving and that's the main thing. Don't rush things at this stage.'

She hadn't seen him smile, really smile before. She knew he was attempting to ease her obvious embarrassment, but the difference it made to his normal stern persona was riveting. Her own smile a little shaky, she said again, 'I'll be ready to start in the house after Christmas for sure.'

'We'll see. Perhaps the New Year. And it will ring in a new century this time—hopefully the beginning of a better time for you and your sister and brothers.'

'Oh, I know it will, now we're here,' she said warmly.

Again they stood regarding one another, and for no reason that she could fathom she felt a kind of breathlessness in the air. This time she couldn't pull her eyes from his.

After the merest hesitation he nodded, turning towards the door as he said over his shoulder, 'It's a tradition on Christmas Eve that everyone comes up to the house before sunset for their Christmas boxes.' He opened the door before facing her and adding, 'My mother makes all the ladies a hamper, and the men are given a more liquid gift. The children also receive a little something. I'm sure your sister and brothers will enjoy it.'

Her eyes widened. She knew from the labourers' wives' gossip when they popped in to see her now and again that every single one of them considered themselves lucky to be part of this farm. It had been in the Hudson family for generations, and each successive master had apparently been strict but fair, and progressive in his views. The present master, like his father before him and his father before him, demanded unquestioning loyalty and hard work, Rose had told her on one of her visits, but they weren't mean and crabby, like some farmers she could name.

'But we've only been here a short time,' Connie said awkwardly, 'and you've been so generous as it is. We don't expect to be treated like the others, sir. You've given us more than enough.'

There was a pause, and then he said, 'You really mean that, don't you?' And it was a statement, not a question. Nevertheless she nodded. He was frowning slightly, as though her words had displeased him, but for the life of her she couldn't think why. 'I want you and your sister and brothers to come to the house,' he repeated quietly. 'All right?'

'Yes, sir.' She wondered how his eyes could look so hard and cold and yet sad too. He was a complex individual.

They stared at each other for another moment and then he stepped outside into the crisp air, shutting the door behind him.

Luke stood for some moments outside the cottage, his frown deepening. He didn't know why he made these visits to see how she was. They never did him any good. He always felt disturbed and unsettled afterwards. Ramming his hat on his head, he strode towards the stables. A damn good gallop on Ebony, his black stallion, would sort him out, he told himself irritably. Blow away the cobwebs. It was a beautiful day; it'd be a crime to waste it. And staying around the farm wasn't an option somehow.

Once in the stables, little Charlie Todd—the youngest son of one of his labourers, whose eldest two sons took care of the huge shire horses, truly gentle giants, along with Ebony and also his mother's brown mare—came running up to him. The lad was only seven years old, but liked nothing better than to be in the stables with the animals and his big brothers once he was home from school and in the holidays.

'Ebony let me feed him an apple this morning, master,' he said excitedly. 'Took it out of me hand, he did. An' he was as quiet as a mouse an' all.'

'Is that so? Well, you watch him nevertheless, Charlie.' Ebony was a high-spirited, temperamental animal, inclined to moodiness, and had been known to bite.

'I do, master. If he looks at me like this—' the small boy snarled, wrinkling his nose '—I know he don't want company. But if he snorts and snuffles and bobs his head he's all right.'

Luke smiled down at the boy. 'I can see you'll follow your brothers into the stables when you're old enough,' he said, nodding to one of the older lads who had entered Ebony's stall and brought him out into the main building, where he deftly saddled him. Charlie was watching, eyes agog, the whole time.

Once he had left the stables, Luke's smile faded. Charlie was an engaging little lad, always smiling and as bright as a button—much as he would have expected his own son to be if he had lived. Even at three months Jack's toothless smile had lit up his face.

He dug his heels into Ebony's sleek sides, encouraging the horse into a gallop and letting him have his head. It was some time before they stopped at the crest of a hill, the horse's snorting breath white in the icy air.

Why was it that since Connie's arrival at the farm the ache in his heart for his son had got worse? He didn't understand it. And he wasn't sleeping well. Umpteen times a night he woke, hard as a rock in spite of having scourged his body into submission with hard physical work during the day. More than once he had been tempted to do what many of his contemporaries did and go into Sunderland or Newcastle and visit one of the brothels for release, but somehow the thought of paying for it was repugnant.

He smiled bitterly. He was a fool. He knew he was a fool. There were several women of his own standing in society who had made it plain they would welcome his attentions, and one—a dark-eyed beauty whose husband had a mistress or two—had let him know a relationship between them would be without strings. He should take what was on offer and ease himself. Live for the day, the moment. No one would blame him, and there was no reason not to.

In spite of himself the picture of a heart-shaped face with deep blue eyes and a mass of chestnut hair came on to the screen of his mind. Today her hair had been drawn back, as usual, into a decorous bun at the back of her head, but once or twice when she had still been bedridden it had fanned out on the pillows in a glorious blaze of colour, silky and soft and as seductive as hell.

'None of that.' He spoke out loud, his voice deep and guttural. Not on his own doorstep. And she was little more than a child—not so much in age as in the way she was. Innocence shone out of her. It was clear she was sexually unawakened. Whatever went on in some of those dwelling places in the town, where humanity was crammed in together to the point where life was obscene, she had been brought up by parents who had maintained moral decency. When she gave herself to a man it would be with a wedding ring on her finger, and that was something he would never contemplate again.

Even if she had been from the same social strata as himself. So the thing was impossible all ways.

He scowled into the distance, his countenance thunderous, before turning the reins and riding the horse down the incline stretching out white and glistening before them.

When she started to work for his mother in the house she would become just another of their employees. It was this unreal situation due to her illness which had made things... He couldn't find a word to describe what he felt and made a harsh sound of irritation in his throat.

'To hell with it.' He nodded at the words. After Christmas things would return to normal, and it couldn't be soon enough as far as he was concerned. One thing was for sure, it was the last time he'd play the Good Samaritan. Didn't the good book say one was rewarded for such things? If this, the way he'd been feeling of late, was a reward, he hated to think what a punishment would feel like.

He grinned darkly. And it was like that, with the twist to his lips giving his face a cynical broodiness, that he rode slowly home in the crystal and white world surrounding him.

CHAPTER FOUR

IT WAS now the end of May, but only three weeks since
the snow had finally disappeared. The winter had been
hard and long, and everyone on the farm—apart from
its newest inhabitants—had been bemoaning the fact.
For Connie and Flora and the boys, however, each day
in their snug cottage had been a continuing delight.
There might be cold and slush and bitter winds to deal
with, but what were these if you could come home to
your own cosy fireside and a laden table?

Connie had seen her sister and brothers gain weight
and develop bright eyes and rosy cheeks and it thrilled
her. They all worked hard: she in the farmhouse and
Flora and the boys at the hundred and one jobs there
were to do round the farm once they were home from
school. The days were long; Connie rose at six
o'clock to get the porridge for breakfast on the go and
the packed lunches for the children ready before they
left at seven-thirty for the long walk to school. Once
Flora and the lads were home in the evening they all
rarely finished work before seven o'clock in the

evening. Then it was eating their evening meal and getting ready for bed for the children, whereupon Connie would sit by the fire, sewing and mending their clothes or darning the boys' socks or working at clippy mats for the bedrooms, until gone eleven o'clock, the wind moaning round the cottage and rattling the windows.

Tommy, David and Ronnie had loved preparing and feeding the cows their pulped turnips, hay or crushed corn during the winter months, when the cattle had been kept indoors at night, and since Seth's wife had fallen on the ice and broken her leg Flora had taken on the task of seeing to the pigs' bran and feeding the chickens. The children had risen to their responsibilities with a single-minded fortitude that made Connie proud of them.

But the sun was shining at last, and suddenly there was even more work to do. Connie glanced at the other women on the farm as they laboured in the hop garden. During the winter months nothing had been seen of the plants but the slightly rounded mounds stretching away in symmetrical rows, but now the warmth of the sun had brought up the shoots, and the bines had to be trained to the strings that were stretched criss-cross from pole to pole. It was a delicate procedure to twiddle the bines into place, and unlike the rest of the women Connie was new to the task, but within a little while she'd got the hang of it. It was a break from her normal work in the farmhouse, and she was enjoying being in the clean fresh air for a few days. As though to make up for lost time spring had arrived with a vengeance, and the sun was hot enough to burn noses and turn skin rosy pink, even under the bonnets they wore.

'So? You fell out of favour with the mistress or something?'

Connie glanced at the girl who had spoken to her. Of all the folk on the farm this was the only person she didn't like. Alice Todd was the eldest daughter of Hannah and Walter Todd, and she had already made it clear she resented Connie working in the farmhouse— a job she believed should have gone to her, considering she'd been born and bred here. Tall at eighteen, and with corn-coloured hair and large green eyes, Alice was very pretty and she knew it. It was common knowledge she liked the master. Rumour had it Walter had taken the whip to her last summer, when he'd caught her lying in wait on the road leading to the farm for Luke Hudson to return from town one afternoon.

'No, I haven't fallen out of favour,' Connie said shortly.

'Why you out here with the rest of us, then, instead of inside?' Alice said tartly. 'Bit queer that, if you ask me.'

Connie stared at the smooth-skinned face. It was on the tip of her tongue to tell the other girl to mind her own business, but for the sake of harmony she bit back the hot words hovering on her tongue. 'Mrs Hudson thought I ought to learn what went on.' She turned back to the bine in her hands. 'See how different things work all over the farm.'

What Luke's mother had actually said was, 'Time for you to get out of doors for a few days and get some colour in your cheeks, lass. I'll miss you, but I'll manage fine for a bit.'

'Huh.' Alice tossed her head in the pert way she favoured.

The exclamation was loud, but Connie didn't rise to it.

A few minutes later, after checking the other women were out of earshot, Alice sidled close enough to murmur, 'Think you're in with the door shut with the mistress, don't you? But you won't get his eye like that. Not with a red-blooded man like him.'

'What?' Connie looked into the green gaze and it was seething with jealousy. Coldly, she said, 'I don't know what you mean.'

'You might fool the others with your butter-wouldn't-melt-in-your-mouth air, but not me. Well, let me tell you the master would never look the side you're on. Not in a month of Sundays.'

'Of course he wouldn't,' Connie agreed, with a cool disregard which clearly took the other girl aback. But not for long.

There was a moment of silence, and then Alice whispered, 'You trying to tell me you're *not* after warming his bed?'

She'd had enough of this. Connie faced the other girl and didn't lower her voice as she said clearly, 'Don't judge others by your own questionable standards, Alice. And I don't have to tell you anything, by the way. Now, I suggest you do what you're paid to do and work, and leave me to do the same.'

One or two of the other women had raised their heads and narrowed their eyes, clearly wondering what was going on. Alice flushed hotly and then flounced off, but not before the green eyes had shot daggers. Connie knew from things Flora had said that more than once Alice had referred to her as an upstart when she wasn't within earshot, and this latest wouldn't exactly help matters. Still, she wasn't going to allow the other girl to think she could walk all over her and say whatever she liked.

She continued to work on quietly, but Alice's words niggled at her—not least because they'd brought to mind the dreams she'd been having of late. It made her blush to think of them, and every one had featured her employer, Mr Hudson. But she hadn't called him Mr Hudson or sir in the dreams; it had been Luke…

Had Alice guessed how she felt?

Almost immediately she answered her own question with no. Alice was jealous because she didn't have the same access to the farmhouse and therefore their employer as she did. Not that it would have done Alice any good if she had, of course. If he ever decided to marry again it would be someone like his late wife, without a doubt—a wealthy farmer's daughter or someone of the same social standing. But then Alice wasn't necessarily looking for marriage, if half of what Connie had heard about her was true.

She had to stop thinking about him all the time.

Connie nodded mentally to the thought, irritated with herself. Her heart raced every time she saw him these days, and it made working with his mother in the house more difficult than it should be. She was always on tenterhooks in case he'd appear.

It was only an hour or so later that Rose came hurrying into the hop garden, calling her name. 'Quick,' she called as Connie met her halfway. 'It's the mistress. We were in the dairy and she came over bad. The master's gone for the doctor, and he said for you to come and sit with her while he's gone.'

As the two of them hurried back to the house Connie's stomach was churning. Mrs Hudson must be bad if Luke had gone for the doctor himself, rather than sending one of the men in the horse and trap. Ebony would cover the distance in half the time, and he must have thought that important.

Luke had apparently carried his mother upstairs, and Rose and Bess had helped her undress and get into bed. When Connie went into the bedroom she was shocked at the change in the plump, rosy-cheeked woman, although Mrs Hudson was still giving orders right, left and centre.

Gesturing for Connie to come to the head of the head, Luke's mother turned to the other two women, saying, 'You two go and finish churning that butter, and make sure it's done right. And we want some cream before evening, Rose. I've none on the cold slab in the pantry. And bring half a cheese while you're about it.' When the two continued to stand looking at her, their faces showing their distress, she said impatiently, 'Well, go on, then. And take those looks off your faces. I'm not six foot under yet, nor do I intend to be for many a long day.'

As the two scurried off, Connie said quietly, 'What do you want me to do, Mrs Hudson?' She looked awful, Connie thought. As though all the blood had drained out of her. And her lips had a funny bluish tinge to them, and she was breathing funny.

'Sit yourself down there, lass, and keep me company. Orders from the master.' She always gave her son his title when speaking to others. 'I'm going to shut my eyes for a minute. I'm feeling a mite tired, but I'll be all right after a little nap.'

It was quiet in the bedroom, muted sounds from the farm filtering through the open window but not really disturbing the peace. Sunlight slanted across the floor which, like all the bedrooms, had a large square of carpet covering it, so only a foot or so border of floorboards was visible. Once a week Connie sprinkled tea leaves over the carpets and then brushed them off to bring the pile up. It was one of the many things Mrs Hudson had taught her since she had begun work.

As though Luke's mother had followed her train of thought, she now said, with her eyes still closed, 'You'll be able to take care of things while I'm laid up, won't you, Connie? You'll manage?'

'Aye—yes, of course,' she said quickly. 'Don't worry.'

'You're a grand little cook and an able housewife. You'll do all right. You learn quicker than a cartload of monkeys, lass.'

Mrs Hudson was talking as though she was going to be in bed for some time. Connie stared at the grey face and concern for the older woman washed over her. She suddenly realised she had grown very fond of Luke's mother over the last six months or so.

The doctor confirmed his patient's suspicions once he had examined her. Leaving her sleeping deeply after the draught of medicine he had insisted she take, he came down to the sitting room just as Connie carried in a tray of coffee, along with a decanter of brandy from Luke's study. He had been as white as a sheet when he'd returned with the doctor, and she felt he needed it. As she went to leave, Luke motioned for her to stay, so she quietly shut the door and stood by it as the doctor took a sip of the coffee she had poured for him and then spoke.

'Heart,' he said flatly. 'But then we've suspected that for some time, haven't we? So has she, although she'd never admit it.'

Luke's mouth had tightened, but otherwise his expression had not changed. He nodded before saying, 'How is she?'

'Comfortable now, and at last accepting she has to be sensible. Bedrest for the foreseeable future—and I mean complete bedrest. I don't want her coming downstairs until I say, Luke. If she does what she is told now her quality of life will not be too severely limited once she is better. If she doesn't…' He shook his head. 'This attack will have damaged her heart. How much only time will tell, but complete rest is of the utmost importance. Can you make sure she behaves herself once she starts to feel better and thinks she can carry on as before?'

'You can count on it,' Luke said grimly. He glanced across at Connie, adding, 'You understand how things are?'

She nodded. 'Yes, sir. And I can see to the house and things.'

'Good, because I will need your help. Perhaps you'd go and check on her now while I talk further with Dr Taggart?'

Connie slipped out of the door and after making sure Mrs Hudson was still fast asleep went downstairs to the kitchen. It was as clean as a new pin. Mrs Hudson wouldn't have it any other way. She walked into the well-stocked pantry, glancing round the shelves and opening the cold meat safe. She would make some soup for Mrs Hudson when she woke up; she'd manage that even if she didn't feel like anything else. Rose had obviously brought the cheese in, although there was no cream as yet. Luke could have some slices of ham from the large joint on the cold slab, and she would fry some of these cold boiled potatoes with a couple of onions and eggs to go with the ham.

She had just got the pan of soup simmering on the range when she heard a movement behind her and turned round to see Luke standing in the doorway to the kitchen. Flustered, she stammered, 'I—I'm doing some soup for your mother. I thought she might be able to eat that. It'll just slip down, so to speak.'

'Thank you.' His face straight and his voice flat, he said, 'Do you think you will be able to manage everything here as well as at the cottage? You'll be doing the work you and my mother did together alone now, as well as seeing to her needs and supervising the women in the dairy, and countless other things.'

He didn't think she was up to the task. Trying to keep all trace of indignation out of her voice, Connie said quietly, 'Of course I'll be able to manage.' Compared to the twelve gruelling hours of back-breaking toil at the pickling factory this was easy. Well, no, not easy, she qualified silently. But doable.

'My mother won't be the easiest of patients, I warn you now. Not once she's feeling a little better. The enforced idleness will drive her mad, and she'll probably take it out on you. Such is her nature she'll find it hard to relinquish her grasp on the household.' The dark eyes were tight on her. 'She's never been able to sit and twiddle her thumbs. She's not made that way.'

'Then I'll have to try and make sure she feels she's still in charge.' Connie's chin had risen a little. He definitely didn't want her here. Who did he want? Alice Todd, maybe? With her voluptuous figure and come-hither eyes?

'You think you can do that? Convince her she's still at the helm?'

For a moment the doubt in his voice compressed her lips. Then the hurt and anger she was feeling caused her to speak rashly, and in a way she would never have dreamt of doing normally. 'I think it's about time you gave me the credit for being stronger than I look,' she said tightly, 'and brighter too. I'm not about to make your mother feel redundant, whatever you may think.'

He blinked. This was a side to her he hadn't seen before, he thought, studying the flushed face and sparking blue eyes with fascinated surprise. He had suspected that glorious hair might indicate a temper, but until now she had always been very circumspect. There were definitely hidden depths to Connie Summers.

He could tell by her face that she had suddenly become aware she had spoken out of turn. In spite of the circumstances he found himself wanting to smile when she added a small, 'Sir.'

Keeping his face straight, Luke nodded. 'Good.' Folding his arms, he leant against the door. 'You'll be giving orders to the other women in my mother's place—even a few of the men from time to time. You will do this with authority from the beginning and inevitably it will set you apart from the rest of them. Will this trouble you?'

She stared at him for a long moment before saying, and very seriously now, 'I don't think I was exactly a part of them anyway. Most of your employees were born here or have been with you for a long, long time. They've always been farm folk. I'm from the town, after all. That makes me an outsider to some extent.'

'No one has been unkind to you?' He'd have their guts for garters if so, he thought grimly. He was having none of that.

'No, no, everyone has been lovely.' Not counting Alice Todd.

Her eyes flickered as she spoke, and now he pressed. 'Are you sure, Connie? I would prefer to know if that's the case.'

'Everyone has been kind,' she said more firmly, 'but nevertheless I'm aware I'm different. I've had a lot to learn and still have, especially about everything outside, but I know I can handle the house and all that Mrs Hudson might expect from me.'

She was different, all right. As different as a rose in a patch of nettles. Such thoughts had ceased bothering him. They were so frequent these days. Since the New Year, when she had first shyly presented herself on the doorstep, he hadn't known a moment's peace. As day had followed day he had become more surprised at himself, but try as he might he couldn't put her out of his mind for more than two minutes. It was irritating and annoying and damn inconvenient, but there was something about her. He couldn't put a name to it, but it was there. And she was right about one thing. She might look as though a breath of wind would blow her away, with her tiny waist and slender frame, but she worked hard enough for two women. She had won his mother round in a couple of months, and that wasn't easy by any means.

Gritting his teeth against the feeling he kept under control at all times, he said quietly, 'I know my mother would prefer you to become our housekeeper rather than a stranger from outside. And that's what this will mean. She will be able to do very little in the way of physical work from now on. This present situation has been coming on slowly from the time my father died, but she wouldn't admit to it—as the doctor mentioned earlier.'

Connie nodded, but said nothing. This was the first time he had spoken so freely. Normally he was so stiff and correct.

'And...and the death of her grandchild hit her hard.'

'Yes, it must have done.' Unconsciously she gentled her voice. There was pain in his eyes—pain, and something else she couldn't fathom but which she put down to the agony of losing his wife along with his son. He must have loved them so much, and for them both to go within days of each other...it was cruel.

'Of course she wouldn't listen to either the doctor or myself. Stubborn to the last.' He forced a smile, but it was a mere twist to the firm, often stern mouth. 'Now she has to listen.'

She dragged her eyes from his lips and said softly, 'I think your mother is a very brave lady. She gets on with what has to be done, that's all.' He stared at her for so long after this that she became uneasy by his continued silence. Had she been too familiar about his mother? Was he angry at the way she had spoken to him earlier? 'I...I better see to the soup, if there's nothing else, sir?' she said at last.

'What? Oh, yes, yes.' She watched him rouse himself, and then he surprised both of them when he said abruptly, 'My wife and mother never hit it off. Not from the first day I brought Christabel to live here. My mother did her best, but...'

Connie stared at him. She tried to think of something to say and failed utterly.

'I hope that wasn't another thing that has brought her to her present state.' The grey eyes were asking for comfort. She gave it.

'I'm sure it wasn't. I think your mother is very strong in spirit in spite of her body. Perhaps this...this attack is just a way of her body telling her she has to take it easier. It happens to everyone eventually,' Connie said gently.

He nodded, turning and leaving the kitchen as abruptly as he had spoken, and closing the door quietly behind him.

Connie found her hand was trembling as she stirred the soup. He had spoken to her, *really* spoken to her, for the first time since she had been working in the farmhouse. Of course he must be terribly upset about his mother, she being all the family he had, but it had been *her* he had shared his concern with. Her heart was thumping so hard it threatened to jump out of her chest, and she could feel her cheeks were burning.

Of course it didn't mean anything, she warned herself in the next moment. He had made it very clear in the last months that she was just another employee, and that was fine—of course it was. She expected nothing more. But still, if she was going to be the housekeeper now it would make her job easier if he just smiled occasionally and was less hostile. No, not hostile. He had never been hostile, more… Standoffish? Unapproachable? What?

She shook her head at herself. She didn't know what he'd been, but it was very different from the last five minutes. And then, horrified with herself that she could feel such a sense of gladness when his poor mother was lying upstairs so poorly, she resolutely put the whole incident to the back of her mind and concentrated on preparing lunch. She was going to have more than enough to do over the next weeks and months, from the look of it, and she needed to focus on keeping things running as smoothly as she could. Ifs, whys and maybes could wait.

CHAPTER FIVE

'OH, THIS is grand. To be out here after all those weeks lying in bed. It's driven me half mad, being confined to that one room, nice as it is. But then you know that, don't you, lass?'

Connie smiled at Luke's mother. Yes, she knew that. When Mrs Hudson had had another attack ten days after the first, whilst trying to come downstairs—ostensibly for a glass of water—in the middle of the night, the doctor had told her quite bluntly she had put her recovery back weeks. And so it had proved. But now it was the middle of a hot August, and a few minutes previously Luke had carried her downstairs and into the front garden, where she and Connie were now sitting in the fresh warm air.

'And my son tells me it was your idea to have this bench made?' Maggie said softly, her eyes on the heart-shaped face in front of her. 'And you sewed the flock cushions for it yourself?'

Connie nodded. 'I thought it would be nice for you to sit out here when the weather's clement. When you have time, that is,' she added hastily. She had been careful to keep up the pretence that Mrs Hudson would be back to normal eventually.

Maggie sighed, leaning back against the sun-warmed wood, her eyes on a lark in the fields beyond that had suddenly risen from the rich green grass into the blue of the sky, singing as it went. 'I think we both know I'm not going to be able to do what I once did, but I shan't mind so much if I can get downstairs of a morning. I shall feel more like myself then. Less of an invalid.'

Connie put her hand on the older woman's. It spoke of how close they had become that she felt quite at liberty to do so. 'You've made marvellous progress,' she said warmly. 'Marvellous. And in a couple of weeks the doctor said he sees no reason why you shouldn't come downstairs every day. But you have to take it slowly. He said today will tire you, and you must expect to rest in bed tomorrow. But see how you feel in the morning. All right?'

Maggie glanced round the garden. 'It all looks bonny. How have you found the time to tend my flowers with all you have had to do?' Her tone was not that of an employer to an employee but as friend to friend, and both women felt this was the case.

Connie smiled. 'This was pure pleasure.' She let her eyes feast on the bursting flowerbeds, where fragrant sweet peas and pinks, pansies and mignonette, larkspur and catnip all vied for supremacy. Honeysuckle and morning glory hung their perfumed bells and horns over the two trellises either side of the farmhouse, and Canterbury bells, their porcelain delicateness fragile against the metallic blue of a host of delphiniums, stirred softly in the warm breeze. 'I've never been able to look after a garden before, but I can see why you love it so.'

'It feeds the soul, doesn't it?' Maggie said quietly.

Connie nodded. That was it, exactly. Out here she could forget about the man who never could, never would be hers. A sated velvet bee tottered drunkenly out of the flowerbeds, humming lazily as it buzzed off into the blue beyond. She watched it until it was out of sight, envying the little bee's uncomplicated position in life. And then she shook herself mentally, telling herself to stop her griping. This time last year she had been working in the stinking pickling factory and worrying where their next meal was coming from. She was lucky. They were all so, so lucky, and she mustn't forget it.

Connie placed the book Luke's mother had brought out with her in the older woman's lap as she said, 'I have to go and make sure Rose and Bess are all right in the dairy, and I've some bread proving on the fender. Once it's in the oven I'll bring you a cup of tea, Mrs Hudson. If you need me, ring your handbell.'

'Don't worry about me, Connie. I'm fine now I'm out here. You get on with what you have to do and forget about me, lass.'

Once back in the farmhouse, Connie walked through the sitting room and into the hall beyond, past Luke's study, where he was checking the farm accounts, and into the passageway leading to the kitchen. She knew he would go and sit with his mother shortly. She also knew he would not have done so if she had remained in the garden. Her soft mouth tightened and her shoulders straightened.

For the first little while after his mother had taken ill
she had hoped he would be more forthcoming with her,
and that had happened for three of four weeks. Then it had
seemed the more his mother had recovered the less
friendly he had become again. And she didn't think she
was imagining it. And as he had withdrawn so she had
found rising up in herself a strong sense of hurt—and
something else. Pride. She'd told herself she would do her
job and do it well, she'd be the best housekeeper in the
world, but she wouldn't lower herself to grovel for a kind
word or smile from him. And she hadn't. It appeared she
was very much her father's daughter, she thought grimly,
walking through the kitchen and into the large scullery
beyond, where a narrow door opened into the dairy.

After checking Rose and Bess were aware of what
was required from them for the day, Connie returned to
the kitchen and popped the loaf tins in the bread oven.
Knowing Luke's mother's liking for drop scones, fresh
from the griddle and dripping with butter, she decided
to make a batch to take out with the cup of tea. She'd
just prepared the thick batter, and was about to put the
first spoonful on the greased griddle, when Luke came
into the kitchen.

She started slightly before controlling herself and
saying, politely but coolly, in the flat tone she adopted
with him these days, 'I'm making some drop scones to
go with the cup of tea I'll be bringing out to your mother
shortly.' She did not say the mistress. She would not give
Mrs Hudson that title any more than she would call
Luke master. 'Shall I bring a cup for you out there too,
sir? Or would you prefer a tray in your study?'

Luke stared at her. She was wearing a blue linen dress that she had made with some material his mother had put by before she had become sick. His mother liked giving Connie and her family things, and she treated them differently from anyone else on the farm. It had been she who had suggested Flora and the lads join Connie in the farmhouse kitchen for their dinner each night, rather than Connie having to nip backwards and forwards to the cottage preparing and cooking the meal. She wouldn't have dreamt of allowing such familiarity with any other of their workers, though some of them had been with them from birth, and their parents before them. Part of him was glad his mother saw Connie as being different and got on so well with her. The other part of him was terrified by it. The larger part.

He blinked, aware she was waiting for a reply, and said quickly, 'I'll have a cup with my mother, thank you, Connie. I wanted to ask you how you think she's coped with coming downstairs from when you sat with her.' It was a lie. What he'd done was to give in to the overwhelming impulse that came on him at times just to look at her and have her look at him with her full attention. The knowledge of his weakness and the power, albeit unknown to her, that it gave her over him made his voice curter when he added, 'Did she appear breathless, for instance? Or in any way distressed?'

'No, she didn't appear breathless. Just very happy to be in her garden. I think she is becoming resigned to the fact that she won't be able to do what she once did, even when she's fully better.' Connie's voice became more animated as she went on, 'I think it would lift her spirits if she could be out in the garden more when the weather's fine enough. Perhaps Jacob could make a table and another bench to go with the first? That way she could entertain visitors out there, and even perhaps have her meals in the sunshine if she so wishes.'

Her concern for his mother's well-being probed a fresh depth of pain in him. She wasn't like Christabel, he knew that, so why the hell did he become more panicky the more she became entwined in their lives? He knew his treatment of her wasn't right, but he didn't seem able to help himself pushing her away. The tension in his body held him stiff as he said, 'I'll have a word with Jacob this morning.'

Connie nodded. He looked big and dark and broodingly handsome as he stood watching her. She wondered what was going on in his mind. He was a deeply unhappy man, that was obvious, but then who wouldn't be if they lost the woman they loved and adored and their baby son in one fell swoop? Her thoughts softened her voice and—unbeknown to her—brought a tender light to her eyes as she said, 'I think your mother is going to be fine, sir, and I'll make sure she doesn't do too much when she's up and about properly again.'

Sir. Mr Hudson or sir had become increasingly irritating and painful of late. He wanted to hear her say his name. He didn't want a reminder of the chasm that was between them when she spoke. And yet, no, he had to be honest with himself here. It was a chasm of his own making. Oh, there might be a few eyebrows raised if he defied convention and introduced her into so-called polite society. Whispers, gossip, tittering behind closed doors. The world in general would think he was a fool, most likely, in associating with a woman they considered to be below their class, but he had never worried about what people thought. It would only touch him if it touched and hurt her. He knew this. But here on the farm she would be protected from the worst of it. The farm was a world in itself, after all.

'Connie—' He stopped abruptly. He couldn't take that one step which would bring this thing that was between them into the light. And she felt something for him beyond gratitude. He felt it in his very bones, his whole being. But once he began down that path the inevitable conclusion would be making her his own—and not in a hole-and-corner affair either. It would be marriage or nothing for her. Her parents had brought her up well. And so it was impossible. He could not—he would not—lay himself open to being manipulated and used again. The first time he had been swept away in the throes of boyish adulation and infatuation. That was his only excuse for the disaster which had been his marriage, a disaster which ultimately had taken the life of the one innocent being in all of it.

As the silence stretched and lengthened between them, Connie said tentatively, 'What is it, sir?'

'Nothing.' He shook his head. 'I'll go and have a word with Jacob now while you cook the scones.' She wasn't like Christabel—but then Christabel had been sweet-tempered and amiable before they had become man and wife. Women could do that—become whatever a man desired them to be until they had got what they wanted. If he had been taken in so completely once there was no reason it couldn't happen again, and he would rather slit his own throat than risk that hell on earth again.

He turned away, his mental anguish concealed behind an expressionless mask, and walked out of the kitchen.

When he joined his mother in the garden she smiled at him, patting the space beside her on the bench as she said, 'Come and sit in the sunshine awhile. This bench is so comfortable I could stay here all day. And I feel so well, Luke. Really.'

'You're certainly looking much better.' Luke sat down, stretching out his long legs. 'And the fresh air will do you good."

'I feel much better, but then with Connie caring for me so well how could it be otherwise? It was a good day's work when you brought her here, Luke. But then you know that. And those brothers and sister of hers are good little folk too. Hard workers, the lot of them. They're a nice family altogether, don't you think?'

He nodded, but said nothing. His mother often came out with things like this. He knew she didn't understand his attitude to Connie. More than once she had complained she thought he was a trifle chilly with her. He never defended himself at these times. How could he? His mother was justified in her gentle accusations.

He allowed a few moments to go by, and then began to talk of farm matters, knowing it pleased her when he involved her. They were still chatting quietly when Connie arrived with the tea and scones, which she served quickly before going indoors again.

The scones were delicious. Everything Connie

cooked was delicious. He couldn't fault her. And therein lay the problem. No one was that perfect. He just didn't believe it.

He glanced at his mother, and as she caught the look she said, 'What? What is it? What's the matter, Luke?'

He didn't say what was in his heart because he knew that if he did she'd defend Connie to the hilt. His mother was like that—where she loved, she loved, and where she hated, she hated. She had hated Christabel after Jack had been born and his wife had rejected their son so completely, and she'd made no secret of the fact. It hadn't made life any easier, but he'd understood it.

He shrugged, his voice slightly teasing as he said lazily, 'Can't I look at my own mother? Even a cat can look at a Queen, you know. And you're a bonny sight, when all's said and done.'

'Oh, you.' His mother nudged him with her elbow before reaching for another scone, smiling at him as she did so.

Luke returned the smile, but he felt no amusement inside. Not that that was unusual. Laughter, gladness, joy had all been wiped out two years ago, and the intervening months had not changed this. He could now take some form of pleasure in ordinary mundane things—a tasty well-cooked meal, a fine wine, the feel of a nicely cut coat—but these were things that touched his body and senses, not his emotions. And he wanted it to remain that way. It *would* remain that way.

He wiped his fingers on the napkin Connie had provided and stood up, looking over his fields where the blackbirds and thrushes and meadowlarks sang their refrains.

No good would come out of letting himself feel again. The paroxysm of grief that had taken him after Jack's death had both shocked and horrified him with its intensity. He had lost control, he'd been powerless against the feelings that had reduced him to crying like a child. He had felt so ashamed in the following weeks and months, humiliated and mortified. Grown men did not cry, whatever the reason, and yet for some time in the quiet of the night he had not been able to stop. And he'd despised himself.

'I'm going into town later.' He glanced down at his mother and she nodded. 'Is there anything you particularly want me to buy after I've finished at the bank? A magazine? Some chocolate?'

'No, I don't think so.' Her gaze had drifted to the flowers and her voice was uninterested, almost vacant, when she added, 'But check with Connie. She'll know.'

Luke's mouth thinned. He wanted to say, I don't want to ask Connie. I'm asking *you*. And don't forget that Connie is our housekeeper, nothing more. If she wanted to up and leave tomorrow she would be at liberty to do so. There is nothing tying her to us. But then he glanced down at his mother's feet. Her ankles over-flowed her soft slippers. The swelling which had come with the first attack seemed to get worse month by month. In spite of the fact her appetite had picked up and her breathing was easier, she was far from well.

Impulsively he bent and kissed the top of her head before walking away—not to the house but to the stables. There he saddled Ebony himself, reflecting that had it been in his power he would have galloped over the sun-drenched fields spreading away from the farm for ever. But he had responsibilities, obligations—not merely to his mother but to the families who worked for him, who had been part of the farm for generations. They all looked to him for their livelihood and he could not do as he pleased.

He directed Ebony to a corner of the farm where he knew Jacob was working, giving him the order regarding the table and bench before making for the fields, where he let the horse have its head and gallop in the sunshine. It felt good to have the wind rushing through his hair and to feel part of all he surveyed, but of late it had not provided the satisfaction it once had. He was becoming more at odds with himself all the time, and he didn't like that. He didn't like it at all. It had to stop.

He inclined his head to the thought before smiling sourly. How the hell that was going to be accomplished was quite another thing.

CHAPTER SIX

CONNIE walked out of the farmhouse with Flora at her side, straw bonnets on their heads and their arms weighed down with the food and drink in the huge baskets they were carrying. It was haymaking time, and everyone on the farm from the youngest to the oldest was lending a hand with the harvest. She had been baking all morning to provide the workers with their lunch of slabs of fruit loaves and wedges of cheese, all washed down with beer or cold tea, and milk for the children.

The fields were lit with a golden haze as they approached, and everyone was hard at work, the warm air carrying an intoxicating fragrance as the men's scythes and the women's sickles did their job. Little hedgerow birds flitted hither and thither over the workers' heads, anxious to whittle out their tiny share of whatever was going, and the harvest mice scurried away to hide till night-time.

The summer had been a hot one, and the harvest was good, but the old timers had sensed a storm brewing in the last twenty-four hours or so, and Connie knew Luke was anxious to get the harvest safely gathered in. Her eyes had searched for him as she and Flora had neared the others, and she saw him at the far end of one of the fields almost immediately, his tall frame and jet-black hair standing out against the other men. As she neared him she felt her heart miss a beat or two. He was dressed more casually than usual, even when working out in the fields, his corduroy trousers tucked in calf-length leather boots and his white shirt open at the neck with the sleeves rolled up. At some point he must have discarded his waistcoat and hat.

Her mouth had gone dry by the time she reached Luke and Jacob, who were using a horse-drawn machine to gather together the crop in readiness for stacking it in sheaves. His open-necked shirt showed the springy black hair of his chest, which was just as soft and luxuriant on his forearms, powerful muscles rippling under the thin cotton as he controlled the massive shire horses.

He looked hard and tough and uncompromisingly virile—utterly at ease with his own body, Connie thought shakily. She, on the other hand, hardly knew where to look—which was stupid, so stupid. He was fully clothed and quite decent. It wasn't as though she had walked in on him in a state of undress or something. Just the thought brought a rush of burning colour into her cheeks which she hoped everyone would put down to the heatwave they were enjoying. She pulled her bonnet more firmly on her head.

Flora having taken her basket to the workers in the neighbouring field, Connie proceeded to unpack her own supply of food and drink, which brought everyone to her—Alice Todd included.

She might have known the buxom blonde would have engineered things so she was working close to Luke, and she didn't feel it was an accident that Alice's blouse had a couple of buttons missing at the neck, so the soft swell of her breasts was visible. Connie masked her thoughts with a smile as she handed everyone their lunch, glancing at Luke and Jacob, who had just finished walking the horses. Jacob joined Rose, who was sitting some distance away, and Connie walked over to Luke, who had flung himself down on the ground near the horses, her heart racing.

'This is welcome.' He smiled up at her, the grey eyes glittering in the bright sunlight. 'My tongue has been sticking to the roof of my mouth the last hour.' He took the food and flagon of beer she proffered, but when she would have turned away said, 'Sit a while and wait for everyone to finish. It will save you making another journey shortly.'

Connie stared at him, taken aback. Since the beginning of the harvest two days before she had returned for the empty tin jugs and flagons after an hour or so, when work had resumed in the fields. Feeling a mite self-conscious, she did as he bid, folding her dress round her knees so only the tips of her boots were visible. He drank with gusto, and had eaten half of the fruit loaf she'd give him before he settled back on his elbow, his gaze holding hers, as he said, 'This is one of those rare blue and golden days which sometimes come at this time of the year. Do you know what I mean?'

She nodded, blushing slightly as she said, 'My da used to call a day like this an Eden day.' He raised his dark eyebrows enquiringly and she went on. 'Working under the ground as he did, Sundays were the only days he really saw the sun for any length of time, but he loved the outdoors. He always imagined the Garden of Eden must have been like a summer's day when the trees are greenest, the sky bluest and the clouds most snowy white.'

'I know exactly what he meant.' Luke paused. 'He must have found it hard to be shut away from the light all day, feeling like he did. Did he ever talk about doing something else?'

Connie shook her head. 'My grandfather and great-grandfather were miners; it was expected he would go down the pit. I'm just glad Tommy, David and Ronnie don't have to follow him down now, because they would have. There were two other lads born after me and before Flora, but they died in infancy, otherwise they'd have been down the mine too. But my da never let it get him down. He used to say—' She stopped, embarrassed, suddenly aware the two of them were sitting talking quietly away from the others as though they had con-versations like this all the time. Which they didn't.

'What did your father say?' He had sat up, his knees bent as he leant forward, his rugged, handsome face curious.

'Just that he felt he saw more on the one day God allowed him above ground than others saw who were above ground every day of the week. Just as there's no rest without toil, no peace without war, no day without night, no true joy in life without grief, so there can be no real appreciation without need and desire. That's…that's what he used to say,' she finished awkwardly, becoming aware he was looking at her in an odd fashion.

He sat quite still, staring at her for a full ten seconds. Something—she wasn't sure what—had thickened his voice when he said, 'And what if the toil or the darkness of the night or…the grief blinds you to what follows it? What then?'

She looked back at him, and her eyes were very blue and steady beneath her straw bonnet. 'I don't know,' she said quietly. 'Except everyone has an element of choice, don't they?'

'You think so?' His voice was harsher. 'You really believe it?'

Sensing his displeasure, she put her chin up a notch. 'Aye, I do. The way I see it, life is a constant stream of choices till we die.'

'Like you had a choice when you had to work in that factory?'

He was deliberately misunderstanding her. Taking her courage in both hands, Connie said, even more quietly, 'It wasn't the workhouse, though, was it? And I thank God for it.'

'Coming from the situation you found yourself in, I find it difficult to fathom how you can believe every cloud has a silver lining.' His tone was contemptuous, even mocking.

'I didn't say that.' As once before she forgot he was her employer, and master of the farm, her voice low but angry when she said, 'And having seen inside the workhouse I never would—because if ever there is a place without hope or joy, it's there. But I tell you one thing.' She fixed her eyes on him and they were dark with the force of her feelings. 'If you never have to fear that place then there is something to be thankful for every day, and I don't care who you are.'

For a long moment their eyes held, and Connie felt the temperature drop by ten degrees. Unable to stand it a second longer, she rose hastily to her feet and without a word left him, her hands trembling as she carried the empty basket home. Fancy her daring to say all that to him. She must have been mad. What if he took umbrage and threw her and the others out of the cottage? But, no—no, he wouldn't do that. But the way she had spoken to him... She groaned inwardly. How was she going to face him again? He'd be furious with her. She should have apologised before she left. She doubted even his mother would have spoken to him in the tone of voice she had used. In fact she was sure she wouldn't.

Once in the farmhouse, she leant against the scullery sink, her mind going over their conversation again and again until, after some minutes, she straightened. He had obviously taken what she'd said personally, which was why he had got so mad, but she hadn't actually been preaching at *him,* if that was what he thought. And— her mouth firmed—she had only said the truth after all. It must have been terrible, awful, for him to lose his wife and baby like he had, and she wasn't belittling his loss, but if he couldn't see he was better off than those poor souls in the workhouse... And then she groaned again, holding herself round the middle as she swayed back and forth. How could you measure the sort of grief he must have felt—what he was *still* feeling—against anything else? You couldn't. That was the thing.

By the time Flora returned to the farmhouse some twenty minutes later, Connie was a little calmer. She couldn't take the words back she reasoned, as she carried a tray of tea through to Luke's mother, who was sitting in her favourite spot in the front garden. And she had plenty to do today without worrying about how she was going to face him and what she was going to say.

When the harvest was over it was tradition for Luke to give a supper for everyone on the farm, and this was happening tomorrow. One of the barns had been swept out, the cobwebs brushed down from the rafters, and two rows of trestle tables set down the middle of the building. She had already cooked three huge joints of roast beef, pork and lamb, but she and Flora had all the baking to see to, which would take the rest of the day and the next morning. The beer was standing by, along with plenty of homemade blackberry wine, but there was lemonade to make for the children. She needed to concentrate on the job in hand.

Luke's mother had long since retired to bed and Flora had been despatched home with a cold supper for herself and the lads to eat in the cottage by the time Connie heard him enter the house by the front door. The deep twilight made the fragrant evening a mass of mauve and charcoal shadows, and there was an unusual hush on the farm which the end of a harvest day always brought. Connie had the kitchen windows wide open, to dispel the heat from the range a little, but a good proportion of the baking for the next day had been done, and for this she was thankful.

She had a steak and ham meat roll steaming on the range for Luke's evening meal, and she had set out the decanter of fine brandy by his favourite chair in the sitting room. The bowl in his dressing room off the master bedroom was already full with warm water for his ablutions before he changed his clothes. Instead of going straight upstairs to wash, however, as was his normal custom when coming in from the fields, she heard his footsteps in the hall. Her stomach churning, she turned and faced the door.

'Hello, Connie.' His voice was quiet and even as he surveyed her from the doorway. She had not yet lit the oil lamps about the house and his face was in shadow. She could not determine his expression in the darkness.

'Sir, about what I said earlier,' she said quickly. 'I'm sorry if I spoke out of turn. I was just saying what I believe—'

She fell silent as he raised his hand, his voice still flat when he said, 'It's a beautiful evening and I think I'd prefer to eat outside at my mother's table—if that's not too much trouble. Where are your brothers? They left the fields with the other children a short time ago. Are they not hungry?'

'Flora and the lads are having a cold supper at the cottage tonight, sir. I knew they would be tired, and it means they can go straight to bed,' Connie said quietly, wondering if she should broach the matter of their earlier conversation again. He was obviously still annoyed with her, although he wasn't showing it.

He nodded. 'And you?' he asked softly. 'Are you tired?'

'Me?' She stared at him in surprise. 'I'm all right.'

'You work all day every day and not a word of complaint.' As she still continued to stare, not knowing what to say, he added abruptly, 'Have you eaten your evening meal yet?'

She blinked. 'Not yet. There were things to do…' She waved her hand vaguely towards the range, where his meat roll simmered. She didn't know what to make of him tonight.

'Then would you care to join me outside? It seems foolish for you to eat in here while I eat alone.'

Suddenly becoming aware her mouth had fallen open, Connie shut it with a little snap. On the occasions when his mother was too tired to stay up for the evening meal and retired to her room, he mostly ate on a tray before the sitting room fire, but otherwise in the dining room. From one or two things his mother had said in the past Connie had gathered the pair of them had eaten informally in the kitchen before she had taken over as housekeeper, but since she had begun work this had not happened. She understood this. The proprieties must be observed, and she was merely an employee like any other. What she didn't understand was why he should suggest this change now—especially after her words earlier that day.

If she did as he suggested and someone saw them, what would they think? That she was more than his housekeeper? That she was what Alice Todd had been angling to be for some time? Yes, they'd probably assume the worst. Folk were like that. And her reputation mattered to her. It would be sensible to make some excuse now—that she had work to do before she ate, or must return to the cottage for the night. That was what her father would have expected of her in these circumstances.

She looked at him where he was leaning against the open door, the white of his shirt standing out in the dim half-light. 'Thank you,' she said quietly. 'It would be nice to eat in the fresh air after being in the kitchen all day.'

He nodded. 'I'll go and change. Shall we say five minutes?'

Once he had disappeared, Connie stood staring at the place where he had stood. Whatever had possessed her? This was madness, she told herself silently as her heart hammered against her ribs. It would have been the easiest thing in the world to make some excuse, so why hadn't she?

Because she wanted this one brief interlude with him. The answer was there. It had been there ever since the first time she had laid eyes on him. Something like this would never happen again, and she didn't fool herself that his invitation meant anything to him beyond male logic. If she'd had Flora and the lads with her as usual, or his mother had been up, the evening would have been as normal. But it wasn't. It wasn't normal. And the thought of being able to sit with him, just the two of them, to be able to share a meal and be in his presence was too heady to refuse. She might regret it—she almost certainly *would* regret it if anyone caught sight of them—but she would regret it much more if she didn't take the once chance fate had presented her with to have an hour of companionship with the man she loved.

The last thought brought forth an involuntary gasp of denial even as she acknowledged it was the truth. She loved him. She loved Luke Hudson, who was as far away from her as the man in the moon. That was why every little single thing he did or said affected her so deeply—why his brooding silences and the odd smile had her emotions see-sawing like one of the swing boats at the Michaelmas Fair.

She sank down on one of the hardbacked chairs, her cheeks flaming. He must never know. She must never let him guess. She couldn't bear it if he thought she was like Alice Todd. He had been so good to them all. He'd saved them—there was no other word for it—and she'd die if he thought she was trying to take advantage of her position in the house and her closeness to his mother.

She stood up, beginning to pace the kitchen before she brought herself up short. Shutting her eyes tightly, she told herself to calm down. He didn't know. Everything was just the same as it had been ten minutes ago. He looked on her as his housekeeper, that was all. Loving his wife as he had, as he still did, it would never occur to him in a thousand years to look at her in *that* way, or that she would care for him romantically. And that was the way it had to remain. She had to appear natural tonight. In spite of being the owner of this big farm and having lots of friends and acquaintances, he was a lonely man. She knew that. She had sensed it all along. And if he could just unbend enough to talk to her sometimes, if she could be some kind of comfort to him, that would be enough for her.

It would have to be. The thought brought a grim smile

to her lips. Because there was no way on earth she was ever going to be anything else to him and she knew that.

By the time Luke came downstairs, Connie had set the small wooden table Jacob had made with two places and had taken the meat roll off the hob. Slicing a generous portion for Luke and a smaller one for herself, she then added the roasted vegetables which had been gently cooking in the oven for some time.

She gazed at her plate with some disquiet. How she was going to be able to eat she didn't know. Her stomach was tied up in knots and her heart seemed determined to jump out of her throat.

'Can I carry anything through?'

As he spoke from the doorway, Connie jumped violently, spinning round and then saying quickly, 'No, no, it's fine. I'll be out shortly. I'm just finishing off in here.'

He nodded. He was dressed in fresh clothes, but probably because of the humidity was not wearing a jacket over his full-sleeved shirt and waistcoat. She had lit the oil lamp while he had been upstairs, and in its flickering light his thick dark hair and the shadow of stubble on his chin showed black against the whiteness of his shirt. Warm, curling quivers flickered in the core of her, heating her blood, but as she turned back to the food she heard him leave the kitchen, and for a moment her legs felt trembly. Oh, she was daft, she was. Plain daft.

She stared at the plates as she took several deep breaths to steady her nerves, then smoothed her dress and tidied a wisp of hair behind her ear before she reached for them. She was going to eat a meal with him, that was all. An hour, maybe less, to last a lifetime....

The twilight had all but gone as she joined Luke outside. A late blackbird was singing a piercingly clear lone song, the succession of low flute-like notes all the sweeter for the rest of the birds having gone to sleep. The night was warm and the moon had risen above the farm, the barns and outbuildings clearly outlined like ink silhouettes against a slaty-blue star-speckled sky. Not a breath of wind stirred the still air, and Connie almost felt she should whisper as she said quietly, 'It's a beautiful evening after such a hot day.'

'Beautiful.' He took the plate she proffered, gesturing to the flagon of wine he must have brought out with him as he said, 'Can I pour you a glass? It will go well with the meal.'

She was going to say she would have a glass of water from the jug she had brought out with the cutlery earlier, but, as this was a magical step out of reality, instead she said, 'Thank you, sir. That would be nice.'

They ate in silence for some minutes, and she was glad the moonlight kept her face in shadow. The blackberry wine was rich and dark; she felt it create a warmth inside as she swallowed, and it left a pleasant sweetness on the tongue. She had never tasted strong drink before. All she'd had previously was a glass or two of ginger wine when she and her parents had attended a neighbour's wake four years ago. That had been weak, watered-down stuff, though, and nothing like this. This was delicious.

'You are an excellent cook. This is as good as anything my mother used to make.' He refilled his glass as he spoke, his voice smoky soft. 'Better, in fact, but don't tell her that.'

'I'm grateful to her for teaching me so well.' She didn't add that before she had come to the farm her cooking expertise had been driven by the need to make a penny stretch to a shilling. Broths and stews had been the order of the day, likely as not made with scrag-ends and spotted vegetables sold off cheap at the end of business. Even before her parents had died it had often been impossible for any of them to have a hearty meal. She didn't like to dwell on this, however, or want to give the impression she was giving a hard luck story whenever she spoke about her past life. There had been an excess of love within her family if nothing else, and for that she would always be thankful. No amount of money could buy that.

'She could teach you because you were so willing to learn.'

'How could anyone not be with your mother's big kitchen and all the food provided?' She still found it hard to believe that they could eat at every meal until they were full.

'You'd be surprised.'

There was a different note in his voice now, a jarring note, and her eyes opened wide for a moment. She could see little of his expression as he sat across the table from her, however, just his eyes glittering now and then when the moonlight allowed it. 'I love cooking,' she said after a moment or two, when the silence had stretched and become uncomfortable, at least to her. 'Although perhaps not always for the amount I've been preparing food for today. It's almost all ready by the way, sir. The harvest thanksgiving meal.'

'Connie—' He stopped abruptly. Then, before she could speak, he continued, 'When we are alone like this, when it is just the two of us, I would prefer you do not stand on formality. My name is Luke. I would like to hear you say it now and then.'

The world stopped spinning. For a moment the night was shining, like a star. Then reality crowded in. He was being kind. He was always kind beneath the gruff exterior he portrayed sometimes. But, however kind he was, it wouldn't be right. Quietly now, her head slightly bent, she said, 'Thank you, but I'd be too worried I might forget myself when we're not alone if I did that, sir, and speak out of turn.'

'Would that matter?'

He had bent forward, close enough for her to see his face in a ray of moonlight and it was unsmiling. She hesitated for a second before murmuring, 'I think so. Folk…folk might misconstrue your kindness to me.'

'I don't see why.' His voice was deep in his throat. 'You said yourself you are different to the rest of them, and so is your position here. My—my mother thinks very highly of you.'

She didn't know how to answer. She only knew she couldn't do what he asked—not loving him as she did. Simply saying his name shouldn't make a difference, but it would. To her. It would make how she felt unbearable somehow. She couldn't explain her feelings even to herself, but she knew it to be true.

The moments ticked by as he waited for her to speak, but for the life of her she couldn't. After what must have been a full minute, he moved irritably into the shadows again, his voice curt as he said, 'No matter. Forget I spoke of it. I had no wish to embarrass you. If you wish things to continue as they are, so be it.'

The night was spoilt, the magic was gone, and as the tears pricked at the backs of her eyes she was grateful for the darkness. Somehow she managed to pick at enough of the food to make a pretence of eating it, and as soon as his plate was empty she stood to her feet, saying, 'I'll bring out your pudding, sir. But I'd better get back home to Flora and the lads, if that's all right. They can play her up sometimes if I'm not there.'

'Of course. I should not have kept you.'

She reached for his plate as he went to hand it to her, and in the brief confusion their hands touched. A tingle as sharp and sudden as icy water caused her to draw back. But it wasn't cold she was feeling, but a singing through her veins like warm honey. Stammering an apology, she retrieved both plates and fled to the sanctuary of the kitchen as though the devil himself was hot on her heels.

And really, she reflected shakily, fetching the apple dumplings out of the oven and covering a large portion with thick cream, she *felt* as though the devil had been on her heels this evening. Why else would she be wondering how she could stay in paradise feeling like this?

CHAPTER SEVEN

CONTRARY to what Connie had expected when she woke up on the morning of the harvest supper, after just a few hours of troubled sleep, that day and the ones following it went quite smoothly on the whole. The intense awkwardness she felt around Luke began to fade after a little while, although she continued to be careful they were never alone if she could help it.

It helped that he had reverted to being his usual cool and withdrawn self. At least most of the time it helped. In the daylight hours, when she was thinking matter-of-factly. But when she was in bed at night, Flora snoring gently beside her and the rest of the world fast asleep, she found herself wishing he had shown some reaction after their eventful meal together. Disappointment, even annoyance, *anything* to show he cared just a little. But that was the thing. He didn't. And he probably didn't consider the evening had been eventful at all.

When these thoughts came she berated herself for her continuing inconsistency and muddled thinking. If he had shown some sign of disappointment or irritation and repeated his request, where would that have led her? Into a worse mess in her head, most likely. At least this way it was easy to continue in her role of housekeeper and nurse to his mother, which provided a roof over their heads. She couldn't ask for more. And Luke was a fair and generous employer. She knew from the other workers on the farm that some farmers paid their employees monthly, thereby cheating them out of a month's wages in the course of the year, but Luke paid his people every week—and handsomely too. Even the children who had specific jobs to do once they were home from school and at weekends received payment—ranging from sixpence to a florin in some cases—and her present eight shillings a week meant she had been able to buy Flora and the lads new boots and coats for the winter already. They lived rent-free, and logs were provided for fuel—oh, yes, she couldn't ask for more.

She did, though. In the dark of the night. And then every morning she would recant her feverish prayers of the night before and resolutely count her blessings. Till the next time.

At the end of September she and Flora and her brothers accompanied the rest of the workers on the farm to the annual Michaelmas Fair on Sunderland's town moor. Shortly after arriving there they joined forces with some labourers and their wives and families from a neighbouring farm some miles past Hawthorn Farm. Connie knew the folk vaguely, she caught sight of them every Sunday morning when everyone attended the parish church on the outskirts of Bishopwearmouth, but as she always had to get back to the farm quickly in case Luke's mother needed anything she never dallied after the service to talk to anyone. A smile and brief nod was all she'd indulged in before.

During the course of the evening, however, she found herself in the company of a young man called Reuben Longhurst—mainly due to his good-natured persistence. She didn't mind too much. He was tall and blond, with a twinkle in his eye, and he made no secret of the fact he was smitten with her. It eased the ache in her heart a little, even though she was careful to give him no encouragement, knowing it wouldn't be fair to him.

By the end of the night she found she'd thoroughly enjoyed herself, however. Reuben had made her laugh, and had treated her with the utmost respect, and it had been a welcome change to feel young and carefree for once.

Alice Todd had made no secret of the fact that she was taken with Reuben's older brother, and he with her, and as the two parties made their goodbyes at the end of the rough dirt road leading to Hawthorn Farm, Reuben said quietly, 'Bart has asked Alice to walk out with him on Sunday afternoon. If I accompany him when he calls at the farm, would I be welcome, Connie?'

Blushing hotly, and speaking in a low voice so the others could not hear, she said, 'I like you, Reuben, really I do. But not…not in that way, just as a friend. I'm sorry.'

'Is there someone else?' he asked softly, making no effort to disguise his disappointment. 'Someone you like, I mean?'

'No. Yes. I mean…' Connie paused. She wasn't making any sense, and after he had asked her to walk out with him he deserved some explanation. 'I do like someone,' she said shyly, after a moment or two, 'but he doesn't feel the same.'

'He doesn't?'

The blank astonishment in his voice and the look in his blue eyes in the moonlight was balm to her sore heart. Connie smiled into the young fresh face. He was nice. He was very nice, and she knew lots of girls would be eager to be seen on his arm, but... He wasn't Luke. 'I'm sorry,' she said again. 'In spite of that my feelings for him haven't altered, so it wouldn't be fair to give you any hope.'

'Then how about I call on Sunday and we go for a walk as friends?' Reuben said quickly as the rest of his party walked off. 'Just friends—not as a courting couple or anything, I promise. You can bring Flora, if you want, your brothers, too. I don't mind. And I'll bring some lads and lasses with me. Yes?'

Connie stared at him doubtfully. 'There's no chance I will change my mind, Reuben, so why would you want to do that?'

'Because I enjoyed your company tonight, and we had fun, didn't we? I could be wrong, but I get the impression you're not used to having fun. I'd like us to be friends if we can't be anything else. I mean it, Connie. I'm quite serious.'

She shook her head. 'It doesn't seem fair to you.'

'I mean it,' he insisted. 'Look, how about we give it a try on Sunday and go from there? There's a whole bunch of us who often go walking of a Sunday afternoon. You met a few of them tonight and we're all pals.

Everyone needs friends, Connie. It's what makes the world go round.'

He was grinning as he spoke, backing away in answer to his party, who were calling him from some distance away. Before she could object further he'd turned and run after the others, calling over his shoulder, 'Till Sunday, then.'

Connie stared into the darkness which had swallowed him up. For the life of her she didn't know whether to be annoyed or amused. Sunday afternoon and evening was supposed to be her half-day, but ever since she had adopted the role of housekeeper she hadn't taken her free time, carrying on working in the farmhouse as though it was a normal day. Like Reuben and his friends, Alice and some of the others always took a walk on Sunday afternoons, if the weather permitted, but Connie had never joined them—although they had invited her a few times. But she *could* try it. She could leave Luke's mother's afternoon tray all ready, and they always had a cold supper on Sunday evenings, so she could prepare that too before she left the farmhouse.

Becoming aware that Flora and the others were calling her, and almost lost from sight on the road to the farm, she hastily hurried after them in the moonlight.

She'd give it a try on Sunday, she decided. It was her half-day, after all, and Luke's mother wouldn't mind. She knew that. It had been she who had persuaded her to join the others tonight, gently scolding her for never leaving the farmhouse. As for Luke, she doubted he'd even notice she wasn't around.

* * *

'Connie is doing *what* and with *whom?*'

Luke stared at his mother, and Maggie Hudson repeated patiently, 'She's going for a walk after lunch with some friends. She will leave my afternoon tray ready in the kitchen, and also a cold supper for the pair of us, so we won't be seeing her until tomorrow morning. It has all been decided.'

'And you told her that was acceptable?'

'It's her half-day, Luke. She is entitled to it. And don't look at me like that. Surely you don't begrudge the girl a few hours off, the way she works for us?'

Ignoring this, Luke said flatly, 'Who are these friends, exactly? What are their names and where do they come from?'

'Some young people from Stone Farm, as I understand it.'

Luke frowned. Young people. That would mean a number of young men. Connie was as innocent and ingenuous as a child, unlike some of the lasses round about, who would give you the eye as soon as look at you. Alice Todd, for one. And lads would be lads. It was the same the whole world over. Fine for *them* to sow their wild oats.

'You should have stopped her,' he said gruffly. 'I don't like it.'

'Stopped her? Why on earth would I presume to stop her seeing her friends, Luke? Hasn't it occurred to you that Connie is still a young lass, in spite of her having to have an old head on her young shoulders for much of her life? It can't be much fun for her, seeing no one but us for most of the time, day in, day out. And, regardless of all that, like I said—this is her half-day, and she can do as she pleases.'

His frown deepened. 'She's never bothered to take it off before,' he said mulishly. 'And we don't know these people.'

After a moment or two Luke became aware that his mother was staring at him with an odd look on her face. Then she said, 'Connie is a bonny lass, Luke. Perhaps she has attracted an admirer. I don't know. If she hasn't already, she will one day. Make no mistake about that. And whoever gets her will be a lucky man, in my opinion.'

He glared at her. 'She's not ready for anything like that.'

'Of course she is. She'll be eighteen next year, as you know.'

'Well, be it on your head if she's taken advantage of.'

When her son stomped out of her bedroom, Maggie continued to stare after him for some time. Then she said to herself, 'So that's the way of it. Well, I hope he does something about it before it's too late.' But her voice carried no conviction.

When Connie got in from church she busied herself with the dinner, having sent Flora to set two places at the dining room table for Luke and his mother. It was a shame Mrs Hudson didn't feel up to making the journey to church these days, she thought, after slipping the roast potatoes in to join the joint of beef she'd put on before leaving that morning. But at least she managed to come downstairs most afternoons. Luke never went to church. According to Rose he hadn't set foot in the place since they had buried his son, in spite of Parson Lindsay having come to see him at the farm several times.

Her mouth tender, she was thinking, Poor, poor man, when a cold voice from the kitchen doorway brought her turning round from the range. 'I understand you intend to leave the house for the rest of the day after lunch?' Luke said thinly.

Connie's eyes widened. By, he was in a state about something. She'd never seen him look like this. But surely it wasn't due to her taking her half-day? It couldn't be. Mrs Hudson had been fine about it when she'd mentioned it to her. She'd even said she was pleased she was going to get out and blow the cobwebs away for a change. No, it couldn't be that. But something had upset him.

'That's right.' She bobbed her head. 'I'm leaving your mother's tea tray ready, and your suppers will be on the cold slab in the—'

'What if my mother needs you while you're gone?'

'What?' She stared at him bewildered.

'I said...' He paused, his voice insultingly slow when he ground out, 'What...if...my...mother... needs...you...while...you're...gone?'

The muscles of Connie's heart-shaped face tightened as she looked into grey eyes which were almost black with what she recognised as suppressed rage. He was objecting to her going out. That was it. How dared he? How *dared* he when she had spent every day for the last nine or ten months at his mother's beck and call. And his. Oh, yes—and his. 'I assumed you would be here, sir,' she said crisply, 'if she needed anything.'

'Really? And you didn't see the need to check with

me first? That would have been courteous if nothing else, surely?'

'Sunday afternoon is my half-day. I'm not supposed to be here. I thought you realised that.' She was standing as stiff as a ramrod now, her sense of injustice and hurt making her cheeks as fiery as the red tint to her chestnut hair and her tone as cold as his. 'For that reason I saw no need to check.'

Luke's voice had a steel thread to it as he said, 'And that is all that matters to you? Not my mother's welfare?'

'I think of your mother's welfare every day, as you very well know.' She was glaring at him now, more angry than she had ever been in the whole of her life. It didn't matter that he was the master of all their destinies. He was being grossly unfair and she wouldn't be bullied like this. 'And Mrs Hudson is quite happy for me to take my half-day—especially considering it is the first time I've ever done so since I came to work for you.'

'Mrs Hudson is not the master of this farm.'

'I'm aware of that,' she snapped back, even quicker than he had. 'But it was you who set my half-day the same as the others.'

There was a short silence as they stood facing each other, and into it Flora came, sidling past Luke in the doorway and then glancing at each of their faces before making herself scarce in the scullery. Connie just hoped her brothers wouldn't come in yet from seeing one of the farm cats' new litter of kittens in the hayloft.

She bit tight down on her lip before asking grimly, 'Are you telling me I can't go out this afternoon…sir?' She knew the pause before the sir was insolent, but something outside of herself was urging her on, all the heartache and smothered dreams of the last months coming into play.

Luke stared at her, bitterness like bile on his tongue and the rage that had had him in its grip since his mother had first spoken entirely unabated. He knew he was being unreasonable, that he had gone about this all wrong, but the knowledge only made him the more angry. 'You must do as you please,' he said thinly.

She inclined her head. 'Then, as your mother is comfortable and the meals are prepared, I shall join the others,' she said in a voice unlike her own, so harsh was it. 'And I shall be taking my half-day every Sunday from now on, sir. Just so as you know and can be aware of it. Unless your mother is unwell, of course.'

'Oh, please don't let us put you about at all,' he said with acidic sarcasm, before turning and leaving the kitchen.

Connie put out her hands and gripped the edge of the kitchen table, her legs threatening to give way. She was trembling from head to foot, her face chalk-white except for two bright scarlet patches along her cheekbones.

She could hardly believe that one minute she had been feeling desperately sorry for him, wishing she could wipe away the grief which still held him in its grip, and the next she had been rudely catapulted into a scene of momentous proportions. He had been horrible, *horrible,* and she hated him. She did. She loathed and detested and hated him, and she would for the rest of her life. However could she have imagined herself in love with him? She must have been mad. He was an arrogant brute of a man.

Then she sank down on one of the stout hardbacked chairs, laying her head down on her arms on the kitchen table and beginning to sob. She heard Flora come through from where she had been waiting in the scullery and felt her sister pat her shoulder in silent sympathy. It wasn't until her brothers came in and—after a whispered explanation from Flora—began to pat her too that she managed to pull herself together.

'It's all right.' She wiped her face with her handkerchief and sniffed a few times before forcing a shaky smile. 'A storm in a teacup, that's all. Look, we need to set the table in here, and Flora—' she turned to her sister '—you start to warm the serving dishes for the dining room. We want to be ready when they arrive from Stone Farm, don't we? Mrs Hudson will be down any minute, and once she's seated we can take in the dishes and then eat ourselves.'

'Are you sure you want to go, Connie?' Flora's voice was low and she still looked worried to death.

Connie looked at her sister and brothers. 'Quite sure,' she said firmly. 'And from now on my half-day is a time for us, when we do things together. We might go for a walk with the others, like today, or just stay at home, or whatever. But I shan't be working here, all right? It's going to be family time. I should have done it before now.'

Flora nodded uncertainly. Tommy, David and Ronnie just stared at her, their eyes wide.

'I don't mind what I do six and a half days a week,

but I won't be taken for a mug,' Connie continued, half to herself. 'Not by anyone. And you can put that in your pipe, Mr Luke Hudson, and smoke it.'

And with that she stood up, smoothed down her dress, raised her chin and set about seeing to the Sunday lunch.

CHAPTER EIGHT

THE month of October passed by fairly uneventfully on the whole. True, Britain's first troops to return home after the end of the Boer War received a heroes' welcome, the Tories were re-elected with a huge majority, and many folk lost their lives in the severe floods which struck the north at the end of the month, but these happenings barely impinged on life at Hawthorn Farm, apart from a brief mention by the parson in his Sunday sermons. All Connie was really aware of was how difficult life had become in the last little while, and how miserable she felt all the time.

Not that anything had changed. Not really. And yet everything had. Luke had been waiting for her in the kitchen on the Monday morning after their disagreement, and he had made a stiff little speech where he'd apologised for his sharpness the day before and assured her her half-days were her own and she would not be called on during them. Nor had she been. Oft times she had seen him in the distance when they had returned in a laughing group to the farm late Sunday afternoon, but he had never acknowledged their existence.

The thunderclouds and rain of October gave way to a November of sharp frosts and thick fog first thing in the mornings. Every twig on every tree and bush was outlined in silver tracery, sometimes until nearly mid-day, and the older farmhands spoke grimly of a bad winter in store. By the time December was ushered in no one doubted they were right. The snowstorms had come with relentless monotony, the wind like a carving knife as it cut unprotected hands and cheeks, and even when mittens and mufflers were worn the wool froze like boards and became caked with ice.

The normal jobs of the farm had to go on—wall-mending, milking, cattle-feeding, watering—and the cowhouses and stables had to be cleaned, the hens, calves, pigs and sheep fed and kept safe. Turnips had to be chopped, bran mashed for the pigs, corn scattered for the hens and slices of dry clean hay cut from stacks for the cattle.

There were long days at a time when they were snowed in, and the children of the workers couldn't get to school—something Tommy, David and Ronnie greeted with relish. Flora had taken to reading to Luke's mother by the farmhouse's sitting room fire on these occasions, and the two appeared to have become quite close. Connie's three brothers would sidle in now and again, sitting at Maggie Hudson's feet as quiet as mice. Usually this was when Connie was drying out their boots and coats on the farmhouse's massive kitchen range; due to the harsh conditions myriad jobs were found for all the children if they were not at school.

Connie knew Luke had walked in on her sister and

brothers during these times because they had told her so, but she did not know what he thought of his mother allowing—no, *encouraging* such liberties. He was always civil to her, and she to him, but both of them spoke only when they had to, and then often as not in monosyllables. It was hateful, but that was the way it was.

With the snow reaching the tops of the hedges they had not seen Reuben and the others from Stone Farm since the middle of November, but Connie did not mind this. She liked Reuben, and now counted him as a friend, but they were both aware that was all it would ever be on her part. When Reuben had been around, though, she had been able to put her misery about the situation with Luke to one side to some extent, at least for an hour or two. She didn't want to love him, she would give the world not to, but it seemed nothing he did or said could kill the emotion. Her only comfort was that Luke was completely oblivious to the feeling that seemed almost to consume her at times.

On the first Sunday in December, with Christmas three and a half weeks away, there came a respite in the weather. The snow was still deep, and the ice thick, but there had been no fresh falls for some days. Paths had been cleared and remained cleared, the tramped-down snow in the fields and around the farm was easier to walk on, and each morning brought winter sunlight that turned the crystal and white world into something beautiful.

Connie had taken to feeding a little robin which came to the kitchen windowsill every morning since the worst of the weather, and it was now so tame it would take cake crumbs from her hand. She hadn't been long in the farmhouse kitchen, and was far earlier than usual, having forgotten to prepare the porridge for Luke and Mrs Hudson the night before—usually her last job— when the robin made his appearance, fluttering up and down the window.

The rest of the farm was still asleep, it being just gone half past five in the morning, and Connie found herself smiling as she opened the window. 'What are you doing here?' she chided softly. 'It's still dark. You should be tucked up with your head under your wing, like all the other birds. I suppose you noticed I'd lit the lamp? Is that it? You're one on your own, you are. Still, if you've decided it's breakfast time I'd better get you something. Wait there.'

She turned, and Luke was directly behind her. But for his hands shooting out to steady her she would have fallen as she jerked backwards in shock and slipped on a patch of dampness on the stone flags—the result of the snow on her boots melting.

He continued to hold her, his eyes narrowing slightly as she gasped, 'What—what are you doing up? It—it's early.'

'I could ask you the same thing,' he said, very softly, his eyes on her mouth. 'I wanted a cup of tea. And you?'

'I forgot to put the oats in soak for the porridge. I only remembered in bed last night.' She drew back a little, and he immediately let go of her, but she could still feel his fingers burning her flesh through the wool of her dress.

He nodded slowly. 'It wouldn't have mattered. We could have had something else before the bacon and eggs.'

'But you like porridge,' she said weakly.

They stared at each other, just a breath apart, and then he ran a hand through his hair in a gesture of what looked like bemusement. He hadn't shaved that morning, and Connie suddenly noticed he had lost some weight. The chiselled cheekbones were more sharply defined. It made him look even more handsome, harder, tougher…

'I've been wanting to talk to you,' he said abruptly. 'But—'

Her mouth had gone dry, and she moistened her bottom lip with her tongue. His eyes followed the action. She swallowed hard before saying, 'But what? What's the matter?'

'I didn't know how to begin, what to say to put this—' he waved a hand '—this matter right. But it's gone on too long.'

Again their eyes held, and now the moment stretched and lengthened, and she felt her heart pounding so hard against her ribcage it actually hurt. It was a small clicking noise that drew her attention to the open window and the robin, who was clearly getting impatient, dancing from one tiny foot to the other.

Luke had followed her gaze, and now he said, a touch of amusement colouring his voice, 'I wondered who you were talking to. I take it he's not a stranger? He seems quite at home.'

'I feed him,' she admitted shakily, before drawing in a steadying breath. Why did he have to look so good?

'The original early bird that catches the worm? Or in this case I suspect perhaps other titbits?' And then, his voice turning huskier, he said, 'He clearly trusts you.'

'Yes.' She smiled at the robin. 'Yes, he trusts me.'

'Sensible bird.'

She didn't know what to say, but the look in his eyes was flustering her. Nervously she turned and reached for the cake tin, opening the lid and crumbling a little of the fruit cake in her hand before walking across and offering it to the robin. As usual he immediately took a beakful, darting to the windowsill and gobbling it up before flying to her hand and repeating the process. In a minute or two the cake was gone, and then, with a quick tilt of his head and a little chirrup of thanks, so was the robin. And now she was alone with Luke.

Connie shut the window after drawing in a deep breath of the sharp icy air, then turned and faced Luke as she exhaled silently. He had seated himself on the edge of the kitchen table as she had been feeding the robin, the dark brown loose shirt accentuating his broad muscled shoulders, his charcoal trousers tucked into knee-high brown leather boots. The powerful masculine aura that was such a part of him was stronger than ever, and it dried her mouth and made her all fingers and thumbs as she walked to the range and began to stir the porridge.

'Would you like that cup of tea you mentioned now?' she said awkwardly when he remained silent. 'The water's just boiled.'

'Thank you.' He inclined his head without taking his eyes off her.

She was vitally aware of him watching her as she brewed a pot of tea from the big black kettle she had put on the hob on first entering the kitchen, and after she had poured two cups, adding milk and sugar—which had been such a luxury when she had arrived at the farm but which now she was used to—she handed him his, being careful not to touch him.

'I haven't been fair to you,' he said suddenly, pinning her with the dark, unrevealing stare she was used to.

She sat down at the kitchen table at the far end from Luke, knowing her trembly legs wouldn't support her much longer. 'I don't understand,' she murmured.

'That I've been guilty of being unjust and blinkered and opinionated? What's not to understand?' he said gently. 'Of course you want to be with people of your own age, and be free from responsibility for a few hours sometimes. It is only natural. You are young. You have the rest of your life before you. It was crass of me to cause such a fuss about it.'

Connie stared at him. She didn't really want to be with anyone else but him, but she couldn't say that. Neither could she say she didn't feel young in the way he meant. She didn't think she ever had. She had been so used to looking after the younger ones and keeping the house running from as far back as she could remember, due to her mother's frailty. It was second nature to her. She found people of her own age a mite silly on the whole.

'This young man, Reuben, from Stone Farm. Farmer Griffiths tells me he is a good worker and a young man of principle.'

Connie's eyes opened wider for a moment. He knew about Reuben? And he had asked Reuben's master about him?

In answer to the expression on her face, Luke said quietly, 'Flora talks to my mother when they sit together.

I just wanted to make sure the man was of good character, that's all. Young men can be…knavish, even deceptive, and you have no experience of the world. I was worried you could find yourself in a situation you were unable to handle. Farmer Griffiths tells me this would not be the case with this particular young man.'

He thought she and Reuben… Connie blushed hotly. And he was talking as though he himself was ancient, when she knew for a fact he had turned twenty-nine this year. That wasn't old. Quickly, she said, 'I think there has been some misunderstanding. Reuben and I are merely friends.'

For a second the mask lifted, and she saw something glitter in his eyes. It revealed how deliberate his air of control was. But almost immediately the thick lashes hid the expression, and when he next looked up his gaze was cool and steady. 'But he thinks very highly of you. I'm sure it won't be long before he makes his feelings plain.'

'He has. Made his feelings plain, I mean. And I told him I couldn't see him in any light other than that of a friend,' Connie said firmly. 'Reuben is in no doubt of my feelings, none at all, and I certainly haven't trifled with his affections,' she added, in case he thought so. 'Right from the beginning of our friendship I told him—' She stopped abruptly, aware she had been about to let her tongue run away with itself. 'I told him he could only be a friend,' she finished flatly.

He stared at her. Again there was something she couldn't put a name to in his eyes, but it was enough to send the blood rushing through her veins and cause her heart to beat faster. *He liked her.* Suddenly lots of little things over the past year came together in one blinding flash. Of course she was just his housekeeper, and he was the master of this big farm, but if things had been different, if she had been of his class…

Whether he was aware he had given himself away Connie wasn't sure, but she saw a muscle jerk in the hard square jaw a few times, and despite his apparent relaxed stance she sensed he was as tense as she was. She took a few sips of her tea, utterly at a loss to know what to say or do to ease the situation. Never had she wished so hard she knew more about men—what made them think and act as they did.

No, not men, she corrected in the next heartbeat. This man. She wanted to say she loved him, and that she knew there would never be anyone else who would measure up to him. To assure him she expected nothing from him and would be content to remain his house-keeper and be part of his life in that way. But then that last wouldn't be true, perhaps, in the future. Loving him as she did, she knew she would have to leave Hawthorn Farm if he began to court someone of his own class, if he married again. She wouldn't be able to face watching him love someone else. So perhaps her love wasn't as unselfish as she would like it to be, in spite of all he had done for her and Flora and the lads.

'Connie, I need to tell you something.'

When she looked up, he'd moved to stand in front of her. He drew her gently to her feet, cupping her small jaw and forcing her to look at him when she would have drooped her head.

She sensed immediately that he had guessed how

she felt about him. The knowledge was there in the darkness of the smoky grey eyes. For a second she wanted to blurt out that it was all right, that she would never presume to expect he would become entangled with a woman other than from his own class, but another thought had taken hold, and the shock of it stilled her tongue. Was he going to suggest she become his mistress? She wasn't so naïve she didn't know some wealthy men thought nothing of such things.

But, no, no. Luke was not like that. How could she have thought so for one second? 'What is it?' she whispered. Something in the twist to his mouth was telling her she wasn't going to like what she heard, and the blue of her eyes was almost black with apprehension.

'I'm sure you have been acquainted with the circumstances of my marriage and my wife's death,' he said quietly, his tone indicating he was well aware of the gossip of his workers. 'I was placed in the position of a grieving young husband and father, but this was only partly true. My wife and I...' He hesitated. 'The marriage was far from being a happy one. Christabel never should have become a wife. She would have been far happier continuing to be the pampered darling of her parents for the rest of her days. Marriage...disgusted her. *I* disgusted her. Within days we both realised we'd made a terrible mistake, but it was done. She had a husband whose demands she found odious, and I had a wife who had been a figment of my imagination. But then our son was born.'

He drew a steadying breath and Connie remained absolutely still, horrified by the pain she read in his face.

'You know the rest of the story,' he said, releasing her and stretching out his arms as he clasped the edge of the table, his head bent. 'Would that it could be undone. But it cannot. It happened. My son died, and he took with him something of me that day. I cannot explain it except to say that it wasn't exactly hope or trust or joy or peace, but an element of all those things. I do not like the man I have become, but I cannot change. I will not change. I am not good company, Connie.'

He raised his head and looked at her. 'Do you understand what I am saying to you?'

'If…if you met someone else, someone you could love, you might feel differently,' she said helplessly.

'I have met someone I could love.' He straightened. 'I think you know that. And I have had a battle going on inside me since the day I met you.' In spite of his words, there was no softening effect upon his face. 'But you deserve, you *need* someone of your own age— someone with no past, no demons. Someone who will make life joyful for you, and you for him. I should have been big enough to rise above the jealousy I've felt long before this and wish you well. I am sorry. Forgive me.'

Connie forgot the rigid rules of society that declared nice girls were never forward. She forgot everything but that he had told her he loved her in one breath and that she must find someone else in the next. And for no reason other than that he wouldn't let his love for her have free rein. It wasn't that he considered her beneath him, or that he was worried what his contemporaries would think of their liaison—that would have held her tongue. But this…

'There is no need to be sorry.' She stepped close to him but did not touch him. 'I love you. I know I will never love anyone else—'

'No.' He moved his head impatiently. 'You are young. You will meet someone. You are on the threshold of life, whereas I feel I'm as old as the hills at times.'

'Don't assume my affections are so fickle.' For the first time that morning a thread of anger made itself felt. 'And don't keep on about my being so young. You are not exactly ancient yourself, besides which you're not the only one to feel old inside. Physical age has little bearing on the soul and spirit.'

He stared at her, his eyes moving over the creamy softness of her skin, the deep blue of her eyes and her impassioned mouth. He took a step backwards, away from temptation, but Connie followed him, her voice soft as she said, 'I love you. I do. I don't care what you're like sometimes; it makes no difference. I can make you hope again, and trust, and all those things you said. I know I can. Love can conquer everything.'

'You're talking like a child.'

'That's better than how you are talking.'

'Possibly.' When she opened her mouth to say more he silenced her with an upraised hand. 'But your feelings could change. You haven't allowed for that. Feelings do, Connie. All the time. There could come a time when you look at me with dread in your eyes, when the bedroom door closing is enough to make you half hysterical. Marriage is a very physical union, not a romantic, airy-fairy thing. And I am a physical man.'

'I understand that,' she said steadily. 'And I'm not Christabel.'

'You have no idea what marriage involves,' he said, anger darkening his voice. 'You don't, do you? And till death us do part can be a hell of a long time for some folk.'

'You don't think I love you?'

'I think you imagine you do, but girlish fancies are very different to harsh reality. Love has to be sustained—'

'You don't trust me.' She stared at him, deep hurt in her eyes and voice. 'You don't believe my love would be constant.'

He paused, and then, as though it was torn out of him, he muttered, 'I don't trust in love. That's different.'

No, it wasn't. She didn't know how to reach him, how to find the words to convey how she felt about him, so instead, guided purely by instinct, she reached up on tiptoe, placing her hands on his shoulders and put her lips to his.

For a second she thought he wasn't going to respond, and then he crushed her to him, his mouth telling of his frustration and desire as it ravished hers.

It was her first kiss, and it wasn't the tender, gentle caress portrayed in *The People's Friend* or *The Lady*— two magazines one of their old neighbours had passed on to her mother each week. For the merest fraction of a moment she felt frightened and all at sea, and then everything within her rose up to meet his need. She leant against him, her arms going round his neck, and her head tilted back as she responded with a touchingly inexpert hunger of her own.

They swayed together in the dim light from the flickering oil lamp, and it was some moments before his head jerked up. He drew a ragged breath, putting her from him as he ground out, 'This is madness—madness.'

'I don't care.' She stared at him, dazed and trembling.

'Then I must.' He raked his hair back from his forehead with a shaking hand. 'I must,' he repeated grimly, before turning away and striding out of the kitchen.

She stood quite still for a minute or more, unable to believe that he had gone, that he had left her. She looked round at the familiar objects in the room and they seemed strange, remote, and it wasn't until the smell hit her senses that she was galvanised into movement.

The porridge was burning.

CHAPTER NINE

THE tin clock on the kitchen mantelpiece over the range showed twelve o'clock, and Flora and the others had just returned to the farm after the morning service at the parish church. Connie had remained at the farmhouse, due to the fact that when she had taken Luke's mother her breakfast tray she had discovered Luke had gone for an early-morning ride—ostensibly to visit friends who lived some miles away. She did not believe this. She had noticed that when he was troubled in any way he would often ride Ebony for long periods, but she didn't say anything to the older woman, merely informing Maggie she would be in the kitchen if needed. Since Luke's mother's heart problems Connie didn't like to leave her alone unless Luke was around and within earshot.

She heard Luke return and join his mother, who was now in the sitting room, as she and Flora set the table in the dining room. But once all the dishes were on the table she sent Flora to inform them Sunday lunch was ready. She couldn't face Luke. Now she had had time to think, she was mortified at her actions. She had thrown herself at his head. There was no other name for it. It had been *she* who had kissed *him,* and she couldn't believe she had so far forgotten herself as to instigate their embrace. Even Alice Todd, brazen as she could be, wouldn't have done such a thing. What must he think of her?

Having dished up their own dinner at the kitchen table, Connie merely picked at the food on her plate, and once she had sent Flora to retrieve the dirty dishes from the dining room she rushed through the washing up, anxious to be away. She would have to face Luke some time, she knew that, but not now. Not today. Tomorrow she would manage—somehow, she assured her aching heart. For now all she wanted was to hide herself away and cry and cry.

As she and Flora and the lads left the farmhouse, however, they met Reuben and the group from Stone Farm. They were standing and talking to Alice Todd and her brothers, and the other youngsters in the yard.

'There's a big lake frozen over by the old quarry, and it's a perfect day for skating,' Reuben's brother assured them all excitedly. 'They're going to have a bonfire, and old Joseph from High Ford is bringing his brazier to roast potatoes and chestnuts. You've got to come. It'll be canny.'

Alice had already slipped her hand through her beau's arm, and everyone was clamouring to be off, but when Connie told Flora to go without her, her sister was having none of it. 'I'm not going without you. You know they won't listen to me if you're not there,' she said, indicating her three brothers with a wave of her hand. 'And anyway, you'd enjoy it. I know you would, Connie. Please come. Oh, say you will.'

She was about to refuse again, and insist Flora take the boys herself, knowing there would be enough folk around to call her brothers to order if they needed it, when she noticed a horse and trap approaching the farmhouse. She recognized the couple as friends of Luke's mother. They called fairly often, and always stayed for two or three hours. She didn't think for a moment Luke would take advantage of their being with his mother to seek her out to discuss what had happened between them earlier, but just in case—*just in case*—it was probably safer to go with the others.

'All right. I'll come.' As Flora darted off happily, Connie glanced up and caught Reuben's gaze. He smiled at her, his eyes bright under his cap and his good-looking face rosy with cold. She forced herself to smile back, as though the turmoil within wasn't making her feel sick and heavy with despair. Why couldn't she have fallen in love with Reuben? Everything would have been so straightforward then. She remembered how Luke had commended him and her mouth tightened. Luke had all but offered his congratulations that they were a couple. He clearly didn't have any objections to her being with someone else. If that was his idea of love…

Once everyone was ready they started off in a gay laughing crowd, the children pelting snowballs at each other or sucking the icicles they had broken off the water butts and cottage windowsills. Although bitterly cold, it was a dry, feathery cold—the sort that sharpened the lungs and numbed noses but in a pleasant way. They passed bushes still laden with shining scarlet berries, tiny footprints bearing witness to countless birds and tiny creatures making use of the easy food.

The sky was blue and high, the air fresh and clean, and all nature had transpired to make the day a beautiful one. Furthermore, Connie thought, she and her family had been able to afford new winter boots and coats, and they would be going home to a warm cottage with a banked-down fire waiting for them, along with a well-stocked larder. She ought to be the happiest, most thankful girl in the world and count her blessings, but she couldn't. She just couldn't. Perhaps tomorrow. For the present she was having her work cut out pretending everything was the same as normal to Reuben and the rest of the company.

Once they neared the old quarry they could smell the bonfire even before they saw it, and the winter afternoon was full of laughter and shouting. There were far more people than Connie had expected on the ice, a few with skates, but the vast majority just sliding on the frozen lake and having fun. The man with the brazier had just got the lighted coals glowing nicely, and the smell of roasting potatoes was beginning to waft on the air. All around the glistening sparkle of the snow touched the joyful scene with magic.

Connie realised she had made a mistake in coming. The mass happiness, the laughter and joy and excitement, only served to highlight how wretched she felt inside. She should have stayed in the cottage and got on with some of the endless darning and mending her brothers provided by way of their clothes and socks, as she'd intended when she left the farmhouse, but it was too late now. She had to make the best of it and go on pretending.

Never having tried to slide and skate on ice before, she found herself flat on her bottom several times during the next couple of hours. Reuben wasn't much help either. Quite a lot of the young men and girls, and especially the children, seemed to skim effortlessly to and fro, but she and Reuben slipped and slithered and clutched hold of each other in a tottering and painfully slow progress around the lake.

Increasingly cold and damp, Connie was glad when the daylight began to give way to a fiery sunset that bathed the mother-of-pearl sky in rivers of red, gold and indigo. Soon the twilight would deepen, and everyone would begin to go home. Already the bonfire was all but out, and old Joseph, having exhausted his supply of potatoes and chestnuts, was packing up.

When she heard the shouts and screams she didn't immediately understand what was going on. It was only when Reuben—who had just fallen over for the umpteenth time—struggled to his feet and said, 'I think the ice has cracked over there, towards the middle,' that she realised folk were in trouble.

She frantically began to search the crowd for Flora and her brothers, but such was the level of confusion and panic that she was knocked clean off her feet as men and women, boys and girls fled the frozen lake.

And the she heard Tommy shouting for her. She knew it was him even before she managed to stand up and scan the scene in front of her. The ice was almost clear of folk now, and what she saw made her blood run cold.

Tommy and David were being restrained by Reuben's brother and another man, not far from where a large black hole had opened up in the centre of the lake. There were one or two other people standing a little way behind them. She recognized Flora and Alice, who had their arms round each other and seemed to be crying, but then her eyes followed where everyone was looking. One of Reuben's friends was stretched out on the ice, holding on to what looked like his coat which he'd obviously flung to the two small figures floundering in the inky black water.

Ronnie. One of them had to be Ronnie, the way Tommy and David were struggling to reach them.

Shaking off Reuben as he tried to stop her, Connie stumbled towards the middle of the lake in seconds, reaching Tommy and David just as she heard Reuben's brother say, 'The ice is still moving. Get him back or he'll be in too.'

She could see Ronnie now, and the other small boy was Alice's brother, Charlie Todd. Their eyes were wide with fear, and they were holding on to the coat with all their might, but she knew it could only be a matter of moments before the cold numbed their grip and their bodies.

With no conscious thought but that she couldn't let her brother die, Connie fell on her stomach and began to inch her way to the young man holding the coat. As she reached him she actually felt the ice creak and move, but she grasped the coat muttering, 'Get back. You're too heavy. I'm lighter. Go on, get back, or we'll all be in.'

He did as she bid, but she felt him stop and hold fast to her ankles. The solid contact spurred her on. 'I'm going to pull the coat and both of you out of the water,' she gasped, but even as she spoke she saw Ronnie's eyes close. Without thinking about what she was doing she lunged forward and grabbed both boys' arms, her own feeling as though they were being wrenched out of their sockets. 'Hang on to me and climb out. Try—please.'

Charlie seemed to be in a better state than Ronnie, immediately scrabbling with his legs as he worked up her arm like a small wiry monkey, before grasping the neck and shoulder of her coat and hauling himself out of the hole, half strangling her as he did so. She could now hold on to Ronnie with both hands, but her little brother's eyes were still closed and he was a dead weight. She attempted to pull him out of the water but it was useless. And then, as the ice creaked again, she heard the young man behind her swear before saying, 'You have to get back. It's cracking. It'll go any minute. I know the signs.'

She didn't answer him, but desperation gave her a strength she didn't normally have and she heaved Ronnie's inert body with all her might so his small torso came clear of the water. Grasping the back of his jacket and his trouser waistband, she heaved again, half dragging, half sliding him past her in order for Reuben's friend to grab him—which he did. The young man inched backwards with Ronnie, who appeared unconscious, and Connie began to do the same—only to freeze as a startlingly loud crack pierced the air at the same time as the ice seemed to separate beneath her.

One moment she was lying on the ice. The next she'd tipped headfirst into water that was so cold the shock of it caused her to gasp, and she took in great lungfuls of the freezing blackness.

As the water closed over her head she flailed with her arms and legs, somehow managing to twist and right herself, her head breaking the surface for a moment as she spluttered and coughed. Her fingers clawed uselessly at the edge of the glassy deathtrap even as the weight of her boots and clothes drew her under again, their power like a concrete block attached to her feet.

She was going to drown.

As she looked upwards through the greeny black water she kicked again, but the struggle with Ronnie had already tired her, and this time she didn't rise enough to break the surface and take breath. And then, before she could continue down into the black depths, she felt her hair being torn out by its roots. The next second she was breathing air again through her choking, and as she grabbed at the source of her deliverance she heard Luke's voice say, 'Steady, steady, or you'll drown us both. I've got you, Connie, don't fight me. I won't let go of you, my love. Trust me.'

She was being held under her arms now, and as she opened her eyes she saw his face, close to hers. She had stopped struggling, and now she saw Luke was lying on what looked like the long thin trunk of a pine tree, or something similar, and a group of men were holding the other end of it some little distance away on the lake. She couldn't speak as he slowly, very slowly, started to pull her out of the icy tomb. She was too terrified for one thing, but she was also still coughing and trying to clear her lungs, and she was shivering uncontrollably.

How long it was before she was clear of the water she didn't know, but all the time she was frightened the ice would crack again and they would both drown. But then he had his arms tight round her waist, and she was half lying across Luke and the precious trunk of wood as the group of men pulled them further and further away from the ominous black hole.

After some good few yards he eased himself off the tree and knelt a moment with her in his arms. She felt sick and dizzy and light-headed, and so cold it was unbearable, but the main thing that held her in a grip of paralysing fear was her brother. 'Ronnie?' she whispered through blue lips.

'Ronnie's going to be all right.' Luke held her to him, so tight she could feel his racing heart pounding against her. 'Oh, my love, I thought I'd lost you. I thought I'd lost you.'

She heard the words through a kind of mist, and it was only when she found herself still in his arms, but now covered with coats and next to the glowing embers of the bonfire, Ronnie equally wrapped up in Flora's arms next to them, that she realised she must have fainted. She looked up at Luke dazedly.

His eyes were waiting for her. 'You'll feel better in a few minutes. It's the cold,' he murmured. Weakly she glanced around. Everyone was standing quiet and still. Alice Todd was sitting with Charlie, who was also enveloped in coats, his hands held out to the bonfire. 'Reuben's gone to the farm to fetch one of the big hay wagons and some blankets so we can get you all home,' Luke said quietly. 'Just lie still and try and get warm. That's the important thing for now.'

She glanced up into his dark face. She didn't want to move. If she could stay in his arms for the rest of her life like this she would be content. The twilight was deep now, the sun all but set, and in a whisper only Luke could hear, she said, 'How are you here? I mean—'

'I know what you mean.' He smiled down at her, their breaths mingling and their eyes holding. 'I came looking for you. I heard some of the children shouting where you were all going before you left, and I thought I'd wait to see you when you returned to the farm. But I became impatient—' He stopped abruptly, his voice thickening as he said, 'My stubborn pride could have got you killed.'

Surprised, she protested weakly, 'No, you saved me.'

'But I should never have let you leave without saying how I felt. It was just…' He shook his head. 'After the way I behaved I wasn't sure if you would tell me to go to blazes.'

'How could you think that for a minute?' She couldn't believe that this man, this hard, strong, taciturn man, could be so unsure and insecure. But maybe it wasn't surprising after what his wife had put him through.

'After this morning…' His voice dropped even lower, his eyes travelling the whole surface of her face before he continued huskily, 'After this morning I knew that come what may I couldn't let you go. Maybe you ought to have the chance to meet someone else, someone fresh and young with no past, but I don't want you to. I love you. I love you with all my heart and soul and body. This morning, when I was riding Ebony, I told myself over and over again that I could master this, but I can't. A part of me doesn't want to feel this way—' for a moment his bewilderment at his helplessness was uppermost '—but I know now that whether I am with you or without you you're in my soul, the very air I breathe. And I want to be with you. Hell, how I want to.'

She listened without moving, barely daring to take a breath. Never in her wildest dreams had she thought to hear such words from him.

His eyes devoured her again, his smile shaky as he murmured, 'You consume me to the point of driving me mad, my love. For such a little wisp of a thing you have the power to terrify me. You hold my life in those tiny hands.'

'This feeling frightens me, too.' She lifted one hand free of the weight of the coats and touched his square jaw, feeling the rough stubble beneath her fingers with a little jolt of longing. 'But I don't want to feel any other way for the rest of my life.'

'This is not the time or the place—I ought to be on one knee, with a ring in my pocket—but I have to ask now. When I realised it was you out there—' He stopped, his Adam's apple moving up and down as he swallowed hard a few times before he could go on. 'I died a thousand deaths.'

'Oh, Luke.' It was the first time she had spoken his name, and the tenderness in her tone was nearly his undoing.

He closed his eyes, striving to fight the weakness that had him wanting to cry like a woman as he clasped her to him as though he would never let her go. Then he moved her back just a little, looking down into her face that was starting to regain some colour. 'Will you marry me?' he asked softly. 'Will you do me the honour of becoming my wife? Will you be the mother of my children and grow old with me, loving me and letting me love you all the days of our lives together? Will you let me cherish you and care for you and adore you, my own, sweet, precious love?'

She smiled mistily, the rest of the world fading away. 'Yes,' she said. 'A thousand times yes.'

CHAPTER TEN

THE banns had been called at the parish church for three consecutive Sundays, the last one being the day before, and it was now Christmas Eve and Connie's wedding day. The whole farm was aware of the furore the hasty wedding had caused in some quarters of society, but they could also see the master and the young mistress— as they had already taken to calling Connie—didn't give a jot.

'And why should they?' Rose said stoutly to Jacob as they dressed themselves in their Sunday finery, ready to board the two big farm wagons pulled by the shire horses that were going to take everyone to the church. 'If ever a pair deserve some happiness, they do. And what's the point in waiting when there's no good reason for it? Daft, I call it. Don't you?'

Jacob nodded. He knew better than to argue, even though he was sure that if it had been anyone but Connie and the master his wife would have been deeply affronted at the flouting of convention. But it *was* Connie and the master, and he, for one, wished them all the happiness in the world. If ever a man had changed in the last weeks, the master had. Just showed what the love of a good woman could do.

He glanced across at his wife, his voice soft as he said, 'You give the lass that garter you made, then? Right pretty that was, love.'

Rose nodded. 'For something blue. And she's wearing the mistress's wedding dress for something old, and Hannah's mother-of-pearl hair combs for something borrowed. Hannah can't do enough for the lass. Well, you can understand it—Connie saving her Charlie, an' all. Ee, I bet she'll look bonny, Jacob.'

Connie did look bonny. She was sitting in front of the long looking glass in Luke's mother's bedroom, and Flora was putting the finishing touches to Connie's upswept hair before they fixed her delicate veil in place.

Maggie was ensconced in a big armchair, watching them, a benevolent smile playing about her lips. After a moment she said softly, 'You look radiant, lass. Radiant. There has never been a more beautiful bride.'

'It's your dress.' Connie turned and smiled at the woman she already thought of as a second mother. From the moment they'd arrived back at the farmhouse that fateful evening three weeks ago, and told Luke's mother their news, Maggie had been beside herself with delight and fully supportive of their not wanting to wait a day longer than was necessary to become man and wife. And she had made sure everyone knew it.

The wedding dress was indeed a beautiful thing. Made with folds of wonderful antique lace, the bodice covered in tiny seed pearls which were reflected in the edging to the veil, the ivory dress was exquisite and as delicate as spider webs.

Maggie had offered the dress and veil to her the day after their announcement. 'I've kept it safe since I wed,' she had said a little tearfully as she had unwrapped the dress and fragile veil from their layers of gossamer-thin paper. 'I always imagined a daughter of mine wearing it, but the good Lord only granted us one child. I think you know I already feel you're a daughter, Connie. Your Flora too. I think of your little family as mine.'

Connie had been utterly enchanted with the dress, and it had only needed the waist nipping in a little. She had flung her arms round Luke's mother that day, and although they had been close before, a deeper bond had developed since.

'And you, Flora,' Maggie said now. 'You're as bonny a bridesmaid as I've yet to see.'

Flora was wearing a deep scarlet dress trimmed with ivory lace, and Maggie had insisted on buying both the sisters long, luxurious hooded capes in ivory silk and lace, lined with rich scarlet velvet to keep them warm, and tied with scarlet ribbons.

The Christmas colours were also reflected in the beautiful little posies they were to carry, which the farm women had made the day before and shyly presented them with that morning. The deep red berries and shiny green leaves of holly, the delicate seed vessels of rosebay willowherb and cow parsnip, tiny brown and honey-tinted fir cones, winding ivy, and the pure white berries of mistletoe, along with other winter flowers, had all been laced through and held together with thin scarlet and ivory ribbons and pieces of lace. Connie had been touched and reduced to happy tears when she had seen the posies, recognising the work and affection that had gone into them.

Once the veil was in place Connie stood up and surveyed herself. She could barely comprehend the fragile, ethereal vision in the mirror was her. She touched her face in wonderment. The lace and tiny seed pearls had given her skin a luminescence, and even Flora was silent for once, gazing at her with something like awe on her face.

Was all this a dream? Was it really happening? For a moment she felt light-headed and strange, and then she glanced down at the ruby and pearl ring on her engagement finger. When Luke had placed it there he had said words of love she knew she would treasure for ever—words which had both humbled her and made her feel like a queen. *This was real.* All of it was real. And, unseemly though some might think her if she voiced how she felt, she couldn't wait to become his wife in every sense of the word. To show him she wanted all the love he could give.

Luke had revealed a little more of how his life with Christabel had been since they had become engaged, and now Connie was aching to show him how much she loved and wanted him. Whatever marriage entailed— and she had to admit she had no knowledge of the bedroom part of it, because her mother had considered it immodest to speak of such things—she knew she would welcome it. It meant she was irrevocably his, and he hers, so how could she do otherwise?

'Ready, Connie?' Maggie had risen to her feet. 'It's time to leave. When you come back here you'll be Mrs Luke Hudson.'

Declaring that it was the height of bad luck for the groom to catch a glimpse of the bride on their wedding day, Maggie had despatched her son off the night before, to stay with his best man, a married schoolfriend who lived on the outskirts of town. Luke had protested, but eventually gone with good grace.

Connie nodded. 'I'm ready,' she said softly. More than ready.

'Lass, I'm going to say something, and then it will never be mentioned between us again. There will no need. A new life for the two of you will have begun. You are as right for my lad as the other one was wrong, and I knew it long before you two became betrothed. My only fear was that because of what had gone before he wouldn't have the courage to commit himself again. But somehow—I don't know how—I would have tried to get the two of you together.'

'Thank you.' Connie hugged Maggie tightly, careless of her dress and veil.

Downstairs, Tommy—as the eldest brother—was waiting in his role of giving the bride away. Everyone else had now left for the church, and the farmhouse was hushed. Only Charlie Todd's two elder brothers remained. They were driving the two horses and traps to the church, and when the little wedding party came out of the front door they all clapped at the way the two brothers had decorated the horses' manes and tails and the traps in the wedding colours.

It had snowed the night before, but someone had had the foresight to sweep the path leading from the farmhouse to the traps clean. Connie paused on the front doorstep, the others behind her. She looked across the white fields in the distance and at the bright blue sky above. The night frost was still holding, clothing the undisturbed snow with diamond brilliance, and as though on cue the robin flew almost at her feet, looking up at her with his bright black eyes before tilting his head to wish her good luck before he flew away. Or at least that was what Connie felt he had done.

Her heart full to bursting, she picked up the hem of her dress and began to walk down the path.

'Don't keep turning round, man. You're making me nervous.' Gregory, Luke's best man, smiled at his friend.

Luke attempted to smile back, but he was too het-up for it to carry any substance. All morning, from the time he had first opened his eyes, he had had the feeling something would go wrong. It was too perfect, *she* was too perfect, and he didn't deserve her. What if there was an accident? Or his mother was taken ill? What if the horses bolted on the way to the church? He wouldn't know any peace until she was standing beside him and they had said their vows. Only then would he begin to enjoy his wedding day.

In spite of Gregory's tutting, he glanced behind him again. The small church had been beautifully decorated for Christmas and it was jam-packed full. A good number of the folk would be back tonight for the Christmas service, no doubt. *Tonight.* His heart leapt, but as he felt himself grow hard he steered his mind from the carnal path it had been following. He was in church, for crying out loud, he told himself wryly. There was a time and a place for everything.

He was conscious of the stir outside in the church's little porch area a second before the organ struck up, and as Gregory hissed, 'Face the front, Luke,' he obediently turned his head to face the smiling parson. But only for a moment. He couldn't help himself. He turned again and saw her. His heart stopped beating. All the colour in life, all the beauty he had ever seen and the sweetest sounds he had ever heard drew together and were embodied in the figure of the woman walking towards him on the arm of her small consort. He couldn't take his eyes off her, and had he but known it the look on his face reduced most of the female members of the congregation to tears before the service had even begun properly.

Then she had reached him, and regardless of protocol he reached out and took her hand, entwining her small fingers in his, where he wanted them to remain for ever.

The service was simple, but beautiful, and when the parson pronounced them man and wife Luke lifted her up and twirled her round in his arms as he kissed her until she was breathless, with everyone laughing and cheering in the background.

They emerged from the church to a shower of rice and dried flower petals, and the trees and bushes bordering the path down to the road sparkled with frost crystals in the sunshine, as though nature had conspired to make the day especially beautiful.

Luke's mother and Flora were following in the

second trap, the lads having piled into one of the wagons with the rest of the farm folk, and as they began the journey home Connie sat nestled into Luke's side, the two of them exchanging long, lingering kisses.

'We're married.' She lifted her face up to his, her eyes starry. 'We're really married, Luke.'

'So that was what this morning was all about,' he teased lazily, before tracing the outline of her face with the tip of one finger. 'I love you, Mrs Hudson,' he said, very softly.

Luke had suggested they have a small wedding breakfast for immediately family and a few close friends at a hotel in town when they had first discussed the wedding arrangements, but Connie had wanted everyone to join in the celebrations for the day, so they had decided to have the meal at the farmhouse. She, with Rose and Alice and Hannah, had been baking all week in preparation for the huge buffet now laid out in the dining room. Luke had brought in a barrel of beer, along with bottles of whisky and brandy, and there was hot mulled wine, spicy ginger beer, plus endless lemonade for the children.

They had invited several of Connie's old neighbours—all of whom had eagerly accepted—and it was during a lull in the proceedings midway through the afternoon that Mrs Briggs came up to Connie, her rosy-cheeked face beaming. 'By, lass, but this is a good do,' she said cheerily. 'You're set up now and no mistake. And I wasn't surprised to hear about the nuptials, you know. I saw the way he looked at you that night you were taken bad—couldn't take his eyes off you. I said to Mr Briggs, once you'd gone to the farmhouse, that man's taken with Connie. It's as plain as the nose on your face.'

Connie smiled. Everyone had been so nice, and the day had been wonderful, but she was longing for the moment when she and Luke could escape to the master suite, which had its own little sitting room as well as a dressing room off the bedroom.

She glanced across the room to where Luke was standing by the enormous Christmas tree Flora and the lads had had such fun decorating the night before. His dark, well-tailored tailcoat and trousers fitted the big masculine frame in a way guaranteed to make any female's heart beat a little faster. The oil lamps had already been lit, as the sky had become heavy with more snow in the last hour or so. In their soft mellow light his black hair gleamed like raw ebony, and the ruggedly handsome face was faintly brooding.

She discovered why in the next moment. As Flora claimed Mrs Briggs's attention, Luke made his way over to her, his voice low and smoky as he murmured, 'Isn't it about time some of them began to take their leave? It will be getting dark soon.'

'It's Christmas Eve,' she chided gently. 'Everyone's in a holiday mood, and this *is* a wedding.'

"I want to be alone with you.' He reached up and touched the shining coils of her hair, free now of the veil. 'I want to tell you how much I love you and what a fortunate man I am.'

She smiled, her eyes loving him, wanting him. 'You'll have to be patient just a little longer,' she said softly. 'Jacob and some of the others have already left to take care of the animals. It won't be long before those going into town leave too.'

In spite of her words it was nearly seven o'clock before the last of their guests were gone. She and Luke stood on the doorstep, waving to the occupants of the final horse and trap as it disappeared from view, and as they did so the first fat snowflakes began to fall from a laden sky.

'Christmas Eve,' Connie whispered gently. 'I couldn't think of a more perfect day for us to get married.'

'Not in the summer, when it's warm and the evenings are long?' Luke turned her round in his arms so he could kiss her.

Connie shook her head firmly. To wake up beside him on Christmas Day, to know that they had the rest of their lives before them, who could ask for more? 'No, today is perfect.'

'You're perfect.'

Behind them in the farmhouse they could hear Flora loudly marshalling the lads up to the large sprawling bedroom they were to share, Flora having a smaller one across the landing, next to Luke's mother. This left two more spare bedrooms besides the master suite, and all the rooms were spacious and comfortable. Connie experienced a moment of intense longing that her parents could see how they had fared and what a wonderful man she had married. But perhaps they could, she comforted herself in the next second. Perhaps even now they were smiling down at them, rejoicing in her happiness. It was Christmas Eve, after all.

Luke's mother had already retired to her room an hour before, tired out by the exertion of the day, and when they went into the sitting room only Flora remained to say goodnight to them, then she too skipped off upstairs.

'I think everyone is being wonderfully tactful.' Luke's voice was deep as he took her into his arms, kissing her long and passionately in a way he hadn't done before. Then he took her hand in his and led her up the stairs to their rooms. By the time they were standing in their private little sitting room, where a fire glowed in the grate, Connie had to admit her anticipation was threaded through with apprehension about the unknown. She wanted to be everything to him. She wanted to love him and please him and erase all the bad memories of the past and the way Christabel had made him feel. But what if she didn't know how? What if she wasn't enough for him?

She watched his mouth as it came closer, shutting her eyes and praying this first night together would be wonderful for him. She felt his lips touch her eyelids, one after the other, before working round the whole of her face, her ears, her throat. She hadn't been aware of how tense she was, but as he continued to slowly rain little burning kisses on her skin she relaxed, her mouth ready for his when he finally took it. He explored the inner sweetness with voluptuous pleasure, and she began to tremble as it brought forth sensations she'd never experienced before.

'You're beautiful, soft, exquisite…' His voice was shaking with desire, but still he took his time, beginning to undress her slowly and encouraging her to do the same to him. She was shy and fumbling at first, but his fingers guided her when she was unsure, and then he was clad only in his trousers and boots, his magnificent chest and shoulders bare to her wandering hands. She felt his muscles clench and move beneath her fingertips, awe at the power of his body drying her mouth, but he gave her time to get used to feeling and touching him before he peeled her chemise away from her breasts and put his lips to the hard peaks.

She jolted with the impact of his mouth on her engorged nipples, the fire in the grate reflected in her body as ripples of heat turned her liquid. She was barely aware when at last she was naked before him, but as he gathered her up in his arms and carried her into the bedroom, again lit by the flames of a crackling log fire in the fireplace, she turned her head into his shoulder, suddenly shy again.

'It's all right, my love. I won't hurt you.' He laid her gently on the satin quilt covering the big bed, peeling off the last of his clothes before lying down at the side of her and kissing her again and again. 'Trust me. I love you….'

Slowly, like before, she relaxed against him, and when she was once again fluid he began to touch and taste her with delicate eroticism. In her innocence she had no idea of the control he was displaying, but he was rewarded by her feverish delight as he led her on and on in the game of love, constantly checking his passion until she was ready for more intimate caresses, knowing it would be a crime to rush her.

It was a long, long time before he carefully eased

himself between her thighs. In spite of her desire she was very tight, but then the brief hindrance was gone and her softness welcomed him. She held on to him with all her might, exulting in the knowledge that she was his, that this was what it meant to be a wife. And then the warm throbbing in the core of her being became stronger and stronger, and she ceased to think, only to feel. She was unaware of the little moans of pleasure she was giving, but Luke wasn't, and his gratitude at her complete giving of herself so generously urged him on as he a carved a place inside her for himself.

When the climax came it took them to a place outside of themselves, a place where only lovers could go, a place of light and sensation and burning bliss. She was dazed, enraptured by the sensations he had brought forth, her voice holding a note of wonder as she murmured, 'I never knew…'

'Nor did I, my love. Nor did I." He eased the covers from under them and gently drew them over her as he fitted her into his side, his arm round her and his other hand brushing wisps of hair from her flushed face.

'What if we had missed each other that night I fainted in the snow?' she said after a few moments, turning to look into his face. 'What if you had been a few minutes earlier or later? What if you hadn't saved me? What if—?'

'No more what ifs.' He placed a finger on her lips, the brooding quality to his dark face absent for once and the lines of his face almost boyish. 'We were meant to find each other, Connie. You are the other half of me. I believe that with every fibre of my being. It's not just that I love you…' He raised himself on one elbow, taking up a handful of her rich silky hair and letting it run through his fingers. 'You're in the essence of my soul, my spirit. I could not have suffered this life without you and been the man I was meant to be.'

'And now you don't have to.' She smiled at him mistily, reaching up and drawing his mouth down to hers.

It was much, much later, when they had loved again and Connie was fast asleep, curled into the crook of his arm, that Luke gazed down at his sleeping wife in the dim light from the flickering fire. His voice husky with a gratitude that was inexpressible but which he knew he would feel towards her till his dying day, he murmured, 'Now I don't have to, my love. But it wasn't I who saved you that day. It was never that, but you who saved me. And one day you will come to understand that.'

He could hear the faint distant sound of the church bells, welcoming the Christ Child, and for the first time since he had lost his son he could allow himself to picture Jack's little face and hold him close to his heart again. He wasn't gone. He was in a different place, that was all, and he mustn't shut him out through pain and grief but be thankful he had known him, if only for so short a time. Jack deserved that. He deserved to be re-membered with joy.

His eyes wet, he clasped Connie tighter to him, and even in her sleep she murmured his name and curled closer.

And so it was always to remain.

* * * * *

Tilly of Tap House

Carol Wood

Carol Wood says: 'Writing has always been a wonderful hobby! My medical stories are based on my experiences in a lively doctors' practice and published by Mills & Boon. In the millennium came historicals, as I'd recorded all those tales that drifted down through my family. The first book, *Lizzie of Langley Street*, was published by Simon & Schuster.

With family living on the Isle of Dogs, colourful parties always rekindled the fascination of the East End. As a youngster, I wrote much of it down. One vivid memory of an elderly doctor inspires this story, *Tilly of Tap House*. I hope to continue writing in both genres and have lots of good ideas stored up to add to those books I've already written. I've web pages on the internet, with both Mills & Boon and Simon & Schuster, where all my books are listed—and hopefully those yet to come!'

Carol writes as Carol Rivers for Simon & Schuster.

With grateful thanks to the Island History Trust,
the Island History News and the curator
of the Trust, Eve Hostettler.

CHAPTER ONE

October 1928

'CRIPES, look at them shoes! They're posher than I've ever seen in me life!' exclaimed the skinny little girl with copper coloured curls bouncing all over her head. She was peering from behind the heavy chintz curtains of the tall window of the basement room.

'Shh, Cessie,' whispered the extremely thin fourteen year old boy standing next to her. 'Miss Tilly will hear you and you're supposed to be in bed.'

'I ain't tired.'

'Well, you should be.'

'What's going on?' thirteen-year-old Molly demanded as she came to join her brother and sister. 'What's all the excitement about?'

'Him!' Seven-year-old Cecilia—Cessie to all who knew her—pressed her nose against the window, bringing a blush to the glass as she returned the smile of the man standing on the steps outside.

The three children crowded closer, trying to get a

better view as they inspected the stranger now frowning slightly under their scrutiny.

'Is he coming in 'ere?'

'No, he's just lookin'.'

'What's he doin' lookin'?'

'I dunno, do I?' Frank answered his sisters impatiently. 'I ain't a mind-reader, am I?'

'You gonna open the door?'

'No, 'cos he ain't knocked yet!'

'Children! What are you doing?' a voice called from across the room. The curtain immediately fell back into place and all three heads bounced to attention.

'There's a gent on the steps, Miss Tilly.' It was Frank who pulled his two sisters beside him and added anxiously, 'And a bigwig by the looks of him. Got a pair of shoes you can see yer boat race in. He might be one of them children's inspectors, do you fink?'

Tilly frowned at her three charges, her very blue eyes hidden slightly by her shining fringe of straw coloured hair. 'Not very likely at this time of night, Frank,' she assured him, causing all three to let out a big sigh.

'Is someone gonna come and 'ave us all locked up, then?' Cessie demanded dramatically, her brown eyes as big as saucers.

'No, course not, Cess,' Frank assured his little sister. 'Not if we've got Miss Tilly to speak up for us.'

'But Dr Tapper don't approve of us livin' down here,' Molly added worriedly. 'And it ain't like we got somewhere to hide, is it? We ain't got no parents and no 'ome either!'

Tilly's kind heart squeezed with pity, just as it had

when she'd first seen the children, two months ago. They had stumbled through the surgery door awash with lice and scabs. Cessie had been running a fever, and all three had been half starved. Her orphans of the storm, as she called them, were unwanted, unloved and utterly dependent on her now. How could she turn them out? Hadn't life been cruel enough already? Their father had abandoned them and their mother had died from tuber-culosis. They had been passed from one distant relative to another and finally thrown on the streets.

Molly still suffered nightmares, and Cessie's health had only just improved. If Frank hadn't had the presence of mind—and the courage—to bring them to the sur-gery, Cessie at the very least would be dead by now.

But even Dr Tapper, as good and compassionate a man as he was, had warned her they couldn't stay at Tap House. It was all very well taking them in whilst Cessie recovered. But to provide a permanent roof over their heads was out of the question. For how could she, Tilly, of no great means herself, hope to feed and clothe them on her small wage?

Yet she still hoped for a miracle to turn up, just as it had twenty-six years ago for herself. Only a few days old, and left in a filthy sack to die of the cold at Tiller's Wharf, she had been found by the kind Sisters of Mercy and taken under their wing. She'd been given a second chance at life. Now she wanted these orphans to have one too.

A loud rap came on the door. Three sets of brown eyes gazed up at her.

'He knocked, then!'

'He wants to come in!'

'He might be an inspector after all!'

Tilly smiled reassuringly. 'Stop fretting, Cessie. Of course he's not. Now, run along all of you, and put on your nightclothes.'

Reluctantly, they all trooped past her and disappeared along the passage to their room.

Pressing her hair neatly into place, Tilly went to see who was at the door.

'Good evening.' A tall young man stood there. His dark hair and even darker features were only just illuminated in the light. She noted, as had Frank, how well dressed he was, in fashionable narrow trousers and a single-breasted jacket fastened over a broad chest.

Tilly was a little put out to be caught in her uniform. After a busy day's nursing the starch had all but disappeared from her white apron. 'Yes?' she asked politely. 'How may I help you?'

'I'm sorry to disturb you and your family…' He faltered as he glanced over her shoulder. A raindrop fell from the gutter above and landed on his nose. With a fine large hand he carefully removed it. 'But I'm looking for Dr Tapper.'

Tilly gave him another discreet inspection. Without doubt this man was not the usual sort of visitor to the surgery. Dr Tapper's patients consisted entirely of the poor and destitute of the Isle of Dogs: a horseshoe shaped piece of land surrounded on three sides by water, and the heart of London's East End.

'Have you knocked hard on the door above?'

He nodded slowly. 'Yes, indeed. But there was no reply.'

'Well, that's odd.' Tilly was puzzled. 'I left the doctor there not thirty minutes ago. We'd finished surgery and no one was left to see. And I'm certain he had no calls to make.'

'And you are…?' he asked politely.

'I'm the doctor's assistant—Mrs Dainty,' Tilly replied a little haughtily, mirroring his slightly aloof air. She pulled herself up to her full five feet four inches, aware that for some reason this dark-eyed stranger wasn't bringing out the best in her. And yet there was something about his handsome features, a long aquiline nose and generous mouth, that softened the contours of his face and added a gentle elegance to his bearing. 'You're sure you gave a hefty knock?'

'Of course. Twice, as it happens.'

A man of very little warmth, Tilly decided as they eyed one another cautiously, although for a few moments as he stared at her she felt a little shiver go down her spine, and in confusion she blushed. Trying to compose herself, she saw no alternative but to go up to the house and investigate.

'Please step in whilst I get my coat.' She was trying hard to remember her manners, although it was not at all easy in the presence of this stranger, who had such a dark and enquiring gaze that she really didn't feel quite herself.

Once inside, he stood stiffly as his gaze swept the room. All seemed to meet with his approval. Even though the 'airey,' or basement floor, of Tap House was not lavish, it was clean and cosy. All her beloved furniture was here, and the bits and pieces that she and her late husband, James, had saved so hard for.

'A very charming room,' he said admiringly.

'Thank you.' Tilly was proud of her small domain, with the fire burning brightly in the grate, and the two large armchairs either side, overflowing with cushions. Although the scarlet settle in the corner sprouted horse-hair from its seams, it still looked gracious. Her big oak dresser opposite was stuffed with china and books. And Tilly was proud to say that she had read every one of them. At least once!

Leaving him to his thoughts, she made her way to the children's room. On entering, she nearly knocked them flying.

She arched an eyebrow as they assembled themselves in front of her. 'Well, I dare say you heard every word?'

As usual, all three heads nodded.

'He ain't an inspector,' said Frank with a degree of relief in his voice. 'He's just looking for Dr Tapper.'

'And he don't like leaky gutters,' said Molly.

'And you're going upstairs to let 'im in,' Cessie added cheerfully, twirling round in her nightgown.

Tilly kept a straight face and clapped her hands. 'In bed, all of you!' She indicated the big iron bedstead the girls slept in and the single mattress on the floor that Frank used.

'Do I 'ave to go too?' Frank objected. 'These two are much younger than me.'

'A good night's sleep won't do you any harm,' Tilly told him. 'You've a long day ahead of you at the market tomorrow. Now, goodnight and sleep well.'

Last week Frank had found a temporary job. A boy had been needed to roast chestnuts on the market brazier. Now Frank often brought home a big bag of chestnuts for roasting on the fire. He always complained he had no privacy with his sisters, though quickly admitted the arrangement of sleeping in the same room was better than on the cold and draughty streets. He loved his sisters to distraction, and considered himself their protector. Tilly admired him greatly for his attitude.

In her own room, she took off her apron and put on her coat. Glancing swiftly in the mirror, she saw a slender young woman with a serious blue gaze. She hoped she looked presentable to the visitor outside. Though she had no real reason to care so much about her appearance—other than her pride! And in some strange way this young man was testing it.

They found the house in darkness. The three-storey building comprised the airey, Dr Tapper's practice on the ground floor, and his living quarters above. It looked very gloomy without light.

Tilly knocked twice.

'Just as I thought. No one is home,' her companion observed.

Tilly could think of no reason why the doctor would be out. If an emergency arose he would always tell her first.

She opened the door with her key. A strange quietness filled the air. The surgery was to the right, and the passage regarded as the waiting area to the left, whilst a short staircase led up to Dr Tapper's private quarters.

'That's very strange.' Tilly put on the gaslights. Shadows cast themselves over the shabby walls and danced on the row of empty wooden chairs.

She led the way into the surgery, where the young man looked up in surprise at the variety of coloured bottles and jars filling the shelves. Tilly was quite used to the sight of Dr Tapper's unique dispensary, the many herbs, lotions, creams and balms that were his armoury against disease. Tilly felt obliged to explain their contents, but then a loud groan came from the examination room.

They went in. An elderly man lay on the floor, struggling to sit up.

'Uncle William!' The young man rushed to help him to his feet. 'What happened, Uncle?'

'I don't know, Harry. I must have blacked out.'

'Let me get you to the chair.'

Tilly pushed a cushion behind his back as he sat down.

'I'm all right now. Don't worry.' Dr Tapper looked up at the two concerned faces. 'Tilly…this is Dr Harry Fleet, my nephew.'

'Yes, we've met briefly.'

'Uncle, I must examine you.'

'That really isn't necessary.'

'Oh, it most certainly is. You've had quite a bump on the head, by the looks of it, and we must get to the bottom of why you passed out.'

Dr Tapper pushed back his dishevelled grey hair. He looked up at Tilly. 'Could I ask you, my dear, to make us all a cup of tea upstairs, and we'll join you soon?'

'Of course.' Tilly had never heard Dr Tapper mention his nephew before, but they rarely had time to discuss personal matters. Their lives were full enough as it was with their patients' ills. But now poor Dr Tapper had ills of his own!

* * *

'How are you feeling, Uncle?'

'Better, thank you, Harry.' Dr Tapper was sitting in his armchair, a bump on his forehead but no bones broken.

Tilly had built up the fire in the drawing room and it was bringing a little more colour to his cheeks. She had also made a pot of hot, sweet tea, which had been drunk and the pot replenished.

Dr Tapper lifted his hand weakly. 'Please sit down, my dear. You're making my head swim, fussing over me like this.'

'Yes,' agreed Harry Fleet, seating himself. 'The fire is warming Uncle William and you have done all you can to make us both comfortable.'

Tilly sat in one of the big chairs. She had tried to insist her employer take a little time off during the day, but so many relied on him that he felt obliged to keep the doors open.

'I'm so sorry I gave you a fright, Tilly, my dear,' Dr Tapper apologised. 'When you left this evening I had no idea that I was about to have one of my little turns.' He sighed lightly. 'It's only to be expected at my time of life.'

'Are you prescribing medication for yourself, Uncle?'

'Yes, a little pick-me-up.'

'Nothing from those shelves downstairs, I hope?'

This brought a smile to the elderly doctor's face. 'I know my dispensary must seem very antiquated to you, Harry, but my remedies have served me well over the years.'

'Quite so. But please allow me to prescribe something for you myself—that is, after I've given you a thorough examination.'

'That really won't be necessary, Harry.'

'I am sorry to disagree, Uncle, but if you don't take greater care of yourself—your heart in particular—you may risk a much greater danger than just blacking out.'

Tilly gasped softly.

'It's all right, Tilly,' Dr Tapper patted her hand. 'It's not as bad as it sounds.'

'But you should be resting!' she exclaimed.

'Mrs Dainty is quite right,' Harry Fleet agreed. 'You must indeed rest. I shall be happy to help you, as I'm on leave from work, and will gladly act as your deputy. The visit to my mother in Bath can be postponed.'

Dr Tapper sighed heavily. 'But you've been abroad for so long, Harry, and your mother is expecting you.'

'She will insist I stay here when she knows of the circumstances,' Harry Fleet said firmly. 'I'm sure I will manage perfectly as I shall have Mrs Dainty to help me.'

'Tilly is a very good nurse,' Dr Tapper agreed. 'And a great tonic to the patients.'

'I am sure we'll get along well. Now, we mustn't keep you any longer, Mrs Dainty.'

Tilly stood up. 'I'll make up a bed in the guest room before I leave.'

The young doctor stretched out his hand. 'Please, don't trouble yourself. I'm quite domesticated, and will see to everything when Uncle William has retired.'

Dr Tapper nodded. 'You can be sure I'm in safe hands, Tilly.'

'Please let me see you out.'

She rose to her feet. 'Goodnight, then.'

'Sleep well, my dear.'

'What time am I to expect you in the morning?' Harry Fleet asked as he escorted her downstairs.

'Seven o'clock,' she replied. 'As you know I have a key, and can let myself in.'

'Good grief! That's dreadfully early! Surely you must see to your husband and children first?'

'I'm a widow, Dr Fleet.'

He looked startled. 'Oh, I'm so sorry to hear that.'

'The children aren't mine,' she added carefully, 'and are only staying with me temporarily.'

He still looked very bewildered, but nodded all the same.

'I always come up to cook breakfast and light the fire before surgery, so that Dr Tapper's rooms are kept warm.'

He was silent for a moment, and then smiled. 'Doing all that whilst I'm here will be quite unnecessary. I'll make certain that Uncle William eats a healthy breakfast. As for the fire, it will take me no time at all to prepare. So if you'd like to delay your arrival until— say—eight, that would be most agreeable with me.' Without waiting for a reply he opened the door. 'Good evening, Mrs Dainty.'

Tilly felt very upset as she left. He seemed not to want her around. And yet she might be misconstruing his aloofness. After all, his suggestion for her to come in to surgery a little later would give her longer in the mornings to prepare herself and the children. What would tomorrow bring? she wondered a little anxiously. And how would the patients themselves react to this unexpected turn of events?

'What's he like, then, Miss Tilly?' Frank demanded at breakfast next morning.

'Is he rich?' Cessie pushed more bread in her mouth than Tilly thought it humanly possible to swallow in one go.

'Has he got a missus?' Molly enquired, scooping the last of her porridge daintily on to her spoon.

'I don't know—times three,' Tilly replied as she filled four large mugs with hot tea. 'Now, hurry up and finish your breakfasts.'

'Ain't you going upstairs?' Molly asked suspiciously.

'No, not till eight o'clock today.'

'I ain't heard Dr Tapper speak of him 'afore,' interrupted Frank as he wiped his mouth on his shirtsleeve. 'He don't sound much like our sort. Don't reckon he'll hang around long.' He grinned under his bushy mop of chestnut curls.

'Will Dr Tapper get better?' Molly asked, voicing Tilly's own thoughts.

'Course he will!' Cessie established, as Tilly dealt with a particularly fierce tangle in her hair. ' He's only got a cold, I 'spect.'

'I'm sure he'll be better very soon,' Tilly said diplomatically as she withdrew the comb from Cessie's hair. She was inclined to agree with Frank, but had no intention of saying so.

'If I said I had a belly ache, would you let me stay

home?' Cessie enquired as she pushed the last crumb of bread in her mouth.

'No, I'd say if you did have a belly ache it was because you'd put too much in it.'

They all burst out laughing.

Tilly was a little nervous as she went upstairs. As she let herself in, all was quiet. Was Frank right? What if Harry Fleet was not their sort at all and disappeared as quickly as he had arrived?

Tilly turned her mind away from her worries and went to the scullery to prepare for the day ahead.

CHAPTER TWO

TILLY wrote the date—Tuesday October 9th 1928—on the top of the sheet and set it aside. In an hour that sheet would be full of names, and she would have turned it over and started to write on the other side. There were always more patients to see at the beginning of the week than at the end. This was because on Thursday and Friday the women were too busy trying to pay off their debts. They had to appease the tallyman or reclaim their Sunday best clothes from "Uncle", the pawnbroker.

None of them expected much money from their husbands. Their pay packets were opened at the pub; a man and his ale could not be parted until time was called and only then did the men arrive home—if their legs were able to support them!

Tilly regarded herself as fortunate not to be one of those poor women. Her husband James had been tee-total, and a kindly man. Though he had been much older than herself, by fourteen years, they had been very happy. They had only been married four years when he'd stepped in front of a tram and been killed. It had been a dreadful shock and one she still hadn't quite recovered from.

Tilly looked down the passage at the careworn faces of the men, women and children of the Isle of Dogs. Many of these poor souls would not see the winter through. The old and infirm, the young and weak. Coughs, colds, sneezes and flu were rife. The children were restless whilst the adults tried to keep order. Already a baby was screaming—she had little Noah's name down for the first to be seen as he was bawling at the top of his lungs and only caused everyone else to shout above him.

By the time the doctor appeared it was chaos. But as Dr Harry Fleet stepped forward to meet his patients the noise ceased.

''Oo's he?'

'Lost yer way, sonny boy?'

'Where's Dr Tapper?'

'Blimey, this toff's orf 'is mark, ain't he?'

Tilly listened to the comments, then made her announcement. 'This is Dr Fleet, who is standing in for Dr Tapper. Unfortunately Dr Tapper is indisposed.'

'What's that in plain English?'

'We don't want no quacks in 'ere!'

'We ain't got no money, if that's what yer after!'

Tilly grabbed the sheet of paper and hurried up to Dr Fleet. 'Good morning,' she said in a professional manner, standing straight in her white apron. But the doctor wasn't listening. His jaw had dropped in surprise at the crowded waiting area. 'Mondays and Tuesday are the busiest,' she added quickly, hoping to soften the blow.

'I'm relieved to hear it.' He smiled bravely at the narrowed eyes all staring curiously in his direction.

Tilly followed him in to his room. He sat down in the chair and straightened his tie. 'How is Dr Tapper this morning?' she asked anxiously.

Clearing his throat, he nodded. 'I'm pleased to be able to tell you he's feeling quite rested. I've urged him to consult a colleague of mine—a specialist in these matters.' He shifted his position under her scrutiny. 'And I'm sure he'll see the sense in it—eventually.'

Which meant, Tilly decided, that Dr Tapper was as stubborn as ever and refusing to do something he didn't want to do. 'Yes, I'm sure he will,' she agreed, a little hesitantly.

'And—er—one thing more, Mrs Dainty. I…er…would like to express my appreciation for all you've done for my uncle. He tells me how well you've looked after him, and with your…er…young people to care for too. I know he is most appreciative.' He looked into her eyes and Tilly felt their darkness lighten, and the smile that edged his lips gave her again that strange feeling inside: a little shiver of expectancy, a shudder of awareness that was almost like excitement as he held her gaze.

'Now,' the young doctor continued as he dragged his eyes slowly back to the desk, 'I think we'd better begin, don't you?'

With slightly trembling hands Tilly gave him her list. She snatched her fingers back quickly, so that he wouldn't see. 'I've written a few notes on some of the patients,' she explained rapidly, afraid her voice would reveal her feelings. 'Not all, as there are just too many to get down at once.' She indicated the passage. 'But there's a small baby outside, Noah Symes. He's six months old and cries a great deal—'

'Yes, indeed. I can hear,' the doctor agreed, frowning at the wails but giving a little smile again.

'Dr Tapper usually prescribes gripe water. Noah has a lot of wind.' She pointed to a tall, thin bottle standing on the shelf.

'You mean one of *those?*' All mirth left the doctor's handsome face. He stood up and cleared his throat once more. 'Mrs Dainty—'

'Everyone calls me Tilly,' she interrupted quietly, straightening her back, relieved that they seemed to have returned to a professional basis.

'Well—er—Tilly, I'm sure I shall come to an assessment of my own, once I have examined the infant.'

Tilly nodded, thinking but not saying that all he would discover, whilst wasting a great deal of time, was an extremely healthy child who fed too greedily.

'Please bring Noah and his mother in.'

'Sadly, Noah's mother died when she gave birth,' she explained before she turned to go. 'The grandmother now looks after him—although, like the rest of the community, she struggles to make ends meet.'

'What of the father?'

Tilly shook her head. 'I'm afraid no one knows where he is. Or even who he is.'

Tilly saw his features soften as he nodded slowly. 'You're right, Tilly, a very sad story indeed. Let's see in what way we can help, shall we?'

It was clear the young doctor intended many changes,

Tilly reflected as she went to find Noah, but thank goodness he also appeared to have his patients' welfare at heart. And she certainly couldn't discount the generous thanks that he had expressed to her when talking of his uncle.

By five o'clock that evening Dr Fleet had acquainted himself with cases like Bert Singer and his wheezy chest, young Emily Tanner and her four brothers, all at various stages of the measles, and an eleven-year-old girl called Grace Mount with what her mother called 'a bout of the vapours.' Stanley Horn, like many veterans of the war, was an amputee. He had lost a leg and was in constant pain. Attending the surgery on his crutches was a feat in itself. Tilly had noted that the doctor had talked at length with this man and offered to return him home by car. But Mr Horn had proudly refused, though he'd confided to Tilly that he been prescribed a new medicine.

It wasn't until half past six that she closed the door and, returning to the surgery, found the doctor absorbed in paperwork.

'I must compliment you on your filing system,' he told her as she stood by the desk. 'The information's been very useful throughout the day.'

'Thank you,' she replied, blushing slightly at the unexpected compliment.

'However…some of the treatments are…' He hesitated, handing her the dog-eared papers to view. 'A little unorthodox.'

Before her were the details of Charlie Atkins'

medical history. As usual at this time of year, he had complained bitterly of the return of his 'agues'.

'These complaints,' mused the doctor, 'are very widespread—from the head downward, covering most regions of the body. On your notes I see that "tincture of camomile, top right shelf" is prescribed to treat them, or, "liquorice pills, third drawer down".'

Tilly nodded. 'Yes, that's correct.'

'But I don't understand.' The doctor frowned. 'Mr Atkins was extremely put out when I asked to examine him fully. In fact he flatly refused and disappeared out of the door.'

'Your uncle usually prescribes the same remedy,' Tilly explained patiently. 'Mr Atkins always comes to surgery before Christmas, and he was probably expecting the camomile and liquorice to be given to him immediately.'

'Camomile and liquorice!' he muttered in a puzzled voice. 'What on earth does he want those things for?'

Tilly's heart sank a little, but she tried to explain. 'The two combined seem to ease the pain of his lumbago and arthritis. His "agues", as he calls them, are caused by his damp cottage—no more than a hut, really—always prone to flooding when the river bursts its banks.'

'But why is he not removed and given somewhere decent to live? The poor man is virtually crippled by these diseases!' the doctor protested.

'Who would give it to him?' Tilly asked simply. 'Where can he go? The other houses on the island aren't much better.' She frowned at him. 'Haven't you seen for yourself?'

He shook his head. 'You forget, Tilly, I'm a stranger here. I haven't stepped foot outside of this place.'

'Then you must certainly go and see for yourself,' she advised.

'Indeed I will.'

She was about to leave when he stopped her. 'Just one thing more.' He paused, appearing to choose his words carefully. 'Some of the patients today informed me that you yourself dispense some of these "remedies"?'

'Yes, quite often,' she agreed. 'If the doctor's busy or the prescription is a repeated one.'

'But isn't that rather a big responsibility to undertake?' he asked doubtfully.

She felt upset at his question. 'I may not have written qualifications, Dr Fleet, but I learnt how to nurse in the orphanage where I was brought up by the Sisters of Mercy. And when I left there I went into service at Hailing House, a charitable institution on the island. I've spent my whole life nursing the sick and destitute.'

'I don't doubt your skills for one moment, Tilly,' he replied quietly, 'but I wonder about these so-called "remedies". How safe are they? Even though my uncle might have the confidence to dispense them, what if a traditional medication was needed, yet not given?'

'I'm quite sure they haven't killed anyone yet! Now, if there's nothing more to be done, I'll go and see Dr Tapper before I leave,' she said, holding her head high.

What a difficult young man he was, she thought as she made her way upstairs. She was still feeling annoyed when she reached the drawing room door. It took her several deep breaths to calm down before going in. Why was it that he disturbed her so?

Dr Tapper was sitting by the fire. 'Ah, Tilly, come and sit beside me. How was your day?'

'Very good, Dr Tapper, thank you.'

'How did my nephew fare?'

She didn't want to upset the elderly man. She thought too much of him to express her true feeling on the subject, which would perhaps send him into a relapse!

'He's patient—and thorough—and I'm sure he'll soon accustom himself to this type of work,' she managed to answer.

Dr Tapper looked thoughtful. 'You must make allowances for him, Tilly,' he advised her in a gentle tone. 'The East End is very different to his normal environment, working in the colonies.' He patted her hand. 'We're very lucky that he thought to pay us a visit.'

Tilly wasn't convinced that luck was entirely on their side. Although it had to be said very few would have taken on the workload that was Dr Tapper's. However, it remained to be seen whether the young doctor would maintain his interest after a few more gruelling days in surgery.

She quickly busied herself by drawing the blanket over Dr Tapper's legs and tucking in the sides to keep out the draughts. As she did so she noticed that the fire had been well stoked. A small array of medicine bottles was on a table at his side. There was a jug of water and fruit to hand, and all the little comforts—a newspaper and book, his slippers on his feet, and his pipe had been provided too. Harry Fleet did have a few redeeming features, then, she decided reluctantly.

'You're very kind, Tilly, but you must go home now. The children will be waiting for you.'

She nodded, waiting for the next question which she knew must come.

'Have you decided what to do with them?'

'I'm thinking hard, Dr Tapper.'

'An institution, you know, is a far better prospect than living on the streets.' He smiled tiredly. 'Don't leave it too long. You've had enough heartbreak in your young life, my dear. And with every day the bond will grow stronger.'

She looked into his dear face, with his bushy grey eyebrows over kind eyes that made him look like a guardian angel. She knew he was only thinking of her welfare. But how could she tell him that the bond between her and the children was already glue-tight?

He stifled a yawn. 'I'm sorry, my dear, I seem to be very tired of late.'

Tilly propped the cushions behind him and dropped more coal on the fire. When she had kindled the flames, she turned to ask him if there was anything more she could do.

His head had dropped forward. He was fast asleep.

Quietly, Tilly closed the door and went downstairs. She was disappointed to find Dr Fleet waiting for her. Standing very tall in his dark suit, he looked tired, but he offered a small smile. Tilly thought that if he tried just a little harder there could possibly be a dazzle to it. However, that was not to be.

'Thank you for your help, Tilly.'

'Can I bring up a meal for the doctor and yourself?'

'No, thank you. I have it all in hand.'

As she went to walk out he opened the door for her. His arm fleetingly brushed against hers as they reached for the lock at the same time. She jumped a little. The collision seemed to have the same effect on him as he looked, somewhat startled, into her eyes. Tilly felt that same excitement flash inside her—a sensation that disturbed her so much her cheeks were quick to redden and her heart started to beat very fast. Why did she feel intrigued and attracted by his presence as his dark gaze bore down on her? Why did it take all her self-control to try to act as normal?

Forcing her eyes away from his powerful gaze, she turned. 'Goodnight, Dr Fleet.'

'Goodnight, Tilly.'

Holding herself erect, she walked into the night. Before she entered the airey she stood still and recovered her breath. Her body seemed to be suffering from a severe case of anxiety. Dr Harry Fleet was a most unsettling and disturbing man!

Because of the wet weather, the patients' complaints were plentiful over the next few days. The young doctor worked long hours, often well into the evening, and Tilly was at his side, although she was still annoyed at his questioning. However, her anger had cooled slightly and she felt much relieved that Dr Tapper had agreed to rest. But on Friday evening Dr Fleet summoned her.

He had a worried look on his face. 'Tilly, I've per-

suaded Uncle William to do as I recommend and seek
further advice on his condition. I'm going to drive him
up to town on Monday for a consultation with my colleague Dr Wolf at St Mary's hospital.'

'I'm very glad to hear that he's agreed,' Tilly said, truly
relieved that Dr Tapper had at last listened to reason.

'Uncle is, of course, reluctant to be away from Tap
House for any length of time, but I've assured him that
we'll be back by midday if we start out early. I'm afraid
I'll have to leave it to you to ask those who come on
Monday to wait for my return.'

'Everyone will understand, I'm sure,' Tilly assured him.

He smiled, a rare but charming warmth lighting up
his face, making him look so different. 'That's all
settled, then,' he added with a twinkle in his eye.

'As you'll have a long day ahead of you, would you
like me to cook breakfast before you go?' Tilly tried
again, encouraged by this little happening. 'Dr Tapper
will need building up before the strenuous journey to the
hospital, even though you have your very comfortable
car to take him in.'

'On this occasion that might be a good idea,' he
agreed, with another accommodating smile that made
Tilly's heart twist a little. But then he paused, crook-
ing one dark eyebrow. 'However, I wouldn't want you
to leave the children unsupervised—what are their
ages, Tilly?'

She was a little wary at his question, but his face held
genuine interest. 'Frank is fourteen, Molly thirteen and
Cessie just seven,' she told him evenly.

'Quite a handful.' He nodded. 'May I ask how they

come to be—?' He was stopped by a sudden knock on the door.

'Oh, dear! Am I at the right place?' a young lady enquired when Tilly opened it. She was very well dressed, in a smart wrapover coat with a fur collar, and a cloche hat over her neat short hair. Her very large brown eyes looked startled as she gazed into the shabby interior of Tap House.

'Who are you looking for?'

'It's all right, Tilly,' Harry Fleet interrupted. 'This young lady is Rosalind Darraway—a friend of mine.'

The girl entered and embraced him, a cloud of sweet perfume flowing over Tilly as she did so. They seemed to know each other well, falling at once into animated conversation.

Tilly went to find her coat. By the time she returned they were ascending the stairs and didn't notice her leaving. They made a very handsome couple, she thought, he so tall and dark and she so elegant.

Was she the doctor's young lady? Tilly wondered as she hurried downstairs.

For some reason, instead of feeling grateful that she had been relieved of his interrogation about the children, she felt quite put out again.

On Saturday afternoon Tilly took the girls to the market. Frank gave them a free pennyworth of chestnuts to eat by the brazier. It was a special treat to browse through the stalls, and though every penny was accounted for now that she had a family to feed, Tilly always found a few coppers for sweets on the way home.

On Monday Tilly rose bright and early. She left Frank to look after the girls whilst she went up to the house to cook breakfast for the two men whilst they prepared for their journey to town.

Complaining heartily that it was all a lot of fuss and bother for no real reason, Dr Tapper finally allowed himself to be driven off in the big car.

Soon after eight o'clock, the patients poured through the door. Tilly explained that there was no one to see them, and they would all have to wait until midday, but Ted Barnes, a burly docker, held out his arm.

'I'll have bleeded to def by twelve o'clock,' he objected, unwrapping a bloody cloth and displaying the injury.

Tilly saw that the cut had just missed an artery. It needed to be cleansed and stitched immediately.

This was well within her capabilities, and Tilly saw no reason why she should watch a grown man faint away on the passage floor!

Once she had attended to Ted Barnes, another casualty followed. Arnold Wise was the landlord of the Two Fighting Cocks, and had suffered a gash to his hand from a broken bottle. Tilly felt obliged to do as she had done for Ted Barnes, and made swift work of attending to the problem.

By one o'clock there were many complaints at the young doctor's absence. After waiting all morning, the women with families had to get back to their children, and the men to work, if there was any to be had, waiting on 'the stones' as they called it, for casual labour in the docks. At two o'clock, a queue stretched to the pavement. Objections abounded.

Elderly Mrs Stopps had waited all day for attention. 'You always do me ears for me, Tilly gel. Why can't you do 'em again?'

Tilly tried to explain that Dr Fleet frowned on the old 'remedies.' Furthermore, he was not agreeable to her dispensing them.

'What's he gonna give me instead, then?' Mrs Stopps demanded loudly. 'A new pair of ears?'

'No, but he'll examine—' Tilly shouted back but the elderly lady shook her head.

'Look, I'm as deaf as a post, Tilly gel. If I sit on that chair any longer me bum will take root to the wood. Now, himself ain't gonna know you've put camphor and oil in me ears if no one tells him, is he?'

The blackmail worked, and Tilly saw to Mrs Stopps. As word got round that Tilly was 'seeing,' the queue slowly diminished.

But when Mrs Mount arrived with Grace it was a different matter. 'My girl is worse than ever today. Just look at her! She ain't gonna be able to walk 'ome.'

Grace looked very ill as she slumped on the chair. 'We'll lay her on the couch and try to make her comfy while you wait,' Tilly said at once.

With Mrs Mount's help she took the child to the couch under the stairs that was used for very sick or fainting patients. Tilly shooed away the children who were scrambling all over it, and drew a blanket gently over Grace's thin, fevered body.

'The young doctor didn't know what it was the other day,' Mrs Mount complained. 'He told me to bring her back the next day if she weren't no better. But what wiv one fing and another I was too busy. There's other kids at home, and I have to get me neighbour to come in and watch them while I'm away.'

Tilly knew how difficult it was for people like Mrs Mount. Most island families comprised five or six children at least, some as many as ten or thirteen. Catering to their families' needs wore the women out very quickly.

Mrs Cribbens tapped her on the shoulder. ''Ere, Til, give us some of that green linctus, ducks, will you? The one you always doles out for me cough. Then I'll be off and out yer way.'

And so it went on. By half past three Tilly was still tending to the needs of the sick and distressed on her own. She was no longer concerned about the young doctor's approval. If she was able to help alleviate suffering, she did her best to do it.

CHAPTER THREE

IT WAS close to half past four when the doctor returned.

'I'm sorry to be late,' he apologised in a breathless voice to Tilly, who was on her knees in the surgery, attending to the swollen ankle of eight-year-old Georgie Parker. 'Uncle is staying for a few days at St Mary's. There are tests that need to be done and can't be rushed. I stayed to see him through some of them, which of course delayed me.'

'But he had no personal effects with him,' Tilly burst out, climbing to her feet.

'I saw that he had all he needed,' he replied, swiftly removing his coat and hat. 'Now, may I ask why you are wrapping this boy's leg in a particularly strange-looking bandage?'

Giving the young doctor the benefit of the doubt— he had endured a long and difficult day at the hospital for the benefit of Dr Tapper—she returned her concentration to the invalid. 'Georgie was kicking his ball and went over on his ankle. This is a compress soaked in arnica, a herb that's reputed to help reduce swellings.'

He looked very confused. 'What old wives' tale is this?'

Before Tilly could reply the door opened and Georgie's mother stood there. 'Is he done yet?' demanded Mrs Parker, looking flustered. 'Only I got the rest of the family to see to and me husband's dinner to cook.' She nodded to the doctor. 'Is it all right if I give yer me sixpence at the end of the week, Doctor, as I'm skint at the moment?'

Dr Fleet nodded abruptly. 'Yes, that's quite all right, Mrs Parker.'

'Good, I'll see yer gets it.' She took one look at her son and crooked her finger. 'Come on, Georgie, take me arm and 'op the best you can.'

Tilly helped Georgie to his feet. 'You must see that he puts his leg up and rests, Mrs Parker. And a teaspoon of Milk of Magnesia if he fails to obey.'

'Yer—two teaspoons I shouldn't wonder,' agreed Mrs Parker, and Georgie let out a loud protest—the first he had made during his treatment. His mother grabbed his arm and propelled him out of the room.

'Milk of Magnesia!' The bewildered expression was back on the doctor's face. 'Why, I've never heard of such a thing! Milk of Magnesia should only be used in a case of constipation or indigestion!'

'But Georgie doesn't know that,' replied Tilly calmly. 'As you saw by his reaction, he hates the very thought of it. The threat is enough to make him do as his mother tells him.'

With a frown on his face, the doctor took his seat at the desk. 'Well, you had better tell me who else you've seen to whilst I've been gone.'

Tilly decided the long list—and the explanations—could wait. 'I think you had better see Grace Mount first.'

'Grace Mount? The young girl who came before?'

'She's much worse, I'm afraid.'

'But why didn't her mother bring her back the following day if she wasn't any better?'

A scream outside caused them to rush into the passage. Mrs Mount was in tears as she shook her daughter's shoulders. 'I can't wake her!' she screamed. 'What's happened to my Grace?'

The doctor firmly took hold of her and sat her down on a chair. After briefly examining Grace, he lifted her into his arms and carried her into his room.

Tilly tried to restore calm in his absence, though Mrs Mount was very distressed, and it wasn't until a few minutes later that Tilly was able to join the doctor.

'She's very ill, Tilly,' he confirmed as he drew the blanket over Grace. 'I must get her to hospital quickly. It will take too long to call an ambulance, so I'll drive her there myself. I'm sorry, but everyone must wait again.'

After he had taken Grace out to the car and driven off, Tilly tried to comfort Mrs Mount. 'What's going to happen to my Grace?' she sobbed.

Everyone crowded round and offered their sympathy. All the pale, anxious faces stared up at Tilly. They had all seen the little girl in the doctor's arms and knew she was very ill. The whispered word amongst them was what they all feared, and Tilly had seen it before, in the infirmary of the orphanage and amongst the poor and sick of Hailing House.

'The Dip', as diphtheria was known, was a cruel

disease that could spread rapidly in the community. Was Grace the first to suffer its symptoms?

It was seven o'clock and all the patients had been seen— though Dr Fleet had been very quiet on his return.

When the doors were closed, and Tilly had tidied and swept the passage, she went into the doctor's room. He had removed his jacket and was rolling up his shirtsleeves.

'Tilly, where do we keep the carbolic?'

Tilly's heart sank. Carbolic disinfectant was used liberally when an outbreak of disease was threatening. 'It is diphtheria, then?'

He shrugged slightly. 'It's yet to be confirmed, but I'm afraid it looks like it.'

'What will happen to Grace?'

'They're transferring her to an isolation ward. All we can do is hope that it was caught in time and she has a strong enough constitution to fight it.'

Poor Grace, Tilly thought sadly. She hoped the little girl would be strong enough to endure, but she was so thin and undernourished, and the terrible disease was heartless.

'I will call this week to examine the rest of the family. Meanwhile we must set to work.'

They filled two pails with water and poured in the strong-smelling disinfectant. Tilly would have mopped the floors herself, but the doctor insisted on helping. When everything had been cleaned, there was a rap on the door. Tilly went to answer it.

'Sorry to bovver you, Miss Tilly,' Frank said as he stood outside. 'But we was wondering if you was all right? Molly tried her hand at cooking ternight, and it's going black in the stove. I dunno what it was like in the first place, mind. You know what Molly's cookin' is like.'

Tilly glanced at the big wall clock. It was almost eight. She hadn't realised it was so late. 'I'm coming now, Frank. Tell Molly I'm on my way.'

'Another patient to be seen?' the young doctor asked when she returned to his room where he was cleaning his desk.

'No, it was only Frank. He was wondering where I'd got to.'

'I'm sorry I've kept you so late.'

'It couldn't be helped.'

'I don't want to alarm you, but please watch Frank, Cessie and Molly for any relevant symptoms. A fever, swollen glands and unusual spots or sores. I'm sure you know well enough what to look for.'

'Should I be in the least bit concerned, Dr Fleet,' she assured him as she put on her coat, 'I would be knocking on your door no matter what time of night it is.'

Before she left he put his hand on her shoulder, and Tilly jumped at his touch. As she turned to look at him his eyes flickered gently, a soft, warm expression filling them even though seconds before they had looked tired and exhausted. His fingers lingered, seeming reluctant to let her go, and his words were gentle when he spoke, filled with deep concern. 'I hope you mean that, Tilly. I shall always be here for you if you want me.'

She nodded silently, unable to find her voice. Returning him a hesitant smile, she tried to calm the butterflies his words had set loose in her stomach. Once more she had to try to calm her scattered emotions as she left and ran down the airey steps. His touch had sent everything out of her mind!

Molly was waiting anxiously downstairs. The table was set and something that looked very much as if it had once been a pie was standing in the centre of it.

'I left it to cook a bit long,' Molly announced as her red curls bounced around her sticky face. 'We can eat the middle bit, though. That ain't burnt.'

When Cessie and Frank came into the room, they all began laughing. Tilly joined in the fun too, beginning to recover from the intimate moment she had shared with the doctor. She also kept quiet about her plans for the rest of the evening. A soak in carbolic was what every child dreaded. Many pans of water would have to be boiled on the stove and the tin bath brought in from the closet. Everyone hated the clinging, overpowering smell that lingered on the skin and hair for days and was the invisible badge of disease.

Tilly tried to break open the rock hard crust of the pie with a spoon.

'You need a saw for that,' Frank laughed.

'A sharp one,' Cessie giggled.

When the crust broke in two there were cries of delight and more laughter as the pie was divided between them. Despite having to chew very hard, most of it was eaten.

As they enjoyed themselves, Tilly's thoughts, having at last settled, strayed to Grace. Had the doctor got her to the hospital in time? Did any of the other children have symptoms? Would there be an outbreak—the outcome every family dreaded?

Tilly knew that word would have spread quickly by now. Women all over the island would be filling baths of carbolic tonight, just as she would. It was the only weapon they had, and one that even Dr Fleet had been swift to use to fight the disease.

For the rest of the week Tilly watched Frank, Molly and Cessie very carefully. She reminded them to wash their hands regularly and avoid when possible all the coughs and sneezes that abounded. As Dr Tapper always reminded her, it was better to be safe than sorry. The doctor, meanwhile, informed each and every one of his patients that any sore throats, fevers or skin infections should be reported immediately.

Consequently the passage was full each day. There was no word on Grace, but on Friday, after the last patient had been seen, Dr Fleet called Tilly to his room. He had returned to his rather withdrawn disposition, but every now and then she thought she caught a glimpse of something in his eyes, though what she couldn't describe.

'On Sunday I was going up to St Mary's to visit Uncle William,' he told her. 'But in the circumstance I've decided against it. Although we've no confirmation about Grace's illness, I don't want to risk Uncle's health. Instead I'm writing to him, saying nothing of our concerns here, and will suggest that after his treatment he recuperates with my mother in Bath. As I have no immediate plans to leave the country I'll reassure him that I'm happy to act as his replacement until he is well enough to return. If you would like to add your letter to mine?'

Tilly nodded. 'Thank you. I'll write tomorrow and put it through the letterbox.' Even though she missed Dr Tapper a great deal, she knew it would be foolhardy for him to return, even if he was feeling better. She also understood that the young doctor was tactfully suggesting that she said nothing of the recent developments in her letter.

'And one thing more,' Dr Fleet added quietly. 'Miss Rosalind Darraway, the young lady who visited the other night, has kindly offered her services as she has some nursing ability. I'm sure you'll make her welcome.'

Tilly was confused again. Why did Dr Fleet want someone else to assist in surgery? Was he dissatisfied with her work? Was he angry with her for treating the patients in his absence? Because of the possible epidemic they had been so busy she hadn't been able to explain her side of the story. And even if she could, would he have listened? She thought they had been growing closer, but now she wondered.

It felt a very long day and an even longer night as she sat by the fire after the children were in bed. What would it be like to work with Miss Darraway? Perhaps she would prove a great help if there was an outbreak of illness.

On Saturday she wrote to Dr Tapper and mentioned nothing of the dramas that had taken place. Instead, she wished him a speedy recovery and told him that all his patients hoped he recovered soon. That night she slid the letter, care of Dr Fleet, through the letterbox upstairs.

On Monday when she arrived at work Dr Fleet was

already in surgery. He was unpacking two very large boxes of books.

'Good morning, Tilly.'

'Good morning, Dr Fleet.'

'As you can see, I've been busy.' He smiled an almost lovely smile. 'Don't worry, my uncle's medical effects are safely stored in the scullery cupboards.'

Tilly could hardly believe it. All the shelves were empty! Dr Tapper's dispensary had vanished. In its place were rows of handsomely bound books and piles of papers.

'Thank you for your letter, Tilly. I enclosed it with mine and have posted them off, together with a few medical periodicals. I'm certain our news will cheer Uncle William, and I took care to assure him that his patients are in safe hands and will be well looked after.'

Tilly wasn't convinced they would be after what she had seen today. Her thoughts must have shown on her face as he frowned at her. 'You're looking a little pale,' he observed, his dark eyes pinned to her face. 'Now that Rosalind will be coming to help, would you like to take a short leave?'

Tilly looked startled. 'No—no, that's not necessary. I'm quite well.'

He frowned and put down the books he was holding. 'Please don't upset yourself over this small change. I know we haven't always seen eye to eye, but I would like to assure you that I am not unsympathetic to my uncle's methods of medicine. But, just as Uncle trusted *his* techniques, so I trust mine.' He sighed softly as he studied her disappointed face. 'I'm not asking for your approval, Tilly, just your co-operation. I hope this will be possible from now on.'

Quietly she left the room. She just never knew what to expect with this young man. How long would it be before Dr Tapper was well? What was going to happen next? How she missed James at moments like these! She wanted his comfort and advice. Why had he had died and left her so alone?

Arnold Wise was the first patient of the day. 'Come to have me stitches out, Tilly gel. Can you make it snappy, love, as I got the brewery 'orses arriving to-day? Wiv your light touch, I reckon I'll be as good as new again.'

A suggestion, Tilly decided, that was certain not to meet with the young doctor's approval.

The following morning, Miss Rosalind Darraway swept in. She was dressed in a very regal beige coat with a high collar, and a black cloche hat with a bow on the side, and she carried a travelling bag made of the finest soft leather.

'Where is Harry?' she asked immediately, frowning at the gawping patients.

'He's with a patient at the moment,' Tilly replied as she returned twelve-month-old Tommy Knox to his mother's lap. His face, hands and knees were filthy, but he had a big smile on his face.

'When will he be free?'

'Very soon, I should think.'

'Are all these people to be seen today?' Miss Darraway's expression was shocked as she surveyed the curious faces staring up at her. At Tilly's nod, she waved her hand. 'Well, you must tell them we shall be away for several hours, as my father is collecting us for lunch.'

Tilly thought she heard an almost audible gasp from the passage. She wondered if she should explain that the people here, once seen, would quickly be replaced by others. Lunch for the doctor and herself comprised a cup of broth and slice of bread. This was usually eaten rapidly, between patients.

But Tilly decided the news would be better coming from the doctor himself. As she returned the mop to the bucket, little Tommy escaped from his mother's grasp.

'Our Tommy's taken to you, miss,' called Mrs Knox, casting a toothless but friendly smile at Miss Darraway. 'You can pick 'im up if yer like. He won't bawl. He's a good little chap, is Tommy.'

'Oh!' Rosalind exclaimed, looking perplexed. She stepped back quickly, out of the child's grasp. 'Where can I change?' she asked Tilly hurriedly.

Tilly pointed along the passage. 'The scullery is warm and has a mirror on the wall.'

Rosalind gasped. 'I'm afraid a scullery won't do. Please tell Dr Fleet that I'm using his rooms,' she called as she ascended the staircase.

'Blimey, is royalty paying us a visit?' Fred Larkins chuckled as he watched her go.

'Well, she ain't gonna hold out her hand for you to kiss, Fred Larkins,' Mrs Knox wheezed. 'You'd have her rings orf her fingers in no time at all.'

This caused a great deal of amusement. The mirth

was still circulating when the doctor appeared. 'It's refreshing to see my patients have a sense of humour,' he smiled, unaware of the cause. 'Now, who is next?'

'Us blokes are gonna wait for the new nurse,' Fred Larkins teased.

'Miss Darraway, he means,' Tilly explained, a little embarrassed at the comment.

'Just gorn up to make herself a cuppa tea and put on her dress,' Mrs Knox nodded. 'Ope you left it tidy up there, Doctor!'

Dr Fleet quickly returned to his room. Tilly followed. 'I'd like you to show Rosalind where everything is kept when she comes down. Now, shall we have the next patient?'

'Your new girl ain't too keen on kids, by the looks of it,' Mrs Knox said as she entered.

'No doubt she will get used to them,' Dr Fleet replied as the woman made herself comfortable in the chair. 'Now, what's wrong with this young man?'

'You tell me, Doctor.' She removed the child's nappy and dropped him on the doctor's lap. He carefully adjusted Tommy, and began an examination of the spotty parts.

'I hope you know you'll have a long queue of healthy blokes outside yer door?' Mrs Knox pointed out. 'All waiting to see her Royal Highness?'

Tilly noticed Dr Fleet pretended not to hear.

'I hope she's got a strong stomach when they has to drop their trousers, though,' continued Mrs Knox, undaunted. ''Cos she might never recover from the shock of it if my old man is anyfing to go by!'

Tilly smothered her amusement at this comment, but it was impossible not to laugh aloud when Tommy decided it was time to relieve his tiny bladder over the doctor's clean trousers.

It was the end of the week, and confirmation had come from the New Cross hospital that Grace had diphtheria. Tilly did then what she always did when there was an outbreak of one disease or another. She prepared a bowl of water mixed with disinfectant and stood it on a table in the passage by the surgery door. She asked the patients to wash their hands, and she was constantly cleaning and scrubbing, taking every precaution possible to prevent infection.

Rosalind Darraway—or Nurse Darraway, as she preferred to be called—disliked intensely any close contact with illness, and had only acted in a nursing capacity to her invalid aunt. Miss Darraway spent much of her time upstairs in the doctor's quarters, attending to the 'correspondence'. This was when she was not meeting her father, Sir Joshua Darraway, for lunch.

Sir Joshua lived with his wife and two daughters in the country, but came up to town to visit his sister—the invalid aunt—with whom Rosalind was staying. His arrival meant that his daughter required a warm fire upstairs to change by. Her expensive-looking dark blue dress, termed as 'uniform', would be replaced by a more fashionable outfit for lunch. Hot water also had to be on hand, and a refreshing drink of some kind. These tasks were allotted to Tilly. Ones that she had to slip in between her duties.

Tilly was relieved, however, to note that Dr Fleet was unable to accompany Rosalind at such times. As the young lady vanished soon after midday and returned nearer to four than two, Tilly dreaded to think of the queue that might have formed in his absence!

On Friday evening she was in the kitchen, sterilising the instruments and washing the cloths that had been used during the day, when the doctor appeared. He looked slightly mystified. 'Have you seen Rosalind, Tilly?'

Tilly paused, indicating the front door. 'As far as I know, she hasn't come back yet.'

'Where has she gone?' He seemed unaware of Miss Darraway's busy agenda.

'Her father called for her earlier.'

'Oh, yes—of course.' He nodded vaguely. 'It's just that I've mislaid Stanley Horn's notes.'

'Did Miss—er—Nurse Darraway have them?'

He nodded. 'Yes—she was going to rewrite a few pages for me. I expect they're with the correspondence. I'm sure they'll turn up somewhere.'

Tilly tidied up each evening after Rosalind had left. The doctor's desk upstairs was laden with effects, but Tilly had noted only fashion periodicals.

'Stanley Horn has a leg infection,' the doctor went on a little glumly. 'I prescribed a cream, but it seems to have had little effect. I thought I would review his notes…'

'Dr Tapper always prescribes the Jamaican balm,' Tilly said without thinking.

'You mean one of his *remedies?*'

'It's just arrowroot, really, grated up and boiled and

made into a pap,' Tilly blurted. 'The plant comes from the West Indies and…er…is known to have healed the wounds of injured Indian warriors.'

For a moment he just stared at her. *'Indian warriors?'* he gasped softly, and his face fell. 'But this is 1928, Tilly! We are living in the twentieth century in the City of London, not the Wild West!' He pushed his hand through his thick dark hair. 'Please bring me some fresh bandages and hot water. And please, whatever you do, don't bring up the subject of one of those— *remedies*—in front of Mr Horn! I'm having quite enough trouble as it is, trying to convince him to take another prescription!'

With that, he turned and marched out. Tilly filled the kettle and took a fresh roll of bandages from the drawer. How could she explain to the young doctor that the patients trusted Dr Tapper and his methods? Sometimes the old remedies worked and sometimes they didn't. But in the absence of another alternative—normally a very expensive one—it was Hobson's choice. For many amputees like Stanley Horn the future was bleak enough. Dr Tapper tried to give them hope and a little relief. It was all these people had. And sometimes it was all they needed to help them through their troubles.

The following week several cases of diphtheria were reported in Poplar, the hamlet closest to the island and often cut off by the tide. It was only the lifting bridges that allowed ambulances, fire engines and motorised traffic to travel to the docks. Stories of people dying in the ambulance whilst waiting for a 'bridger' abounded.

Combined with terrible tales of the rampant disease, the passageway echoed with stories.

The smell of carbolic soon filled the streets, and as the weeks went by, it became unremarkable. East Enders were resilient people, and at their best in a crisis. This was another of Dr Tapper's sayings, and Tilly repeated it often to the patients.

Despite all her efforts to keep the children well, they all got colds. Frank insisted on going to work, as November was very busy at the market, but Tilly let the two girls stay at home. She didn't want them to spread their germs, and she didn't want them to catch anything else either.

It was a grey Saturday after morning surgery when the doctor gave her the news that his uncle was leaving London for Bath.

'He's well enough to travel by train,' Dr Fleet informed her. 'I'm going to drive him to the station from the convalescent annexe of the hospital. If you'd like to write a letter, I'll be happy to give it to him.'

It was almost five weeks since Dr Tapper had gone away. She was beginning to feel less certain of the future. What would happen if he didn't come home?

'I was wondering if you had a free hour tomorrow, Tilly?' The doctor broke into her thoughts. 'After seeing off my uncle I would like to—er—look round a little. Not in the car, as I always seem to travel, but on foot. I really haven't had time to investigate the island properly yet.'

Tilly was very surprised at this request, but she agreed. 'I could spare a little time in the afternoon.'

'That will do nicely. Will the young people come with us?'

Tilly was even more shocked at this. 'No, they'll be quite fine at home for a short while.' She couldn't imagine the doctor fitting in with the children at all.

'In that case I won't keep you long.' He smiled. 'If you would like to write your letter to Uncle and give it to me later?'

'I'll put it through the letterbox this evening.'

He smiled again—a rather nice smile, Tilly thought, and one that made his dark eyes come quite alight.

That afternoon she wrote her letter. She tried to say everything that would keep up Dr Tapper's spirits. But at the end she couldn't stop herself from saying how much she missed him!

That evening, she took the letter up. It was becoming foggy—a dense river fog, mixed with the smoke of coal fires, thick and yellowy, rolling around the lamplight and along the pavements, tumbling against the doors and windows. As she came to the top of the airey stairs she saw a car draw up. Waiting where she was, she watched Rosalind Darraway climb out. The air cleared for a moment and her evening gown glistened, partially covered by a short silver cape and fur collar. She was assisted by an older gentleman wearing a cape and top hat.

The door of Tap House opened and the young doctor stood there. Light spilled out into the swirling fog. Tilly's heart rushed quickly as she saw the tall, lean shape of the young doctor step forward to welcome them. He too was dressed in a formal evening suit, his dark hair slicked smoothly back across his head. Rosalind was soon in his arms, stepping up to kiss his cheek.

Tilly returned to the airey. She didn't want to be seen in her dull coat and the same shoes that she always wore for work. Once they had felt very fashionable, but after seeing Rosalind's changes of clothes and footwear for the past few weeks, Tilly was ashamed of looking the way she did.

'Ain't you posted it, then?' demanded Molly as she went in.

'Not yet.'

'Why?'

'The fog's too thick.'

Cessie came running in from the bedroom. 'I ain't half hungry.'

Tilly was released from Molly's suspicious gaze as she hurried into the kitchen. She pushed her letter in her pocket and hung her coat on the peg behind the door. Very soon she was busy making supper, helped by the girls and in one instance hindered, as Cessie dropped the bread pudding dish on the floor but quickly scooped up the contents with her sticky fingers.

But when Tilly sat at the table with the children to eat she felt lacking in appetite. Not that she had a good reason for it. Perhaps it was a case of indigestion? she told herself, as she rubbed the hard little knot under her ribs. It had been there ever since Rosalind Darraway had thrown herself into Dr Fleet's embrace.

CHAPTER FOUR

HARRY examined his reflection in the mirror. He'd changed from his flannels into a dark grey suit, and with the addition of an overcoat to combat the November breeze he regarded himself as adequately dressed for a stroll. Last night's fog had thankfully disappeared. Every so often the sun slid from behind the clouds and reminded him of early spring. But he'd been glad of his warm jacket whilst waiting for the train to arrive. Platforms were cold and draughty places at the best of times, and he'd been eager to find a comfortable compartment for Uncle William. When the journey ended at Bath a driver would be there to meet his uncle and take him to the house, with a hot meal waiting on his arrival.

He reflected on his uncle's condition as he drove back across London to the East End. All in all Uncle William had recovered well. But the hospital tests had been prolonged and tiring. However, with the new regime of tablets Dr Wolf had prescribed, the outcome was looking better.

Harry frowned into the dark, rather sombre face regarding him from the mirror. He regretted the awkward situation that had arisen between him and Tilly. She greatly disturbed him, in a way no other woman had ever done before. When he looked into her beautiful eyes a warmth filled his chest and his heart raced. There was something about her that deeply attracted him, and yet he could tell she was suspicious of him. He had tried hard to allay her fears, but he found himself at a loss, daunted by her grace and strength of character. He knew why his uncle cherished her, and somehow he had to break his news gently—though neither he nor his uncle had been able to come to a decision about the future. But in all fairness Tilly had to be acquainted with the situation. There was her accommodation to consider, not to mention the children's!

And what of those three young souls? Harry wondered, a little perplexed. Uncle William had explained Tilly's background in more detail. An orphan herself, she had had a very hard life. It was no wonder she was sympathetic to the children's' plight. But the fact remained that something must be done about them. He wanted to help her with the problem, but had to tread lightly. He sensed she was a proud and independent young woman. What could he do to reassure her of his sincerity?

As he trod lightly down the stairs, a smile touched Harry's lips. If Sir Joshua were to see him now, would he still approve of his potential son-in-law? For last night, a world away from the poverty-ridden streets of the East End, he had spent at the Ritz. Whilst dining in the company of Rosalind and her family he had been offered a proposition by Sir Joshua, who had just bought at auction certain properties. Amongst them was a handsome country house. Sir Joshua had hinted that it could be converted to be part surgery—both a home and a lucrative medical practice. An idea that had merit, Harry acknowledged, *if* he were to marry Rosalind.

But did he love her? He liked her well enough. She was amusing and good company, and their families were on good terms, having known one another from before the war, when his own late father had been the Darraways' private physician.

Life had been good then, with a bright future. But the war had changed all that. At least for him. He'd seen bloodshed on the battlefield in France, watched men die and, worse, seen them torn apart before they died. As a young and inexperienced trainee doctor he'd volunteered to go to the Front. Somehow he had survived those nightmare days in the French trenches. But he could never forget them. For eight long years after the end of the conflict he had chosen to travel and work around the world, trying to rid his mind of the images of war.

Now he was thirty-two. But the ghosts were still there…

Harry looked down at his hands. Sometimes, after the fighting, the tremors had been so acute he had administered morphine to himself in small quantities. He'd known a little peace for a while…but not for long.

Now he took life neat. Work was his liberation. But how long must he continue to roam in order to forget? Was it possible that he could settle down to life in the country with Rosalind as his wife? Become a family physician like his father before him?

Harry found himself downstairs, staring at the front door. He pulled back his shoulders and blinked his eyes. Taking a deep breath, he opened it and the chill breeze blew in.

He adjusted his hat and stepped out.

It was time for his appointment with Tilly. And he was immensely looking forward to it.

They took the Westferry Road to Totnes Cottages, a row of tumbledown dwellings, one of which was home to Charlie Atkins. The doctor stood still on the cobbles as he studied the impoverished conditions. Above the roofs of the cottages a forest of masts rose into the sky. The children on the other side could be heard playing in the mud and clambering over the moored barges.

'The river is so close that it's no wonder the cottages are flooded,' Tilly said. 'Some of the residents go away whilst their homes dry out. But Mr Atkins has no relatives.'

'A deplorable situation,' the doctor said quietly. 'And a very unhealthy one—especially as there seem to be plenty of those.' He nodded to the scurrying balls of fur that darted between the tin sheds.

'Everyone's used to rats.' Tilly shrugged. 'When there's too many to kill the rat man comes with his dog. Then the water soon brings them back again. You can even see them jumping from the tall ships to the roofs as the vessels come right up to the walls and hang their bowsprits over the houses. Nevertheless the figureheads are so beautiful, and the sails whistle in the breeze like an orchestra. It's a wonderful sight.'

He frowned down at her. 'So the river can be forgiven for her cruelty?'

'You won't find many that complain.' Tilly smiled. 'Even people like Charlie Atkins. He's happy enough with what Dr Tapper gives him, and life just goes on as it always has.'

They strolled on through streets of smoke-blackened houses, past tall factory chimneys and railway sidings that bordered concrete backyards and lines of washing, all encircled by the river and the traffic of the busy port. They paused at the dock walls and the big iron gates of the dock authority, where Tilly indicated 'the stones'— the place where the men lined up to be selected for dock work if they were lucky.

'Is there no secure employment?' the doctor asked.

'The strikes and unemployment have made competition fierce even for even the smallest job,' Tilly explained. 'The most desperate of the men, those who have so many mouths to feed they will do any work, will volunteer for the skin boat, where the cargo is often contaminated with Anthrax.'

He looked shocked. 'You mean the port authorities allow a diseased cargo to land?'

Tilly shrugged. 'The holds have to be cleared and the infected skins burnt. But by then it's too late for the men who moved them.'

They walked on to pass the two attic rooms that were shelter to Noah Symes and his grandmother, and the noisy, cramped terraced house in which the Mounts lived.

As the sun began to set Tilly was thankful for her warm scarf and gloves—quite old now, a gift from her previous employer, Lady Felicity Hailing. She had worn her best coat too—a smooth fawn camel that, many years ago, had been a donation from the Ladies of Charity. James had told her that she looked like a little deer when she wore it. The expensive weave was smooth and soft. This memory brought back her husband's face—not handsome, but regular and dependable. A small man in stature but big in heart, often dressed in his smart chauffeur's uniform, pale grey, with a flat cap and highly polished boots. She had been very proud of him. Why had he been taken from her so soon?

'Are you cold, Tilly?'

She looked up at the young doctor. His handsome chiselled features and dark eyes were so different from her husband's. But the picture of James in her mind was becoming vague. Now all she seemed to see these days was the dark and intense stare now studying her.

'No, it was a chill, that's all.'

'I think I'd better walk you back now.'

'One last stop,' she said, aware of the doctor's dejected expression. 'It's only a few minutes away. From Island Gardens we can look across to the South Bank. It's such a beautiful sight I should hate you to miss it.'

He smiled and offered her his arm. 'Please lean on me, then, and we'll continue our journey.'

Tilly accepted his offer. She didn't feel it was quite right to be so close to him. He didn't feel at all like James. Harry Fleet was tall, lean, and his arm was strong, his step steady, instinctively slowing when they stepped into the road, his hand lightly sliding round her waist to guide her across.

A distinctive smell came from the river as they approached Island Gardens. The tar and the oils from the ships, the scent of timbers packed like sardines on the barges and a ripple of sweetness from the pickle factory. In the distance, the hooters and bells from the water traffic, the whine of the machinery in the warehouses. The cries of the children playing shoeless on the river-bed where the tide was out and they searched in the mud for treasures. Who wouldn't admire the view from Island Gardens, where the small green patch of parkland gave way to the banks of the slippery grey river dividing the heart of the city?

'How extremely mysterious,' was the whispered comment at her side as they stopped to gaze across the water. 'So compelling that one doesn't want to take away one's gaze.' His dark eyes were fixed on the South Bank, just beginning to vanish under the evening mist. A single glint from the roof of the Observatory sparked like a daytime star. Then in the mists of evening the vision was gone and all of Greenwich vanished under the cloak of grey.

Tilly sighed contentedly. 'This view lifts the heart, don't you think?'

'Yes, without a doubt.' He looked down at her. 'You often come here?'

'Not lately,' she admitted regretfully. 'But when I lived at the orphanage I used to bring the children. The Sisters liked them to take the salt air as they believed it was a cure in itself.'

'Very wise women,' the doctor agreed. 'Salt is important in the diet. Not too much, not too little—a happy
balance. And,' he added, turning to gaze at her, 'you
yourself are evidence of that, Tilly.' He was studying her
very carefully. 'Tilly, perhaps this is the moment I
should share something with you—news that I have
been reluctant to impart. It's about my uncle.'

She let go of his arm. 'What is it?'

'Dr Wolf has discovered that he has suffered a series
of small strokes.' He paused, frowning slightly. 'I suspected this on the night we found him, guessing that, as
an experienced physician, he already knew this himself.'

'But why hadn't he ever told me?' Tilly felt distraught.

'Both you and I know he is a man of great indepen-
dence. I find it quite understandable that he kept the
knowledge to himself.'

Tilly felt a cold hand grab her heart. 'Is he very ill?'

'Let us say his health is fragile and he must rest.'

'Will he—? Can he—?'

'Ever work again?' He shrugged. 'In a small capacity,
yes. But certainly not to the degree that he was. I'm afraid
the pressures of the practice are much too rigorous.'

Tilly turned her face away. 'I'm so sorry.'

'You care for him deeply, don't you?'

'He's been like a father to me.' Her voice caught in her
throat. 'To think that I didn't give you my last letter to him.'

His brow creased. 'I *was* expecting it.'

Tilly recalled her reluctance to meet Miss Darraway
last night. But she couldn't tell the doctor that. 'Does
Dr Tapper know you're telling me all this?' she asked.

'Indeed. But neither he nor I wish you to distress

yourself.' He reached out and turned her gently towards him. 'God willing, with a period of recuperation, he will recover.'

She tried not to let her dismay overwhelm her. She couldn't bear to think of Dr Tapper unwell. He had done so much to help the people for so long. Why hadn't she noticed he was ill? Perhaps she could have averted this somehow?

'I only want him to get well.'

'Yes. Of course. But for the near future I will continue in surgery, until he has recovered enough to decide what is going to happen to the practice. In the meantime, please be assured that he has your welfare and his patients at heart.'

Tilly nodded. 'I know that.' She lifted her chin. 'I think we'd better walk back now.'

She took his arm again and they set off for home. She had walked this way many times, once before with a heavy heart, after James had died and she had come down to the river for comfort. The familiar landmark of the big round globe, entrance to the foot tunnel, brought back memories of their life together. They had often walked through it to Greenwich on Sunday afternoons. In summer they would take a picnic and catch a bus to Blackheath and the beautiful green common beyond. The trees and hedgerows would be filled with birds and wildlife, a little haven of peace away from the noisy, grimy streets of the island. Yet as they had strolled back to their quarters at Hailing House the island had always seemed welcoming. It had been their home, and Tilly loved it as much as she had loved James. Now her life was set to change again, and she must accept the fact that her time with Dr Tapper was over.

When they reached Tap House it was dark. The doctor escorted her down the airey steps and waited as she opened the door. Three scrubbed and shiny faces gazed back at them.

'Molly's cooked a big tea,' Cessie burst out. 'And Frank's made up the fire.'

Molly nodded. 'I cooked another pie, Miss Tilly. And it ain't burned this time.'

'I brought home some chestnuts,' added Frank as he pushed his sisters back and opened the door wide. 'And Mrs Shiner on the fruit and veg gave me a bottle o' stout for the doctor.'

'You are coming in, ain't you, Dr Fleet?' Cessie looked up at the tall, dark-eyed young man hesitantly waiting on the doorstep.

'I'm sure the doctor has other more important things to do,' Tilly said, looking reprovingly at Cessie.

'Why, none at all,' the doctor said delightedly. 'A pie sounds wonderful, Cessie.' He gave them all one of his rare and perfectly dazzling smiles.

The next day Georgie Parker was having his ankle inspected when Rosalind Darraway arrived.

'Tell the doctor I'd like to see him as soon as possible, Tilly. It's very urgent.'

With that Rosalind hurried upstairs, leaving the scent of an expensive perfume behind her.

'Cor blimey, it's enough to put out an 'erd of elephants,' one woman said to another as Rosalind disappeared.

'P'raps it's a new disinfectant.' The other nodded.

'Better than carbolic,' agreed her neighbour.

'Wants to watch the wasps with that,' observed a man, holding his arm wrapped in a filthy sling. 'She'll have 'em swarming all round her.'

'Well, it's better than my old man's breath,' laughed another.

The joke was still going round when Georgie reappeared.

'What's the verdict?' asked Mrs Parker, catching her son by the scruff off his neck as he made to run out.

'He's quite recovered.' The doctor smiled. 'No damage at all done to his ankle.'

Mrs Parker frowned. 'You don't have to tell me that! Tilly's stuff worked the very next day. It was his spots I come about. You said to report anything new!'

'His spots?' Dr Fleet looked at the scowling child. 'I can't say that I noticed any.'

'You didn't look in the right place, did yer? They're all over his backside.'

There were smiles from everyone as the doctor urged Georgie back for another examination. A few minutes later the boy was released with a pronouncement of nettle rash.

When Tilly gave the doctor Rosalind's message he looked slightly irked, but went upstairs. On his return he told Tilly that he would be out to lunch the following day with Sir Joshua.

Other than this small delay, the morning progressed. It was mid-afternoon when the trouble started. Mrs Tanner came running in, her three small children close behind her. 'It's my Emily,' she cried, wringing her hands as she tried to catch her breath. 'The doctor's got to come! He's got to come now!'

'What's wrong with her?' Tilly asked, trying to calm the woman.

'She's come over all faint like. I thought it was just her putting on an act, like she does sometimes to get out of school. But then I heard a thump and there she was! Laid out on the floor upstairs like she was dead, not a breath coming from her!'

By the evening, Emily Tanner had been admitted to hospital. The next day there were two more cases reported of suspected diphtheria. The doctor cancelled his plans for luncheon. Tilly noted that Miss Darraway seemed very put out as she followed him into his room and banged the door.

'It's really too bad, Harry,' Tilly and all the patients overheard her complain. Tilly didn't want to listen, but the door had opened slightly with the force of the bang. 'Father had arranged the meeting especially. You know how taken with the house he is. It would be the perfect place for a country practice, and with all the right sort of people. '

'I'm sorry, Rosalind. But I can't leave just now. There is an epidemic looming.'

'I'm sure you're making a great deal of it, Harry. There is our future to consider, you know. We must set a date for our engagement, amongst other things.'

Tilly moved to the door then, and closed it. She looked round at the row of silent faces. Their expressions were enough to tell her that nothing had been missed, and soon the intimate conversation would be public knowledge.

Tilly herself was unsettled by what she had heard. It was clear that Dr Fleet and Miss Rosalind were to marry. After which they would move to a practice in the country more suited to their social level. But the most worrying comment of the doctor's was that an epidemic was looming. So far he had given a tactful warning and tried not to cause distress. But his decision to cancel the meeting with Sir Joshua and what he had told Rosalind could mean only one thing. He was preparing for the worst.

For the next few days the doctor was besieged. But Tilly never knew him to refuse anyone. Sometimes he was already at his desk in the morning, having had no sleep the previous night. By the following week, the newspapers reported that four more victims had been sent to the isolation hospital.

One November morning, when the river mists were at their worst, Tilly felt very strange as she went to work. There was a heaviness on her chest and a she had a cough.

'Go home and rest,' Dr Fleet told her as she blew her nose and sneezed. 'Rosalind's here. We'll manage.'

Tilly felt too poorly to argue.

'I'll come and see you later,' he told her as he ushered her out of the door.

'There won't be any need for that. It's just a cold,' Tilly said stubbornly.

'We'll see.' He smiled. 'Now, straight to bed.'

Tilly went in to a quiet house. The girls were at

school. Just as she had fallen asleep on the chair by the fire, Frank burst in.

'Are you all right, Miss Tilly?' He looked worried, pulling off his cap and scarf and falling on his knees beside her.

'It's just a cold, Frank.'

'Are you sure?'

'Of course I am.' She smiled. 'What are you doing home?'

'The other kid came back to the barra.'

'Don't they want you any more?'

'Not till Christmas. Look—I got me pay. We can get somefink nice to eat now.' He tipped the coins into her lap.

Tilly reached out for his hand and squeezed it. 'You're a good boy, Frank.' She was, however, very worried. What was going to happen to them all if Dr Tapper didn't come home and Dr Fleet went away? She herself could always get work somewhere, but the children were homeless.

'Let me 'elp you to bed,' Frank said in a grown-up fashion, and she smiled, taking hold of his arm. 'Then I'll go and make you a nice cup of tea.'

Tilly almost didn't hear him. She was too weary. As she lay on the bed she slipped into sleep. A sleep that she couldn't fight against, no matter how hard she tried.

CHAPTER FIVE

FOR more than a week Tilly was confined to bed. In between bouts of heavy coughing and nausea she couldn't keep anything down; it just came straight up again.

The girls stayed home from school and looked after her. Sometimes Tilly felt as though she was living in another world. It was a dark one, with voices, though she couldn't make out people's faces. One minute she was so hot she couldn't bear the bedclothes to touch her, the next she was shivering and freezing. She remembered waking up to the doctor standing over her and making her drink a very unpleasant liquid. Before she fell into the dark again, she knew it hadn't got halfway to her stomach before it came up.

Her dreams were wild and frightening. She was running down Westferry Road, calling out for the children. She saw them sailing off in one of the fever ships used for the sick many years before. They were calling to her, and she couldn't hear what they were saying. She wanted to dive into the murky grey water and swim after them. Her arms automatically lifted as she threw herself into the cold, grey river and sank beneath the surface...

'Tilly! Tilly!' Someone was calling her name. She opened her eyes slowly. They felt as though they had lead weights on them. 'You're quite safe. You're not drowning.'

'They're taking the children away,' she mumbled.

'No, they're not,' the doctor assured her as she blinked her eyes. 'Here, take a small sip. Not too much at first.'

The cold water tasted like a mountain stream. Or what she imagined a mountain stream might taste like. 'How…how long have I been here in bed?'

'A little while. You've been quite ill.'

'What with?'

'The flu. It was a very bad attack.' He bathed her head with a damp cloth.

'You should be at the surgery.'

He grinned as he sat down beside her. 'Would you have me working at midnight too?'

'Midnight!' she croaked, trying to sit up. But he pressed her gently back.

'Lie still, now.' He wrung out the cloth in a china bowl full of cold water and smoothed it again on her forehead. 'You've had a fever—a very high one. But it's broken tonight, and I think I can safely say you're on the mend.'

'Oh, dear,' Tilly said weakly.

He smiled. 'What's the "oh, dear" for?'

'I've caused you a lot of trouble.'

'No, but I'll admit to being worried.'

'I don't know what to say.'

'Don't say anything—which might be a little difficult for you, but do try. Just until you're on your feet.'

This brought a smile to her lips. She felt very tired again, but in a pleasant way.

'Rest now,' he told her. 'Sleep is the healer.'

Tilly's eyes closed. This time she didn't fall into a deep dark chasm. Instead she was resting on a soft white cloud, blown along by the breeze.

Harry glanced at the darkened surgery and once again missed Tilly's presence. Despondently he ascended the stairs and entered his rooms, took off his coat and lowered himself into the big fireside chair. Resting back his head, he inhaled the scent of the ashes in the grate, the fire long-ago burned out. Every moment he had to spare he spent with Tilly and the children. He had come to know them well whilst Tilly had been ill, and there was no finer young man, in his opinion, than Frank. He would make a grand, upright young fellow one day, and Harry knew all three were devoted to Tilly.

Harry's eyes opened slowly. He heaved a breath as he loosened his tie and the studs of his collar. His long, lean body was exhausted, but his mind was alert still, despite the long hours at Tilly's bedside. He had discovered in the time she had been sick that his feelings had deepened for her in every respect. He admired her so much—her strong spirit and delightful nature. Her beauty was unquestionable, and as she had slept uneasily, tossing and turning, struggling to fight the infection, he had wanted to draw her into his arms, to comfort her and whisper that he would always be there for her. But instead he had watched at her bedside, tried to keep her fever low and acted out his professional role in front of the children. It had only been when they had gone to bed that he'd been able to take her hand and whisper his thoughts. Thoughts that had only just crystallised in his mind as the fear of losing her persistently haunted him.

Harry leaned forward, shaking his head, as if trying to shake off a pain. Angrily, he thumped his knee with his fist. His knuckles showed white as he frowned. What would he do if he ever lost her? He couldn't bear the thought! She was so tiny, so fragile—like a porcelain doll. And yet so strong within. She had every chance of regaining her health; she was over the crisis, he was sure. And yet he still tortured himself. Having found something so precious, was he to lose it again?

Tilly soothed him, made him forget the past and remember the future. She had given purpose to his life, reminded him of his true calling. For the first time in years he was at peace with himself. But what would happen if this was taken away?

Harry stood up and went to the window. He looked down on the street, and the moonlight streaming ladders to the earth, and pressed his forehead against the glass.

'Get well, Tilly, dearest girl,' he whispered, and his breath gently dappled the window, coiling up in a cloud like a little prayer to heaven.

Tilly woke with a start. Cessie's nose was an inch away from her face. 'I fawt you was dead.'

'No,' Tilly assured her as she sat up in bed. 'As you can see, I've plenty of life left in me.'

Cessie ran out and returned with Molly. They were carrying a pitcher of water and a tumbler.

'I ain't half glad you're better,' Molly said as they filled the glass and handed it to Tilly.

'So am I.' Cessie nodded.

'You was really ill.'

'So the doctor said,' Tilly agreed as she drank.

'He come every morning and night to look after you. He was worried you might have caught the dip.'

''Cos you had all the simpsons,' Cessie added knowledgeably.

'Symp*toms,*' Molly corrected. 'But it wasn't the dip. Just the flu—like what they had after the war.'

'And the flu was bad enough, 'cos it killed a lot of people too.'

Tilly raised her eyebrows. 'You're both very well informed on the subject.'

The two girls nodded. 'Frank told us what the doctor told him.'

Tilly looked puzzled. 'Dr Fleet told Frank?'

'Frank's been helping the doctor upstairs,' Molly explained proudly. 'Dr Fleet bought him a new pair of trousers and a white shirt and said he's done a very good job an' all.'

Tilly smiled as the two young girls, sitting on her bed, began to tell her about all the things that had happened in her absence.

That evening Tilly put on her warm dressing gown and sat by the fire. Her legs felt very weak, as if they were filled with feathers. She didn't tell the girls that, though, as they would insist she went back to bed. Reluctantly she consented to a little more fuss, but warned them that soon she intended to resume normal duties. Molly assured her, however, that Frank had made such a good job of supervising them and helping the doctor that he was becoming quite a dictator. Tilly smiled. She knew they were very proud of their brother.

When Frank came in from the surgery he looked very smart in his new white shirt and trousers. He smelt highly of carbolic and had smoothed his curly red hair back with some kind of oil, making himself look much older. Tilly was impressed at the transformation.

'I see to everyone as they come in, just like you do, Miss Tilly,' he explained as he sat down beside her. 'Make sure they wash their hands and don't breathe heavy over each other.'

This brought giggles from the girls. 'You gotta let them breathe, Frank, or they'll die!'

'You soppy dates,' Frank teased his sisters.

'We ain't soppy,' Cessie protested indignantly.

'You'd better go and see to the supper.' Frank laughed, pulling their plaits. 'Dr Fleet'll be along soon for his.'

The girls ran off and Tilly frowned. 'Did you say Dr Fleet was coming here?'

'Yes, Miss Tilly. Since you been ill he ain't missed a night. As soon as he closes them doors upstairs he's down here to tend to you. Sits by yer bed till he dozes off, so the girls cook him supper. Makes a handsome pie now, does our Molly.'

Tilly went red. 'Well, that's very good of him.' She pulled back her shoulders. 'But I'm better now, and I won't need to trouble him any more.'

Frank scratched his head. 'I don't fink he thought it was trouble.'

Tilly changed the subject. 'I hear from the girls you've been a very good help?'

Frank nodded eagerly. 'I've kept everything clean as a new pin. Washes all the floors, and I'll even mop a boot or two if they don't lift up their feet.' He laughed. 'They moan every day 'cos you ain't there.'

Tilly looked at this fourteen-year-old boy who had suddenly grown up overnight. He even looked taller now, in his new clothes and tamed hair. 'You've done very well, Frank.'

He blushed. 'Thank you, miss.'

'Is there any news of Grace and Emily?'

'The doc said he's heard they ain't got no worse.'

Tilly knew this was indeed a good sign, as the first weeks were the most dangerous. 'How is Rosalind—I mean—Nurse Darraway?'

'She don't do much nursing, if you don't mind me saying. Spends most of her time upstairs doin' writin', and waiting for her old man. And he ain't too keen on hanging round either. Last week one of the kids in the street frew a stone at his vehicle.'

'Oh, dear!'

Just then there was a knock on the door. Frank and the two girls rushed to open it, and there was much giggling and ordering by Frank to keep quiet.

The doctor entered. 'Tilly, how wonderful to see you sitting up!' He strode forward, a delighted smile on his face.

Tilly felt light-headed as she stood up to greet him.

It must be the last of the flu that made her feel so dizzy, she told herself as he took hold of her hands and pressed her down into her chair again.

The meal was over. A very tasty one, Tilly decided, even though Frank had asked his sisters when they were going to cook a proper dinner. The vegetable and mince pie had been delicious, if a little repetitive, added to generous helpings of the soft, succulent bread that Tilly had taught Molly to make.

'We'll wash up,' Frank ordered. 'You and the doctor sit by the fire, Miss Tilly.'

'I'm really quite well enough now,' Tilly protested, but the doctor caught her arm and led her to the chair.

'It'll please them to spoil you.' He bent to tip some coal on the fire. 'It will be a few days before you recover your sea legs.'

Tilly smiled. 'I'll be happy enough if my land ones come back.'

He laughed. 'They will, I promise you.' He sat beside her and frowned. 'You know, I'm very worried that you caught the chill whilst out on our walk. You were cold, if you remember. I feel responsible for having made you walk out, and now I intend to make sure your health is recovered before you return to work.'

'I'm sure it wasn't the walk,' she insisted. 'I was quite wrapped up.'

'Well, in any case, I insist you stay at home for the next few days. We'll see how you are on Monday. And don't forget I have Frank to help me. He's a very capable young man. Actually, I wondered if he could continue to help out with the heavier work on your return? That is, if you're agreeable?'

Tilly knew Frank was very proud of himself, and it would build his confidence. 'I'm sure Frank will be very pleased to,' she replied.

'Has he told you about Emily and Grace?'

'Yes. I hope their progress continues.'

He nodded as he sat back and folded his arms. 'Let's hope they are over the worst.'

They sat in companionable silence, listening to the noise coming from the kitchen. Frank's authoritative tone punctuated by laughter from the girls. Tilly smiled as she gazed into the fire. She liked to hear them around the house. A feeling of contentment spread over her as her companion stretched out his long legs and crossed one ankle over another.

When Cessie and Molly came in they sat in front of the fire, and Frank drew up one of the dining chairs. He straightened his back and crossed one leg over another in much the same way as the doctor.

'Can we sing some carols?' Molly asked.

Cessie jumped up. 'Yes—yes!'

'We mustn't tire our patient,' Dr Fleet reminded them.

Tilly nodded happily. It was a wonderful time of the year, and she wanted to join in the fun. For the next half an hour they sang all the carols they knew. 'Silent Night' and 'Away in a Manger' and 'Hark the Herald Angels Sing'. The doctor's voice was a very clear baritone, and Tilly sang a descant in her light, sweet tone. The girls clapped hard when they'd finished, and Frank went out to make the tea.

Tilly thought it had been the perfect seasonal evening.

Before the doctor left he warned Tilly again to rest. But, as much as she tried, she couldn't sleep that night. Instead she lay awake, thinking of the happy evening that had passed. She had felt part of a real family—but of course it was all just wishful thinking. If Dr Tapper didn't return and Dr Fleet left, who would come then?

It was on the first Monday of December that Tilly returned to work. A letter from Dr Tapper had arrived on the mat.

My dear Tilly,

Harry tells me you have had a bout of the flu. I do hope you're recovered now, but I must impress on you to take care. I myself have had to heed this advice! As you know by now, my health hasn't been at its best, but my sister Mary has looked after me very well, and my waistline has expanded!

I apologise for not writing before, but I wanted to give you good news. And, dear Tilly, I think I can safely say that I am beginning to feel my old self again. You must be wondering what's in store for the future. Although I can't say at the moment, I'm sure providence is looking after us all.

I promise to write again soon. Get well, and take care of your very good self.

My very best wishes as always, Dr Tapper.

Tilly carried the letter with her all day. She decided to write back that evening, as the letter she had intended to post before she was ill was still in her pocket. Now she would have lots of news to tell him—including the fact that she had returned to work.

Frank was a reliable worker, and insisted on doing all the fetching and carrying for her. The surgery was in very good order, every spot clean, and whilst she attended to the patients Frank was always close by.

'The young doc called on me the end of last week,' Tilly was surprised to learn from Charlie Atkins. 'Said he was sorry he wasn't familiarised with me treatment and that I was to call here so's we could have another chat.'

Tilly was curious as to what the chat would be about. She found out very quickly, when the doctor called both her and Mr Atkins into his room.

'I seem to have been a little too hasty in refusing one of Dr Tapper's—er—remedies.' He rubbed his chin thoughtfully. 'I understand the camomile and liquorice help your agues a great deal, Mr Atkins?'

The older man nodded, looking as surprised as Tilly. 'But I ain't taking orf me clothes for one of yer so-called examinations,' he protested swiftly.

Dr Fleet smiled. 'An examination won't be necessary now, Mr Atkins. Tilly, would you kindly bring in the appropriate dosage from the scullery cupboard?'

Tilly was shocked at this request, but hurried out to do as she was asked. 'As I'm not an expert in these realms,' the doctor said on her return, 'Tilly will see to it.'

'Just what the doctor ordered.' Charlie Atkins rubbed his gnarled hands together as Tilly scooped out the required amount. The elderly man eagerly took the brown paper bags and produced a shilling. The price of a consultation.

'Not this time,' the doctor told him. 'It was my mistake, not yours. But if you would like to try this—a very small dose of a painkilling substance...' He drew a glass phial from his bag. 'It won't do any harm to try it as well.'

After Charlie Atkins had gone, the doctor had a satisfied smile on his face.

'It was a compromise, Tilly. And in view of this success perhaps we'll reinstate the camomile to the top right shelf and the liquorice pills to the third drawer down?' His dark eyes twinkled as he smiled at her. 'I think we have enough space on the shelves for the best of both worlds, don't you?

Tilly had promised the girls she would take them to the market on Saturday afternoon. Frank was going too, to meet some of the friends he'd met whilst working on the barrow.

Soon it would be Christmas. Although there was no money to spend, Tilly knew the girls wanted to look at all the decorations. The market was at its best at this time of year, with holly and mistletoe strung over the stalls.

At the end of Saturday morning Frank looked excited. 'The doctor says he ain't visited the market yet.'

Tilly looked suspicious. 'Did you tell him we were going?'

'Only mentioned it in passing.'

'I doubt he would be interested.'

'Indeed I am,' the doctor broke in as he appeared

from his room. 'I have a few things to buy for Christmas. When Frank mentioned the market, I thought it was just the place to find them.'

'Cox Street isn't a very big market. Chrisp Street or Petticoat Lane have a larger variety.'

'But there's lots to choose from at Christmas!' Frank exclaimed. 'And you can buy a nice cup of tea and a plate of jellied eels.'

'Can you, indeed?' The doctor laughed. 'Well, Frank, the tea takes my fancy, though I have yet to acquire a taste for eels.' He turned to Tilly. 'On a cold day like this, perhaps I could drive you there? After all, bearing in mind your recent illness—'

'I'm quite recovered,' Tilly broke in a little sharply, and Frank's face fell. 'A walk will do us good.'

'Well, if you change your mind I shall be going out at two o'clock,' the doctor answered hesitantly.

Ignoring Frank's dejected face, Tilly hurried off to the scullery. She had been almost rude to the doctor. But why did he make her feel so uncomfortable? Why was she so confused? She didn't understand her feelings.

Harry looked out of the window. It was a quarter to two. He was unsure whether to wait until he saw Tilly, Frank and the girls emerge, or go down and wait at the car. He felt like an adolescent again, excited and full of anticipation. Tilly and the children made him feel something that he hadn't felt in years. Whilst he was in their company life took on a simplicity, a joy of just being alive, that had been missing for so long.

Yet he was sensible enough to know this state of

affairs couldn't last. He had far greater responsibilities. Sir Joshua, for a start, and the country house that would make his future practice, and of course Rosalind.

Rosalind…how did he feel about her now? he asked himself as he stared down at the street. Since admitting his feelings about Tilly he hadn't given Rosalind any thought! And yet as young people before the war they had got on very well. She was seven years younger than he was, and he had always teased her, laughed with her, played the older brother. But the question was, was this enough to commit himself to her for the rest of his life? And yet what was the alternative? To return to his wanderings and take up his old existence again?

Perhaps he should stay at home this afternoon and consider the matter. Sir Joshua had been patient, but he wanted the best for his daughter. Harry was aware that he was expected to propose to Rosalind soon, and just thinking about it now dampened his spirits.

Yes, this afternoon he would sit down and give serious thought to his future. If he was to do his duty by Rosalind he must keep her waiting no longer.

He was about to take off his coat when he caught sight of Frank. Following closely were the two girls and Tilly. Forgetting entirely his resolution to sit down and consider his future, he straightened his tie in the mirror and hurried downstairs.

The stalls were decorated with holly and mistletoe and pretty glass balls. They glistened in the pale afternoon sun, and the excitement of Christmas was everywhere. As Tilly and the doctor strolled along the busy market

street their breath curled into the frosty December air.
Frank had disappeared with his friends, and the girls had
gone off to explore the toys, sweets and games that
were piled high on the stalls. Both had a sixpence in
their pockets, courtesy of Dr Fleet, and were eager to
spend some of it.

'Are you hungry?' he asked as they passed the pie and
mash stall. 'The smell of onions is delicious! Let my buy
you and the girls some hot food.'

'No, we've already eaten, thank you.'

He pointed to the jellied eels, whelks and winkles set
out on little enamel trays. 'Or maybe those would interest you?'

Tilly smiled. 'We have winkles for Sunday tea sometimes. The girls like to pick off the eyes with a pin.'

'I'll have to try some.' He grinned. 'But perhaps not
now.'

A man sitting in a Bath chair was selling ribbons and
laces. The doctor frowned as he read the notice pinned
to the chair. 'A war veteran,' he said quietly. 'Poor chap.
He's lost both his legs.'

Tilly nodded sadly. 'It's very hard for them. Selling
from their chairs is the only way to support their families.'

'I think I'll give him some trade.' The doctor dug in
his pockets. 'Perhaps you'd help me to choose some
gifts, Tilly?'

They approached the man, who was flexing his
fingers as they turned blue with cold.

'What colour ribbons shall I buy?' the doctor mused
as he stopped by the chair and smiled.

'The red and green would be suitable for an older

lady; the pink for a younger one,' Tilly pointed out, wondering if these were intended for Rosalind.

Dr Fleet nodded, frowning for a moment. 'I'll have all you've got, good man.' He placed three silver coins in the small box.

'Thank you, sir.'

'No, my thanks to you,' the doctor said quietly, and Tilly watched him bend to read more of the handwritten notice on the tray. 'I see you were at the Somme?'

The man nodded.

'Is that where you lost your legs?'

'It was—though it wasn't the mortar that did it. It was the cold and wet in the trenches.'

'Trench Foot.' The doctor nodded. 'A despicable thing.'

'How do you know that?'

'I'm a doctor, and I treated such cases.'

'Was you at the Somme?'

'No,' the doctor said quietly. 'Verdun.'

A look of respect filled the man's face. 'Then take your money back, sir. To my mind all those that was in that hell came out an 'ero.'

'I assure you there is nothing heroic about what I tried to do,' the doctor replied. 'Most of the time I had little or nothing to help the poor devils with—only a few words of comfort, a miserable offering for a dying man.'

The man's face darkened and his whiskers seemed to stick out on his chin. 'It was a man like yourself that took off me legs and got me back to me wife and kids. I'm grateful to him to this day, but sometimes I wonders if saving my country was worth the loss of half of me body.' The man reached out. 'I'd like to shake yer hand, sir.'

'And I am privileged to take yours.'

Tilly watched the silent tableau as the last of the sun dropped out of the sky. The tall, elegantly dressed young man, and the other, poor and weak. But their hands were locked as firmly as their eyes. Though no words were spoken, the understanding between them was complete.

Then the doctor took his ribbons and carefully folded them into his pocket. The man in the chair disappeared into the crowd and the doctor held out his arm. Tilly took it, and they walked in silence through the bustling market street.

How deep her respect had grown for him! she thought then. His compassion for the poor man had touched her heart, and with this came another feeling, a warmth and intensity that left her in no doubt about what was happening. Her perceptions of him had changed as she had got to know him, and the regard that she felt for him was melting into a deeper sensation— one that she had never experienced before. All the same, she knew what it was, as every woman knew when it happened to them. But still she tried to resist the truth as despair slowly filled her breast. For what future could they possibly have together? He was destined to marry a woman of his class and standing, Rosalind Darraway, and nothing, not even Tilly's deep and secret affection, could change that.

The next day, Monday, Rosalind Darraway arrived in high dudgeon. 'Harry, I'd like to speak you immediately!'

'Can't it wait till later, Rosalind?' the doctor said as Tilly showed in the first patients. 'We're beginning shortly.'

'This won't take a moment.' She glanced upstairs. 'Surely you can spare a few minutes to discuss our future?'

He inclined his head to the stairs and Rosalind floated up them.

'What's up now?' wondered Mrs Fish, rocking her baby in her arms. 'She ain't got the dip, has she?'

'No, of course not. Now, please take a seat.' Tilly urged her to a vacant chair. 'The doctor won't be long.'

Half an hour later, Rosalind came down the stairs. 'I shan't be here today, Tilly. I hope you'll manage without me.' She strode out to the street, where a car was waiting for her. The chauffeur drove away very quickly.

A moment or two later, Dr Fleet came down the stairs. He looked very serious. Frowning at the waiting patients, he nodded, smiled politely, and disappeared into his room.

Even Frank's good-natured banter couldn't bring much of a smile to his face as the day progressed. Tilly wondered what was wrong. Rosalind had remarked on their future and the importance of a swift discussion. What had happened to make him so preoccupied?

Tilly found out before she left that night.

'Tilly, please come in.'

She went into his room. He was pacing around it, his hands behind his back. Finally he stopped and stood still. 'Something has happened to change my plans. Sir Joshua is leaving England on January the first for the Far East.' He coughed. 'So at Christmas Rosalind and I are to be engaged.'

Tilly knew she should wish him every happiness.

But when she opened her mouth the words faded away. She was grateful that he didn't seem to notice as he began to search the drawers in his desk.

'Ah! Here it is.' He brought out a small blue box. 'I wonder, would you look at this for me?' He opened the box and removed a little pad of blue velvet. The ring inside was set with three oval stones that sparkled brilliantly.

'What do you think of it?' he asked.

'It's beautiful,' Tilly gasped.

'You are about the same size as Rosalind. Could you try it on? I really have no idea as to how it would look on her finger.'

'But I couldn't—' Tilly began, only to be stopped as he nodded firmly.

'You see, the ring is my grandmother's. I'm quite baffled as to whether Rosalind would like it, or whether she would want to choose one of her own. Of course the ring has immense sentimental value for me, but as I've never actually seen it worn it's very hard to come to a decision. I would deeply value your opinion, Tilly. Here—let me help.' He lifted her hand. Automatically her fingers spread out. 'You have very dainty hands, Tilly.' He slipped the ring on.

Tilly stared down at the breathtaking sight. The little diamonds caught the light, sparkling like a brook on a summer's day. It was a treasure, and one that any woman would adore. 'I'm sure it will be most suitable,' Tilly said, a catch in her voice. 'The link with your family will make it even more special.'

He smiled. 'My grandmother was very special to me. My father was her only son, and I'm sad to have lost them both from my life. This ring is her legacy and I've always cherished it.' He paused. 'But now you've reassured me that Rosalind will like it too.'

Tilly slid the gold band from her finger. It had been a perfect fit. The space where it had covered now felt very bare. 'Miss Darraway will be honoured to wear it.' She placed it back in the box.

'This has all been quite sudden,' the doctor said as he replaced the box in the drawer. 'It will, I'm afraid, mean I shall not be able to return here in the New Year.'

'Oh!' Tilly felt full of panic.

'I have a house and a practice to arrange, you see, and I must set about these things as soon as possible now…' His voice drifted as he turned his back and walked to the desk. 'I hope that we shall hear soon from Uncle William.'

Tilly quietly left the room. What was going to happen now? Would Dr Tapper sell the practice if he couldn't come back?

Would she and the children be homeless?

CHAPTER SIX

ON WEDNESDAY afternoon it rained very hard. The wet weather drove people from the streets and the passage was deserted.

'Tilly, I've received another letter from the New Cross Hospital,' the doctor told her as he stood at the window, considering the wet streets. 'Grace and Emily have been moved into another ward and are now classed as out of danger.'

'Does that mean they'll be home soon?' Tilly asked, but the doctor shook his head.

'They have to build up their strength first.' He frowned as he rubbed his chin thoughtfully. 'I'd like to see for myself how they are, so that I can give their families some idea of the situation. This afternoon may be the perfect opportunity to visit the hospital. You're most welcome to join me, if you'd like to see the girls.'

'I'd like that very much.' Tilly nodded.

'Then we'll leave as soon as you're ready.'

Tilly hurried to fetch her coat, and the doctor gave Frank his instructions. 'Don't worry,' Frank said as he stood at the door. 'If anyone turns up I'll give them a cup of tea and sit them in the passage till you get back.'

'I shouldn't think anyone would venture out in this,' Tilly said as she buttoned up her raincoat.

'No major operations whilst we're away, now, Frank,' the doctor teased as he took his umbrella from the stand.

Very soon Tilly was sitting in the car beside the doctor. He started the engine and it gave a splutter. They surged forward and Tilly grabbed the side.

'You're quite safe,' he assured her calmly.

'I should hope so.' Tilly felt nervous as the vehicle picked up speed.

'Have you never ridden in a car before?'

'No. My husband James always promised me I would one day. Unfortunately, he died before I had the opportunity.'

'I'm sorry to hear that,' the doctor replied softly. 'But I'm sure you'll enjoy it.'

Tilly thought how luxurious the car felt inside. It was much smaller than the big car Lord and Lady Hailing used, but the seats were all leather and button-backed, and very comfortable.

'What form of transport has my uncle used in the past?' the doctor asked as he turned the steering wheel.

'He drove a pony and trap until recently, but then the pony went lame. Even so, he insisted on walking to those who were bedridden or too sick to attend the surgery. He would go out in all weathers, much as I tried to persuade him not to.'

The doctor drew a deep breath. 'No wonder the pressure on his heart became too much.'

The car slowed as a bicycle appeared in front of them. The man riding it was soaking wet and had his head down, battling his way in the downpour. The doctor applied the brakes and fortunately avoided him. With a little grunt he pulled a knob on the instrument panel and the headlights went on.

'I'm always amazed at the fact that this car is so well equipped. It even has a hood that is collapsible, yet unfortunately it has nothing to help clear the rain except this silly hand-operated gadget that makes practically no difference at all.' He turned a lever and a long blade swept across the windscreen.

Once more the car began to move. Tilly had always wondered what it felt like to ride in a car. How exciting it was to be sitting high up and looking down on everything!

She recognised the long stretch ahead as the East India Dock Road, and soon they entered the Blackwall Tunnel. The noise of the rain had stopped, to be replaced by the whoosh of other vehicles as they passed. Soon daylight appeared at the other end of the tunnel, and a sign read 'Greenwich Point'.

When they came to New Cross, the big Victorian hospital looked very forbidding. Dr Tapper had once told her that the hospital had been used as an asylum, and later for the isolation of smallpox victims.

It was bleak in appearance on the outside, but inside was worse. Long corridors everywhere, and a peculiar smell. Whilst the doctor spoke to the woman at the desk Tilly looked down a corridor. A little girl with a shaven head was sitting in a Bath chair. A boy, also without hair, hobbled along very slowly on his crutches.

Were Emily and Grace down there?

She jumped as the doctor touched her arm. He said in a whisper, 'I had to persuade her to let us in, as it's not yet visiting time. They seem very strict about the rules.'

Tilly inclined her head. 'Why do those children have no hair? Is it their disease?'

'It's removed for cleanliness' sake,' he told her quietly.

'But they look so frightened and alone.'

'It must be very upsetting for them,' the doctor agreed, with a great deal of conviction in his voice. 'But at least these sufferers are being attended to. We must remember that.'

A nurse came to march them off. Tilly was separated from the doctor, and in a small changing room was told to wash her hands in disinfectant. Then she was given a white cloak, mask and cap to wear. She managed to smooth down her damp blonde hair behind the clumsy strings, but there was no mirror.

Whatever would the girls think when they saw her dressed like this?

Dr Fleet reappeared, also clad in white. 'Don't worry,' he said in a voice muffled by his mask. 'I am told these precautions are still necessary to prevent infection. However, I'm eager to make enquiries as to when the girls will be moved from such depressing surroundings.'

A nurse strode towards them, her footsteps ringing out loudly. 'We can allow a short visit,' she said, looking annoyed. 'But it's most unusual without prior notification.'

The doctor nodded. 'Thank you. Can you tell me when the girls will be discharged from here?'

'Only the doctor can tell you that, and he's not here.'

'That makes things rather awkward. I was hoping to speak to him today.'

'You will have to make an appointment.'

Tilly saw the doctor's eyes look very cold behind his mask. Once more they were marched along endless corridors. Eventually they came to a door marked 'Visiting Room.' The nurse opened it.

'Please take a seat on this side of the room. The two patients will sit on the other.' Tilly and the doctor walked in and sat down as instructed. The nurse added abruptly, 'There must not be any physical contact between you and the patients, of course. And nothing passed over or given.'

With that, she was gone.

'I've known more relaxed drill in the army!' the doctor exclaimed. 'I'm sure a few pleasantries wouldn't have gone amiss!'

Tilly knew he was annoyed. How could anyone get well in this desolate place, without any human warmth or kindness?

They sat and waited. The odours of the hospital were thick and pungent, and seemed far more offensive than any fresh air that visitors might bring in.

Eventually the door opened and Emily and Grace entered. Standing in long white gowns, and wearing masks around their shaven heads, they looked like two little ghosts. Immediately once the nurse had gone they held hands.

Hot tears sprang to Tilly's eyes. She wanted to get up and hug them, and tell them everything was going to be all right. She must have leaned forward, because the doctor reached out to stop her.

With great tenderness he spoke to them. 'Grace—Emily, it's very good to see you. Do you remember me—Dr Fleet? And this, of course, is Tilly.'

They both nodded, huddling close together.

'We must look very frightening in these clothes, but underneath the masks we are just the same people. Now, won't you sit down and tell us how you are? Then perhaps we can give you some news of your own families.'

The girls sat down. Tilly had to stop herself from running over. Like the other children, they looked so lost and alone. The doctor explained that they were getting better, and that he intended to find somewhere else for them to go to recover.

His gentle words seemed to cheer them. Tilly knew they were listening intently when their eyes filled with tears at the mention of seeing their mothers.

It was very quiet in the car on the way home. Tilly felt very sad. They had had to leave Grace and Emily inside that bleak room without even a hug goodbye. The nurse had returned all too quickly and told them the visit was over. The doctor, however, had promised them it wouldn't be long before they saw their families again.

Tilly could see he was preoccupied, his face white and tense, as he drove them home. The memory of the hospital would remain in her mind for ever. The terrible smell of disinfectant and the underlying odour of illness was still in her nose.

'What shall we tell their families?' she asked faintly. 'We can't say what it was really like because it would worry them too much.'

'Yes, I agree. I was trying to look on the bright side when we entered the place, but there was very little to recommend it. I shall write immediately and say that I want the girls transferred to a convalescent home. Somewhere close to their families, where the Mounts and Tanners can visit. I've heard that there is a place in Poplar that might be suitable. What they need now is clean air and good food and visits from their loved ones to maintain a recovery.'

'I don't see how anyone could be expected to get better at New Cross. I'm glad Mrs Mount and Mrs Tanner didn't go to visit there. It would have broken their hearts.'

'Quite so,' he agreed quietly.

At last the journey was over. Frank was there to greet them, and looked very pleased with himself when the doctor patted him on the back.

'No one turned up,' he said, a little disappointedly, 'but I gave the place a good clean.'

'Thank you, Frank. You've done very well. You must go and have your supper now, and a well-earned rest.'

After he had gone, the doctor took off his coat. 'I apologise, Tilly, if our trip today caused you distress. It was a step into a world that radically needs changing. We do our best for the sick, but in some cases it really is not enough. In time, modern methods will help the poor souls who fall victim to disease, and one day there will be new cures without having to undergo such experiences.'

'I hope it happens quickly.'

'I have full confidence it will. Only recently a professor at the very same hospital my uncle was at—St

Mary's—isolated a substance that can be used in the fight against diseases such as diphtheria. The medical world is very excited about it.'

'Will it help Grace and Emily?'

'I'm afraid it won't be ready in time. But, God willing, Professor Fleming will help many thousands— no, millions—in the years ahead, with his discovery of *penicillium notatum.*'

'That sounds a bit like something Dr Tapper would put on his shelves! He used to call camomile *matricaria recutita.* Liquorice had a Latin name too, but it was always difficult to remember.'

'Then maybe one day we shall see *penicillium* on the shelves too—though of course it will never be given in its raw form, like camomile or liquorice, though the culture was discovered quite by chance, in fact, on a patch of mould left out on a plate. Professor Fleming noticed the rings around the mould were absent of bacteria, and from this deduced that a chemical in the mould was defeating the bacteria. However, isolating the chemical is very complicated—unlike your tried and tested method of simply spooning camomile into a paper bag!'

'It sounds very long-winded to me.'

'Yes, it is—as all science tends to be. But one day the cure to many diseases will be in our hands. And after what we saw today, Tilly, this must be our goal.'

The doctor's eyes shone with intensity and hope. When she looked into them she understood why he was so eager to use new and improved methods. He really cared about his patients, and it had shown today.

'Now, it's time you were on your way,' he said quickly. 'I'm sure one of Molly's pies will be awaiting you, and I shouldn't like to see it spoiled.'

'I doubt that anything could spoil one of Molly's pies!' She was about to leave when she stopped. 'If you've nothing prepared you're welcome to share supper with us.'

His face brightened. 'How very kind. What time would be convenient?'

'Say in half an hour or so?'

'Perfect. And…er…Tilly?'

'Yes?' She smiled as she met his eyes.

'Won't you call me Harry—when we're not in surgery?'

A request that brought a hot flush to Tilly's cheeks.

Frank jumped up from the chair, yawning. 'I sent the girls off to bed and ate me supper by the fire. I must have dozed off.'

'You've had a long day, Frank.'

'Yer, but the doctor thought I did all right.'

'You did very well.' Tilly smiled as she took off her things. 'I'll go and say goodnight.'

Molly and Cessie were fast asleep when she went in. She could only see the tops of their heads poking out from under the covers. The sound of soft snores drifted into the air as she closed the door.

In her own room she hurriedly changed from her working clothes into a soft grey dress with long sleeves and black velvet cuffs. She usually wore the dress on Sundays, but for some reason tonight she wanted to look her best.

As she looked into the mirror, at the big blue eyes under a halo of corn-coloured hair, her pale cheeks flamed. Was she really going to be able to call the doctor Harry?

'I'm falling asleep on me feet,' Frank told her when she returned. 'And I've got be up early in the morning.'

'But the doctor's coming down for supper.'

'Yer, but I've had mine. And I just can't keep me eyes open. I've made up the fire, and Molly said the potatoes is on the stove and the table's laid out. Goodnight, Miss Tilly.'

'Goodnight, Frank.'

Tilly felt very strange without the children around. What would she and the doctor—Harry, she reminded herself—have to talk about?

When a tap came on the front door, Tilly felt her heart race as she hurried to open it.

Harry finished his meal. 'That was excellent, Tilly. Thank you.'

'Shall we sit by the fire?'

'I'd like that.'

As Tilly cleared the supper things and prepared a tray of tea, the doctor went to sit in one of the big armchairs by the fire. She watched him make himself comfortable and stretch out his long legs. He was still a little preoccupied. Whilst they had eaten they had talked about Grace and Emily, but she felt he had something else on his mind.

When she joined him, he smiled up at her. 'You're spoiling me, Tilly.'

'You've been working very hard.'

'Not as hard as I would like,' he replied as she sat down. 'I'm frustrated at not being able to achieve more.'

Tilly frowned. 'Whatever do you mean?'

'I'm only just beginning to know the East End and its people. I can understand my uncle's desire to be where it matters. Helping those who really need help. Yet I am frustrated, with so little time left…'

Tilly nodded slowly. 'Yes, of course—your forth-coming marriage.'

'And now medical practice,' he added heavily.

'I'm sure it will be very satisfying.' She added quickly, 'Instead of people banging on your door at all times, you'll have proper hours and a social life.'

He looked at her over the rim of his cup. 'You know, that was exactly what I dreamed of once. A comfort-able home and married bliss. A few rural pursuits— shooting and fishing—evenings spent in leisurely companionship with neighbours and friends.' He sighed softly, gazing into the fire. 'But that was long ago, before the war.'

Tilly saw that distant look return to his eyes. She rec-ognised it as the same expression in Stanley Horn's when he talked about his disability, and in the man they had met at market who made his living from his Bath chair. She had heard from the war veterans she had helped to care for at Hailing House how their lives had been changed. She had seen their wounds and knew the mental scars would never heal. The doctor too, seemed to be living still in a world he could never forget.

'Time will help,' she said quietly.

'Yes, I thought so too.' He nodded. 'That was why I

travelled and took posts with the government instead of facing the fact that one day I would have to settle down. The ideal could wait, I told myself, until I had rid myself of all memories.'

'But you haven't?'

'Have you forgotten your past, Tilly? Your years at the orphanage, the austerity of your upbringing and the loss of your husband? I think not.'

'James wouldn't want me to mourn him for ever. He was a good man. He would urge me to try to find happiness again.'

'And have you?'

'I've found peace here at Tap House,' she answered quietly.

'A peace that has been put under threat since my arrival,' he said heavily.

'I can't expect to stay here for ever.'

'But you would like to?'

'Work amongst the poor and needy is very fulfilling.'

'Yes.' He nodded. 'I have found that too.' He smiled. After a pause he added, 'There's so much to be done, with so few resources to do it, yet each day is a challenge and worthwhile. I hope I will be able to say that of my country practice in the years to come.'

Tilly glanced at her companion—at his handsome profile, his high forehead and long, straight nose, and the dark, troubled eyes that were gazing into the fire as if expecting to find the answer there.

A little shiver went down her spine. As he turned slowly to meet her gaze there was something else, an intensity that drew her heartbreakingly towards him.

Heartbreakingly because Tilly knew that soon he, and moments like these, would be gone from her life for ever.

Harry stood alone in his uncle's surgery. He had just left the warmth and comfort of the airey and Tilly's calm presence was still with him: her big, soulful eyes that seemed to fill her face, her pale, flawless skin and soft mouth, always turned up in a ready smile. He would have liked to stay longer and enjoy her company. They had discussed so many things that seemed common to both of them.

But then he'd remembered with a little start that he had been thinking more about Tilly and his work here than his forthcoming engagement.

Marriage and a family was what he had always aspired to before the war. Even on the battlefield he had clung to the thought that one day the nightmare would pass and life would be normal again. Whilst he had been trying to repair the shattered bones and broken flesh of the injured troops under the roofs of those flimsy tents pitched not five hundred yards from the Front he had still believed in the future. England again—the green hills of home. A new beginning, far away from the thunder of the guns.

He would forget the wholesale slaughter, the men dying without pain relief. Forget the absence of clean water, dressings and morphine that should have been a man's right to survival.

Forget and start afresh…that had been his hope.

A long, deep sigh came slowly up from his chest. Gradually he breathed rhythmically again, and the memories sank back like a sly fox into the thicket.

Harry sat down at the desk, took out the letter from the hospital he had received about Grace and Emily and, with determination etched deep on his forehead, began a reply.

It was early on Friday morning when Tilly found an envelope on the mat. She recognised Dr Tapper's handwriting. Was he coming home at last?

The girls were still in their nightdresses. 'Who's it from?' Molly asked, rubbing her eyes.

'Dr Tapper.'

'What's he say?' Cessie said, all ears.

'I don't know yet.' Her heart beat fast as she opened the envelope.

'Is he better?'

'Is he gonna come back to Tap House?'

Tilly pointed to the table. 'Sit down and eat your breakfasts while I read it to you.'

'"My Dear Tilly,"' she began. '"I hope you and the children are keeping well. I'm missing you a great deal and wonder how all my patients are. This ancient body of mine is slow to progress. I would dearly like to be able to say I will return soon, but my hopes for the future have been a little ambitious. In time I shall get stronger, but I understand from Harry that it's time we don't have. He is about to become engaged, he tells me. I'm sure my nephew deserves great happiness, and I hope he will find it with Miss Rosalind Darraway. This turn of events, however, makes it necessary for me to do one of two things. I must consider selling Tap House or engage a temporary doctor in my absence. My dear

sister tells me I'm a fanciful old man, and that returning to Tap House is out of the question at present. I have
therefore instructed the papers in London to advertise
for a temporary replacement, and Harry will interview
them on my behalf. He will acquaint the successful applicant with your circumstances, and the fact you will
assist him as his nurse. My pressing concern is the
children's future. I have therefore written to Lady
Felicity Hailing and asked for her help in the matter of
their accommodation."'

Here Tilly stopped reading. Cessie and Molly were
staring up at her.

'What's acomm—acomma—?' Cessie stammered.

'Accommodation is where a person lives.'

'But we live *here!*'

'You won't always be able to,' Tilly said gently.

'Where we gonna go, then?' The blood had drained
from Molly's face.

'You can cook now, Molly. If you went to live with
a family you would be able to help in a kitchen.'

'What family?'

'I'm not sure, but—' Tilly hadn't finished before
Molly ran off.

Cessie threw her arms around Tilly's neck. 'I never
wanna leave here, Miss Tilly. I never wanna leave *you.*'

Tilly nodded. 'I know that, Cessie.' But, as much as
she yearned to keep the children with her, Tilly knew it
was impossible.

When everyone was in bed Tilly read the letter again.
Tomorrow she would have to go to Hailing House and
speak to Lady Hailing.

CHAPTER SEVEN

LADY FELICITY HAILING had received Dr Tapper's letter, she told Tilly, but she would like to hear the children's story again.

Tilly explained how Molly, Cessie and Frank had become orphans, then received cruel treatment at the hands of a distant relative and finally been thrown on the streets.

'A very distressing beginning to three young lives,' Lady Felicity said, a kind smile on her aristocratic face. 'And it was very kind of you to take them in, Tilly. But I'm sure we can find a solution to the problem. There is still a need for domestic help in the bigger houses of the city.' She turned to Molly. 'How old are you, my dear?'

'I'm fourteen next week, ma'am.' Tilly was relieved to hear Molly responding politely, as Molly had been fiercely against this visit.

'And I'm seven,' Cessie said loudly, before being asked.

'Frank is also fourteen,' Tilly added.

Lady Felicity nodded. 'Young, but not too young to be entered for domestic service.'

Tilly glanced at Cessie and Molly. They were still

trying to absorb the large, elegant drawing room and the handsome young woman with fair hair and kind eyes who sat in front of them. Felicity Hailing was the eldest daughter of Lord and Lady Hailing, known for their charitable works amongst the poor. Tilly had been very happy to work for them once, and to live at the Hailings' island residence.

It was here that she had met James, the family's chauffeur. Dressed in his smart uniform, he had been helping Lady Felicity into the big car when she'd first seen him. Theirs hadn't been a passionate love, but a friendship that had blossomed. When they had married they had lived in rooms below stairs and had been very content. But when he had died so unexpectedly Tilly had known that her life at Hailing House was over.

Tilly blinked, for a moment lost in bittersweet memories. Then, as she saw the tears brim in Molly's eyes, she came quickly back to the present.

'Please don't be upset, Molly,' Lady Felicity said gently. 'Just think—you won't ever have to live on the streets again.'

'But I want to live with Tilly.'

Lady Felicity sighed. 'The best we can do is find you a position with a good family where you'll make friends with the other staff and be secure. You can always visit Tilly on your day off.'

'Where will Cessie go?' Molly asked tearfully.

'She's too young to accompany you, my dear. We'll have to arrange schooling.'

'You'll put her in a home, won't you?' Molly's voice rose.

'I don't wanna leave me sister,' Cessie wailed as Molly hugged her tightly.

'Molly—Cessie, Lady Hailing is doing all she can to help us. It's very good of her to take such an interest.'

'I hope I can be of help.' Lady Felicity smoothed down the fine grey silk of her dress.

'That's very kind of you.'

'What plans have you made for yourself, Tilly? I don't suppose I could interest you in coming back to us?'

'Dr Tapper has arranged for me to stay. At least for a short while.'

'Yes, but will you be happy there without him?' Lady Felicity asked, although she didn't wait for an answer. 'We miss him greatly at Hailing House—almost as much as we miss you. He was always so good with the poor and needy. Now we have no assistance at all for the sick.' She paused. 'Perhaps the new physician would like to take up a charitable surgery with us?'

Tilly didn't know about that. She didn't know who would come in Harry's place.

'I hear young Dr Fleet is very good.' Lady Felicity arched a curious eyebrow.

'Yes, he is.'

'But he is to be married, I hear?'

Tilly nodded.

'A loss to us all, I'm sure.'

Tilly had at first thought it was a great loss when Dr Tapper had been forced to leave. But now, having come to know Harry, it felt just as bad. She had only known him for two months, and yet it seemed like for ever.

'I'll ring for Alice and have tea sent in,' Lady Felicity said, and she stood up and pulled a long cord by the hearth.

But even the delicious cucumber sandwiches and hot scones couldn't bring a smile to the girls' faces. They sat quietly without a word.

All the while Tilly's mind was in turmoil. What would happen to Cessie? What kind of a family would Molly go to? And what would Frank say when he heard their news?

After tea, Lady Felicity escorted them to the front door. 'I'll be in touch with you soon,' she assured them.

Tilly was relieved the meeting was over. The girls held her hands very tightly as they walked home.

She didn't want to think of her family being broken up.

But how could she stop it?

That night, the mood in the airey was sombre. After they'd told Frank what had happened, Cessie and Molly went to their room. Frank soon joined them. Instead of the usual noise and laughter coming from behind the bedroom door there was only silence.

Tilly sat by the fire alone. She felt as though she had let them down. What could she do? Her own future was uncertain. Lady Felicity had been very kind, but she couldn't keep Molly and Cessie together.

Tilly tossed and turned in bed that night, her dreams filled with a feeling of apprehension. But when she woke the next morning the sun was shining and the sky looked blue. It was a bright December day. She decided to take the girls to church and then to the market— Frank too, if he would join them. The Christmas spirit and the carollers would cheer them up. Perhaps Frank would see his old friends?

When no one appeared, Tilly went to wake them. She opened the door of the bedroom quietly and let out a gasp. The two beds and Frank's mattress were empty.

Frank and the girls had gone!

Harry was entertaining a special guest. Rosalind, having arrived at the crack of dawn, sat on the edge of her seat, one finger crooked daintily as she drank her tea.

Her hair was cut in the latest of styles and her fine orange and cream spotted silk dress looked as though it hadn't seen a day's wear in its life. Her wit, as usual, was delightful, and most of the names she mentioned were society names—people with whom he would soon be mixing and no doubt treating on a professional level. Rosalind had already assured him her friends were eager to find a good physician. Their home in the country would become renowned for the skill of its practitioner. She would be very proud of her famous husband.

He smiled as he listened, content to be entertained on this lazy Sunday morning when the sun outside seemed to hint at an early spring. Perhaps he would take Rosalind out to lunch? Then a stroll in Hyde Park, where she could indulge in the society chit-chat that she enjoyed so much.

'Harry, you must really concentrate a little more,' she was saying to him, and he suddenly realised he had been daydreaming. 'Father is arranging Christmas as our engagement. Mummy is in an absolute whirl of activity…you *will* be down for the Christmas Eve party, won't you?'

Harry's brow creased slightly. 'It will be late when I arrive. I'll travel after I have finished surgery here. As it will be my last day I intend to say goodbye to everyone.'

'Surely that isn't necessary?' Rosalind sounded put out.

'These people have been my patients, Rosalind, albeit temporarily, and there is Tilly and the children to take leave of too.'

'Well, I suppose that will have to do.' She laid a hand on his arm. 'And now we must decide when to buy the ring.'

Harry smiled broadly. 'I have something to show you first.' He went in search of the blue box in his desk downstairs. When he returned Rosalind could hardly contain her excitement.

'Oh, Harry! What have you got there?'

He placed the box carefully on her palm and watched her face, alight with expectation, as she flipped open the lid. Under the blue satin his grandmother's ring sparkled. She took it out.

'Do you like it?'

'Oh—er—yes. It's—sweet.'

'Let me put it on for you.'

She gave him her hand and Harry watched her changing expressions as she angled the cluster of diamonds to the light. 'Where did you buy it?'

'It's my grandmother's ring.'

'Oh!' Her face fell. 'I see. Well, it does feel rather tight.'

'It will be no trouble to alter.'

Tilly's finger was slender, he reflected, unlike Rosalind's rather plump hand. 'This ring is of great sentimental value to my family.'

She took it off and dropped it back in the box. 'Harry, I don't think it's very suitable.'

'Why not?'

She laughed. 'Why, it's very charming, but a rather old-fashioned design. A girl usually chooses what she likes, you know. Something more fashionable. We can go shopping together for one this week!' she exclaimed, then, lowering her eyes, added petulantly, 'That is if you can spare a day from your precious surgery?' She held out her hands, beckoning him towards her. 'We'll have lunch out, and talk about our wedding—I think the spring would be perfect. Mother and Father will have enough time to make all the arrangements, and—' Rosalind stopped, her expression annoyed as a loud banging came from downstairs. 'Who can that be on a Sunday?'

'I'll go and see.'

'Do you have to?'

'I won't be long.'

'Please send them away quickly.'

Harry hurried downstairs. When he opened the door it was Tilly.

'I'm sorry to disturb you.'

'Come in, come in.' He took hold of her arm. 'What's the matter? You look very upset.'

'I am,' she gasped breathlessly. 'I've looked everywhere. I've been to the park and the school, but of course it's closed, and down to Island Gardens, but they're nowhere to be found!'

He sat her down on one of the chairs. 'Take a deep breath, then tell me who you're talking about.'

'The girls and Frank! They've just—disappeared!'

'Where to?'

'I don't know. But it's all my fault.' Tears sprang to her eyes.

He was trying to comfort her when Rosalind appeared on the stairs. 'What's going on, Harry?'

'I don't know, Rosalind. I'm trying to find out.'

'Is it so urgent it must disrupt our morning?'

'Tilly is very upset.'

'I see. In that case I'd better leave.' She reached out for her coat.

'Please give me a moment, Rosalind. This is most unfortunate, I know, but I must see to it. Why don't you wait upstairs?'

'Because I'll be waiting for ever, knowing you,' she snapped as she came down the stairs. 'I do hope that when we're married this kind of thing won't happen. Your first duty will be to your *wife,* Harry, as of course mine will be to you.'

Without acknowledging Tilly, she walked away. The front door banged and Harry sighed.

'I'm sorry—you must forgive Rosalind. She is a little…er…distracted at the moment.'

'I shouldn't have come.'

'Of course you should. Now, tell me what's happened.'

Tilly didn't know where to start. They had run away, but why—and where to? She began by telling him about Dr Tapper's letter, and then their visit to Hailing House.

* * *

They went to the market and searched through the stalls. Tilly thought Frank might have taken the girls there. Carollers sang around the braziers and people stamped their feet to keep warm. But they couldn't find the children anywhere.

'Let's separate,' Harry suggested. 'I'll go this way and you go that.'

Tilly pressed her way through the crowds. Though people didn't have much to spend, they were cheerful. Many couldn't afford the luxuries spread out over the tabletops. An orange, an apple and a few sweets was the most any child here could expect in their stockings.

All her savings had gone over the past three months, but she had planned to give the children a surprise on Christmas morning. Two pretty rag dolls for the girls, and a pair of boots complete with metal studs for Frank. Though there were no funds to buy a tree, she'd intended to wrap up their gifts and hang their stockings on the hearth. On Christmas Eve, as they sat by the fire, she would tell them the tale of the selfish old banker Ebenezer Scrooge, and how his life changed for the good with the appearance of ghosts. Then they would read from the Bible of the true meaning of Christmas. The story of Caesar Augustus and his decree that the entire world should be taxed, which caused Joseph and Mary to travel to Bethlehem on a donkey.

But this would be impossible now.

Tilly stopped breathlessly. She had looked everywhere and asked everyone who knew Frank if they had seen the runaways. But they seemed to have disappeared without trace.

'We'll take the car and search again,' Harry decided as he joined her. 'It's not dark yet. There's still time to find them.'

Tilly nodded. But what would happen if they didn't find them? Cessie's health was delicate. They had taken their coats and hats from the cupboard, but the night would grow cold. Where would they sleep? What would they eat?

'Don't worry—they can't have gone far,' Harry assured her. But even as they drove through the streets it seemed like a fruitless search.

Tilly slept in the chair that night. She listened for sounds, starting at every noise, hoping that some miracle would bring them back. When morning came she rushed to their room. It was empty.

'Any sign of them?' Harry asked when she arrived upstairs. She had waited till the very last minute in case they returned.

'No.'

He touched her shoulder gently. 'We'll look again later.'

Tilly tried to concentrate on her work, and the morning was very busy. There were only eight more days to Christmas. Everyone wanted to be well for the seasonal celebrations. Dr Tapper's cough linctus was always very popular at this time of year. If Tilly hadn't been so worried about the children she would have laughed when Harry asked her to retrieve it from the shelves.

That evening they drove out in the car again. The headlights illuminated the dark roads as they drove slowly along. But at last Harry stopped the car and shook his head.

'We must stop for tonight.'

Tilly knew now that however much they searched they weren't likely to find them. After the visit she had made to Hailing House with the girls Frank had decided that he and his sisters would be better living on the streets again than enduring life apart.

Tuesday morning brought a Dr Middleton to the surgery—a frail looking elderly gentleman. 'I've come, having read the advertisement in the newspaper,' he said, so faintly that Tilly could hardly hear. 'This is my son, his wife and their four children, who will be living with me if I should decide to take up the position.'

Whilst Dr Middleton spoke to Harry the children ran noisily up and down the passage. The parents seemed to have no control as their offspring invaded every nook and corner. The patients all glared at them, tucking their feet under the chairs as the noisy, clumsy pairs of feet sped this way and that.

'Blimey, I hope we ain't having that old codger,' muttered Arnold Wise as he removed his corns from harm's way. 'He looks as much use as a chocolate teapot!'

'And them kids want a good hiding,' Mrs Cribbens whispered back.

The next applicant, a Dr Darke, arrived at teatime. He was of middle age, wore a black hat—and a scowl to match his name.

'That one looks a barrel of laughs,' Bert Singer wheezed as he watched the tall figure depart without acknowledging his prospective patients.

''Spect his face'd crack if he smiled,' the woman next to him agreed.

Tilly knew it would be very difficult to find a replacement, and she tried not to think the worst; Harry would have to pick the best of the bunch.

When surgery was over Tilly went out into the street. No light sprang up from the basement window—not that she'd really expected to see one. But she had kept a small hope in her heart. Perhaps Frank would relent and bring the girls home. It was so dark and cold. They must be hungry and afraid. But all she could see was the river mist creeping along the street and over the houses.

Where was her little family? Would she ever see them again?

Two more candidates arrived the next day. The first was a well-dressed young man who, after talking with Harry, took one look at the crowded passage and fled. The next was a widower, accompanied by his two daughters. The women inspected the quarters upstairs and could be heard disagreeing on the decoration and the close proximity to the surgery.

'I shall dispense with the chairs,' their father told Harry as he stood in the passage, noting the occupied seats. 'It's much healthier for the patients to wait outside in the fresh air.'

An audible gasp came from the assembled company.

'That old misery wouldn't give a spot to a leopard,' someone yelled after they left.

'Did you see them women? Fat as a rabbi's cat!'

'That type wouldn't give two penneth of Gawd 'elp us to a dying man.'

At the end of the day Tilly sat quietly in the scullery. The patients hadn't liked any of the applicants for the doctor's vacancy and neither had she. None of the applicants had asked about the work or the people they were to treat. Tap House was a fine home, despite being in the middle of a slum, and it was the accommodation that really interested them.

She sighed as she gazed out of the kitchen window to the dark night. Her thoughts turned to the children. The longer they were away, the more chance there was of her never seeing them again.

'Tilly?'

She jumped up. 'Has another doctor arrived?'

Harry smiled gently. 'No. I've closed the doors now.'

'I'll get my coat.'

He took her arm as she passed. 'There's been no news, I take it?'

'No, none at all.'

'We'll take the car out again tonight.'

But she shook her head. She was grateful for all he had done, but she had to accept the fact that Frank had lived on his wits before and would do so again if it meant he could keep his sisters with him.

It was Thursday when the young doctor made an exception to his rule. He explained to Tilly that he would be accompanying Miss Darraway into town at lunchtime for at least two hours, on a matter of some urgency.

Rosalind looked very handsome as she entered the surgery, wearing a brown and beige suit trimmed with a thick fur collar. Tilly thought she looked the picture of country elegance.

'Are you ready, Harry?' She pushed open the surgery door and, ignoring the line of patients as usual, entered.

All heads inclined to get a better view.

'Mappin and Webb are thought to be very fashionable at the moment,' she was heard to say. 'But Father would prefer us to visit the family jeweller.'

All heads resumed their normal position as the doctor appeared. He inclined his arm and Rosalind took hold of it. Though all consultations had been officially postponed, this event was worth waiting to see.

'He's gonna tie the knot, then, is he?' someone asked Tilly as the chauffeur-driven car outside roared off.

'A right to-do that's gonna be. Frills and fancies galore.'

'That little madam will make sure she has 'em an all.'

A general nodding of heads confirmed the fact.

'Now, Tilly gel,' said Bill Shiner as he stood up and put his hand on his hip, the celebrities soon forgotten. 'Gimme some of Dr Tapper's cure for me back, will you? A nice rub will do me the power of good.'

Tilly went to the kitchen to find the renowned mixture of camphorated oil, turpentine and lard. She would quietly restore it to its former glory on the shelves in the doctor's room. The New Year always brought with it a surfeit of aches and pains...

Tilly stood still. Tears sprang to her eyes.

The New Year!

She would enter 1929 without the people she loved. Cessie and Molly and Frank, and Dr Tapper too.

But now there was someone else...someone who had

crept into her heart and stolen it away. A person so dear to her that the thought of being apart from him made her feel desolate.

A tear slid slowly down her cheek as she remembered Harry's soft touch as he'd slid his grandmother's ring on her finger.

CHAPTER EIGHT

THE days leading up to Christmas were even busier, and Tilly was glad to be occupied. In between assisting in surgery she hung sprigs of holly over all the doors. The patients brought what they could beg, borrow and in some instances steal, to show their gratitude to the young doctor. Bottles of ginger ale and homecooked pastries stood on a table in the passage.

'A medicinal tipple for our patients,' Harry told Tilly on Saturday morning as he brought down a tray of glasses and a bottle of port from upstairs.

Everyone heartily approved. Tilly made a frantic effort to clean the glasses as they were used, but mugs were soon brought in. When the port was exhausted, mulled wine was suggested as beneficial for the heart and lungs.

Most people refrained from asking who the new doctor was going to be. Like Tilly, they had favoured none of the candidates. When asked if there was any news of the children, Tilly just shook her head.

'You did your best,' people assured her.

'Keep yer chin up, gel.'

Tilly was trying very hard to act as normal. But she missed the sound of the girls' laughter, and Frank's jokes, and the happy routine they had fallen into— although now she realised that that was what made life all the harder now. She had lived alone since James died, and had accepted a solitary existence. But since finding her little orphans life had taken on a new meaning. And then Harry had come along! She had believed no one could fill Dr Tapper's place. But her opinion had soon changed. It was clear to her now that this feeling that made her heart ache was not a love as she'd had for James, who had been so dear to her, but something that frightened her because it was so strong.

'A penny for your thoughts?' The familiar voice brought Tilly out of her reverie. Harry was standing beside her.

'Oh, I was daydreaming!'

'You look very charming when that happens.'

Tilly blushed. 'I didn't think I did it very often.'

'Occasionally.' He smiled. 'Now, I have some news which will cheer you up. I received an answer to my last letter to the hospital doctor. I put some pressure on the authorities and Grace and Emily are being discharged from New Cross. They are being sent today to recover in a decent home for invalid care.'

'Oh, what wonderful news!'

He nodded. 'It's well within walking distance for their families—the one I had in mind, in fact.'

'Do Mrs Mount and Mrs Tanner know?'

'We'll go and tell them.'

Tilly wanted to throw her arms around him and hug

him. But instead she hurried to find her coat and hat, and a few moments later they were on their way.

The Mounts and the Tanners were overjoyed. 'I wish you was staying 'ere for ever, Dr Fleet,' Mrs Mount cried through her laughter and tears of joy.

'Gawd bless you, sir,' Mrs Tanner repeated, over and over again.

Plans were quickly drawn up, and they left the two families making arrangements for a visit the very next day.

That night, alone in the airey, Tilly kept busy. She cooked sweet mince pies for Monday's surgery— Christmas Eve.

On Sunday she went to church. The Sunday school children had made a small stable of straw for everyone to look at. They had placed chipped but colourful china figures of the Holy Family, the shepherds and their sheep and the three kings in the centre. A star made of shiny paper had been unsteadily glued to the roof. A lantern was lit and put beside it, reflecting the faces of the Holy Family.

Long lines of children paraded past.

She thought how Cessie, Molly and Frank too would have stood with her, lost in wonder as they gazed at the tableau. She missed them very much and said a prayer. "Wherever they are, please take care of them."

CHAPTER NINE

IT WAS Monday the twenty-fourth of December, 1928. Christmas Eve. Dressed not in her apron but in her Sunday best frock, with her hair washed and combed so that it curved like a silver halo around her head, Tilly opened the doors to a deserted street. Even in the East End, as poor as they were, the people were preparing to celebrate.

Dr Tapper always ended his surgery at midday on Christmas Eve. Each year Tilly would go upstairs and share a glass of cream sherry with him. Afterwards she would walk to Hailing House and help with the Christmas dinner being prepared for the poor and needy. One slice of roast turkey, a spoonful of roast potatoes, peas and carrots for everyone. It was a welcome hot meal for the starving and homeless, and they were grateful for it.

'How quiet we are this morning,' Harry observed as he came down the stairs. He was wearing a black jacket and waistcoat, and his thick dark hair was brushed back over his head. No doubt he was expecting a visit from Rosalind, Tilly thought dejectedly.

Just then the door flew open. A woman appeared, a screaming child in her arms. Three more infants followed, clinging to her skirts. 'Got somefing stuck up his nose, Doctor!'

The child was taken into the surgery and the marble removed by bribery as the little boy crammed a mince pie into his mouth.

'I ain't got nothing wrong with me,' Charlie Atkins told Tilly a little while later. 'Just come to wish the good doctor a happy Christmas and thank him for what he done for me aches and pains as I heard he's leavin'. Is that right, gel?'

'I'm afraid so, Mr Atkins.'

'It'll be a loss to one and all, I can tell yer.'

When the doctor appeared he shook the older man's hand, and soon the passage was filled with well-wishers. Mrs Tanner and Mrs Mount arrived, to give an account of Sunday's happy visit to their daughters and tell everyone what the doctor had done for them.

Good humour abounded—with a few minor casualties in between. The question that was on everyone's mind—was who was the new doctor to be? But no one knew.

When everyone had gone, and it was time for Tilly to leave, she took a small parcel from her pocket and gave it to the doctor. 'This is for your new home,' she murmured, her blue eyes very bright.

'Tilly! What is it?' He took the package, slowly removing the thin sheet of wrapping Tilly had tied round it.

'It's a paperweight made out of *papier maché* and weighted with a stone. The children made it and painted on a robin. I'm sure they would want you to have it to remind you of—of—where you once worked.'

His eyes dropped slowly. 'How very kind of them—and you.' Then quite unexpectedly he leaned forward. She looked into his dark eyes and felt the whisper of his lips on her cheek.

Tilly could find no words to reply. He was looking into *her* eyes, and his fingers were wrapped around hers.

'I—I must go.' She quickly dragged them away.

'Won't you wait a while?'

She mumbled about having to go to Hailing House to help with the Christmas dinners. Then she fled. Her heart was beating fast when she got downstairs.

He had kissed her cheek!

She put her hand up to the place where his lips had touched. She knew it was only a friendly gesture and meant nothing to him. But she would never forget it.

Tilly walked to the hearth and sat down. The fire was out, a dusty mess in the grate. It needed to be built up again, to be coaxed into life. A tear brimmed on her lash and slid down her cheek. Followed by another. She let them all out then, like little wet prisoners of love that had been trapped behind a mask of pretence for too long.

The sound of carollers in the street woke Tilly up. She'd thought she had been dreaming the voices, but they were real. She had fallen asleep on the chair! Panic filled her as she realised hours had passed. The mantel clock said half past five. For the first year since James had died she had missed going to Hailing House.

Getting up, she lit the oil lamp. Light radiated around

the dark room—a soft light that flickered and burst into life as she turned up the wick.

The voices outside grew nearer. 'Hark the Herald Angels Sing!' Finding her purse, she took out a penny. Then, brushing her salty cheeks with the tips of her fingers, she quickly patted down her hair.

A cold breeze blew in as she opened the door.

Tilly frowned at the faces in front of her, muffled with scarves and hats.

'We wish you a Merry Christmas…we wish you a merry Christmas…'

She gasped as she recognised the bright red ringlets springing out from the little girl's hat. 'Cessie!'

Suddenly she was being twirled around the airey floor as Cessie hugged her close and laughed aloud.

She caught Cessie's shoulders. 'I can't believe it! Is it really you?'

Molly and Frank stepped forward. Tilly flung her arms around them. 'Oh, Frank—Molly!'

'We're sorry we run away,' Molly said, squeezing her so tight that Tilly had to prise her away.

'But why did you?'

'We don't want to be split up.'

'But you can't live on the streets.'

Frank nodded. 'It was my fault, Miss Tilly. It was a daft thing to do, but I couldn't fink of anything else.'

'Where've you been all this time? How have you lived?' She looked at their clothes and they seemed clean enough. Their faces weren't dirty, but they all looked hungry.

'A lady at the Sally Army took us in. She gave us a

couple of beds, as it was near to Christmas, but we didn't know what we was going to do after. Then all of a sudden the doctor found us.'

Tilly gasped. 'The doctor?'

'Yer—he come this afternoon. Said he'd been out lookin' for us every day since we'd gone and finally found us.'

'But he didn't tell me!' Tilly wailed.

'I didn't want to raise your hopes.'

She spun round. Harry stood in the doorway, his tall figure filling the space. The children pulled him in.

'Oh, Harry—I can't believe it.' Her family was back! She didn't know how long for, but tonight it didn't matter. They were all together again for Christmas, and that was what counted.

'It's gonna be a happy Christmas, ain't it, Miss Tilly?' Cessie cried as Tilly hugged her close.

'Yes, Cessie it is.'

'I'll 'elp you with the dinner, Miss Tilly,' Molly said shyly.

Harry smiled as he put his arm around Frank's shoulders. Tilly was too happy to speak. She didn't want it ever to end.

The airey was warm and glowing. The children had pinned up their stockings by the hearth. Ebenezer Scrooge had been thoroughly booed at, and Tilly had read aloud the story of a stable, a bright shining star and the birth of a special baby boy. All Tilly's dreams had been fulfilled. Now the airey was still; the young people fast asleep. Tilly was sitting where she had dreamed she would sit on Christmas Eve and had never believed her dream would come true—beside Harry.

The fire burned brightly, reflecting on his handsome face. A golden light sparkled and danced across the walls.

'Tilly, let me ask you something.' The doctor took hold of her hand and led her to the door. He opened it, and she shivered as they ascended the airey steps. The street was empty, the night was clear, light burned in the houses. There was no snow, but to Tilly it looked like a picture postcard.

'What do you see?'

She replied without hesitation. 'All that I love, Harry.' It was her island—a special place where the wind from the river swept salt and tar into every breath and where a ship's hooter could be heard at any time of day or night, where men lost their lives and found them again by the grace of the sea.

'And I have grown to love it too. I'm happy here.'

'You'll be happier at your country practice.'

'I think not.'

'You mustn't say that.' She looked up at him, the stars above seeming to reflect in his eyes. 'Because you're leaving. You're going away and I'll probably never see you again.'

He reached out to take her shoulders and turned her gently to face him. His lips came down over hers and for Tilly the world seemed contained in his kiss—all the blue sky and green earth, the deep seas and changing seasons, the shift of the tide, a bird's last evening song and a baby's first breath. It was all hers. The sweetest, most beautiful moment she had ever known.

'Tilly, I've been blind and very foolish. I can't leave—won't leave—I've found happiness here, and great peace.'

She woke up then, her eyes wide. 'But you…and Miss Darraway! You love Rosalind!' she gasped.

'If ever I thought I did I was quite mistaken. Rosalind and I would never have found happiness together. We both know that now.'

'But everything's been arranged. Your engagement, and your new practice, and the new doctor coming here—'

'*I* am the new doctor.' He laughed, his voice filled with joy. 'And before me stands my future wife—if she will only say yes.' He lifted her chin and stared deeply into her eyes. 'Tap House is waiting for us, Tilly. Fill it with your presence—and your orphans too.'

'You mean—you mean Frank and Molly and Cessie?'

'I mean them, dear heart. Of course I do! We'll adopt them and make them our own.'

'Stop—please stop!' Tilly put up her hand. 'Oh, Harry, I must be dreaming!'

He laughed again, the rich, deep sound echoing down the empty street. 'If you're dreaming, my darling, then I'm dreaming too. Say yes, Tilly. Say yes.'

The bells began to ring out over London from every church and tall steeple.

It was Christmas Day!

'Yes,' Tilly breathed as he held her close, shielding her from the wintry wind. Then he kissed her once more under a Christmas moon that cast its silver light to earth and its magic into people's hearts, changing the darkest of nights into a bright new day.

Eighteen months later

A NOTICE placed in the *Island Times,* June 1930:

It is with great pleasure that Dr and Mrs Harry Fleet announce the christening of their son, William Harry, first brother to their wards, Frank, Molly and Cessie. The service will take place at St Nicholas Church, Isle of Dogs, on Sunday June 22nd at two in the afternoon. The family would like to invite all those who know them to join the celebration. A running buffet will be held afterwards at the surgery of Dr Fleet and his retired senior partner, Dr William Tapper, godfather to the infant. Dr and Mrs Fleet look forward to seeing one and all on the day, and to sharing the happy occasion with them.

Wartime romances, extraordinary friendships and hope against the odds

If you love family sagas, you'll love these authors

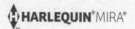

London, 1938.
Meet Daisy Driscoll, the
working class orphan whose
luck may be about to change…

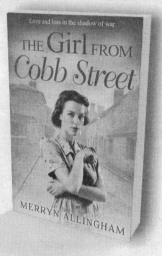

The war has just begun when Daisy meets and falls
madly in love with Gerald Mortimer. But when
Gerald returns to serve in India as a cavalry subaltern,
Daisy is left alone once more and, unbeknownst
to Gerald, pregnant with his child…

Wed by duty, Daisy struggles to adjust to life with her
new husband and soon discovers that Gerald is
in debt, and tragedy is about to strike…

Book 2 in the extraordinary new wartime saga

As a nurse in the rubble-strewn East End of London, all Daisy Driscoll can do during the Blitz is to protect herself—and do her best to help others survive.

Yet this isn't the only war Daisy is fighting—there's a battlefield in her heart as she deals with her husband's cruel betrayal. As Daisy tries to forge a new life without him, she is determined not to become dependent on another man—but first she must face her very deepest fears…

HARLEQUIN®MIRA®
www.mirabooks.co.uk

ONE WOMAN'S PRIVATE WAR...

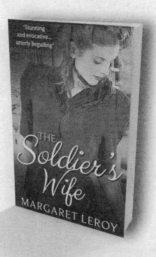

1940, and Vivienne de la Mare waits nervously.
The island trembles to the sound of bombs on the
French mainland. It will be Guernsey next. And
everyone knows that the Nazis are monsters...

Except Captain Lehmann is different...and the
reality of war cannot touch the world they have
built together. Until Vivienne witnesses the casual,
brutal murder of a slave-worker in a Guernsey
prison camp... And her choice to help will
have terrifying consequences.

HARLEQUIN®MIRA®
www.mirabooks.co.uk

POLAND, 1940
A FAMILY TORN APART BY WAR

Life is a constant struggle for sisters Helena and Ruth
as they try desperately to survive the war in a bitter,
remote region of Poland. Every day is a challenge to
find food, to avoid the enemy, to stay alive.
Then Helena finds a Jewish American soldier,
wounded and in need of shelter.

If she helps him, she risks losing everything, including
her sister's love. But, if she stands aside, could
she ever forgive herself?

www.mirabooks.co.uk